HOW TO DODGE A CANNONBALL

OR

The Traitor

OR

The Coward's Journey

OR

The American Future

OR

The Making of the Living Abacus

OR

A Civil War Cartoon

OR

Why We Gamble in Nevada

OR

General Lee Is the Most Overrated Fuckup in Military History

OR

The Yellow Badge of Survival

OR

Allegiance

ACTUALLY JUST

How to Dodge a Cannonball

HOW TO DODGE A CANNONBALL

A NOVEL

DENNARD DAYLE

HENRY HOLT AND COMPANY

NEW YORK

Henry Holt and Company
Publishers since 1866
120 Broadway
New York, New York 10271
www.henryholt.com

Henry Holt® and 🄗® are registered trademarks of Macmillan Publishing Group, LLC.

Distributed in Canada by Raincoast Book Distribution Limited

Library of Congress Cataloging-in-Publication Data

Names: Dayle, Dennard, author.
Title: How to dodge a cannonball : a novel / Dennard Dayle.
Description: First edition. | New York : Henry Holt and Company, 2025.
Identifiers: LCCN 2024042062 | ISBN 9781250345677 (hardcover) |
    ISBN 9781250345660 (ebook)
Subjects: LCSH: United States—History—Civil War, 1861–1865—Fiction. |
    Racism—Fiction. | LCGFT: Satirical literature. | Historical fiction. | Novels.
Classification: LCC PS3604.A98846 H69 2025 | DDC 813/.6—dc23/eng/20240909
LC record available at https://lccn.loc.gov/2024042062

Our books may be purchased in bulk for promotional, educational, or business use.
Please contact your local bookseller or the Macmillan Corporate and Premium
Sales Department at (800) 221-7945, extension 5442, or by email at
MacmillanSpecialMarkets@macmillan.com.

First Edition 2025

Designed by Meryl Sussman Levavi

Printed in the United States of America

1   3   5   7   9   10   8   6   4   2

FOR MY MOTHER, EUGENY HIGGINS.
WHO, FOR POSTERITY, I SHOULD NOTE WAS
NOTHING LIKE THE LUNATIC MENTORS THAT
FOLLOW. WITH HER, THIS WOULD BE THE
STORY OF ANDERS GETTING WISE, LOVING,
INDISPENSABLE SUPPORT FOR EQUALLY
INSANE DREAMS.

THE CIVIL WAR? RIGHT NOW?
YOU MUST HATE PEACE.

—LISA M. GOTAY

GOOD LUCK.

—KADEISH RUSSELL

CONTENTS

HOW TO
DODGE
A CANNONBALL

0.5

———◆———

GLEASON'S NOTES

"This is the struggle for everything. Freedom. Dignity. The American Future. I'm proud to give whatever Columbia requires."

—Tobias Gleason, *To Arms for Liberty* (1861)

"I don't know what's happening. But I know that when the last sword is sheathed, it will have been worthwhile."

—Tobias Gleason, *One Man's War Journal* (1863)

"They died for nothing. Dead men aren't free: they're trapped in wood and dirt forever. The living have even less. A white burial in a clean cemetery is kinder than Black life."

—Tobias Gleason, *The Pyre of Hope* (1863)

1

ANDERS TURNS SEVEN

ood morning, niggers!" announced Anders, waving through the schoolhouse window. Cheer shone through his voice, emanating the joy of being alive and American, in that order. The bulk of the assembled students ignored him, but two waved back. Anders mentally marked them as his friends.

His mother thought he'd gone swimming, which had been true fifteen minutes ago. Anders found the water hard to enjoy: he couldn't figure out floating, and letting the current drag him back to shallow depths tired him out. Now that he'd finished connecting with the Illinois River fish (and the rocks in the riverbed), it was time to learn.

Learning remained a core value, to the extent that he understood what core values were or why they mattered. Thus, it deserved special attention on his birthday. An event that mattered simply because it was his, and lowered the odds of an unprovoked kick from a moody adult. Visiting the only children in town that acknowledged him didn't hurt.

Despite some dampness (overcast weather preempted his usual sun-drying method), he enjoyed his perch. Peering from the window put him above everything, as if he held court. A theater balcony had to look something like this, sans the risk of falling. He resolved to invite one of his two known friends to try it. The stools spread around the room looked shabby, so they'd appreciate the tip.

The teacher eyed Anders the way shopkeepers did, complete with a confused squint. Or practical: the teacher *owned* bifocals but only wore them under duress. Anders gleaned her first name from Mother, but proper learners stuck to last names. Bell never introduced herself, so she was the teacher. Shorter than most adults, equally confounding, and less impatient. She only looked tempted to smack him half of the time. But she always looked tired, even before he got on a roll.

Anders waved again, hoping to stir more of a reaction. Instead of responding, she turned back to her charges and opened a thick blue book. Tiny, tilted, hand-drawn letters dotted the browning pages.

"Are we doing figures?" asked Anders. He liked figures. Numbers made sense, which was why he could count all fifteen kids in the room and their twenty-two shoes. Words got complicated and made everything else complicated. Someone needed to find a way to replace them with numbers, so people could get through books faster. If the Bible used numbers, the world would be at peace.

With numbers, he also knew most of the black kids were older. The oldest were twice his age and had lost general enthusiasm for education. Sitting in on their session felt like capturing a piece of adulthood.

"Today, we'll explore some history," said the teacher. She expertly ignored and answered Anders at the same time. He considered it their personal game.

"How much history? Is there a lot?"

"Who knows why this town's called Liberty Valley?" asked the teacher. She'd only ignored without answering, so Anders was ahead.

A girl two heads taller than Anders raised her hand. Anders might have called her cute, if his mother wouldn't thrash him for that. Instead, he'd call her . . . something else. She was very something else.

"Robin." The teacher acknowledged the girl with a point. The girl (Robin!) stood up (no shoes?) and spoke.

"Because we're free."

"Like me!" said Anders, participating.

"Yes, like you, Anders."

The teacher had answered him without ignoring him. Anders was *dominating* this round of the game.

"We can be mayors," Anders continued.

"No, *we* can't."

"Oh. Well, we can vote!"

"Just you."

"Oh. Then Liberty Valley's a dumb name."

"Now then," said the teacher. It was her go-to strategy when he'd made a point, but she planned to keep going. "Liberty Valley was founded in—"

"Mama calls it NiggerTown, which makes Auntie laugh. I think that's nice, having your own town. Is there a WhiteTown? I hope they have a river."

"It's WhiteTown everywhere, Anders."

"Oh." Anders chewed on the words, and the whiff of venom that had entered the teacher's voice. The sport had left the game. "That's untoward, we should make a NiggerTown."

A younger boy—one of the shoeless ones—in front made a sound between laughter and choking. Other students looked through Anders or made a show of staring at the teacher. For her part, the teacher started and stopped multiple responses, never making it past the first two or three syllables. Finally, Robin gave Anders the first look he could identify as a death stare.

Then Anders caught the edge of a familiar shape in his peripheral vision and let himself fall. He landed hard on his knees but knew worse approached.

Anders, like most surviving children, owned strong instincts. Those instincts told him to move after seeing his mother's shadow. He heard metal ricochet off wood as he dove left, shielding his head with his forearms for the landing roll. By the sound, she'd only thrown a medium lid. That bode well: the medium cookware lacked the arrow-like speed of the small and the brutal heft of the large.

"Boy!" she shouted before launching a medium saucepan. "What in hell are you doing here again?"

"Learning," volunteered Anders. He primed himself for a second roll, watching her hands. Whether she pitched with her main or off hand would shape his next move.

"At the nigger school?"

"It's the only school here."

"Are you a nigger?"

"Maybe?" The question intrigued him. "It's a nigger town."

A small bowl bounced off Anders's forehead, shifting the world to a shaky blur. She'd caught on and brought a mixed set. By the time he rallied and found his feet, she'd be in switch distance.

Drawn by either the noise or a stray projectile, the teacher's black (mulatto? octoroon? there were too many shades) head poked out the schoolhouse window. She peered at Anders, then his mother, and then back at Anders. The bewildered squint returned and faded. She made a small, polite wave, adjusted a small white latch, and let the window fall shut. He was on his own.

His opponent paced around him slowly, stalking her prey. She had the size advantage, speed advantage, and an ocean-blue dress hiding unknown improvised weaponry. He had courage, which never seemed to outclass improvised weaponry. Nonetheless, Anders barreled to the left, taking the slim chance of making it to freedom. He refused to be remembered as a coward by his two friends in the schoolhouse. Or Robin.

He never saw the cookware that took him out.

✣ ✣ ✣

Mother, who other adults called Katrina, dragged him by the shoulder. Her grip impressed Anders, even as its target. The vise had strength beyond her slight form.

"It's supposed to be my day," whined Anders.

"Is it?" Katrina scoffed. "Then you're going to learn," she added, resolute.

Anders flinched by habit. There was nowhere left to roll.

"Not like that," she said, her voice and posture softening. Her grip loosened from iron to a gentler, maternal copper. "I'm going to tell you about our family."

Curiosity earned silence and stillness, two things Anders seldom surrendered. The boy eyed his mother carefully, searching for a hint of the lies adults wove with ease. He found none of the few hints he knew. Katrina looked too tired to lie convincingly to anyone. If she were any less irate, she might have nodded off.

The exhaustion etched into Katrina had a short history. Years of conspicuous effort to avoid a "worker's tan" had recently failed, which seemed to Anders fair for a worker. For her, it was a private apocalypse. Looking one shade closer to the other Liberty Valley residents had put her in a permanent foul mood. Jokes and errors that would have drawn a laugh from her a season ago attracted a projectile instead.

Katrina gently dragged him to the riverbank, where a sizable and unattended fire waited. The display almost impressed Anders, whose only effort at firekeeping had consumed a copse of rare trees. Katrina had let that go, since "Mayor Spade" owned them. Now she sat Anders down on the grass beside her makeshift pit.

"Do you mean Pa?" Anders hazarded. It wasn't his only question, but the others pertained to fire. Why had she started one on a summer afternoon? Why hadn't she taken the time to put it out before picking him up? Whose iron poker was she holding? Such trivia wasn't worth risking a real conversation about where he came from.

Katrina nodded.

"You're seven and ready to work. That makes you a man, in every way that matters."

"Do men have to read more?"

"A gentleman never has to read anything."

"I'm a gentleman?" asked Anders. He reflected on his recent swimming attempt. Gentlemen should float.

"You're a soldier's son. And a soldier's grandson. And a soldier's great-grandson. If any had gotten their due, we'd still be down south. With our own land, and niggers, and future. But they didn't, and usurers chased us here."

Anders bit his cheek, his habit while thinking. Katrina chided him for it, so he'd dialed down the thinking in recent weeks. The new information, however, demanded it. Illinois was his whole world, and he liked it. The idea of a previous, lost life was beyond him.

Except his father's absence. Stories about the man were rare, and time, youth, and multiple falls from trees distorted Anders's memory. All he knew were the two orders relayed by his mother: to pursue an education and avoid asking for hugs. He'd excelled at the latter, and avoided any clutches, grips, or embraces that might weaken his grit. The first still felt out of reach.

"That's good," Anders said. He congratulated himself for contributing to the conversation and waited for Katrina to keep going. If more was coming, it'd be at her pace. She didn't answer or return eye contact, focusing instead on prodding their fire. Sparks danced as she thrusted, floating a few inches too close for Anders's taste.

"The fire's good too." A compliment seemed worth trying.

His mother gazed into the flames for too long, as if they had insight to offer. Anders had almost committed to asking what they said, and if they liked numbers, when she sat down beside him. She put her arms around his shoulder, a gesture generally reserved for Bible study. The fire had finally inspired a response, hopefully about his other parent.

She produced a small glass bottle of whiskey. How it hid or even fit among her pockets was a mystery.

"Here. It's time you learned to handle your liquor."

Anders did his best, pushing through the instinct to spit the harsh wooden flavor out. There were only a few scant drops left. His mother must have given the rest to someone else. Nonetheless, she beamed with rare maternal approval, patting his head.

"You're strong. That's good, the current drags everything else away."

With the heat getting stronger, the current sounded nice. Anders switched between eyeing Katrina and the growing pyre. Sparks now encroached on their family breakthrough.

"What's the fire for?" Anders asked. An explanation hadn't come on its own.

"Underlining the point."

"What's *underlining* mean?"

"You'll see."

"What's that fancy poker?"

"A branding iron."

"Does it underline points too?"

"Yes."

Half satisfied, Anders let the rest of his questions lie fallow. His mother usually had little patience for them, and fewer answers.

"Son, I need you to trust me," added his mother. "You're going to learn about our entire line. Just let me collect myself. It's not an easy lesson." She rolled up the sleeves on her dress and then lifted the fancy poker. "Stick out your arm."

Anders, the son of a soldier, stuck out his arm and began his education. Katrina pressed half a star onto his arm, for half-fulfilled dreams. It only hurt until he blacked out.

2

ANDERS TURNS FIFTEEN

Anders twirled flags for the Union, until he'd been captured and shown the light. Now he twirled flags for Southern freedom. No man deserved to lose his property, human or otherwise.

Tonight, Anders twirled with pride. He was the only flag carrier intelligent enough to be trusted with military intelligence. The others didn't understand a proper spin's role in preserving morale. An underperforming flag-twirler might as well hang his commander himself.

His skill shone better under the sun, with more than a dying lantern to illuminate his sets. But he could use the tent's long shadows and cramped spacing to his advantage. The silhouette was simply another character: a larger, stronger version of the rebel ideal.

The silhouette's sleeves stopped short of its wrists. Anders's jacket once belonged to someone shorter and perhaps younger. He didn't know if they'd died or defected, and never asked. His thoughts stayed with the mission.

"If morale fails, the enemy prevails," Anders whispered under his breath. Croaks and chirrups crept into the tent, distracting Anders from the mosquitoes floating around his forehead. He'd spun through battles, but Pennsylvania wildlife tested him. Perhaps they were Union mosquitoes, scouting for Meade.

He repeated his maxim, shaking mosquitoes and (underperforming) frogs from his mind.

"What was that, son?" asked the general. Anders had drawn the eyes of all his superiors away from the war map. This was like a normal map but with chess pieces. Understanding it was beyond Anders's duties.

"Nothing, sir! I'm being judiciously silent, save responding to your question, sir! Thank you for choosing me as your flag-waver, sir! If another general is a Union spy, I will take the bullet for you, sir! Please send my body to my mother, sir!"

Lee stared without comment, confronted with his first unsolvable puzzle. The others looked amused. Anders wondered what the joke was and resolved to pay better attention. A spy could have already lit a stick of dynamite behind his back by now. He remembered the Union as a pack of wily cowards who didn't even have decent beans in their rations.

"Is the boy touched?" asked General Ewell. He sat in Jackson's old chair and wore his beard in Jackson's old style. When anyone slipped, he even answered to Jackson's name. The war prophet's death had left a hole in the men's hearts and the command chain, and Ewell dutifully filled it.

"No. Maybe. We need to nurture the next generation," answered Lee.

"Nurture a cannonball," said General Pickett. He spat on the war map, drowning a detachment in saliva. Lee grabbed the chipped game piece by a dry edge, wiped it against Pickett's shirt, and replaced it on Cemetery Ridge. Pickett spat on it again.

Distracted by heresy, Anders nearly missed a spin and let the stars of freedom slip out of his grip. Like all the men, he loved Lee like a father. More, since Lee had never abandoned him without strategic benefit or struck him directly. An insult to Lee attacked the very image of a soldier. That image's beard had grown whiter, longer, and more jagged over the current campaign. It had also picked up spots of fresh blood from Lee's new nervous habit of chewing his fingertips. As European intervention drifted further away, the bites grew faster and deeper. This sacrifice of personal comfort and sanity was yet another holy gift to the men.

"I'm detecting some hostility, Pickett. Let's explore that," said Ewell, the only general still seated. One leg rested comfortably over the map's edge. "The Lord respects a still heart."

"Nurture two cannonballs. This plan is a suicidal fever dream, and you're enabling it." Pickett followed this with a few insults that Anders didn't understand. Bayonets didn't even work that way.

Morale, his charge, had sunk deep underwater. Anders stretched his right wrist, and then gave the flag a nervous test twirl. Only his best tricks could save the young nation, and earlier birthdays hung over him.

The family honor was at stake. His great-grandfather had twirled flags for the British, spinning even as the last ship fell to Hessian raiders. He spent the rest of his life looking out for gangs of drunks with tar. Anders's grandmother ran away from home, cut her hair, and bound her breasts to twirl against the Canadians in 1812. This looked foolish in the shadow of the burning White House. She came back thoroughly broken and passed it on to her child. After growing into a broken adult, Katrina met a Texan flag-twirler bound for the Mexican War. Specifically, a mercenary on the Mexican side. They never had a second night together. The romance, long after her rearing days, still left her with Anders. A miracle unstained by martial defeat.

"Promise me you'll never twirl flags for another man's war," she told Anders, once a year, every year. The first time stood out. Her eyes were wild, and the whiskey was empty.

"Mother, I'm afraid of the fire."

"Promise me!" she screeched, drawing his hand closer to the branding iron. The rest was a blur of shouting and pain, punctuated by black oaths. Anders had earlier family memories, but this was the sharpest.

Back to the task at hand. Pickett had torn out a tuft of his own hair, followed by his sword. Bloody roots and permanent hairline damage underlined his commitment.

"Send your own men sprinting into hell!" spat Pickett.

"I'm your superior. They *are* my men," observed Lee. He drew his own sword. "Not that I expect a half-educated wretch from the Pig War to understand the chain of command."

They circled the map, beards bristling with enmity. Pickett took light and measured steps, ready to spring across the table like a wild cat. Lee's steps were loose and confident, informed by the aristocratic surety that death was a peasant problem. Ewell seemed content to watch, tapping a Bible in Jackson's old manner.

No one acknowledged the virtuoso flag-twirling performance unfolding in the back of the tent. Anders sweated through the *Georgian Furl*, *Three-Fifths Shuffle*, and *United Virginia Wave* to no effect. It was heartrending; if the *Sumter Two-Step* didn't remind them what they were fighting for, what could?

Lee struck first. He looked insulted when Pickett sidestepped the thrust, as if some gentleman's agreement had been violated. After block-ing the riposte, he hopped back to cradle his wrist.

"Treasonous oaf," Lee spat.

"Do you academy engineers learn to fight? Or skim that with the books on strategy?"

Lee lashed out mid-quip, and Pickett's sword flew out of his grip. It landed at Anders's feet, halfway through a flawless execution of the *Dead Yankee Twist*.

"Anything else?" boasted Lee.

Pickett drew and leveled his pistol. A German import, without a sport-ing chance of misfire. The confidence and blood drained from Lee's face.

"Listen, the plan is sound. A committed charge is perfect because they think we'd never do it. In the pedestrian Yankee mind, a complete lack of cover for two miles is insurmountable. I encourage you to have more *vision*. What our men lack in terrain advantage, they'll more than make up for in fighting spirit. If we don't seize this chance, historians will mock us for the rest of time." Lee remained remarkably loquacious before the barrel of a gun. Two years on the edge of ruin had served him well.

Pickett shook his head and took aim.

Anders pushed when he meant to pull. The flagpole's base struck Pickett in the side of the head, smashing it against the war map. Vibrations from the accidental blow shook up Anders's arm, down through his legs and torso, and into the earth. Pickett didn't move from that spot. Lee prodded him tentatively with the point of his sword. Nothing. Pickett's chest rose and fell and there wasn't *too* much blood, so he was at least technically alive.

"Perfect!" Lee exclaimed. He patted Anders's shoulder. "Tie him to his horse and smack it in the rear once the charge begins. I expect a full apol-ogy when we've won, preferably in liquor form. We'll be senators yet, my boy."

Ewell perked up and shut his Bible. The dog-ear of a brown-and-gray nude photo stuck out the side. "Ah, good work, lad. Be sure to pass Lee's orders on to the officers. Pickett will be 'indisposed' until the critical moment, after all."

"Excellent thinking, sir and sir!" Anders answered cheerily. He'd come far too close to being flogged for insubordination. It looked like assaulting superior officers helped in small doses.

He tried slumping Pickett over his shoulders but found the general's ten years of officer rations too heavy. Then he tied a rope around his legs and dragged him back to base camp. On the way down, Anders hummed hymns of victory, triumph, and winning. They were both lucky to have a leader with Lee's vision. Tomorrow morning, he'd take the final step shedding the family shame.

3

CHARGED WITH PURPOSE

Anders contemplated trading his flag for a gun. He still treasured the cause and his flag's role in making it real. But everyone else had some kind of weapon. The enlisted men carried well-worn rifles, and officers sported pistols alongside sabers with artisanal hilts and worn, chipped blades. Even the bugle players had scrounged knives from nearby towns, though no one had offered him one. A flag could stir men's souls but couldn't steer a bullet.

He resolved to trust his brothers and leave his doubts with yesterday's dead. They were the best that Alabama (and Illinois, considering Anders) had to offer. Anders had peered into the Yankee heart, and it was empty. His brothers, on the other hand, would die before letting their flag fall.

Besides, Pickett still hadn't reappeared. So a thwack with the flagpole had to be worth something.

Unfortunately, there wasn't time to perfect *Southern Comfort* (the new technique's working title). His regiment had formed six tight rows in anticipation of the decisive charge. Anders stood in the back, close enough to the soldier before him to see the burnt skin and ticks on his neck. He also heard hyperventilating, which proved hard to ignore.

The lack of ambient animal chatter didn't help. The fauna that had heckled last night's performance had fled the battlefield, down to the flies and scavenger birds guaranteed to thrive in the aftermath. In that void, the soldier's hyperventilation could have been a hurricane. For the second time, Anders imagined local insects working for Meade.

"We'll be fine," Anders whispered, leaning as far forward as he could without tipping. "Imagine the celebration afterward. It'll be just like when the Founders killed the king at Bunker Hill."

The soldier's hands shook, which Anders took for excitement. A heroes' feast offered a major improvement on starvation marching. And perfect fuel, God willing, for a growth spurt.

"Do you really believe that?" asked the boy to his left. Bryce hadn't died or run, which was a relief. At seventeen, he had two years of seniority. Anders considered him an older brother, even if he played a bugle. Competition pushed Anders to improve.

"Of course." Anders flashed a smile that went unreturned. Bryce's face had been stuck in a constant, skittish panic since the first day of battle.

"I haven't slept since we got here. Every noise puts me on edge. Even my bugle. *Especially* my bugle."

"That's great! If your horn scares you, imagine the enemy's reaction."

"Gunfire?"

"Retreat. General Lee says the Union's center will shatter like glass. All we have to do is reach it."

Bryce began the same pained breathing as the infantryman in front. Anders hoped it was a bugle-playing exercise. For solidarity, he joined in. The exercise delivered; forcing deep, gasping breaths had a calming effect bordering on meditation. It had to be some kind of spiritualist technique. Bryce kept more books in their tent than Anders had read in his life.

The breathing exercise rapidly spread throughout the two back rows. Anders stifled a chuckle: only three of them were proper bugle players, yet they were all hyperventilating. Comradery could achieve anything.

Anders took occasional breaks to wipe away streams of sweat. The July sun couldn't be routed or negotiated with, and punished him for being born farther north. His hair clung to his neck: as the war dragged on, he'd given up on keeping it at ideal military length. The curls were tied back in a revolutionary ponytail at least eighty years out of date.

"Some of the others said you fought with the Union," said Bryce, between exercises. "I set them straight."

"About what? I was in McClellan's army for ten months."

"Truly?"

"Maybe eleven."

"Was it safer?"

"I don't think so."

Bryce snapped to attention and blew three rapid notes of fanfare. General Longstreet had arrived, with Pickett's unconscious form strapped to the back of his horse. While both of Pickett's legs were secured, his arms dangled freely in the air, swinging with every step.

Even Pickett's saber had been returned, though Anders had no memory of carrying it back to camp. The scabbard dragged in the dirt behind Longstreet's horse, attached to Pickett by a double-knotted length of string. Such precise follow-through helped Anders believe his own words: there was a plan, and they had a place in it.

Longstreet peered down as his horse paced the front line, wielding the aristocratic aura reserved for Southern generals. Anders found his view partially obscured by stinging sweat and fully obscured by the rows of adult men standing in his way. He pushed himself to his toes, putting his eyes just above a pair of gray shoulders. The general had drawn his sword and pointed it at the sky (which was a Yankee blue today), and began his address:

"Look at this clearing. Across two miles of open ground waits a wall of wretches starving for liberated steel. Will we let them go hungry? No. We'll feed every man we find. It's our Christian duty.

"This moment is the fulcrum of history. Some of you can't spell *fulcrum*, or define it. But the slight majority of you can spell *freedom*, and that's the only word you need. Every man, save a few simians, deserves freedom. The men on the other side of this field don't understand that. They want you to live and think their way. I, for one, refuse. I'd rather die or not think at all.

"We've all lost something irreplaceable. Friends. Brothers. Expensive slaves. Remember them as we charge. Right now, we have a chance to honor them. Right now, we can crush the Union's center and throw the continent's largest army into chaos. We can show their senators and newsmen that we will not kneel. I won't mince words: we are one charge away from *winning this war*. But I need you with me.

"Or rather, Pickett needs you with him. I'll be supervising."

Longstreet slapped Pickett on the back with the flat of his sword. The general yelped like a punished dog as he started awake and then gaped at

Longstreet in bewilderment. As he took in his surroundings, the confusion shifted to heartbreak.

"You can't agree with this madness," begged Pickett.

"I can and do." Longstreet slid off the horse and cut Pickett's restraints loose with two dangerously broad slashes. "Now, either I shoot you, or you steel yourself and take your chances with the Yankees. Sound fair?"

Pickett didn't answer. Instead, he eyed the men with an odd, unidentifiable expression. Then he palmed his revolver's grip and eyed Longstreet with what Anders guessed was indecision. Finally, his head and shoulders sank with unmistakable resignation.

"Men!" Pickett shouted. His voice carried bass, power, and minimal conviction.

"Sir!" shouted everyone in earshot. Anders imagined he was louder than the others.

"When I say charge, you *run*. Not canter. Not jog. *Run*. Don't you stop until you reach the other side of this field. No matter what you see or what you hear. Nothing else matters. Understand?!"

"Sir!"

"Good," said Pickett. His skin had taken on a dull gray tint, like cheap rubber. "I'm sorry."

Anders listened for hyperventilation during the countdown. Nothing. There were few audible hints that anyone was conscious, let alone breathing. The regiment held its breath as one as easily as it panicked. A cough started in his chest, traveled up, and died before it reached his lips.

"One!" cried Pickett. His voice broke. Then he fired a shot at the clouds. "Charge."

Anders sprinted. He ran for his father's respect, and his grandmother's honor, and his mother's mind, and his future children's freedom, and the freedom of whoever came after them. And because everyone else was running.

The lines quickly collapsed into one confused, sprinting cloud. Some men were faster, some slower, and some dead. Anders caught his first glimpse of the dead when a cannonball decapitated Roland, the bravest man he'd ever met. This would've made for a grisly corpse, if the ensuing explosion hadn't burnt and scattered the rest of Roland. Charred and pulped pieces of Roland covered Anders's uniform, along with every other lucky-yet-luckless soul standing nearby. Bryce retched to his right but kept running.

Anders started to doubt the integrity of the plan.

Nonetheless, he twirled. He twirled as synchronized rifle fire cut down Arthur. He twirled as impossibly high-pitched screams rang out and ended. He twirled as smoke caked his lungs and red-tinted mud made his uniform unrecognizable. There was nothing else to do.

Except run, which was harder. While the *Secession Twist* had become second nature, endurance running was a new experience. Anders had never been shot but imagined it felt something like the agony in his chest. He looked down twice to make sure that he hadn't, in fact, been shot in the chest. All clear. His heart was simply imploding on its own.

He looked back up. Everyone ahead of him was gone.

Worse yet, so was the music. Bryce's bugle, the morale appendix to the flag's heart, had gone silent. Anders stopped and found Bryce standing still and silent. A slim trail of foam ran from his lips to his collar, moving through the dirt covering his face. Anders defied patriotic instinct and turned around. He didn't have any real friends in any army, but Bryce listened without calling him names.

"You can't stop here. The general said to run."

"We're already dead."

"Just play. Walk and play. You don't have to run, just move. Then you'll make Columbia proud."

Bryce chuckled at nothing, as if he'd remembered history's best joke. That chuckle evolved into teary-eyed Mark Twain belly laughter. The mirthless guffaws cut through the screams of their peers, and multiple backhanded slaps failed to stop them.

Before Anders could make a second plea, Bryce raised his horn and stomped ahead with a full marching band's vigor. He played a slow version of "The Bonnie Blue Flag," imbued with fresh energy. Anders cheered, pumped a fist into the air, and watched a cannonball shatter Bryce's legs at the knee. It failed to explode, leaving Bryce broken instead of burned.

If he lived to reflect, Anders would say he tried to help Bryce. Or at least stopped to see if he was dead. It would be a better story for his children. But to survive long enough to have children, or even lose his virginity, Anders abandoned Bryce. He sprinted in the exact opposite direction, away from the cannons and rifles and bayonets and fists and other tools for ending his life before he was good and ready to go. And he left his flag with them. Whatever officer shot him for cowardice wouldn't need a bright red signal.

Then he tripped.

It felt like a rock or a corpse that had gone stiff. Either way, he found himself face down in the red mud hacking and crying. The second wave of doomed men charged over and on him, leaving at least sixteen pairs of footprints on his back. The pain put an end to any sobbing: wailing didn't work with the breath stomped out of him.

Once his lungs came back to life, he started crawling. The Union had launched their own bayonet charges to clean up the survivors, and he didn't intend to be found. Anders dragged himself into a blackened hole half his height, wrapped both hands around a jagged sedimentary rock, and waited.

A lifetime of instinct said to pray. Yet as the scant survivors of Pickett's offensive met the incredulous Union line, he watched in silence. A few blue uniforms fell over, but the bulk of the bodies were gray. Anders felt the seed of a plan. It would take a different strain of courage than the charge.

Anders stripped off his coat, hat, and pants. After kicking away his shoes, he crawled out of the ditch and toward the closest blue corpse. The black man was taller, but Anders didn't have time to be choosy. He dragged off the corpse's coat and pants, slid into them, and ripped the medal off the coat. Imitating a hero was beyond him. He dropped the glittering pin back into the muck, beside its owner.

He waited for a gunshot from either side to interrupt his second treason. Nothing. Anders dragged the denuded corpse into his old ditch and limped toward the Union lines. Hopefully the food had improved since his last stint as a loyalist.

4

BECOMING B. K. JEFFERSON

According to the unsent letter in his pocket, Anders's new name was B. K. Jefferson. He could do worse. The first initial could be Bryce, after the late trumpeter, and the second could be Katrina, after his less late mother. There was no helping the last name, but Bryce would learn to live with it.

The rest of the letter belonged to the dead. Anders read one line lamenting his wife moving on to a flourishing gunsmith, balled up the paper, and shoved it in a thornbush. His own trauma weighed enough, and he barely even noticed the fresh cuts on his palm.

"Bryce. Bryce." He mumbled the name as he walked, stepping over the odd stone or human. Somewhere beyond the smoke and iron, he could smell opportunity. From this moment, he could write a new life. A mother who never threw or drank anything. A father who stayed local. A girlfriend who existed. Neighbors who resembled and accepted him. And an enlistment that had gone swimmingly, free of even a hint of high treason.

Things were looking up for Bryce.

Bryce followed a trail of black soldiers back toward base camp. Or, at least, a cluster of tents that looked like a base camp. An awkward task, but the black regiments were the most likely to be missing a Jefferson. Recordkeeping was terrible in both factions, and Anders (*Bryce!*) opted to play it safe, even if he didn't have much experience doing so.

The black soldiers meandered past a cluster of patchy tents surrounded by multiple fires, six busy surgeons, and the competing smells of boiling stew, cheap wine, and human fluids. They stopped at a cluster of low tents with one dying fire, a blood-soaked surgeon reading an old *Harper's*

Weekly, and a single chicken head on a spit. By the look of it, the head had already rotted past edibility.

Bryce hovered behind the trees, watching the regiment at rest. Blankets were arranged in clusters of four or five, which might make blending in difficult. Mercifully, everything else looked wildly disorganized. Two open crates lay some distance from the fires (not far enough, in his experience), and soldiers freely claimed new hats or fresh bullets. Bryce doubted any written record of B. K. Jefferson's full name and appearance had survived the first year of the war.

Bryce pinched a blanket from a five-man group and dropped it into a four-man group on the opposite side of the camp. Then he slid underneath and tried to nap until his organs hurt less.

He'd gotten halfway through the usual nightmare about his mother broiling him alive, when a lanky man with an unmarred blue cap shook him awake. The soldier looked down at Bryce with mixed incredulity and irritation. Bryce offered what he hoped was a winning smile.

"Who the hell are you?"

"B. K. Jefferson," Bryce answered weakly. "I'm an octoroon," he added without provocation.

"My squad doesn't have a B. K. Jackson. Or an octoroon. Or even a fifth human."

"Are you sure?"

"Yes."

". . . Really sure?"

"Again, yes. Look, I understand. Your father wouldn't let you enlist, so you snuck over and pinched a uniform. But why a Negro regiment? Have you seen our casualties?"

The familiar accent puzzled Bryce and then snapped into place as the stranger expounded on salary caps and fatalities for black soldiers. The man had taped an education over the standard negro mode, just like Liberty Valley's schoolteacher. Nostalgia for simpler, less lethal years supplanted the initial shock. With luck, this one would be easier to impress.

"A small price for freedom," improvised Bryce.

"Good spirit. But freedom is for survivors," said the stranger.

"That doesn't sound very Christian."

"Mercifully, our regiment doesn't have a priest. Just faded Old Testaments in Spanish. I suspect they're leftovers from the Pig War but lack proof."

"What about the New Testament?"

"General Harrow cut it out. He doesn't want all the red-letter parts about peace and meekness giving people ideas."

Bryce nodded his understanding. He'd stumbled into one of the smarter blacks, capable of finishing a pidgin-free conversation without distraction from a passing bird or thoughts of white women. A friend like that would be invaluable in his new life. The man didn't have glasses, but he had a face where glasses would belong.

"My name's Gleason, by the way," said the negro, who was evidently Gleason. Bryce would have written it down in his pocket journal, but he'd abandoned it with the rest of his Confederate regalia. Forgetting a few names beat a sedition paper trail.

Judging by the loose skin around his neck and wrists, Gleason had once been fat. Extra weight tended to wither during a campaign. Bryce found that both sides fed the common men just enough to make it to the next battle.

"Is there something on me?"

"You used to be fat," Bryce said dreamily. He couldn't remember his last meal. The reflexive honesty earned a glare from Gleason that would have looked better with glasses.

"True," Gleason said icily. Then he looked Bryce over again, and his face softened. "And observant, I suppose."

Bryce hoped this was charisma at work, and not pity. His mother had always found pity pitiable. To this day, Bryce (not Anders!) pitied people who relied on pity and held little sympathy for their misfortunes.

"What's your real name?" asked Gleason. Anders considered the rich myth of B. K. Jackson's (or was it Jefferson's?) military career, which he'd already drafted at length in his head. Letting it go felt like a waste, but he needed the smart negro to help him find food.

"Anders. But I think if I try hard, I can be Bryce. Effort's like prayer, only it works. Not that I'm some kind of apostate or Deist. Unless you don't believe in God. Then we should be friends—I don't have anyone to talk to."

For the first time in their short relationship, Anders had the right answer. The word *Deist* flipped a switch in Gleason's mood. He now watched Anders with a hint of paternal warmth, or at least the bemusement one had for a clever dog. It'd be patronizing, if Anders hadn't given Gleason the same look after hearing his word choice.

"Tell you what, Anders. I keep a few extra rations stored on the side—"

"Because you used to be fat?"

". . . Admittedly, yes."

An ounce of battered confidence returned. He'd finally evolved into a student of human nature. Clearly, the minor trauma of the charge had been enough to shape him into an intellectual powerhouse. Soon the natural balance between himself and Gleason would assert itself. Until then, he'd be patient.

"I'd like that to be your last comment on the matter," Gleason added. "Do that, and we can leave your story as an octoroon alone. And then we can get you some food."

Anders's imagination already started drifting to dinner, or lunch, or whatever meal came after reality had collapsed into bullets and screams. Union fare had never moved him much. Despite far superior supplies, Union brass seemed content to flavor meals with righteousness. But a black regiment offered a change; there was no animal, fruit, or liquid that his Liberty Valley neighbors couldn't deep-fry.

Anders gladly shut up, stood to the side, and watched Gleason reveal a hole beneath one of the less frayed blankets. A leather sack sat at the bottom. Gleason untied it, reached inside, and retrieved what had once been a biscuit in a kinder life. Anders accepted it eagerly. Half the meal slipped out of his mouth as crumbs.

"Take note. This is my method for protecting personal effects." Gleason stretched the blanket back over his hole.

"What if someone steals the blanket?"

"The method is evolving."

"It's probably common. A lot of people don't have one."

"The method is evolving."

"Maybe we could make and sell blankets," thought Anders out loud. More crumbs escaped. "Then we'd be rich, for soldiers at least. And no one would ask us where we came from, or who we fought for, or why you know the word *evolving*."

"The method . . . Pardon?"

A white man on a white horse pulled up beside them and looked straight past Anders. Open disrespect from an officer restored some normalcy to Anders's world. The rider pointed down at Gleason, who stood at rigid attention.

"Coleson."

"Gleason," corrected Gleason. Anders, who would have gone along with the name change, found this bold.

"The rest of your squad's dead," said the officer. "You're the new corporal. Find three other unattached survivors and start a new squad. Keep them alive for an extra ration."

Gleason asked several follow-up questions. The officer rode off without answering, stopped before another survivor, and repeated the announcement. He made three more new corporals before drifting out of view.

"Congratulations," said Anders. "Most regiments don't have squads. So you're really one of the first squad leaders in America. Definitely one of the first black ones. You could be in the history books, if we win. If we lose, Ewell will probably bury your memory, only with fire instead of dirt."

Gleason remained lost in thought. He stared at the empty, now ownerless blankets beside his own.

"Corporal!" Anders added, snapping to attention. He put extra energy into the salute.

"You're going to be difficult to keep alive," Gleason mumbled. "What skills are you trained in?"

"Wit and loyalty, sir."

"Combat skills, Anders."

"I'm an excellent flag-twirler."

The corporal put his hands over his mouth and made a sharp, angry sound. After the human bark, his features settled back into academic poise.

"I also know Confederate cyphers. What do you do?"

"Speculative theater. I write visions of— *What did you say?!*"

4.5

SPECULATIVE THEATER

The Flying Soldier Review: A Black Stage!
BY STEPHEN MASON

∼

Manhattan Market Man Monthly, February 8, 1859

Black theater may very well be the eighth wonder of this world. Just as a well-trained dog might rise on its hindquarters, blacks may be moved to write, perform, and even direct theater! Whatever the quality, its very existence inspires. I now truly believe that in our Eli Whitney era, anything is possible.

So does the auteur (he uses the word!) Tobias Gleason. His latest play—again, of multiple!—is called *The Flying Soldier*. It's a long-form tribute to "The American Future," a matter explained in an idiosyncratic opening monologue. While the speech's length is questionable, the passion behind it isn't. Gleason imagines our nation overshadowing the staid castles of Europa and leaving behind the cruelty that built them. He also imagines negroes as the key, lending the work imagination.

In Gleason's future, soldiers do battle miles above the civilian world, via shoes attached to large balloons. This allows the warmongers of tomorrow (including a black governor!) to hide war's horrors from the people. A pair of mulatto reporters from opposite walks of life set out to expose the truth. But one is not what he seems (the rich one)!

Fanciful? Perhaps. Overwrought? Undeniably. But prop "airship skates" shackled to each actor make this mirror world feel real. And as real violence tears through Kansas, I welcome the distraction. That said, the leads looked tired by intermission, so solid wood "balloon shoes" was an error. A people less suited to toil might have collapsed.

The auteur calls this genre Scientific Theater. I suggest changing the name; science is a dull matter, best left to dull men. Negroes are exciting and excitable creatures, and should stick to exciting words. Only then can black art compete with true virtuosos.

Go out of your way to see *The Flying Soldier.* Lord knows when we'll see another talent unite the pen and the jungle without Frederick Douglass's maudlin hysterics.

5

GLEASON'S OPINIONS

A new morning, alive. No one had strung him up for desertion, defying every unspoken expectation. His new uniform even fit better. If it weren't for the homework, Anders would call it paradise. Instead, he racked his brain in earnest for the first time since he'd fallen from the schoolhouse windowsill. Gleason didn't seem like the type to throw cookware, but Anders kept an eye open.

Writing played a minimal role in his vision of martial redemption. He wasn't averse to it, at least compared to the endless series of doomed charges that comprised most of infantry life. But it was a far cry from the graceful maneuvers he deployed as a morale specialist. By and large, most men fighting on either side were subliterate. Literary inspiration was a dead end, at least compared to the delicate swing of a well-placed flag spin. This, and the teenage attention span, left his writing skills wanting.

Nonetheless, Gleason insisted he write down everything he could remember about Confederate cyphers.

"I don't see the point," muttered Anders. "All they ever did in these messages was argue."

"Over what?" Gleason asked, with all the adult patience he could find in his heart.

"Minutiae. Where to stand. When to stop standing there. How much food there was for standing around. Where we'd stand next. None of the real, Homeric grit of battle."

"Keep writing."

Anders kept writing. He got halfway through an idiot-proof explanation before his mind drifted. Lately, he'd been painfully aware of his exclusively male company. Anders wished that the army were coed, and not for the first time. He suspected whichever side made the change first would win.

In some regiments, the wounded interacted with nurses from the Sanitary Commission. Taking a bullet could earn him some female attention, yet Anders suspected he'd be left alone with infection and The Reaper. And Gleason would still ask after the cypher report as he walked into the light.

Gleason laid a palm on Anders's shoulder. The gesture read as both *take your time* and *hurry up*.

"I know you won't let me down. As Deists, we share a legacy of reason stretching back to the Founders. In a real way, we're their sons. It falls to us to use knowledge to fight for The American Future."

"Mr. Gleason, I might have lied a little. I'm not *certain* what a Deist is. Or most things involving God."

"Ah." Gleason's frown echoed the disappointment that marked most adult faces in Liberty Valley. He'd consider it a quirk of the black mind, but his mother used that expression as well. Anders wondered how many campaigns it would take for his version of that look to set in. He'd have to fight extra hard to avoid it.

"All I know is that God isn't paying much attention."

"Then you're a Deist!" Gleason declared with renewed enthusiasm. His energy left no room for debate: Anders had been drafted into the non-faith. He rolled his wrist, squinted at the slowly filling page, and wondered if Anabaptists had to write less. There had to be a sect dedicated to math somewhere.

Pickett's aides had only let him touch the codes because he liked puzzles (and they were vaguely certain that encoding messages amounted to lying, and thus dishonor). Anders took to the tables with zeal, certain that each message would be the one inquiring about skilled flag-twirlers, and how their value might be better recognized and preserved in the war effort. As he waited, he filtered a bunch of brouhaha about supplies and invasion staging points.

Today, rewriting the tables was easy enough, and not wholly divorced from his love for a good problem. The irritating part was *explaining* the Vigenère cypher in layman's terms. Gleason wanted the system described in terms that no officer could misunderstand, however intoxicated. Anders didn't see the point; their message had little chance of reaching Grant, or even a sober underling.

Then there was the matter of active keywords, which he had to pull from memory. After a few weeks under Pickett, Anders had devised a labor-saving method of decoding messages without a password. But a clear, concise description eluded him under pressure. Gleason watched him while sitting on the same log, leaving none of the distance and mess-about time necessary for good paperwork. He decided to simply list the codes he could recall and leave a truncated note to "Ask for more if you want it." Hopefully that would be the end of it, and no one higher up would care too much about cryptography until Anders felt more settled.

"This should do it," said Anders, folding the page in half. He regretted the gesture immediately, as Gleason looked like he might have a heart attack. But the new corporal accepted the sheet without verbal complaint, slowly sinking back to the baseline level of stress defining his lifestyle.

"Wonderful work. I'll rewrite this more legibly tonight and hand this off to the lieutenant."

"You should give it to the brigadier general yourself. Otherwise, the lieutenant will say he made it, and we won't get any credit."

"A cynical assumption. Up north, we're in this war together."

"Mama used to do it to black ladies back home. Farther north than here. She published ten poems about 'dreaming of free air,' and no one caught on."

"Noted," said Gleason. Anders understood this as officer for *You're right* and left it there.

Finishing the report gave Anders a taste of free air. He spent an hour of it on the same log, bone-tired. The dead men's blankets had been stolen by more alert hands, leaving Anders a choice between the earth and the log. Pockets of stray bullets and soiled bandages littered the earth, so the log won.

He woke up flanked by armed black men. Mortal terror gripped Anders until he recalled joining a black army. Then the terror faded to a low hum. One giant stood on the left, alongside two mortal-sized adults on the right. All three watched Gleason pace in the self-conscious manner of a leader. Longstreet had done the same on horseback. The gesture, however affected, successfully held the quartet's attention. Anders made a note, in case he lived long enough to get his own command.

"Men at arms!"

"Hey, Gleas."

"*Corporal Gleason*, Thomas. We're rising in this world, to our overdue place at the American table. To enjoy it, we must learn the niceties of rank and presentation."

"Sounds great, Corporal Gleas," said the closest negro on the right. "Since we built the table and all." Thomas looked skinny by nature instead of plight. Anders wondered where he hid his food.

"Thank you. Now, this is Anders. He's joining our squad in the struggle for The American Future."

Anders hoped the contradictory initials hand-stitched onto his sleeve weren't visible. Either way, the three privates nodded his way without judgment.

"I'm an octoroon," Anders clarified.

They nodded his way again, with judgment. The giant grunted.

"Now, Anders. You'll learn more about Thomas, Joaquin, and Mole in time. These three are veterans of the greatest Union victory since Antietam."

So am I, technically. For the first time in his loyalist career, Anders held a thought back. Gleason, as if he'd read the entire sequence of thought, loosened with relief. He gave the rest of his speech with true comfort. He wielded the clarity and even pace of an experienced pontificator.

"Violence, of course, leaves a mark on a man. But breathing truth into the promise of freedom is worth it. Even the *misfortune* of Mole's old squad."

The giant crossed himself. Anders searched for a mole-like feature. His eyes looked functional, alongside claw-free hands.

"Men, you might be aware of my status as the most famous Negro writer of our age."

"Frederick Douglass?" Thomas chimed in.

"You might be aware of my status as the second most famous Negro writer of our age."

"So that's why you got promoted?"

". . . Yes."

The men gave a mild but genuine round of applause. Gleason swelled with each clap, as if a missing piece of him had finally snapped into place. Enjoying the effect, Anders clapped a little louder and more rapidly than the others, until he drew a sidelong glance from Thomas.

"I'll admit, I was a little *put off* by the contrast between my former rank and edification," continued Gleason. "But I understand. It was a sacrifice in the name of the world to come. What the poets say is true: America is the home of the new human. Thus, America's character will reflect and shape the era to come.

"I want that humanity to be one where a Black visionary's plays are shown side by side with the words of his inferior yet plucky white contemporaries. Not divided, or panned by critics on racial grounds. I hope you're ready to fight for that world too."

"My children are still slaves," said Mole.

"That's right. We *all* struggle in our own way."

Anders started a new wave of applause. The others followed his lead, Mole a step behind his comrades. The nearest cluster of men eyed them like a fairground sideshow. Anders eyed them right back, inviting them to join in. Small acts of crowd manipulation elevated a flag-twirler's arsenal.

The slowest and most languid claps came from the third man (Joaquin, by elimination). He cupped his hands, coming out louder. Anders resolved to pick up the trick, as soon as he overcame the morale-busting instinct that something about the man was off.

"Well said, sir."

"Thank you. I've had a promotion speech ready for some time."

The officer on the white horse returned. Anders still didn't know his name or rank, but the ire behind his glare indicated at least a lieutenant.

"If you braindead niggers don't stop this noise, someone's getting flogged tonight."

He trotted away.

"It really was a nice speech," whispered Anders.

6

THE PITCH

Gleason said the triumph of their lifetimes was at hand. Anders gleamed with relief: terror and failure had characterized his life of late, and a change in the pattern felt overdue. If the blue army's fortune could turn around, why not his?

To commemorate his divorce from disgrace, Anders decided to become presentable. Ownership around the camp appeared to be fluid, so he pinched a brush from one of the only enlisted men with straight hair. The part in his dark hair hadn't been tended to since Lee's tent. Anders restored it with a hand mirror borrowed from Thomas, who'd stolen it from Joaquin in turn. Mole enjoyed freedom from the squad's circle of theft and counter-theft, doubtless due to the size of his calloused knuckles.

Ideally, Anders would give his uniform a true wash. But privates lacked access to the material niceties of a flag-twirler (which were the borrowed niceties of the officer they twirled for). He settled for thwacking B. K. Jefferson's uniform against a tree, dislodging the largest flakes of dried blood and mud. The effort still made him one of the neatest privates in sight.

When he rejoined Gleason, the corporal tipped his cap.

"Son, you're the picture of an American soldier."

The word *son* lifted Anders's mood for reasons he preferred not to interrogate. He followed Gleason with a borderline skip. They walked past the shabbier makeshift dwellings of the common infantry and lower officers toward the tents of command. These tents lacked holes or unidentifiable scents, just like Longstreet's inner circle.

"It's not easy to get time before a brigadier general," explained Glea-

THE PITCH ÷ 33

son. His cadence reminded Anders of the schoolhouse teacher, filtered through the extra words and casual arrogance of New York. "Our colonel isn't fond of bothering his superiors. Or talking to Black folk. But once I explained that an enterprising young man had cracked the secret of clandestine enemy communications, he got bored and wanted to end the conversation. Now we have ten minutes of Brigadier General Harrow's time."

"Amazing work," said Anders. "How long would it take one of us to become a brigadier general?"

"I'm feeling confident in our work," Gleason continued, ignoring the question outright. "To shore up our odds, I've given your report refined packing. I was saving this envelope for sending my latest play north. But your codes deserve it. Note the frills along the margins. That's Carolina cotton."

"Aren't we fighting to end Carolina cotton? With The American Future and all?"

Gleason wagged his finger. "Carolina cotton is part of The American Future. They should just pay the poor souls collecting it."

Anders let himself relax. Most black men he'd met outside of Liberty Valley carried a chip on their shoulder about one thing or another. They brayed about this insult or that whipping. Instead of that bitterness, Gleason had big ideas and used words from England.

Moreover, Anders resonated with The American Future. Those words bestowed purpose on his first two tours of horror. It was one thing to bleed for a hill Anders couldn't name in a state he didn't think either faction really needed. It was another to bleed for The American Future. The corporal wielded at least three-fifths of a white academic's intelligence and deserved matching deference.

The news hadn't reached the brigadier general's guard. He stopped Gleason and Anders with a silent extended palm. A gesture punctuated by the pistol in his other hand. The tall, red-eyed black man looked upon the corporal and Anders with flat detachment. While he didn't look *eager* to shoot them, he didn't look like it would bother him much either.

"Good morning, Simon," said Gleason.

"Morning, Gleas," said the guard.

"Our fortunes are changing. I have a report for the brigadier general."

"Our fortunes . . . You say that a lot."

"Were our brothers not emancipated this year? Have I not risen to the station of corporal? Was I not granted a flash of divine inspiration, leading to the birth of a script draft in the dingiest battlefields of our bleeding nation?"

"Sounds like yours. Not ours."

"Focus on emancipation. It changes how they see all of us."

Simon relented and holstered his pistol. He eyed Gleason with genuine respect, or at least none of the bafflement that followed most of the corporal's speeches. Anders gave the man a small nod: as a flag-twirler, he could relate to standing in the periphery of important people for hours on end.

Without being asked, Anders held the tent flap open for his superior. Gleason started to thank him but mercifully noticed this would ruin the theater of the moment and strode into the tent with purpose. Anders followed with what he hoped was at least the *impression* of purpose (he wasn't sold on the value of codes, or Gleason's insistence that this effort wouldn't out him as a double traitor). Simon chuckled behind them.

Inside, a familiar face glowered. The first man to call Anders a nigger since he'd become a fake black man. Anders had flinched by instinct, both for his character and the fact that *nigger* preceded most Liberty Valley fistfights. Black combatants used it with ease, whites with intensity.

"Sir!" Gleason said with a salute. Anders matched his timing.

"Ah. Lieutenant Hobbes."

"Corporal Gleason, sir!"

"Until you do something worth remembering, you're Hobbes."

Anders shrank back from the conversation. "Officer" had been an understatement: the white horse's rider ran the whole brigade. Harrow currently sat on a matching white wooden rocking chair, a luxury in a campaign where victories were counted in single boxes of bullets. The general's lip bore a wispy line of fur aspiring to the rank of mustache but falling short. His eyes were sunken and heavily lined, as if he hadn't slept since Fort Sumter. Said eyes flickered between Gleason and Anders, evaluating the soldiers claiming to have information more valuable than sleep.

"Good morning, sir. I hold, in my hands, with the Lord above as my witness, the key to our next victory. And many to follow." Gleason stood tall as Harrow weighed his soul, primed by a lifetime of ignoring dismissive stares. He also held the envelope in question out in both hands, waiting for the brigadier general to bite.

"I'm Anders," volunteered Anders.

"Shut up," volunteered Harrow.

Anders shut up, and Gleason extended the ornate envelope farther. Harrow stared at it like something dirty before finally accepting it in a gloved hand.

"And this is? Better not be any more Baptist nonsense. You'd think you boys would learn. If prayer worked that way, none of you would've been slaves in the first place."

"That's a guide to rebel cyphers, accurate as of yesterday. Including keywords."

"The day a pair of braindead niggers crack that nut, honey will rain from the sky."

That insult again. Braindead. *Nigger* meant that Anders's cover worked as intended, but *braindead* stung. It reduced him and his efforts to a stranger's snap judgment. If possible, he'd talk with Gleason about dropping *braindead* from the camp lexicon and replacing it with something more gentlemanly. The Southerners had been much kinder with their language.

"It's real," Anders squeaked. The brigadier general didn't respond until Gleason repeated it at adult volume. Harrow then, resenting the time and effort each motion ate, tore the envelope open, unfolded the parchment within, and mouthed the first paragraph to himself. Harrow doubled back a few times, swapping the occasional *d* and *b*. The errors added to Anders's estimation of their leader: Harrow must have been exhausted by long, inspired strategy sessions. It followed that he'd resist reading yet another piece of intelligence.

Nonetheless, the general finished the layman's summary of the Vigenère cypher, rotated letters and all. Anders let himself stand a little straighter. He'd resisted earlier, but he liked the sound of intellectual work. *Codebreaker Anders* would see fewer charges than *Private Anders* or *Flag-Twirler Anders* or even *Prisoner-of-War Anders*. He'd spend the rest of his military career with fingers covered in ink instead of dirt and blood.

Harrow struck a long match and brought it to the parchment. It caught quickly, charring hours of labor in seconds. The brigadier general let the fire spread in silence, risking his fingertips before letting the final embers fall. Codebreaker Anders hoped against hope that this was part of maintaining secrecy.

"Why?" asked Gleason, stunned.

"We can't stake battles on black intelligence. Even if it's reliable, it perverts the character of the army."

"But Anders is . . . an octoroon," said Gleason, pivoting quickly. Anders waited for his cleverness to bear fruit. "Maybe even a quadroon."

"Perhaps, but one-eighth nigger rounds up to nigger."

Codebreaker Anders raised his hand to correct the general's math. Gleason gently guided it down.

"What if I said it came *directly* from a Confederate soldier?"

"I'd ask where they were, in order to execute them with the full authority, approval, and force of American law."

One of Anders's feet drifted toward the exit. He caught himself before the drift turned into a sprint.

A familiar sensation returned. During Anders's more involved flag routines, time typically dragged and slowed. He used the time to weigh his pole's momentum, gauge audience reactions, and plot his next move. Bare-knuckle boxers had told him about similar experiences, when they weren't slurring words or asking after his mother. It took the same determination and focus to keep his face neutral as the brigadier general discussed treating traitors like traitors.

The charge had been simpler. Anders just had to run, and fall, and hide among the filth and dead. He didn't have to check his own eyes, mouth, and posture for tells. He was just a gray speck that became a blue speck. Nothing short of a lifetime of gambling could have trained Anders for Harrow's tent.

As his imagination flooded with nooses and firing squads, a miracle unfolded. Harrow looked past and through Gleason, Anders, the dangerous fire in his tent, and the nurse hidden under his straw bedding, and yawned. Napping commanded more interest than anything happening in his tent or the camp outside.

"I executed him myself," said Gleason, seizing the change in energy.

"Now that, Corporal, is work worth remembering. The body count makes Harrow's Harriers special. You may replace Hobbes yet, if the infection gets any worse."

"I'd be honored."

"Sorry to waste your time, boy," said Harrow. Then he turned to Anders. "Yours as well, young man."

"Thank you for yours, sir," said Gleason. Any morale damage hid behind his snap salute. Once again, Anders matched the corporal's movements. Nothing more convincing came to mind. Shadowing others kept him alive, but greatness didn't feel any closer.

6.5

—◆—

A GLOBAL PERSPECTIVE

TRANSLATED FROM FRENCH

General,

I know our own troubles abound. But I thought it might lighten your heart to hear a fairy tale from the United States. Or Northern United States. I wouldn't call a winner yet.

As you know, war rages over de facto vs. de jure slavery. The de facto slavers, as generous heroes, remain divided over letting Black men win their war for them. Don't ask me why, I suspect the entire system of rivers and canals here contains lead.

What matters are the conspiracies. The Disunited States is a paranoid and mystical land, and fertile ground for excellent mythology. Consider, for one, the myth of General James McClellan's ability. The man single-handedly extended the war, one inept stroke at a time. And, in classic American manner, became a folk hero for it. His demotion is a loss for comedy everywhere. But I may have a replacement.

In this case, an old Southern fable has traveled north: that we have installed spies and commandos into the ranks of Black soldiery, to inspire greater brutality against their white countrymen. Reportedly, we've orchestrated this scheme since Kansas fell apart.

Absorb the premise. Hold it in your heart. Breathe in its paranoid fumes.

What if we did it? No major commitment—the ofays will rule here, whoever wins. But let's send a few dozen men of serious salt to keep the conspiracy-minded guessing. And help our brothers in bondage. But mostly get a laugh.

What will the Americans do if they learn? Complain about the free manpower? They're close to strapping guns and blue hats to cows and having McClellan train them.

At the very least, send my cousin Joaquin Geoffroy. The man takes missing the revolution personally. He's always made the other men nervous and could stand to let some of that lunatic energy out. Let him be someone else's international incident.

Life is too short not to laugh.

Yours,

Agent Abel Geoffroy

7

THE WRETCHED AND THE DIVINE

During Harrow's rejection, Anders caught a glimpse of a nurse hiding in the corner. The brunette ducked beneath her own discarded clothing as soon as Anders spied her, distracting him from the grand strategy chatter to his left. A valuable excuse if and when Gleason grilled him about saying nothing in his work's defense.

Her stealth efforts moved Anders, who had quickly and violently learned the value of shrinking beneath notice. She was a natural. Her outline beneath the threadbare covers moved him further. He might have whispered or waved, but that would insult her makeshift camouflage skills.

Life hadn't thrown many nude women in Anders's path. The hidden photos, brothel runs, and war crimes of his peers hadn't appealed to him in past tours. While the last two still didn't, he now saw the appeal of a tasteful photo or twelve. He'd trade several meals for a photo of Harrow's guest. Tastefully. The nurse belonged only in the quality browns of gentlemanly pornography.

"Don't despair, Anders," said the despairing Gleason on the walk back. "We'll have our chance. It'll take time to get before a major general or a brigadier with sense. But these codes could decide the war. We'll be a modern Paris, letting the arrow of intellect fly into a brutish melee."

Reflexively, Anders eyed the general direction of Longstreet's massacre. That felt like more of a turning point than anything on paper. But Gleason had cited the Greeks, and men that did that tended to be correct. Anders nodded assent and marched in his superior's footsteps. When the corporal settled down for a depression nap and/or death between Thomas and Joaquin, Anders followed suit.

Why *did* the Greeks have so much weight? There wasn't much Homer in his schoolhouse windowsill days. He knew their gods were fond of glory, war, and incest. Similar to his God, at a glance around the country. Considering how easily duty and violence had found him, he was glad to be an only child.

His thoughts drifted back from the Greeks to the nurse. She starred as an angel in that night's dream.

Said angel combined competing visions of the divine. Artists depicted women in flowing white robes, a note Anders's psyche had recorded in triplicate. Preachers referred to an afterlife in the clouds, so she had to be able to fly. Then there were the traveling spiritualists, who'd camped in Liberty Valley with some regularity. They examined the biblical record in more detail than local worshippers, a habit that chafed with the preachers. In their writings, angels were a mind-shredding mass of limbs and energy.

The angel unified these concepts with eight shining wings. Anders liked the idea of soft white feathers carrying him away from the current hell of charging, writing, and whatever came next. The molten silver leaking from her ears and eyes was disconcerting, but he could ignore it for her warm smile and impossible proportions. Even the host of flaming eyes dotting each wing failed to diminish her beauty.

"Good soldier, are you weary?" Her voice was both soft and overpowering, like a whispering giant. He saluted by habit.

"Yes. In my bones and heart."

"I'm sorry. No child of God should suffer so," said the angel. She laid a comforting palm on Anders's shoulder. Her arctic-cold touch left his arm numb, which Anders could overlook given his options.

"Thank you, Miss Angel. That means everything."

"I see requests in your eyes, slightly to the left of the trauma. Let them out."

"Can you prevent my future pain?"

"No. That is the domain of God."

"Can you end the war?"

"No. That is the domain of Man."

"May I touch your butt?"

"Yes. It is the butt of all beings who walk in the light."

Anders avoided the disconcerting eyes on her wings and focused on her face. Two eyes filled with pure mercy looked down upon him. The mercy left no room for pupils and stung a bit if he looked directly for too long. But Anders felt and appreciated the mercy.

"I'm honored," he said, resisting tears. "First, can you clarify some things for me?"

"Of course."

"I've been in both armies. Which side has the soldiers of God?"

"There are few soldiers in heaven, Anders. Most sleep in the great fire below."

"Oh. But I'm—"

"Flag-twirlers as well."

Beneath his awe/horror at the divine and his ongoing hormonal rush, indignation stirred. Impressions of the charges, speeches, jokes, fistfights, and breakdowns he'd watched and joined in camps and battlefields across the nation stirred in unison and fought for space on his tongue. He searched for intelligent words. Something Gleason-ish.

"There are principles. People believe in them, and sprint for them, and then Bryce died, and he's probably not the last one, and I'm probably going to die." The venom in his own voice surprised him. "One side has to be right."

"Unambiguously. But letting the question linger was sin."

Anders let the issue go. If angels knew everything, they'd have graduated to the trinity and gotten out of lugging harps and flaming swords around. Arguing with Miss Fancy Bleeding Eyes wasn't worth losing his progress toward touching another human(esque) being. Whichever side of history he'd landed on, he preferred to die knowing he'd lost the fun part of his innocence as well.

"Sorry. If I Hail Mary a bunch of times, can I still touch your butt?"

"Of course, child. But it will require one thousand Hail Marys per enlistment. As a double defector, you must perform three thousand."

Anders got to work.

At two thousand nine hundred and eighty-seven, a weight settled on his shoulders. It jerked him back and forth, side to side, and back and forth again. Each phantom motion made his angel a little blurrier. As her hips faded, a pain equal to the death of his friend slashed at his heart.

Mole was a poor replacement. If any mortal stirred the same feelings, it wouldn't be the eternally frowning black giant shaking him awake. Anders swatted at his hands, emboldened by grief. Mole stepped away, leaving Anders room to punch impotently at the sky before settling down.

"What who why?" said Anders, despondent.

"Patrol," said Mole laconically. His mass blocked out the half-moon above.

Most adults in camp had some height on Anders, save Joaquin. Yet the amount Mole towered above him felt like a slight—or at least a violation of social order. The muscle gap only sharpened the sting. Anders maintained the musculature essential to his duties (former duties, until he had a talk with Gleason) as a flag-twirler, but Private Mole had genuine bulk.

"Ready?"

"Please bring back my angel."

"No, small idiot," said Mole. "In war, avoid angels, the light, and unscheduled sleep. Death hides there."

Anders made a single dry sob, followed by six or so more. Mole waited for him to finish, and then helped/forced him to stand. Anders then accepted a rifle from his unwanted companion. The giant didn't fear handing him a loaded weapon with a rusty bayonet, which only made Anders angrier.

"Whose gun is this?"

"James. He was lucky, until he died. Hopefully you'll be lucky and live."

Anders searched for the ugliest word he knew. "Are you *braindead*?" he spat. "Are you genuinely stupid, or do you think this is funny?"

Mole ambled past the camp, into a patch of tall grass. He clearly expected Anders to follow. The broken stalks behind him made a natural path, annoying Anders further. On top of being alone, he was still small.

Anders spent a few minutes (maybe one, maybe ten) standing still, listening to the crickets play their irritating song. Then the spirit that helped him through 1862 sparked again. He took off down Mole's natural trail, stopping to steal a sip from a neighbor's canteen. If soldiers had to share hell, they could stand to share water.

A stronger flavor greeted him. Whiskey—the smoky kind his mother favored. He coughed like a fourteen-year-old child, straightened himself out like a fifteen-year-old man, and returned to the chase. Better to be scarce when the liquor was missed.

The giant's path seemed to be the standard route—peanut shells and clumps of spent chew dotted the flanks of the trail. Alongside the odd half-finished cigarette. Only luck had spared the Harriers a brush fire. The same luck kept Anders upright. His run was mostly downhill, and a dozen gopher holes threatened his ankles. He slowed down to a jog—he could survive a sprain, but an army doctor might decide to take the whole foot.

"Mole!" Anders shouted as he caught up. The man crouched behind a wide, dead tree that left both shoulders exposed. If nothing else, Anders knew no sharpshooters were about.

Mole returned a shushing gesture. Anders closed the distance in silence. He caught himself creeping forward in an imitation of Mole's stance. Once again, in another man's shadow. Was that his place in the world? Was he a good learner, or a witless follower? Would he ever get to touch anyone's butt?

"I'm a little stupid, and you're a little funny," said Mole, interrupting the spiral.

"Pardon?"

"You asked me."

"Oh. Thank you for answering."

Silence resettled between them. Mole carefully parted sections of tall grass, looking for hints of rebel stragglers, spies, or survivors. While Anders matched his motions, his mind was busy fretting. If they found any of the three S's, they might know Anders. He still didn't have a plan for that, a gaffe he barely had the energy to chide himself for. If they met a friend, he had to either shoot fast, join them, or die.

His mind wandered to hell, a lighter topic.

"Hail Mary," mumbled Anders. "Hail Mary, Hail Mary," he added. His grasp of Scripture was weak, but he *felt* that finishing her challenge should bring her back.

"Are you Catholic?" asked Mole, with a hint of concern. He slowed his trek through the grass a beat but never came to a stop.

"No, but I think my angel is. She took the offer, at least."

"As long as you're not Catholic. Thomas thinks they plan to take over the country, once both sides are tired. It's the next war."

Anders weighed the idea. His mother had similar theories. He'd nodded instead of risking a second branding.

"Gleason says I'm a Deist."

Mole shrugged. "I don't know what that is."

"Me neither."

"He's probably right. Gleason knows such things."

"True. The Greeks."

"The Greeks."

They'd reached something like the same page, which made Anders less tense during subsequent circles around the camp. And all the more surprised when Mole tore off a page nailed against a tree. He thrust it into Anders's chest, nearly bowling him over by accident.

"Read this, please." Mole pointed at the sheet, covered in large black type.

"I'm tired, and reading takes it out of me. Can't you do it?"

"No. I wasn't allowed."

Illiteracy was standard, but *allowed* hung in the air between them. Anders knew, but didn't want to know. He bit back, "Were you a slave?" The endless screech of local crickets was far preferable.

"Yes." Mole read him without a word.

"Sorry," said Anders. "That they did that. In the South."

"Mmm."

"My upbringing was pretty rough too."

"I'm sure. Can you read the sign?"

"My mother was terrifying," continued Anders. The small ground between them felt uneven. "Very mean."

"That's hard," Mole said without irony, making Anders feel lower. Why slaves let so much of their slaveness leak into otherwise pleasant days was beyond him. Wasn't their own war enough?

"I'm from a free state, you know."

"I guessed."

"We never had slaves."

"That's good."

"We're self-reliant, up in Illinois, north of slavery. A day's work, a day's dollar. But we're also generous. I'm going to read this, just to be amenable."

"Thank you."

Anders cracked his neck as if facing physical effort, and then held the sign at eye level. Mercifully, this obscured direct eye contact with Mole. The handbill's block letters remained legible in the limited light, along with a stunningly detailed sketch of an ornate royal scepter. Anders returned his focus to the words, which he read aloud.

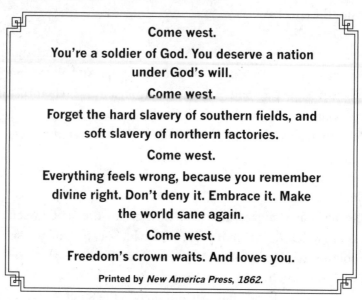

> ### Come west.
> **You're a soldier of God. You deserve a nation under God's will.**
> ### Come west.
> **Forget the hard slavery of southern fields, and soft slavery of northern factories.**
> ### Come west.
> **Everything feels wrong, because you remember divine right. Don't deny it. Embrace it. Make the world sane again.**
> ### Come west.
> **Freedom's crown waits. And loves you.**
>
> Printed by *New America Press, 1862.*

"Enemy propaganda," declared Mole. He mispronounced *propaganda*, which Anders left uncorrected. "They want us confused. Do we report it?"

"No point. Harrow only takes intelligence from white officers. We're black enlisted men."

Mole watched Anders in silence for some time.

"Okay," the giant finally declared.

"I'm an octoroon," noted Anders.

"Okay," repeated Mole.

Their patrol continued without incident, save Mole taking the occasional glance at the handbill. To move things along, Anders folded it in thirds and stuffed it in his left pocket.

On their sixth or seventh loop, Anders took to naming trees. He named the dead oak Mole had hidden behind Bell. A tall, bullet-pockmarked oak was Robin. The healthiest, largest sycamore in sight was Angel. He considered sharing this pastime with Mole but imagined talk drifting back to the handbill and the details of Anders's service. Or, worse yet, bondage. Then he ran out of names, save Katrina. Better to leave that alone.

They made it back to their corner of camp before the sun finished creeping into view. Mole pointed at Thomas and Joaquin, and Anders gleaned his meaning without explanation. They were the next two damned souls charged with facing any hidden danger first and alone. As the newest, youngest, and most suspicious of their pair, it fell to Anders to wake them up.

Anders prodded Thomas with a tree branch until he stirred, cursing softly. He looked just as angry about returning to conscious life as Anders had been.

"Patrol," said Mole.

"Fuck you, cotton nigger. I was dreaming about food. Real food, instead of hard bread and harder pork. I'm going to lose my teeth before a gray gets around to killing me."

Mole handed Thomas his gun. The weapon had the same cooling effect on Thomas as on Anders. If he didn't know better, Anders would think it was intentional.

"Sorry," muttered Thomas. "It was a good dream."

Mole patted Thomas on the back. The soft, stoic gesture made Anders feel *much* closer to Thomas than to Mole. The born freeman stood on the same side of the uneven earth that separated Anders and the former slave. Whatever ills the country had heaped on Thomas, Anders could at least look directly at them without digging out his eyes.

Thomas shuffled over to a dozing neighbor, scooped up his canteen, and found it empty. He lobbed it into the distance without bothering to curse. The sober private sleepwalked down Mole's trail, starting a dirty version of "John Brown's Blood." The words were unintelligible, but Anders had heard the parody before. It described General Lee's wife in some detail.

Anders jostled Joaquin awake with significantly less effort. The man half rolled, half kipped forward, rising like a natural dancer. Stranger yet, he smiled warmly at the notion of potentially finding Confederate scouts or mysterious propagandists. The enthusiasm for danger and a distinctly nonstandard name might have raised a range of questions in Anders if he hadn't deeply desired to be asleep again. For the second time, he found himself relating to the brigadier general that had burned his words. Sloth might hurt the cause, but so did dying of exhaustion.

"Thank you, boy."

Boy didn't fit a warrior of his stature, but he let it go.

Anders laid down without a shred of new wisdom. Just the weight of fresh mental fatigue, lingering physical fatigue, and guilt from lying near a slave. At least if they won, he'd be the last white man to inherit guilt for the black problem. Possibly if the South won too, albeit for different reasons. Either way, peace couldn't come soon enough.

An hour later, he rolled to his feet.

No amount of prayer or begging returned the angel to his dreams. Anders tended to himself by a tree the camp had wordlessly designated for that purpose. He pitied the tree, but everyone made sacrifices for the war.

8

JEFFERSON, JEFFERSON, AND JEFFERSON

Sunlight woke Anders instead of an officer's boot, meaning life had improved. He started the day by digging an anti-theft hole and dumping the enemy propaganda inside. It would make a fine postwar souvenir. Unless he earned a medal, primary documents would be invaluable proof he'd actually been involved.

Then his morning turned south. *Could* he earn a medal? There was no record of him rejoining the Union army. Or doing anything but dying in an anonymous Carolina ditch.

"Gleason! Sir! Can I ask you a question? I think we've bonded. It's a big question, but we've bonded. Have we bonded?"

"Good morning," said Gleason. He peered into what looked *like* a tin cup of coffee but smelled otherwise. For the first time, he looked doubtful.

"I joined under certain circumstances, which we discussed while bonding. Can I still win honors? Or get paid?"

Gleason emptied the cup into the brush before responding. Beetles scurried away from the coffee's landing site, where a smell between copper and sulfur wafted through the air. The fumes could finally put an end to the camp's wildlife problem.

"Anders, this is about more than any one man's honor. It's about the shape of a nation. A man's personhood, whatever shade of armor he wears into the arena of life."

"Of course," said Anders, buying time as he put together the metaphor. "But I want to buy food after the war."

"Quite important. But so is equity. Have I told you my mother's last name?"

"My family doesn't own stuff. There was a house, but it burned down during a birthday fire."

"Her last name was Jefferson," Gleason continued, acknowledging Anders's latest tragedy with a brief pat on the shoulder. "Of *the* Jeffersons. My ancestor enshrined equality in the nation's founding documents. A mission you and I continue today."

That didn't sound right. Anders screwed up his face again, this time with an audience.

"*The* Jefferson was white. Real white, not the fake Irish kind."

"He loved both races, in his heart and his actions."

That sounded more like the president Anders learned about from the schoolhouse window. Though the teacher had always said *Jefferson* in a voice thick with resentment. She must not have known about the love for his slaves that Gleason had inherited.

"Oh! You're a reverse octoroon."

"I suppose."

"Very impressive. I thought you were a normal negro."

"That's my point, Anders. There are no normal Negroes: every American is exceptional. I'll see what I can do about your wages, but first I have to work my way up. Properly falsifying records takes authority."

Or destroying them. The memory of Harrow's matches remained fresh. Along with the other presence in the command tent, but half of that was imagination. He'd seen just enough to realize he hadn't talked to nearly enough nurses over the last two years. Taking a bullet to the foot might work.

"Will that take long? You just became a corporal."

"No. I've got momentum," parried Gleason. "And while The American Future comes first, I'll make sure my men come second. Now get your things and find out where Thomas is hiding. We have an assignment."

Jefferson. Equity. Assignment. Anders left satisfied with the elite, multi-syllabic conversation. He even stood a decent chance of being paid for it.

Eventually, he found Thomas on the former battlefield, reading in a ditch created by a cannonball. Anders almost recalled the pit he'd found his new uniform in but successfully repressed the memory with a deep breath and elbow to his own side. Through the pain, he noted that Thomas didn't look like he wanted to be found, which Anders could respect.

Reading was an admirable hobby, particularly for a spade. He'd consider Thomas another intellectual, but intellectuals always introduced themselves as such. Besides, Thomas had a newspaper, and those never made anyone any smarter.

"Hey, did you know Gleason's descended from—"

"Yes. He's not shy about it."

"A black Jefferson. Can you believe it?"

"Who do you think I'm named after?"

✦ ✦ ✦

As the company (one hundred of the six thousand under Harrow) gathered north of the camp, Anders polled more soldiers on their relationships with Thomas Jefferson. Given God's pique of late, he expected to find more deluded sons of the White House. Half a new stereotype had already formed in his head. But there weren't any others.

Two options remained. Either Gleason and Thomas were uniquely mad, or a Top-Three president indulged in miscegenation. Specifically, miscegenation with *his property*. Words came to mind for that, but Katrina would have slapped them out of his mouth. So Anders pushed them out of mind and kept his eyes open for a new flag.

At the moment, he was a private. In theory, flag-twirlers were below them as decorative baubles outside the command structure. But Anders had gleaned that his odds and lifestyle were better outside the hierarchy than at the bottom. He trusted Gleason to reach the top, but until then he'd find his own solutions.

They stood on a hill of largely dead grass, likely stomped out by thousands of boots. The sun shone in appreciation of the Union's triumph. Anders hoped. His angel had left the righteousness of their cause an open question.

Gleason's squad formed the right half of a ten-man line. Anders had nodded, winked, and waved to the men of the other squad. Nothing. He'd have continued if Thomas hadn't given him a reproachful flick to the ear. Touching a paler child hinted at origins at *least* as far north as Massachusetts. Maybe even Canada.

Then Anders shook his head. *Man*, not child. He was in the army. He'd held multiple guns. Statistically, a bullet he'd fired in battle had killed someone. He was a man. He did manly things his unknown father would be proud of. Like press-ups, and drinking with blacks, and only crying when he was off-duty. *Man.*

A captain loomed over them on a sick-looking horse. Anders didn't know his name, but he could pin an officer's rank by the depth of the furrow in his brow. The red-haired man was a captain. A good one, if he'd gotten past the prevailing ire against papists and men who resembled them.

"Men," bellowed the captain.

"Yes!" said Anders before he could stop himself. He ducked another flick from Thomas. Surprisingly, Gleason stood on the edge of career-killing laughter. Cheer leaked out in two small coughs as the chase continued. Anders guessed the corporal found Thomas's lack of self-control amusing. Whatever the case, the corporal held it in by biting his top lip.

"Through effort and sacrifice, we've taken this hill. But the grandest sacrifices were made by the men no longer with us. I suggest you follow their example in the future. Until then, we're left with you cowards."

A bugle player stood to the captain's left, stiffly waving a flag. Anders marked him as a permanent enemy. Even his *location* was hackwork; a proper routine should be conducted behind the speaker, in order to avoid distracting from their commander's presence. Then speech and flag flowed together, bewitching observers until they reached a zenith of patriotism and bloodlust. As the imposter struggled through a *Sumter Salute*, Anders lost any vestige of professional sympathy.

"Can you believe this?" hissed Anders.

"Boy, if you don't shut the hell up," hissed Thomas.

"Why don't you? Boy," snapped Anders.

Gleason almost laughed again, confounding both soldiers. How a man that took himself that seriously had hid a sense of humor that long was a mystery. When Mole let an open chuckle out, both Anders and Thomas straightened up and stood still. They'd tumbled to the bottom of a hierarchy of five.

Anders returned his focus to the captain's speech, struggling to ignore the obscenity to his side. At the very least, the twirler looked embarrassed. Though that was another error in itself. A flag-twirler's three emotional modes were stoic, jubilant, and furious. Much like men in general.

"This regiment, despite its complexion, has marked history," said the captain. "I'm proud to be a part of it. Take a moment to be proud of yourselves, and General Harrow, and mostly General Harrow. The moment is now over. It's time to get back to work."

The captain borrowed Harrow's cadence, expression, and word choice. His horse was even white (though the appearance that it would keel over at any moment dimmed the effect). Anders could relate to the copycat impulse. Life in the others' shadow had that effect.

"The brigade has new orders, and we're marching out tomorrow. Today's about mop-up. Our company's charged with local resource evaluation and acquisition."

"Looting," Joaquin whispered. It was the first word Anders had heard from him, and he didn't sound displeased.

"Your corporals have your targets. We've saved the men and women of this region from pillaging by Lee's barbarians. Now we'll help them contribute what they can for our trouble. The patriots among them will appreciate it."

The captain turned his horse without fanfare. A moody exit Anders guessed came from Harrow as well. That said, after watching innumerable officers hold for applause, Anders found the change laudable. Applause-worthy, even.

He appeared to be alone. Gleason grimaced like a teenager confronted with a forgotten and hated chore. Thomas pouted like a child confronted with a forgotten and hated chore. And Joaquin, judging by the way he stared imaginatively into the crowds, hadn't heard a word since *acquisition*.

With his mirth gone sour, Gleason glanced hopefully toward Anders and Thomas for fresh entertainment. Once more, Anders cursed his lack of a flag. A *Lincoln Step* could brighten the day of anyone north of Georgia.

"He did say we should be proud," noted Anders.

"You were on . . . Never mind," said Gleason. "It's not palatable, but it's our duty. And as far as looting goes, our target is of prime importance."

Anders squinted at *prime importance*, put together the context clues, and nodded. Success brought Gleason closer to promotion, and Anders closer to some kind of recognition for past, current, and upcoming hell.

"I'm with you," he said. Surely that meant more from a habitual defector. "What is it?"

"A bank?" suggested Joaquin.

"A brothel?" suggested Thomas.

Mole didn't play.

"An arms factory," said Gleason. "While the others fixate on wealth,
we'll keep the brigade armed." He'd recovered the stoic poise of his first
speech, even as Thomas cursed and pitched his hat into a thornbush.
Gleason then snapped, pointed, and waited for Thomas to retrieve the
hat.

✢ ✢ ✢

Gleason led the march into Tinpot, Pennsylvania, in relative silence,
providing only one monologue on the topic of antiquity. It focused on
The Odyssey, and how Odysseus had to lead his men through multiple
acts beneath his dignity to blossom into a legend. This sounded good to
Anders until Thomas asked how many of them would be turned into pigs.
Gleason (who looked surprised that Thomas had ever *heard* of the poem)
then turned to sulking.

The cart pulled by others left little room for sulking. Or energy.
Anders thanked his angel for the thin film of rubber around his side's
handle. Mole and Joaquin's side had naked wooden corners interrupted
by splinters.

"We're soldiers, not horses," grumbled Thomas. "It's going to be even
worse with those damn guns."

"It's a promotion, in a way," mused Anders. "Horses get shot when they
can't work. Soldiers get shot when they do."

"Tell Gleason that. He'll put it in a play," Thomas muttered bitterly.

"That'd be something else. People knowing my name."

"Didn't say anything about credit."

Like many towns, Tinpot was divided among a mansion, a factory, and
the hovels supporting them. As a former hovel dweller, Anders was an
expert. Raiding the factory was good fortune: these people didn't have
much to steal. Based on the disinterested stares they drew from muddy
doorsteps, they didn't even have a stake in the battle's winner.

"A damn shame," said Gleason.

"Huh? Where?" asked Anders.

"Keep moving."

At three stories tall, the factory towered over everything else. Like many factories, it had absorbed prosperity from the surrounding town like a sponge. Still, eager plants were all over the union, and most were formally dedicated to the war effort. Swiping arms a week earlier than they'd be shipped out was beyond Anders, but he appreciated the air of relative prestige about the task. Along with the chance of scoring an officer's pistol, which was much closer to his practical size.

"Jefferson Firearms," mumbled Anders, reading the sun-faded sign. "How about that?"

"Hmm," grunted Gleason, in the manner of great thinkers. His ancestor's name brought out his reflective streak. Like most things.

Thomas, for his part, focused on the present and the literal burden it had placed on him. Equally admirable, in a sense. Surviving America as a work-averse black man spoke to strength of character.

"Did they make you do this in the mine?" said Thomas, glancing back at Mole. Anders quietly wrote the word *mine* out of his memory of the sentence. He deserved some peace of mind.

"I didn't have a cart."

Thomas elaborated on a point about hard labor, the Emancipation Proclamation, and hypocrisy that went unacknowledged by their officer. Instead, the corporal pointed at a vehicle that seemed out of place, and a man that *definitely* was. Thomas quickly trailed off, watching the stranger with mixed fear and befuddlement.

A ramshackle carriage sat by the factory gates. Its driver dozed, likely waiting for whoever occupied the front passenger seat. He wore an unbuttoned gray coat and stained gray pants. The slack uniform contrasted with the thin, neat, closely maintained beard he sported. It implied knife control that they were lucky to catch off guard. With razors going the way of soft bread as the war limped on, grooming pushed enlisted men's dexterity to the limit.

The carriage looked out of place for both the army and the mud town. Nothing else that expensive had touched Tinpot on this side of the century. Some generous aristocrat had likely donated it to the rebel cause, boosting his chances of staying an aristocrat. Anders was clearheaded enough to appreciate the heavy wheels, sturdy construction, and single well-behaved horse. He kept said admiration off his face to avoid uncomfortable and well-deserved questions about his loyalty.

"Odd," said Mole, capturing what the rest of them fumbled around. "Let's tie him up."

The sixth sense for upstart slaves that had preserved generations of Southern men kicked in, and the rider's eyes opened. The rest of him moved before anyone could shout a word of warning. Survival erased the sloppiness that made the encounter possible.

The rider sprang out of his seat, betting everything on a rust-flecked knife. It appeared in the man's grip from nowhere. Then it came Anders's way, threatening the life he'd traded his sense of self to preserve.

A man with stronger instincts might have fired, and a man with weaker instincts might have died. For his part, Anders held his rifle by the barrel and swung it like a wooden club. The blow collided with the rider's temple and nearly sent Anders's own bayonet into his flank. He was lucky enough for it to only slash his coat open. Anders let the gun slip from his now-aching fingers, keenly aware it had come as close to killing him as the enemy.

"Fine work," said Gleason.

"Oh god. Oh god. Oh god," chanted Thomas. He finally got his rifle to bear, in case the limp body rose from the dust. It didn't. The rider remained still as Joaquin stepped through Thomas's line of fire and lifted Anders's gun. He examined it ruefully, like a fresh meal tossed aside by a fat dilettante.

"Gun's broken," said Joaquin, judgmentally. Anders didn't have the presence of mind to place the accent leaking through. "Why not use the bayonet?"

Anders tried to mouth something about trained habits and flag-twirling. Hyperventilation wouldn't let him get a word out.

Mole wordlessly patted Anders down, hunting for stab wounds (both enemy and self-inflicted). It was the closest Anders would get to a hug, so he allowed it. In the worst case, a veteran slave had more experience successfully treating open cuts than army doctors.

"We'll replace the weapon," said Gleason. He sauntered over to the cart and pulled out a fresh repeater. "Sooner rather than later. There's double-dealing afoot. The guns in here could arm a company, and the powder could blow one apart."

"Is he dead?" wheezed Anders. The rider hadn't moved, and Anders hadn't taken his eyes off him.

Joaquin snorted. "Of course."

"—not," added Gleason. "Of course not. You've painted a shining picture of restraint, Anders. Thomas, Joaquin, kindly restrain our prisoner and find him somewhere to rest."

Joaquin grabbed the still figure by the legs. Thomas put a finger to the man's neck, shuddered, and hoisted him by the shoulders. Together, they carried away a man Anders tried to believe was sleeping.

"Do we bury him?" asked Thomas.

"If you can do it alone," replied Joaquin.

As the conversation descended further, Gleason stayed on task. After handing the near-mute Anders his new gun and more ammunition than the boy had ever held, the corporal strode to the thick, high front door. Then he thought better of it and led them to a smaller, unremarkable side door. It bore a single heavy iron lock.

Anders tried to say, "I'm good with locks." Someone replaced his words with "I didn't mean to hurt him."

"Mole. The door."

The giant stomped up to the door, kneeled down, and stuck a bent piece of scrap into the lock. Seconds later, he gently pushed the door open. Competing scents of sawdust and gunpowder wafted out. It wasn't *pleasant*, but Anders welcomed a novel sensory distraction from what he'd just experienced.

"Thank you," said Anders. The corporal marched inside without comment. Mole patted Anders twice before following suit. Left alone for a few precious seconds, Anders bit into his sleeve, screamed, and then limped ahead. It was time to meet the last Jefferson of the day.

8.5

WHY WE FIGHT

"I have three brothers that love guns and hate thinking. If you think I'll be the only old nigger at every family reunion that didn't fight, you're insane."

—Private Thomas Lobdell, On Duty

"They took my house. My father's gift to my sons, stolen over a family spat. I think it's only right I throw a bonfire at Abe's."

—General Robert E. Lee, On Honor

"The warmonger in chief gave up on compromise. We could have come together. After Antietam, I proposed making the negroes under dispute half slaves. From January to June, they'd conduct their usual favors for our brothers in the South. And from July to December, they'd breathe free air. That's what democracy means: meeting in the middle. Find a measure that reaches halfway between you."

—General James McClellan, On Fellowship

"I couldn't afford a substitute. I'm hoping to make officer so that I can afford someone to take my place."

—Pvt. Geordie Evans, On Freedom

"Father said I had to fight. The training was the best part. I don't know why war can't be more like training."

—Pvt. Bryce Orton, On Family

"Do you know what it's like to wake up without your slaves? My daughters do. Emancipation sent their spades scattering like roaches. My Flora just washed her own clothing for the first time in thirty young years, and now no gentleman will have her. I'll never forget the tear stains on that letter."

—General J.E.B. Stuart, On Justice

"I don't see why we're starting an out-and-out war. I love the sales, but I don't get it. The real countries in Europe know how to throw a good shadow war. We can't even keep it in Kansas for a year. Why risk all our new real estate?"

—Slade Jefferson, On Peace

9

REVOLVERS

Liberty Valley never attracted a large factory. A textile magnate had come close, but the entrepreneur disliked the townspeople's mixed air of hope and irritation. A factory needed men who would take their place in line and stay there, not look for less lethal work down the road. Especially when there *was* less lethal work down the road, at either of the family farms least hostile to blacks.

Today, Jefferson Firearms became Anders's first factory experience. Above all, it was humbling. They stalked past seemingly endless identical wooden benches and machines he didn't understand. He'd assumed three floors from the outside, but they stood below a single high ceiling. The light pouring in through three layers of windows recalled a church. He'd found the shrine of the gun. Maybe the dozens that labored there had felt something like divine purpose, whirring away as individual parts of a giant machine.

Shame about the air. It might not be black lung, but Anders could feel himself developing *some* kind of lung. The locals' dejected state made a little more sense. After marching past a stack of half-finished rifles, he tied a handkerchief into a makeshift mask. He looked like a frontier bandit, but they'd come to steal anyway.

The others picked up the idea quickly. Soon, Gleason alone stood unmasked. If they weren't sneaking, Anders would have asked why. Since they *were* sneaking, Anders imagined a speech about the New Human staring down opponents without illusion or cowardice. The theoretical speech inspired Anders, despite having committed his first murder (*kill*, his first *kill*), and he snuck with a little more pep.

They fell into a natural formation. The eager Joaquin in front, followed by the implacable Mole. Thomas trailed behind Mole, enjoying the natural cover his bulk provided. Then Anders, who quietly worked through the fact that the rider outside was *definitely* dead. Finally, Gleason brought up the rear, where he could give orders from a proper, informed distance.

Amid the abandoned scraps, Gleason selected a fully constructed pistol. He cradled the knockoff Colt like a gift from God. J.F. was engraved on the handle and barrel, advertising the brand to anyone that survived it. Gleason spun the five empty chambers, luxuriating in holding a real signifier of rank. Anders, who had entered hoping to find a revolver of his own, tried to keep jealousy off his face. A repeater felt like a con.

"Keep an eye out for ammunition," Gleason whispered. His eyes didn't leave the gun.

"Yessir," said Anders. The others nodded or shrugged without breaking pace. The riddle of the Confederate rider cast a pall of danger over what should have been a satisfying scavenge. Or maybe they just wanted pistols of their own.

Joaquin stopped and held up a fist. This meant nothing to the others, who assumed it was one of his quirks and tramped past him. They halted after his hiss of "Stop, idiots," save Gleason. He waited for "Please stop, *sir*."

Joaquin crept to an adjacent corner, back pressed against the dusty brick wall. He cupped his right ear and leaned as far forward as he could without becoming a target. Gleason followed suit, followed by Anders a polite full-body length behind the corporal and de facto scout. Thomas replaced Gleason at the rear, clutching his rifle with a discomfiting finger resting on the trigger.

"What are we listening for?" whispered Anders.

Joaquin cursed in French, creating new questions. Anders let them go and listened. In the new silence, he could pick out a veteran smoker's rasp. The dry voice carried a boisterous confidence, as if the owner were both sick and in perfect health.

"I'm telling you, get married. I should've done it before Sumter," said the smoker. "You're wasting your freedom. Or what passes for it up here.

"That's the worst part of army life besides the dying. No free female company."

"Nothing's free," said a softer, smoother voice. No more than two cigarettes an hour, maybe three. "And payment comes with discretion and experience. Everything a business or personal relationship needs."

"I see. That's why this shipment's got half the weight and twice the cost."

"You're welcome. Most of my boys fled before the battle. I doubt they'll be done cowering until both armies move on."

Joaquin belly-crawled around the corner. The medley of tools and baubles on him jangled as he went, but correcting him would have been louder. Anders took his preoccupation (and the lack of incoming fire) as a chance to peek around the corner and get eyes on the enemy.

Two marks sat together, feet resting on the same side of a wooden table. A civilian and a soldier. The soldier displayed a slovenliness Longstreet never would have tolerated. His coat was tied around his waist by the sleeves, revealing a shirt covered in scratches and old bloodstains. No sign of a weapon in reach—an achievement in a firearms factory. The remnants of Anders's pride as a Southern soldier took offense. The sword leaned against the far wall implied officer status (along with his facial hair), compounding the Confederate's sins.

The trader occupied his role with much more flair. His suit was genuine night-sky black instead of the off-blue most could afford. Anders's mother claimed that if he ever wore non-matrimonial jewelry, he'd be robbed by real men. Yet the civilian sat comfortably with a glittering silver ring on each finger, on both hands. He had gold hair to match. Both colors dotted his smile; the man's teeth could likely buy someone's freedom.

Despite the brilliant excess of the teeth, Anders focused on the hair. For the second time in as many seconds, he recalled his mother. She'd considered Germans and their descendants somewhere between blacks and people in the local hierarchy. Closer to the latter, but the gap was large enough to dye her natural yellow a more respectable brown. The effort cut into their food budget.

Anders pushed homesickness into his mental cellar, where it belonged. He'd have plenty of time to gloat, or apologize, when peace arrived.

"Not you?" asked the rebel officer.

"Deals keep the lantern oil burning. As long as you and Sherman need bullets, I'll be around."

"But mostly us, no?"

"At the moment. Northern orders are getting stingy. I don't think they expected you to make it past a year. Understandable, considering you're almost out of bullets."

The soldier's smile shriveled. "Careful."

Joaquin rose to a crouch behind the trader's chair. He lingered in the double-dealer's shadow in a state of relative calm—leading the squad by the nose had stressed him more than slinking across the room alone. Anders pondered if simple confidence kept Joaquin from being noticed. His aura was more *eavesdropper* than *assassin*. Joaquin pulled a knife from his belt like he planned on merely peeling an apple.

"Fie. You need me more than you need Davis. Learn from the French: you can't hang your friends until you've hanged your enemies."

"Slade, there are two things I don't do: tolerate dishonor and learn."

Joaquin paused, piqued by the unfolding argument. His eyes betrayed a small, sick hope that the two would finish each other off. That struck Anders as indulgent, to say nothing of the risk, but he wasn't the one creeping around like a savage. Then again, judging by the moody grumbles from the corporal, he wasn't alone in his evaluation.

The confederate gripped the bottle between them by the neck. Then he chortled and drained what was left within.

As the rebel's spirits rose, Joaquin's smile matched. The rebel might put up a fight. He winked at his comrades, which struck Anders as more foreboding than any of the earlier agitated hand signs.

"Slade, I didn't know Northerners with your character still existed."

"Thank you. Unless that's an insult, in which case that's your prerogative. I've already been paid."

"It's a high compliment. If the rest of your kin could put business first, America would still be one family."

Slade extended an arm for a handshake. The officer grabbed his wrist and pulled him into a hug. The post-negotiation gesture was warmer than any family memory in Anders's short life. Making guns looked like a warmer world than holding them. The corporal, less taken by the display, stepped out.

"Hands in the sky," declared Gleason. His voice carried hitherto unheard steel, helped by the fresh pistol in his grip. Slade jumped back from the soldier, detecting that anywhere was safer than his side. "You move, you die," Gleason added.

The Confederate froze, and Joaquin slashed. Then the Confederate made a gurgling sound that would stick with Anders for some time. He pawed madly at the fresh tear in his neck, which leaked freely and generously.

As a man, Anders didn't cry. However, dust did irritate his eyes until they leaked as well. Anders clutched his new repeater like a security blanket and tried to recall the gentle violence of home. The flying pans and forks had been nonlethal and well-intentioned. Now he'd seen more men die than he'd ever spoken to.

"They were complying!" barked Gleason.

"The citizen is complying," replied Joaquin. "The soldier was resisting."

The survivor didn't move. He also said nothing, inferring that the punch line to any setup he gave Joaquin was a stabbing. He kept his hands in the air, far from the ceremonial-looking pistol at his belt.

Joaquin pulled the stranger's pistol out from his belt. He appraised it less like marble-handled loot and more like a stray coin on a lucky stroll. He ambled over to Anders and offered the revolver to him handle first. Obeying the man holding a freshly used knife, Anders accepted. It was heavier than it looked.

"A gift."

"Why?"

"You're the hero of the day. And I feel a little sorry for you. I didn't kill anyone until I was seventeen."

Anders thought, *Someone in the camp is going to steal this from me. They'll feel justified because they'll think I stole it. And they'll be right because we're stealing it now. Please give it to Gleason, who's looking at me like I seduced his fiancée. I think he liked having the fanciest revolver.*

"Thank you," Anders said weakly. Gleason exhaled sharply and turned away, which was what intellectuals did instead of hitting people. Then he pointed at the prisoner.

"Mole. Thomas. Tie Mr. Jefferson up. I'm sure Harrow will have thoughts on his double-dealing."

"You're robbing an innocent man," said Slade. The easy quality had fallen out of his voice, replaced with soft resentment. The insult had emboldened him more than any bygone opportunity to save his skin. "I've armed more of you than John Brown. Ask anyone."

Gleason didn't accept or deny the claim. He ambled around the assembly tables as his two current favorite troops bound the prisoner, hunting for signs of an even more ornate pistol amid the sawdust and half-finished riflery. The corporal kept his pace beneath a run, but each step picked up a little more urgency.

Anders eyed the red floorboards as the corporal made figure eights around the room and then the adjacent room. Then Mole finished his knots and slung the gunsmith over his shoulder. It took all the effort of a yawn. Then the big slave (man? friend?) gave Anders a small nod.

"Don't worry. You're less likely to get robbed now."

"What? Why?"

"You've got a revolver."

10

BUMPY RIDE

This carriage, like everything misappropriated by Davis and his base band of bigoted brigands, is Union property," explained Gleason. The *b*'s *sounded* like negro musicality, but the others flashed Gleason *the look*. Anders had been on the other end many times, without a hint of natural rhyme.

No arguments emerged: memories of the cart and its weight were fresh. Adding the haul from Jefferson Firearms, along with a hog-tied prisoner, would have been hellish. The men just had to scour the factory for everything left of value, which was merely purgatorial.

Here, Thomas came into his own. Conviction that his final, painful death lurked around every corner sharpened his senses and made picking out stray bullets and semi-functional rifle parts easy. He made a natural scavenger, since he didn't take surviving scavenging for granted. A few new, unexplained lumps appeared in his coat and pants pockets, which Gleason generously ignored without discussion.

Hauling the prisoner fell to Anders and Mole, and thus mostly Mole. The other two privates came closer to his height, but Anders gleaned that willingness and ability to follow orders mattered. And Joaquin's hopefully necessary kill still lent him an aura of mixed honor and horror, making Anders's first kill stale news.

The recent violence gave his performance a small uptick, thanks to a lingering rush and painfully rapid heartbeat. Slade Jefferson made the odd kick or curse, which Anders took as the cost of a prisoner worth having. Mole likely had a reaction as well, but Anders didn't enjoy lingering on the former slave's thoughts, lest they ruin his own temper. Fighting had to be enough of a donation to whatever problems of black men fell outside of nature's will. Anyone who disagreed was free to take his place amid the charges and beatings and stabbings.

"Are you okay?" asked Mole.

"Yes. He's just fat," said Anders. His counterpart looked unconvinced. "Why wouldn't I be okay?"

"My son would be your age," said Mole. This didn't strike Anders as an answer to his question.

"Is he dead?" asked Anders.

"Maybe."

"Oh. Well, I won't die."

Mole remained unconvinced.

"I'm not kidding, or blowing smoke, or being patriotic. I've realized that a lot of us don't make it, and a lot of us aren't remembered, and decided that neither of those sounds like me. So I won't die or be forgotten. I'm going to be a heroic survivor, like my father."

Slade Jefferson kicked again, cutting off Anders's introspection before Anders had to do it himself. Mole dropped a heavy elbow onto the gunsmith's forehead, and he was still.

"No no no no," noted Anders calmly.

"He's alive."

"Good work," Anders mumbled.

They dropped their cargo with all the care that morale allowed and avoided putting him on anything that looked like a bayonet. The carriage interior had become crammed with Gleason and Thomas's patriotically reacquired gains.

"We're gonna have to take a few of the guns out," noted Thomas.

"Why?" asked Anders. He was short on real curiosity, but engaging kept other matters off his mind.

"There's no room for us."

For the first time, Anders looked at someone else like a neophyte.

"What's up your ass, ofay?"

"I'm an octoroon."

"What's up your ass, 'roon?"

Gleason stepped in. "Your *compatriot* has observed that a few of us must walk."

"Two trips?" suggested Thomas.

Gleason considered it, which separated him from most officers. Then he shook his head.

"Someone could come looking for these guns. Or these men, even. Both are invaluable, and rebels interrogate Black soldiers . . . enthusiastically."

Thomas spat on the carriage. "You two war-crazy niggers had to kill them, didn't you? Why should I have to walk because murder makes you stiff?"

Joaquin shrugged. Anders exhaled on the slur, relieved that his brilliant cover remained intact.

"When you walk, we rise," said Gleason. "It's a little marching, but you'll be stronger for it. And I'll be one step closer to our shared dream. Remember: a certain statesman once said, 'A house divided cannot stand.'"

Anders nodded. "Grant is a brilliant man."

The others silently evaluated Anders. Their expressions matched the looks he'd drawn at the schoolhouse window, triggering a mote of nostalgia. Satisfied that the issue was settled, and determined not to walk, Anders took half a seat inside what little space remained within the carriage.

The rebels had put it through the paces. Either days, trips, or kills (of which there evidently were fifteen) were tallied on the left-hand door. Two bullet-shaped holes on the roof suggested difficult outings. Sunlight dribbled in through them, shining directly into Slade Jefferson's unconscious face. Anders prodded Slade's forehead with his revolver, eliciting a sound between a snore and a cough. A relief.

Gleason poked his head inside. "The others are walking, so our prisoner falls to you. I have some experience driving horses, so I'll be up front."

"What kind of experience?"

"Speculative Dramaturgy. My first drama featured several men and women imitating horses. I believe my research, along with a few creative insights, should transfer well."

Anders promised himself he'd ask what kind of play entailed that. Or at least what *speculative dramaturgy* meant. Theater belonged to the flowery world of paper and stages and classroom rhymes. Which, from Anders's perch, hadn't made anyone else more prepared for the collapse of society than he was.

"Remember: unlike our prisoner, you're more than cargo now. You're a warrior. If he gives you trouble, do what you did earlier."

Anders gawked. Gleason saluted and shut the carriage door.

Alone with the prisoner, Anders tried another gentle prod with the pistol. Barrel-first this time, now that he had authority. He got another cough-snore for his trouble. Then the carriage crept forward, stopped, jerked forward, and stopped again. The ride could prove difficult. Anders made what comfort he could, gently adjusting a stray bayonet away from his hip. He lost a pocket button but no skin.

The town looked even sadder on the way out than on the way in. They'd made enough noise to inspire curiosity but not enough to generate terror, so a wider range of local vagrants and survivors poked their heads out for a look. Anders knew that as long as he avoided defecting again, the government would keep him at least marginally fed and armed. These people, less so.

"That's not yours."

The gunsmith's acid voice was a relief. He wasn't sure correctly-sized men could survive a hit from Mole. The swelling around Slade's quickly blackening eye seemed like a light toll.

"Be careful. There's a lot of sharp bits in here," said Anders. He shifted another bayonet away from his favorite knee.

"That's not yours," repeated Slade. Venom filled in charm's gap.

"It's my uniform. I earned it. Lucky soldiers never know if they kill anyone. They shoot into a gray cloud and hope their shots went wide. I hit someone, and I know he's dead because his skull made the sound chicken necks make. I killed a chicken for the first time when I—"

"That *pistol's* not yours," corrected Slade.

"This? Spoils of war."

Anders considered twirling the revolver. His mind's eye portrayed an accidental discharge, spooked horses, and consequences somewhere between a scolding and early death via carriage crash. A flight of fancy that, if nothing else, proved some part of him had gotten smarter. The vision was more welcoming than the prisoner's expression.

"I'd respect it if you robbed me yourself. That's the law of the jungle.

Most of my favorite things are stolen. Taking it as a gift from a burrhead, or anyone else, is low."

"Well, I thought it was nice of him," Anders muttered. "And if you wanted to keep your gun, maybe you should've used it."

Slade went silent again. The words sent wheels turning, or whatever turned in a gun factory. He stifled a laugh, exhaling sharply from his nose. The stare that followed had half the earlier contempt. Maybe even a third.

"Maybe there's something to you," said Slade. He adjusted his head to rest on a rifle stock and swung his bound feet on top of a cannonball. The prisoner, to the best of his ability, lounged, a feat enhanced by the random, drastic swings of Gleason's driving.

Under the oppressive duo of daily terror and adolescence, Anders envied that ease. For the dignity of the squad, he propped his feet up on the opposite seat, on top of a pair of hopefully unloaded rifles. The ride continued in silence, half natural, half tense.

"Are you going to interrogate me?" asked Slade.

"I think Gleason can do that. Or Joaquin."

"Is that the nigger with the knife?"

"Yeah."

"I'd prefer you. With all due respect to your pack of braindead niggers."

"Don't say that. That curse belittles the souls of men."

"With all due respect to your pack of braindead monkeys."

"Again? I'm warning you."

Slade chewed his top lip, as if contemplating an ancient riddle. Anders didn't see what was so complicated.

"With all due respect . . ." he began, teasing out each word, looking for the hint, "to . . . your pack . . . of braind—"

Anders leveled the pistol.

"Understood," said Slade. Earnest fear trickled into his voice. As someone used to the wrong end of insults, Anders found the reaction a little too intoxicating. If only he'd been armed earlier in his life.

The gun lingered at the ready for a few minutes, then sagged, then finally returned to Anders's lap. When explicit mortal danger passed, the patience keeping the prisoner silent evaporated. Whatever devil motivated the merchant didn't like silence any more than losing property.

BUMPY RIDE ÷ 71

"Apologies. That wasn't very brotherly of me. We are, after all, Northern brothers in a time of strife, and white brothers among the Mali."

Brothers. Anders didn't have any, but the word came up in both armies. And often. Did anyone who said it ever mean it? What kind of brothers did this man have? They could be riding his way now, with their own well-armed carriage and opinions on property rights.

"Are you a Jefferson?" asked Anders.

"That's the name."

"But *the* Jeffersons. As in the president."

"What? No. Do I look black?"

Anders shrugged, glancing out the window for signs of camp. Futile, since it was all alien to him. The endless roads and rails and biomes that made the nation beautiful all ran together now. Two months into his first Union tour, he couldn't have separated the swamps of South Carolina and Florida, save the accents of the people shooting.

"Son, what do you hope to get out of this war?" asked Slade.

"Repatriation of the rebel states."

"In your words. Those are Lincoln's."

"Black freedom," said Anders, picking two words out of Gleason's hat.

"You're not black."

"I'm an octoroon."

". . . You're not."

Anders leaned in and shook off his contemplative mood. He'd need all the wits at his disposal to win this interrogation.

"Honor and survival."

"That's closer to sense. Though the order sounds backward."

"And, once again, freedom."

"And, once again, that's nonsense. Sherman could line up every slave master in North and South America on the coast, shoot them in the back, and kick the bodies into the ocean, and the blacks wouldn't be free. General Lee could behead every soldier in a blue coat in one flanking maneuver, and the South would still crawl back, hat in hand, to Northern plants and ports within three years. When the last shot is fired, this will be the same country it was in 1861. Just less crowded."

Anders took a moment to imagine the first scenario in very literal terms. It felt like fair postwar policy. The tides would even take care of the cleanup.

"Is any of this sticking?"

It hadn't. Anders gave a perfunctory nod.

"Excellent. Now listen: I'm an important man up north. And down south, and one spot out west. Wherever bullets go, Jefferson Firearms follows."

"Good work," said Anders, sans irony. "Business is hard."

The trader took another beat to think. After deciding he wasn't being mocked, at least overtly, he continued.

"The powers that be—that's your boss, and your boss's boss, and Lincoln's boss—need bullets to keep this war going. Won't keep me caged for long. If at all."

"Oh. Well, that's a relief."

The riddle-solving stare came back. Anders decided to play with the world for a change.

"I felt bad about taking your gun. But you're going to be out soon, and you have a lot of guns, so it's fine."

"... This time, you're playing dumb."

"Yeah."

"Mocking your betters."

"Yessir."

Slade snort-chuckled. The sound could have come from someone half Anders's age.

"*Good work.* You've got a manager's brain. Avoid dying in a muddy hole over a foregone conclusion."

Anders concluded that they'd unearthed some kind of demon. The term fit a man who armed two men and bet on the duel. Someone who joked through his own capture, tried to buy out his jailers, and laughed at his own failed escape. With minimal knowledge of demonology, Anders would have to ward himself. He stuck his tongue out at the gunsmith.

"Childish."

Anders continued the gesture. Slade's jester's grin held for twenty seconds before his brow furrowed. Then the adult returned the gesture. The standoff continued far longer than either would admit in the future.

10.5

---·---

THE OTHER CART

Thomas."

"..."

"A moment, Thomas."

"..."

"Citizen Thomas."

"Mmm?"

"Will they torture him?"

"Let's talk about anything else."

"We should torture him."

"Christ alive . . . I always end up marching with you, and you always have some insane offal."

"True. It's also true that we should torture him."

"Lift the cart without jawing."

"You say I should talk more. You've won, I'm talking. About how we should torture him."

"No one should torture anyone."

"But they do. And we should torture him."

"What do you think, big guy? Is torture fun? Or is Joaquin a crazy nigger that should walk quietly?"

"..."

"He agrees with me."

"Sounds like Citizen Mole agrees with me."

"What's the point?'

"We need information."

"What's left to know?"

"What drove him to betray the nation."

"I'd betray the nation for half what he gets in a day. The whole nation, and every Black and white hand in it. Then I'd be one of the rich Jeffersons."

"That's different."

"How?"

"The nation's already betrayed you. It'd be fair play. A white man double-dealing, however, that's high treason."

"Well, this is Gleason's Salute-and-Sing Squad. We're trying to do better."

"Citizen Thomas. Do you know what the Grays do to captured Black soldiers?"

"No. I won't listen now or read about it later. I plan on dying beside a fireplace forty years from now, not knowing. If I die in this never-ending shit rain, I'm taking a clean bullet. Even if I have to fire it."

"Wise," suggested Joaquin.

"No one's getting tortured."

"They geld the Black men they capture."

"Joke's on you, island boy. I don't know what *geld* means."

11

—•—

DIVERSIONS

The camp appeared unchanged, save smaller clouds of insects around the medical tents. As time moved on from the battle (likely called *The Longstreet Conundrum* in the halls of history), the sick and wounded must have either recovered or died. The ratio favored the latter, which made Anders question the well-worn hammers, forceps, and bone saws the dirt-tired doctors left baking in the sun. If a man was doomed, it seemed better to smother him than rearrange him.

While the scavengers had thinned out, the parasites were still out in force. Idle men pulled ticks and more off their feet with the practiced ease of brushing hair or ignoring medical tent screams. One man resembling a shrunken version of Mole yanked a leech from his forearm. Anders wondered what swamp village he'd looted and if they even had anything worth the trouble.

Stepping out of the carriage, he found the corporal in his element. Gleason looked straight through the grime, insects, and the people in between. His gaze even traveled through the commander's tent and the thin tree line separating their camp from one of history's largest slaughters. He looked into a future where his speeches reflected facts of life rather than hazy conjecture pitched to armed drunks and teenagers.

With no immediate agenda of his own, Anders watched Gleason watch nothing. The recursion lasted until the corporal dismissed him, freeing Anders to enjoy a quick nap-and-cry. Isolated spaces were hard to come by in any camp, but Anders had picked up some skill over two tours.

Now that they'd returned without accident, reprisal, or (successful) bribery, Slade would end up wherever prisoners went. Not dwelling on that genre of question went a long way toward keeping Anders's rapidly escalating heart contractions to a minimum. He was free to dwell on lighter issues, like how much extra food he could trade a revolver for.

"Treasure it," said Gleason, visibly biting back the urge to make an offer. He'd tied Slade to the back of the carriage's freshly liberated horse, making for a more impressive entrance. "The new human shapes his desired future. You and I carry the marks of high officers, and thus will become high officers."

"Oh. Like spiritualists."

"No. Spiritualists make Baptists look like Rationalists. This is simply a matter of attitude."

Anders nodded, his reflex for anything that floated over his head. The corporal occupied a simple moral universe: Whatever Deists and Rationalists liked was good, and whatever Baptists and Spiritualists liked was bad. Especially moral reductivism. While he wasn't convinced, he'd come to appreciate the aesthetic of a gun at his hip, and using it under duress couldn't be any more traumatizing than beating a man to death. The borrowed gun matched his borrowed uniform.

Slade mumbled something to the effect of "nippity ugger" or "tuckity bigger." Instead of the beating for insubordination that had been standard among Longstreet's prisoners, Gleason placidly stuffed a pine cone in the prisoner's mouth and steered the horse toward Harrow's tent. A new spin on a roast pig.

"Sir! One question, before you go."

The corporal nodded.

"Joaquin seems strange. And foreign. And murderous."

"He's a freedom fighter, like you or me."

"He seems like a strange, foreign, murderous freedom fighter."

A thoughtful expression set in on the corporal's face. He evaluated *something* in Anders's eyes and came through either satisfied or indifferent.

"Let me give you a real answer. I keep forgetting you have a type of insight."

Anders planted one arm against a tree and braced. If it were anything like the other truths that had entered his world of late, some degree of madness or psychic pain came attached.

"The new human has a conspiracy theory fixation," began Gleason.

"It's unfortunate, but it's a habit we must live with if we are to correct it. Follow?"

Anders scraped the bottom of his reference pool. Gleason had pulled "new human" from one of the fancier poets. It meant American.

"Conspiracy theory. Like slave power?"

"Not quite, Anders. We're fighting slave power. You had to batter one of them yesterday. Cotton money paid for the soul of the man tied to our new horse."

"Understood, sir," said Anders. To his right, the tied and sullen Slade glared. Chunks of pine cone tumbled from the corner of his mouth to the ground.

"In the South, there's an old paranoid conspiracy about Haitian revolutionaries infiltrating America to free slaves."

"Madness."

"Utterly. Since John Brown took his stand, however, Southerners have been willing to believe anything."

"What's that have to do with Joaquin?"

"He's a Haitian revolutionary here to free slaves. His nickname back home translates loosely to The Reaper, if my French is worth anything."

The new information settled into Anders's mind with a refreshing lack of trauma. For once, the madness came without pain. He could cope with a world that made little sense, as long as it wasn't actively antagonistic. Sleeping in arm's reach of someone called The Reaper set off some of his instincts, but Joaquin had had ample chances to kill him by now.

"Understood, sir. That makes sense."

"Perhaps." Gleason shrugged. "I'm going to drop off our turncoat. I suspect the general will be happy to see a double-dealer brought to justice. And to inherit some product."

"Make sure to mention that you're Gleason, and not Lieutenant Hobbes."

"Thank you, Anders."

"Otherwise he'll think Hobbes did the stuff we did."

"I'm aware of my rivalry with the lieutenant. It's healthy. We share a dream for our people."

"Rivalry? You have one? I thought Harrow just thought you looked alike."

"Perhaps."

"As blacks, I mean. You're taller, and your face is different, but I sort of get it. I distinguish by looking at the eyes. Yours are always a little mad, like the kids who read too much back at Liberty Valley."

"*Thank you, Anders.*"

Having received proper thanks for his input, Anders left the corporal on a high note.

As the day crept toward sunset, Anders found a card game by a bullet-riddled stump. After convincing them he wasn't an officer (the pistol didn't help), Anders injected himself as a dealer. The flashier motions came naturally to him, as did quickly summing up winners and losers. Despite initial resistance, and a few rude questions on who exactly he was, his stump quickly became one of the night's most popular.

The regiment enjoyed casual gambling and drinking as eagerly as the rebels. Anders had scarcely touched dice games, since he found it hard to cheat. The late Bryce had a method requiring sleight of hand beyond him. Cards, however, were kind to anyone who could track past hands without writing them in the dirt with a stick. Longstreet's men enjoyed a poker variant called Dixie, where every spade played at three-fifths' value. Anders tried introducing Dixie to his new players and found enthusiasm lacking. Back to poker.

For all that, he'd never seen a game like Ofay.

Said game had a childish flavor, so Anders avoided participating. He laughed every round, but only in the cool, distant manner that an adult laughed at children. His thoughts were typically on man things, like push-ups, Harrow's nurse, and the time he'd killed someone.

A game could happen anytime, though it mostly occurred during card games or speeches. It started with someone simply saying, "Ofay." The first declaration was low, at either a mumble or whisper. If the speaker overdid it, the word might go unnoticed altogether, making him the de facto loser.

The next player, typically to the speaker's right, had to say "Ofay" slightly louder. Followed by the third in line, who had to say "Ofay" louder than the second. The pattern continued until a white officer noticed.

Losers were thoroughly and professionally beaten. General Harrow wasn't fond of Ofay and felt a little force could break the habit and replace it with wholesome gambling. This lent Ofay stakes that poker couldn't match, for all the crumpled bills and wedding rings available.

Unless someone combined the streams. Joaquin glided into a free spot at the stump, as quiet as disquiet. None of the adults (including Anders, who reminded himself that he counted) gave this much overt reaction. Popping in from nowhere was the kind of thing The Reaper would do. If he had stumbled in drunk, exhausted, and cursing like a normal soldier, something terrifying would be afoot.

"Ofay," whispered Joaquin, with half his standard accent. He'd had practice. The word made its slow orbit around the circle of players, growing one fraction of a decibel at a time.

"Hi, Joe." Anders dealt him in.

"Joe?" Joaquin mumbled, nonplussed. Then he peeked at his cards and smiled. "A lucky nickname. I'll keep it."

"Ofay," said the man to Joaquin's left. Joaquin repeated it at conversational volume, shaving minutes off the game. The player to Joaquin's right stiffened, balking at the escalation, and then followed through. The slur traveled around the circle at double speed, quickly overtaking interest in the card game.

Anders watched Petey J. (was he another Jefferson?), his current pick as the most likely loser. Petey was an immature sixteen, compared to Anders's mature fifteen. He followed the other soldiers like a confused puppy, something Anders stuck close to his squad to avoid. Exactly the type to shout a slur two decibels louder when one would do.

Worse yet, he was a bugler. Losing would be divine punishment. Petey absorbed jokes about his marginally lighter skin without protest, or even a comeback, leaving Anders alone on the outside. Somehow, even black buglers got to glide through the world.

Petey said it like a natural. But side-eyeing Petey gave Anders a clear view of an intruder. Clyburn, one of the white officers Harrow sprinkled across the regiment to "maintain a civilized shade," crept toward the circle with a schoolteacher's authority and a drunkard's stagger. Meanwhile, "Ofay" traveled past Petey, through several men who still looked alike to Anders, and back to Joaquin.

Did they have a signal? Some hand sign for the enemy or cantankerous friendly officers? A squad ought to have signals. It was time to innovate. Anders stuck his thumbs into his neck and flapped his hands like wings. This, unfortunately, drew every eye that could have seen Clyburn coming.

"Ofay!" Joaquin shouted. He looked as pleased as Clyburn did furious.

Clyburn breached the circle with conviction, elbowing Petey aside on the way to Joaquin. He knew the power of a universal, unchallenged slur and would be damned before letting one settle over his people. That, and Harrow looked kindly on disciplinarians. No one missed that Clyburn wore his facial hair in the brigadier general's style.

"What did you say, boy?"

It took Joaquin several seconds to stand, the first sign of the exhaustion from the long march home. He cursed in either French or Island Black before striding to the officer for a conversation. His knife, still coated in oxidized purple from recent use, bounced in the loose knot at his hip.

"I said 'ofay,' as in a devil of a white breed. You are familiar with the term, Citizen Clyburn? Perhaps you hear it in your heart when you feel small?"

The officer wasn't a coward, per se. He understood having the Union war machine's full power behind him, however badly McClellan and lesser divas like Harrow mismanaged it. But he could smell that pushing further meant trouble, and trouble always meant an extra roll of the dice of life and violent death. The best way to make it to the war's increasingly theoretical end was to act with a *sprinkle* of cowardice.

The officer marched off, giving Anders a small nod of commiseration on the way out. Inexplicable. Perhaps Clyburn hadn't heard his story and considered him a real part of the white fraternity. Which he *was*, but he couldn't let word of that travel too far, or questions about his origins might crop up. Anders considered the benefits of buzzing his hair down to match his new lifestyle.

For his money (of which there was little), Ofay had novelty. And now that he finally thrived under deep racial cover, Anders figured no insult was intended. Or at least only seven-eighths of an insult. He'd smiled wider and laughed harder than the black soldiers playing. Likely, looking back, drawing Clyburn in the first place.

The encounter killed the gambling mood around the stump, save Joaquin, who attempted to ante a set of foreign coins, a clean pair of gloves (after seeing winter duty, Anders would have taken this bet), and the long knife still coated in the enemy. The others ignored him and packed up the cards while discussing the joys of avoiding beatings and court-martials.

Then they divided the money, a process that brought them closer to violence than the Clyburn standoff. Petey won a tense stare-down with a man a head taller than he was, which Anders could have done if he tried. Better even. Petey never beat anyone to death. And if he had, it lacked the panache and precision of a trained twirler.

As dealer, Anders lacked the opportunity for a fortune-enhancing win or boredom-annihilating loss. So his players (and the miscellaneous survivors of Ofay) pooled odds and ends together as a reward for his time. They were:

◊ Ten bullets that might or might not fit one of his guns.
◊ A knife with a half-finished caricature of a Native warrior carved into the handle.
◊ A week-old newspaper with minimal bullet holes.

Seeing a chance to challenge himself, he resisted the temptation of the knife and started with the newspaper.

Southern Regiment Disappears, he mouthed. An unlikely title, even with the mixture of rumor, official misdirection, and outright fiction in most papers. He ruled out fiction; any author would treat a nation at war with more respect. As a misdirection, he couldn't see the benefit. Neither side benefited from reminders that escape was an option. As a professional walker, he could attest to the turnover risk.

"Joaquin," he hazarded. "I've got a question. I'd ask Gleason, but he's busy fighting for our medals. But you don't look like you're in a stabbing mood anymore."

"Your honesty's admirable, Citizen Anders," said Joaquin. On the word *stabbing*, he glanced at his weapon and noticed the viscera drying around it. He wiped both sides of the blade against the tall grass, removing almost none of the red-purple coating. "How can I help?"

"What do you make of this?" Anders handed over the newspaper. To his surprise, Joaquin repeated the trick of mouthing the longer words. In this language, they were on equal ground.

"Traitors, most likely. Or rather, since they were already rebels, twofold traitors."

"Is that worse?"

"Infinitely."

Unfortunate news.

"Citizen Anders, the Norse, Protestants, and true men of God all understood one thing: traitors may never step into the kingdom of heaven."

"I heard that *no* soldiers get into heaven."

"From who? Or whom. Whomever?"

"The second one, I think. And I heard it from an angel."

Instead of correction, mockery, or a slap, Anders got a nod.

"Maybe God judges us," began Joaquin. "In that case, he should come down here. So that we can have a *conversation* about the planet he left us. A man should be willing to defend his work. I'd have a lot to say."

Joaquin's gaze drifted back to the paper and took on a thoughtful quality. This spared Anders further discussion of turning against heaven, which didn't sit well with him. It would ruin his chances of encountering another angel on friendly terms.

"Then again, this wasn't long before our last battle. Look what happened to the grays who didn't desert." The Haitian threw a thumb in the broad direction of Cemetery Ridge and the charge that had changed Anders's life and understanding of death. "Always take your best offer. And almost every offer is better than death."

"Almost?"

"Bondage."

"Mmm. Indeed. Okay. Yeah. Thank you!"

Anders drifted in a random direction. He could fight slavery in the factories, fields, and towns. But he didn't intend to *discuss* it.

11.5

DICTATION

Get a clean sheet of paper: Meade's lost his nerve, so we have time for dictation. Yes, I want you to write everything. All of it! That's what dictation *means*. God above, I wish there was a way to pay you coons less. I'll start over.

To the Esteemed Mr. Jefferson,
I apologize, most profusely, for the inconvenience of arresting and perhaps executing you. I hope you find your stay here—or remaining time alive—pleasant. Feel free to ask me or the men for anything.

That said, you <u>have</u> been a bit cheeky. Whose men would Lee have buried with those newfangled repeaters? If the quality was better, I'd be offended. Mercifully for us both, you've cut corners with both sides. More than one rifle pointed my way has jammed, so I'm recommending leniency.

I suspect with the right donations and discounts, you'll be back to work. This time, I suggest sticking with one client. Namely, the one defending free trade, free soil, and I'll say it: free men. The monkeys have earned the right to swing where they please. Chattel slavery is a filthy Mali habit, and beneath white society.

Moreover, I suggest remembering your friends.

I suppose the world's changing. The Mexican War had clarity. Facial hair was trim and proper, and the sides were simple. There were the winners, and Mexico. Now two states call themselves America, claim victory, and enjoy Mexican land. I haven't reached dotage, but I'm starting to feel the years. If you live through this, try to set a better example for the rest of your generation. If we come together, there's plenty of Mexico to go around.

On to your dining options.

We lost our best cooks to a cavalry charge during the battle. Cavalry armed, notably, with your repeaters. There are rations for the alligator bait, but I wouldn't call that food in the strictest sense. It's matériel, simply meant to get boys from one end of a march to the other. Nothing for an adult palette.

However, every town has patriots. When an officer knocks, hat in hand, posture shrunken from hunger, they're happy to open their larders. As for rebels and sympathizers, we open their larders for them.

I've assigned Henrietta to you. The name sounds German, but she's of better stock than that. One of the smaller European countries that falls on and off the map. She's from Maine, but carries her people's fastidiousness and understanding of discretion. If you live, I'm sure you'll remember her fondly. If you're condemned, I'm sure she'll make your last days worthwhile.

Attempt to escape and you'll be shot.

With Regards,

Brigadier General Arin Harrow

That's enough of that. Switch to a new sheet, we're going back to my memoirs. First, I'll paint a fuller picture of how I clinched Cemetery Ridge *in spite* of Meade's bungling. Then, I'll circle back to my youth and some of my more memorable conquests. I want the people to know I'm both a warrior and a lover, and the two are inseparable. The body that inflicts pain and creates death also brings pleasure and creates life.

Are you listening? You haven't switched sheets yet.

Stop writing and *do it*, you worthless ni

12

TO NEW YORK

The morning meal was in an unnatural state: fresh. Anders's tin bowl featured half a fully cooked potato, beef that could be tasted through the salt, and carrots that hadn't been stolen in transit. The savory largess defied all precedent. Even after the bread riots, the South aimed to win freedom by feeding men air. And the Union only fed soldiers as a fine line of distinction from slavery. Even then, when Anders twirled flags in blue command tents, he'd heard rumblings that free soil didn't mean a free meal.

No one nearby questioned it. Anders ate in a huddle with Thomas and Mole, men content to eat without discussing God, country, or the nature of warfare. Anders could make a habit of it. They formed a triangle around the ashes of last night's fire, which still made a natural hub. Mole inhaled his entire bowl before Anders finished his potato. Thomas took a more measured pace, taking time to critique each piece of unexpected gourmet.

"This cow's dry," said Thomas. "If they paid me to cook, you'd feel blood running down your chin. In a flavorful kind of way, not a freshly shot kind of way." He took a large, wet bite between each sentence. When no one seemed to be looking, he wiped his chin with his sleeve.

Anders tried to smother his growing trepidation with beef and failed. Even chewing the tender fat couldn't silence his rapidly growing survival instinct. He hadn't endeavored to develop one, but his mind's shadowy underbelly remembered the real Bryce's death better than his up-tempo consciousness. The morning of Longstreet's Push (Lee's Maneuver? Pickett's Attempt? The newspapers would decide), Anders enjoyed a chicken breast gently coated in every spice he could name and a few he couldn't.

The flavor had still been on his tongue as the first whispers of a "big push" had reached the other men. He didn't regret the meal, or even surviving. But not telling the others what was coming sat heavy.

"We're getting bad news," Anders mumbled.

"There hasn't been good news since 1860," growled Thomas. "The whole damn decade is cursed. I bet that skinny ofay Abe's the only one that smiled that year."

"What makes you say that?" asked Mole.

"He got to be president."

"I was talking to Bry . . . Anders."

"My old captain used this trick. Whenever genuinely awful orders were coming, they'd give privates food from the officers' stash."

"Smart. Odd for . . . you," said Mole with excess honesty.

"Don't be rude," said Thomas. Rudeness was his purview. If they all did it, the dynamic would be ruined.

Mole gaped at them both like strangers, settled something internally, and continued. "What news?"

"I don't know."

"Maybe the copperheads convinced Congress to give up, and all this was pointless. I wish Lincoln would shoot the turncoats and put an end to it."

"I thought you hated Lincoln."

"I love him. He's *my* skinny ofay. I bet he'd only call me a nigger if I actually did something wrong. Him and Grant. I could have a drink with Grant. Or six. He'd only call me a nigger if I couldn't finish six. I like that." Musing on Lincoln, and getting called a nigger less often, put a buoyant grin on Thomas's face.

"Good food. That's worth something," said Mole. He'd wholly disso-ciated from the current thread of the conversation. Likely, by Anders's measure, because he couldn't parse sophisticated politics' finer points like Anders and Thomas. Topical small talk was a free man's pursuit. "I hope there's more bad news later."

✝ ✝ ✝

Once again, Anders stood at attention in a field. He tried not to panic.

Wet grass overpowered the usual sweat-and-dried-blood scent. For the first time, Anders could compare his group with the other four regiments comprising Harrow's "black burden." Their lines seemed thicker, implying a discomfiting casualty gap. He tried to focus on the grass scent.

An hour after the meal, Clyburn and his cohorts had wrangled the lower officers. They, in turn, wrangled the swordless, horseless, and revolverless men beneath them for an address. The long, winding lines of infantry standing at either a patriot's rigid attention or veteran's resigned slouch summoned strong, painful memories of the battle. It didn't help that they stood on the very ground Anders had charged across. His heart pulsed with memory of the effort. The extra weight of another man's coat sat heavier. The July sun bore down with pity, sorting the uncommitted from the warriors. Anders stood a little straighter. He was a warrior. He had to be.

He waited behind Gleason, to the left of Thomas, and to the right of a stranger. The stranger was a sloucher. How many slouchers did it take to unravel a squad, or a company, or an entire army? When he got promoted with Gleason, he would ban slouching. And give everyone a personal nurse.

Gleason radiated renewed purpose. Anders hoped the corporal was an exception to the coming calamity. Or at least a profiteer. The encounter with Jefferson had painted profiteering as one of the sharper human instincts, and he had no desire to repeat Longstreet's Conundrum.

The corporal's new sidearm hung from a hitherto unseen holster. He must have traded something of value or broken his own mantra about property rights among the New Humans. The former was easier to imagine, especially if he had leftovers from New York or the stage. Both were alien to the pastorals he served with, including Anders. The corporal stood at a slight angle, putting the symbol of future office in prominent view.

The general made no sign of recognizing this, or any other change among the men, as he paced his horse. Harrow took his time, letting his aura fall over each company. He bore the same humor Anders had witnessed in the tent: none. Each company's posture tightened as the white steed approached and slackened as it passed. He carried the gravitas Clyburn reached for. Impressive, considering the entire routine was cribbed from McClellan. Anders had seen it all before, in four states.

As the show dragged on, Anders felt his flagpole's absence. He missed it more than his mother. Flags had never branded him, or kept him from a dream, or told him he'd go to hell for kissing a spade. Now, in the midst of near-daily pomp and circumstance, he stood naked.

"I'm losing my grip," Anders whispered. He meant his literal wrist muscles, which risked atrophy without a flag or sacrilegious levels of onanism. But Thomas looked at him with unprecedented sympathy.

"I know the feeling, kid. Let's just get through the general's self-stroking and sleep the rest of the day off."

Before Anders could correct the kind words, the shell-white horse came to a stop. Harrow raised both hands for silence. Minimalism worked to his advantage. Unlike McClellan's three-ring event, neither backup cavalry nor amateur flag-twirlers were present to distract from his well-worn frown.

"This war began with a betrayal. Not Sumter, or any of the other tantrums King Cotton threw before finding a presentable name. But the betrayal of my family. While Sherman became a hero and McClellan became a joke, I was shunted offstage altogether. To babysit a pack of children in everything but name and body. Or so I believed.

"You see, I didn't herd a black brigade into Mexico. I led a company of white men and did it well. We marched from town to town and let them know they were proud Americans. When they disagreed, we clarified the point with iron. When they agreed, we established dominance with iron. I knew that consistency was the key to freeing that territory and set an example for other commanders. We still benefit from the results today.

"Later, a new war came. I left my exchange in the hands of a son I'm certain has already run it aground. Because I love this country, and most people in it. I love that our workers push until they fall. I love our soldiers that do the same, and the women that reward the survivors. That's the spirit of a free worker, a drive that Dixie aristocrats would smother for a little cotton money. There'll always be money for men who know how to supervise. Refusal to change is simple cowardice.

"That love didn't earn me the corps I imagined. Or division. I earned five regiments of dark men, with only a handful of my veterans to fill out the officer's tents. I'll admit, bitterness found space in my heart. The chance to bring back the Harbingers, and show Sherman a proper offensive line, seemed to be gone."

That word again. *Harbingers* didn't recall anything in Anders's pre-Gettysburg memory, despite fascination with army nicknames during his first tour. He tried measuring Thomas's reaction, but the man had mastered sleeping while standing at attention. Gleason remained engaged, but he was the type to stand at attention through an earthquake and recite every word said.

"Harrow's Harbingers," continued the general. "A name that still carries weight. A unit that understands sacrifice. One ready to give the heart, soul, and blood it takes to complete the objective."

And blood. Anders's heartbeat doubled its pace.

"I didn't think you boys understood this. I said the words, but I didn't truly *believe* that everyone here, white or compromised, embraced the Harbinger spirit. But you proved me wrong here, in Gettysburg. You overcame every disadvantage in terrain, courage, and breeding to give traitors their due.

"Other regiments were content to cling to cannons and barricades during Longstreet's Conundrum. But when I asked for a charge, you listened. Only the Harbingers charged onto that open ground, to meet them bullet for bullet, bayonet to bayonet, man to man. I dare say we almost matched the rebel scum's sacrifices. Of that, I'm proud.

"Sadly, we won't be finishing the job. Nor anyone else. Some thin-wristed traitors in New York are protesting their duty, and we have orders to stomp it out. Meanwhile Lee, the only man to kill more of our boys than McClellan, slips away. Until he resurfaces to butcher us again.

"In my army, we'd chase Lee to Virginia, and then hell. But Grant only takes orders from Lincoln and imported whiskey, so we're headed north to save both. That's my prize for saving the nation; an inglorious milk run against men too cowardly to join the scrap themselves.

"Which brings me to the matter of *your* reward."

Anders dared to hope. He'd been wrong about one or two things before, and he'd happily add today's prediction to the list. His focus flitted between the general's posturing and Gleason's profile. Through Gleason's practiced (and literal) stoicism, a crack of a smile emerged.

"I'm well aware that, as the recent descendants of great apes, many of you feel Lincoln's army limits your opportunities. Never. That's a delusion of your half-monkey minds, overstimulated by the first taste of hard work. I have every intention of elevating men that demonstrate leadership, intellect, or valor."

Gleason looked like he was in love.

"Of course, words are vapor without action. Which is why I'd like to call Lieutenant Hobbes forward."

Gleason's romance ended.

"Hobbes has been with the Harbingers since the first days of the war. When the defenders of free soil were less *commanded* and more pointed in rebellion's broad direction."

Gleason's right hand drifted to his gun.

"Hobbes is a writer, which it seems blacks are allowed to do. One of Lincoln's reforms, perhaps. While I don't care for that idea, I do enjoy Hobbes's results in the field: leading four other infantrymen into a facility held by the enemy and capturing a double-dealing merchant of death. Naturally, said traitor's factory shall be seized."

Instinct drew Hobbes's gaze to Gleason. He gently shook his head, with the expressive passion of a man who knew it wouldn't make a difference. Something easily mistaken for a prideful tear fell down his cheek.

"Hobbes, you seem nervous."

"Honored, sir," squeaked Hobbes.

"Well, straighten up. You're a lieutenant now. One hundred men depend on you to embody battlefield honor. Lieutenant Riggs died in the charge, but his badge of rank will live on through you."

The last vestiges of restraint weakened. Gleason's fingertips brushed against the revolver's handle, preparing for the draw that would end the lives of Hobbes, Gleason, and at least one unlucky bystander. The men on either side of the corporal took minute steps to the side.

Anders reached past his formal flag-twirling training. Fate stole his stage, but generations of twirling still lived in his fingers. He could use the *Jackson Lift*. The maneuver, named after the peaceful liberation of land by America's finest president, allowed for the gentle theft of nearby objects without the target's awareness. In Longstreet's army, it earned him enough cloth and hardtack to survive winter.

"You're this brigade's first black officer. In fact, I reckon you're the highest-ranking freeman around. Save that one spade with the hospital. I hope that you'll remain steadfast, humble, and distant from the paler nurses."

Gleason's restraint snapped, and he drew. He clutched air. The corporal turned back, neck only, a few degrees farther than possible. The youngest member of his squad stood with two pistols gracelessly tucked in his pants. Anders flashed the best disarming smile in a lifetime of pandering. When that failed, he launched into a rapid barrage of near whispers. As things stood, sanity outweighed decorum.

"You're disappointed, murder isn't a solution. I mean, you'd feel a lot better, as long as you're past the initial shock of killing. But it's not the *moral* solution, and I know you're big on that, which is why you're willing to anger God with Deism. Which isn't the point. The point is it's also *impractical*, because they'll shoot you. And then they'll search your squad for traitors and spies, and shoot them too. That's not fair to you, or to me and Joaquin, who haven't done anything. Today. And Thomas looks generally suspicious, so they'll shoot him too. And then it'd be odd to leave Mole on his own, and they're very casual about executing blacks, so he'd be next. If you want to lead this brigade, you have to lead this squad first.

"Believe it or not, this kind of thing used to happen all the time in Liberty Valley. We had a hardworking black trader—and I mean real hardworking, not the self-congratulating former slave types—and his white partner would take all the credit, and most of his money, and give his wife a certain *look* when he wasn't around. But look at it this way: your credit's being taken by a *black* soldier. That's a massive step forward. You may be the first black careerist exploited by another black careerist in our generation. The first of many, if we win this war. Isn't that what it's about? Maybe one day your kids can exploit Mole's kids. Assuming Mole's kids are alive. Actually, stuff like that might be more important than your promotion thing. But your promotion matters too! Please don't shoot Hobbes."

"Fine."

"Or the general."

The dead-eyed Gleason drew something in the air with his index finger. Madness may have been communicable, because Anders could see it. The corporal calculated the value of Anders's words on an invisible chalkboard. While Anders didn't need tricks for a quick problem, he appreciated good technique. Hopefully the shortcut led Gleason to the right answer.

"Anders."

"Yeah?"

"You talk a lot."

"I do, sir. Unless freshly traumatized."

"Scale that back." Hints of his old professorial tone returned, tinged with something else.

"I will, sir. If you promise not to murder our superior officer. Either of them."

"For the moment."

"Please. A rank is just a title, and more money, and a sword. You have respect. Everyone here is impressed by your big words, and your bigger words about the value of big words."

"Anders. Corporal is the second-lowest rank in the army."

"I know, sir. That still gives you four men. I have the first-lowest rank, and I respect you."

Gleason returned to something like attention before the general circled back. Harrow was near the end of his speech, or at least the first act. Something about turning black lead to black gold. Anders focused on his heart, which thumped too energetically for him to stand comfortably. And his superior's, which appeared to be dying.

13

BIG BEAST

Anders couldn't get his feet going. They refused direct orders, leaving him in the same stalemate as his environment.

He'd run onto his first train with vigor. It wasn't quite the behemoth he faced now, but it could reach the new army McClellan was strutting around the capitol. Approaching the steel beast had made the scale of the war real: the train was a one-way journey to the arena where men etched their names into history. Or were killed by men etching their names into history. Or crouched in a hole until history died down and a bugle sounded victory.

His mother had given chase, armed with every iron tool one body could carry. She'd aimed to keep him home, even if it was only his corpse. Today, he could see some of her perspective. A train hauled him from DC to Fort Donelson, where he'd found terror. Another took him to Shiloh, where he'd found excess terror. The train to Perryville introduced him to enough terror to change uniforms. His memory had separated that terror from human action and twisted the trains themselves into hideous iron snakes.

Today's train led to New York, a city he'd lacked the confidence to dream of. He could see the heart of American culture and industry, even if he had to crack a few heads on the way. The excitement of the destination couldn't move his legs. His id and ego had simply grown tired of his superego's nonsense. The violence inflicted around, to, and by Anders could only escalate if he repeated the same mistake.

The ashen cloud overhead didn't inspire enthusiasm. They were downwind of the engine car, and the smog recalled a lifetime of hushed coal mine warnings. How much healthier could the machine be? With a rational complaint to latch on to, half of his superego joined the embargo.

Gleason's quintet stood last in line to board the rear car, slackness the corporal forswore less than a day ago. Now their leader observed Anders's frozen form with meager interest, like the only white performer in a black freakshow.

"My legs won't move."

"Mm-hmm," grunted the corporal. He eyed his other men, who respectively sighed, shrugged, and tittered. Then he eyed the other companies, who filtered into their cars without incident. Loitering officially Looked Bad.

"Sir?" said Anders, expecting something more loquacious.

"Could you try harder?"

"Sir!" replied Anders. He then tried harder. Motion followed, which was inspiring until he noticed his feet dangling above the ground. Mole had picked him up by the collar with one hand and started trudging ahead.

"Put him down," said Gleason. "It's a block of the mind. A powerful and sensitive machine. If we push him without fixing it, it might break."

"Kid's the sanest one here," said Thomas. "Maybe we can get a protest for white pay rates going. They get thirteen bills for every ten we get, while we eat thirteen bullets for every ten they get. He's a rough mascot, but we could smear some coal . . ."

The line won a rare laugh from Joaquin. "Not shoe polish?"

"Nah, Frenchie. Around here, that's for comedians. It's gotta be coal dust."

Both paused on reflex, waiting for a reprimand referencing the New Humanity's entertainment standards, money's irrelevance on the stage of history, or the side effects of inhaling coal dust. Instead, Gleason wordlessly observed Anders's shaking hands and still legs. Slade had worn the same puzzle-solving frown.

"I'll be back. Make sure he doesn't move."

"Aren't we trying to do the oppos—"

"You're not funny, Thomas."

"House Negro," mumbled the private.

"Enjoy the field. Now wait."

Anders figured out why houses and fields mattered while Thomas seethed. The terms were familiar, but all the house and field slaves Anders had seen both lived in shacks.

"So they're really all shack slaves," Anders mused aloud. He prayed the insight distracted from his condition. The angel in his dreams had judged him, but there had to be others voting in the Democracy of Heaven. If not, he would double down on Deism.

The corporal reappeared, miraculously, with a short flag on a long wooden staff. Gleason planted the pike in the dirt beside him, sat down on the train car steps, and waited.

Professional honor made Anders lean in. A standard union model, mass-produced. But its last owner hadn't loved it, allowing the instrument to absorb several wounds meant for the player. The heat that rose whenever he saw an inferior flag-twirler (or any bugle player) returned.

"What in the Lord's name is this?" asked Anders. He stepped forward, yanking the abused flag out of the earth.

"A Union flag," Gleason submitted.

"Hardly."

"I see twenty stars."

"I thought you were an artist," Anders mumbled.

"The best alive. But that's not our topic."

"This flag is a professional disaster. The stripes have six unstitched bullet holes, and the stars are all faded. Someone's carved his initials in the shaft. If v.f. is dead, he deserved it."

Anders tested the weight. The staff spun easily around his left forearm, into an underhand catch in his right palm. It had a heavy, non-bruising impact. Perfect. He let his new best friend rest over his shoulder, where a rifle might sit if he lacked taste.

"This mean the protest is off?" asked Thomas.

"I'm afraid so, Mr. . . . . Thomas. I forgot your last name. But we can talk about that shoe polish later. Not the coal dust, it's bad for a fighting man's health. And a non-fighting man's health. Not sure it's bad for a woman's health, the local mine only had two ladies working in it, and they died in a cave-in along thirteen—"

"Good, you're back," said Gleason. "Get in."

Anders bounced inside with new vigor. Even if the train was one giant, intimidating phallic object, he now had his own to match. New York wasn't ready for a properly executed *Sumter Strut.* Though he'd have to change the name. Perhaps a *Manhattan March.*

✣ ✣ ✣

They shared the train car with fifteen other enlisted men. Five maimed and traumatized privates languished in semiconscious torpor in front, leaving the healthy-adjacent remnants to fill time. Their car provided much more space than past shipments of black men, forcing only two men to a seat, with enough room for two men to pass each other in the aisle.

This comfort, like the quality meal, sat poorly with Anders. Inhumanely stuffed trains meant more men at his side. Pleasure rides meant that they might be even with the rioters, or even outnumbered. He gripped his new flagpole tight and found it provided some comfort. Cards had the same effect on the others.

The train's demonic clamor challenged efforts to sleep or think. The latter fell outside a private's typical duties, but Gleason had set them to an atypical task. Per managerial habit, it began with a speech.

"Art, my first love, unites men. The stage is the elegant face of that love, carved from black marble. Performance is the firm, rounded thigh. And language is the soft mouth that kisses men goodbye as they pull away from New York, perhaps never to return. Alas for Sophia. Maybe I can visit her after the riot . . ."

"*Obsidian* would be artier than 'black marble,'" suggested Anders. Gleason then palmed thirty pages of cursive writing into Anders's stomach. They were tied together with blue thread, a luxury as bullet holes spread through Union uniforms.

"*The Living Abacus: A Steam-Powered Pascaline,*" Anders read aloud. Gleason had self-consciously nice handwriting, like the schoolhouse kids. Perhaps all literate negroes did? It bore later experimentation.

"A fine title, I'd say," said the author.

"What's the point of a steam abacus?" asked Anders. "Wouldn't it burn your fingers?"

Gleason folded both his arms behind his back. The order of the world, in which he explained life to the unwashed, had restored itself.

"The point is invention. Ideation. Innovation."

"So you built one?"

"Metalwork isn't for learned men. Speculative Dramaturgy is."

Anders waited for the definition of Speculative Dramaturgy.

"Scientific Theater."

Anders waited for the definition of Scientific Theater.

"Remember what I said about the future?"

Anders scraped his memory and found, "The American Future is coming, but also already here, as we make it in the present. Which makes us the new humanity, because of a Walt Blackman poem."

"Exactly," said Gleason, accepting the spirit of the law. "The New Humanity needs stories about a better future to reach it. Inventing the genre took me many long, sleepless nights. My early failures, like *The Flying Horse*, *The Time-Galloping Horse*, and *The Worthwhile Religion*, could fill this car. But Scientific Theater is a blueprint and shared imagination for The American Future."

"Swell."

"Thankfully, I had the Theater Noire—known as Nigger Stage among the rabble—to stage my work. I had the vision, and my sister had the land, capital, and connections. We started small, with *The Man-Like Machine and Subsequent Ethical Quandaries*. A modest success. Later, we could barely fit attendees of *The City Where Blacks Rule Over Whites* in the building. I'd even agreed to run *The Woman That Could Hear the Future* on white stages when the war erupted. Then I had a cause that trumped art. Well, I thought I did."

Anders liked the name Nigger Stage a little more. It sounded rebellious. But he'd absorbed enough black life as B. K. Jefferson to keep the idea inside.

"I like Nigger Stage better," said Thomas.

"Noted."

"And a Black theater? Lincoln's doing well by you."

"It's older than Lincoln, who doesn't strike me as much for theater."

"Well, thank him anyway. Then you might get promoted."

Gleason palmed a second script, bearing the same title, into Thomas's face. This met Anders's standard for friendship, a concept he'd shouted into the schoolhouse with little tangible return. He liked seeing people get along.

Their leader explained the project twice, took questions, and explained it again. They'd spend the ride memorizing their parts in *The Living Abacus*. After they beat the latest bout of white panic, he would use the opportunity for a brief detour to Theater Noire, which no one that wanted a decent role should call Nigger Stage. There, he would stage an impromptu performance, raising the morale of the men, the community, and future speculative dramaturgists. Then he carefully reopened the floor to questions.

"Who are you playing?" Anders asked.

"I'm directing. Not that I'd ever act. I live in the light of the truth, and acting is applied falsehood."

"People say that about writing."

"Yes. A sure sign they've never written anything worth reading."

"So you built a living abacus?"

"There's no such thing as a living abacus. That's what makes it real."

Anders flipped through the pages, faster than he or anyone else could read. Feigning comprehension might force others to follow. The dreamier children at the schoolhouse had been prone to this kind of creativity, until set straight by the taunts and fists of their peers. Gleason had, somehow, shrugged off similar influences across an adult black life. That marked either madness or genius, both of which helped leaders.

"Thank you for the role. I'll approach it with all my skill as a soldier."

Gleason looked concerned.

"I'll approach it with all my skill as a flag-twirler."

Gleason looked mollified.

A third copy of *The Living Abacus*—again, handwritten—went to a peer Anders couldn't name. The thick-bearded soldier, who Gleason held even less authority over than Thomas, didn't resist or jeer. He accepted it with mixed anticipation and curiosity, like one of the newspapers they routinely seized from occupied towns. Then he walked it to his circle of strangers and started running lines.

"You know him?" asked Anders.

"Scarcely. Another corporal."

"Why's he listening to you?"

"I'm directing." Satisfied that he'd explained everything, the director claimed a full bench, laid out, and tugged a faded blue cap over his eyes.

Knocking out at a whim amid the train's clamor seemed impossible, but Gleason had grasped some measure of peace. He lay still and content, without a snore or turn of the body.

✣ ✣ ✣

Typical rehearsals likely ran longer than a single train ride to a desperate mission. Anders had some performing insight: learning the *Madison Twistover* alone in the shed behind his house (which was also a shed) had taken him two weeks, and he'd still dropped the flag in front of the other students. Nonetheless, he trusted the process. Or, at the very least, that army discipline would speed things along more efficiently than creative drive.

Mole, who remained illiterate, gripped the script with reverence. Anders, along with two unfamiliar theater recruits, stared up at the lines. A human podium felt like the best compromise: with Mole holding the pages aloft, everyone had to crane their neck, instead of just Anders. If his costars disagreed, they swallowed it out of respect for Mole's enthusiasm/mass.

Anders played the titular Living Abacus, who could talk. As the best mathematician present (unless Haitian guerrillas had a secret form of algebra), Anders admired the casting choice. Though he found many of the ten-dollar words in the Abacus's dialogue taxing—the thing sounded more like a Living Dictionary. One tortured line read, "My artificial cerebrum has determined that compromise over Homo sapiens' bondage is anathema to sociopolitical survival." Incomprehensible. He'd add some visual flourish onstage to give his fellow monosyllabics something to look at.

A *little* of the Bible treatment Mole gave the script had merit. It used some of the finest paper Anders had ever seen, even with the odd creases and grease stains of infantry life. How Gleason had preserved this many thin silky sheets, and used none of them on letters to family (or whoever Sophia was), sat beyond Anders's threefold expertise in pole tricks, arithmetic, and avoiding death.

"Does Dr. Prometheus say much?" asked Mole.

Anders fluttered through the pages.

"She's the main human character."

Terror spilled from Mole's eyes. Nothing similar had appeared during their two combat outings together. Anders tried smiling. Reassuring someone twice his size and age was a mystery.

"I, uh, can read it to you. Out loud."

Mole didn't look relieved.

"I mean it. I'm not the *best* reader, but I can do it."

"It's not the words. It's the stage."

Anders nodded, noting another piece of How Other People Thought. Public speaking chilled a soul that had survived enslavement, multiple battles against General Lee, and Harrow's shotgun approach to tactics. This matched Katrina's attitude to crowds, where she feared to hit him with even the smallest object in sight. How that fit into Anders's love of pageantry and a comfortable number of witnesses, he couldn't say. But he could *reverse* his thinking and then imagine how Mole thought. Anders called it other-thinking, and with it he could slowly step into an ex-slave's shoes.

"Remember that God put you here for a reason, and you should show it off. Unless God's fake or the Deists are right. Then there's no reason, and nothing to worry about."

"God's a cruel beast," whispered Mole.

The swinging of the back door spared Anders philosophical reflection, pulling in the full clamor of the impossible machine soaring across fresh railroad track. The cacophony deafened Anders's side of the car as Lieutenant Hobbes pulled himself in. The lieutenant had adopted a new, straight-line posture. His fresh uniform lacked a single rogue thread. With other-thinking, Anders could hazard that Hobbes aimed to make his officer status a tangible, visible reality.

The lieutenant took slow, measured steps toward Gleason. When the director yawned instead of drawing a weapon, some of the tension left the lieutenant's body.

"The men in my car are agitated, repeating the same nonsense over and over. They're something called extras?"

"They struck me as the type."

Hobbes shifted his gaze to the other men. Instead of reproach or approval, his face betrayed deep confusion. He waited for Gleason to try to make sense, a more mundane strain of mercy than their last interaction. Meanwhile, the enlisted men ran lines.

"And what's going on here? The white child is yammering about an abacus."

Gleason sat up, with none of the urgency rank demanded. He watched Hobbes with all the academic superiority he spared the men, even during games of Ofay. Anders noted that pretense could be taken on and off, like a coat or sidearm. Too many seconds passed before his answer.

"My home city assumes Blacks and rustics lack the sophistication for acting," said Gleason. His voice had taken on a peaceful, settled quality. "As a dedicated dramaturge, I know that acting requires no sophistication. Our men will perform as well as any of Manhattan's waxed mustaches. Better, if they read the entire script."

"Gleason. Friend. Is there time for mummery?"

"Mummery keeps their minds sharp. And refers implicitly to satire, a childish arena I avoid when possible. Is there a problem, *Lieutenant* Hobbes?"

"Of course not. Just checking the welfare of my favorite men."

"Your favorite men are doing well, *Lieutenant* Hobbes. They're rehearsing a play, *Lieutenant* Hobbes. And they need space to focus."

A fight had seemed like the safe bet. But for the moment, Hobbes remained determined to make a friendship out of the gentle hatred in the air. He spent several seconds staring at the ceiling, as if he'd find an answer scrawled there by another soldier. It was blank. The lieutenant turned back to Gleason.

"A Black play . . . I always thought you were blowing smoke. Have room for one more?"

"Perhaps. But shouldn't a *lieutenant* be busy? You have a hundred men to watch."

"They're mostly in this play."

"The more inspired ones, yes. The rest require watching, *Lieutenant* Hobbes."

"Corporal," said the fresh-minted lieutenant, straightening his spine and inflating his chest. "Enjoy your show. But remember that I run this company."

"Of course you do. Mole, could you walk the lieutenant out?"

The private turned from the script and expanded to his full height.

Hobbes, still straight as a beam of light, took to the exit with more speed than the heavy door should have allowed. He stole repeated worried glances at Mole, then at Gleason, and even one desperate look at Anders. Anders waved back and hoped it improved Hobbes's day. The army was a tough place to be alone.

13.5

NINE THESES

To the Mayor, Governor, and "President,"

In Paris, the armies of tyrants could not take the streets from their people, nor people from their streets. The rest is history. In New York you'll find the same spirit, save the ending. We are united in our stand against tyranny, senseless death, and miscegenation. And no Napoleon will undermine our purpose.

Our demands are simple. We do not need a hundred sans one points to be mollified. Only nine. Nine simple changes can spare us all the bloodletting of revolution.

1. An immediate end to forced conscription in New York.

2. The immediate return of all conscripted New York citizens.

3. An immediate ceasefire with the former southern states.

4. The immediate return of negro property to its owners.

5. The immediate disbandment of the New York Police Department.

6. The immediate expulsion of all voluntary Union army members from New York State.

7. The immediate resignation of the governor and elimination of his office.

8. The immediate resignation of the "President" and elimination of his office.

9. The immediate creation of a new national executive office rooted in the will of the people and the mandate of heaven.

I expect you to reject this out of hand. You are small men with small visions, and no place in the new world. You can fight for the scraps of the old nation, while we build the next.

Still, you may surprise me. Vagabonds can only ignore the word of God for so long, and a stray bullet from playing soldier may have dislodged some of the cotton from your ears.

Best,

Wendy Ross
Voice of the Sons of Columbia

14

THE QUIET CAR

The army attention span (half or twice a civilian's, depending on who you asked) ran out minutes after Hobbes's humbling. Bench activity drifted from thespianism to snoring, gossip, and comparing stashed liquor supplies. Anders had more interest in the train itself, which thundered across once-treacherous terrain. He wound up next to Joaquin, who wasn't his first, second, or eighth choice. Nonetheless, inspiration struck.

Thirty miles an hour. Like an arrow from God.

Anders liked the line as soon as he thought of it and repeated it to Joaquin. His compatriot lacked any interest in the rapidly changing world outside their window, making his window-seat monopoly galling. Anders contemplated trading his pistol, which he had no intent of using. But he could already hear Gleason pontificating about symbols and temporary inconvenience.

"An arrow?" scoffed Joaquin. "Doesn't God have a gun?" The soldier busied himself rolling a penny from one finger to the other. Anders couldn't see the trick's appeal or why he refused to teach it.

"I'm speaking poetically."

"You're a codebreaker, no? Not a natural fit for poesy."

Obvious bait. Anders avoided it, which made the insult stronger. Being the bigger person felt like intellectual surrender. Restraint shaved a millimeter off his confidence, and he needed all of it. Another lesson in a year he'd grown tired of lessons.

"I'm taking a walk," said Anders.

"Where?"

"Other cars."

"I don't think you can do that," noted Joaquin. *Either* went unsaid.

"I will," Anders said with more defiance than planned. "I can do a lot of things. I'm one of the best doers here. Unlike 'The Reaper,' who . . . can't act. You're awful. You'll reap tomatoes."

The infiltrator looked at him like a new person. Anders took the opening to leave, hopping over his snoring comrades' legs. The impulse was fading, but he had to follow through to keep his newfound respect.

Each door bore a heavy, elaborate, and thoroughly rusted lock. Those didn't set Anders back for long. Most locks were easier than codes, if you listened. Under Pickett, he'd supplemented dinner with extras from the officer stores. Anders reasoned that they were only locked away; if they were important, command would put real effort in. He'd dropped the habit in the Harriers, where black enlisted men seldom went unwatched.

Falling between cars looked dangerous, so he didn't. He did appreciate a wider view of a passing town. The army train attracted waves from some townsfolk and single fingers from others. Anders returned whatever he received.

He took a break between the second and third car, to try rolling a freshly removed bolt between his fingers. Why not teach something so simple and small? Anders gave out flag-twirling tips without anyone even asking. Joaquin (Was that his real name? It had to be. A fake one would blend in) still treated him like a sideshow. But proper sideshows got respect, and tips, and flirtatious glances from local bachelorettes. He needed a date.

The bolt slipped between his thumb and forefinger. One more try.

Why weren't there women in the army? The nurses were too overworked or traumatized to flirt with anyone, and the escorts trailing the army made Anders nervous. If his love life thrived, or existed, he wouldn't be flicking rusty metal back and forth, angry at his squadmate for less than nothing.

The timing eluded him, so he slid the bolt back into the subpar lock and got moving. He picked up more sideshow glances in the third car but let them pass. People got used to anything with exposure, and he'd win them over eventually. Even smug Petey, who sat with a script in his smug hands, smugly reading when everyone else had moved on to drinking or disassembling locks. Damn Petey. Always hunting for approval and getting it.

Petey waved. Anders pretended to miss it.

If they won black freedom, he'd be happy for the others. Particularly Mole, given the dark silences that followed any mention of family. But the number of people allowed to condescend to Anders would also increase, and he didn't look forward to that. Wherever he went, he attracted disrespect in a new accent.

The fourth car down took a little longer to enter. It featured a nearly rust-free lock designed by someone that had at least heard of lockpicks. Behind him, the men shouted mixed support and jeers. Like most events between battles, Anders became the subject of betting. He overheard Petey bet more than Anders owned, spurring him past the final tumbler. Anders saluted his captive audience before forging ahead.

He stepped into paradise.

Or at least wealth beyond his vocabulary. Lee's photos of his lost estate came close. The general prized them as reminders of what he fought for: property, human or otherwise. Like any attendant with hands and eyes, Anders took the first opportunity to sift through the master strategist's things. The estate photos were more lovingly preserved than the lone photo of Lee's wife, which sat beneath some maps, books, and extra clothes.

Lee's mansion had an understated beauty, designed to remind the observer just how much more the general owned. Free servants—an odd phrase, on reflection—loitered around the estate's Ionian pillars, doing their best to look elegant, busy, and idyllic at the same time. Whippings weren't an option in DC, but penury and starvation sufficed.

This car crammed that luxury into a box and understated nothing. A heavy wooden desk sat in the center, immobile despite the shakes, twists, and jumps of the train. Each wall featured a realist painting of an unknowable European noble, the kind of art that only changed hands through inheritance, auction, or theft. A chandelier wider and heavier than the desk hung above it all. Unlike the desk, it shifted with every stray bump and turn, remaining attached through forces beyond unlanded ken.

Anders would be impressed if he weren't livid. Slade Jefferson lounged on top of the desk like the king of the republic.

No chains, no cuffs, no guards. In fresh clothes free of any sign of being violently dragged from anywhere. The demon picked at a half-eaten steak beside untouched white cheese, with no intention of finishing either. He grinned at Anders like an old classmate, encountered by chance in a city tavern. His silver teeth caught flecks of incoming light, making him even harder to look at.

"Hey, junior. Save the republic yet?" Slade then stuck out his tongue.

"Hands!" Anders shouted, drawing his/Slade's/their revolver. Empty, but he could keep *some* things quiet. Slade followed orders, putting both hands behind his head. He let his silver plate fall, confident someone else would pick it up.

"This again? I know a stalwart young man like you wouldn't shoot a guest."

"You mean prisoner of war."

"I mean guest. Do you drink yet?"

Anders recalled empty whiskey beside the branding iron. A warm memory, in the worst sense. He'd still give anything for his mother's advice in this moment. Or his absentee father's. Or someone's from the car behind him. Anyone whose brain wasn't on fire with confusion, rage, and shameful fear.

"Focus, son. Don't drift off with *my gun* pointed at me. The trigger's sensitive."

Anders homed back in on the present. It remained loud and dangerous. With a gun raised to an unarmed prisoner, he could only imagine what happened when he put it down. Any influence that kept Slade's head on his shoulders could smother Anders like nothing. Because he was nothing. He wouldn't even get a chance to defect again before the hanging.

Unless he fired.

The gunsmith's smile cracked—he must have seen Anders's thinking change. Then he pointed at the half-corked bottle resting on the desk.

"Wine?"

"You're an enemy agent. That's enemy wine."

"No, I'm a double-dealer. It's everyone's wine."

That didn't sound too treasonous. Anders pointed at the bottle with *his* revolver. Slade had no idea how to interpret that, so Anders tried words. The prisoner of war quickly filled two cups. Anders pointed at one cup, and then the wall, which was also incomprehensible.

"We're using the same cup. I'm not getting poisoned."

"I like that. Very native."

Slade carried the cup in both hands, in grim mockery of a stereotype Anders couldn't place. The dealer tiptoed across the car, muttering a parody of an unfamiliar language. After a lifetime on the sidelines of the white-black grudge match, hearing another pool of jokes and insults unsettled him. The cruelty was fresh. He snatched the cup without ceremony.

Anders sniffed the wine for poison, watched Slade Jefferson take a sip, and then drank. The flavor ambushed him. Nothing since recruitment could compete. He waited for Slade to take the obvious opening, and the moment never came.

"Good stuff," Anders guessed. He'd need to try a second wine to rank it.

"Wonderful, you can finish it. I'm four cups in. Should I call a serving girl for some food?"

"We don't have serving girls."

"*You* don't have a serving girl. Shame, really. Does a lad good."

"No serving girls," declared Anders. He didn't want to be outnumbered. His teenage imagination came second.

Slade shook his head. The baseborn didn't know how to enjoy anything.

"Why aren't you in a cell? A proper cell. No equivocation or tongue twisters. Or sticking out your tongue. You're an adult."

"General's orders. I'm still being held—I don't know how you got through that vault lock—but he knows who I am. Harrow figures I'm as likely to go free as hang, so he's kept me comfortable. It's a good bet. I might split another drink with him."

"You don't sound too worried about execution."

"The road goes where it goes."

"That's sophistry," said Anders, using a Gleason word. "You don't know danger, so you don't respect it."

"An unstable child's pointed my gun at me twice."

Child. The word lingered, just like *junior*, and Joaquin's dismissive glance. He didn't need help feeling small. The world he'd set out to conquer blew him around like a leaf in a windstorm.

"Don't get offended, junior. People lash out when they're on their back foot. Be proud when insults and accusations fly. It's what winning sounds like in America." Slade eyed the freshly ruined lock. "Talented people should enjoy themselves. Wine?"

Anders shook his head. Slade refilled the cup anyway, moving with sleepy ease. He'd either forgotten the gun in the room or chosen to filter it out of his mind. Maybe a lifetime around gunpowder made it easy. Or maybe his deals had ended at gunpoint before.

Junior. Anders snatched and drained the cup, without taking an eye or barrel off of the prisoner. Who, for his part, looked impressed.

"You seem to get how things work. Not in your head, which is full of schoolhouse nonsense. But in your heart, which keeps that gun trained on me. Could you do me a favor?"

Anders didn't reply.

"It's a paid favor. And I'll remember it. Recall that money and medals are for paler regiments, as far as Meade and company are concerned."

"They'll turn around. People come before profit in The American Future," recited Anders.

"Great. What's your plan in the American present?"

Anders returned to silence, while Slade finished the bottle. He drank straight from the lip, without the mirth or desperation that accompanied a standard binge. Before he finished, the door opposite Anders creaked open and a nurse stepped through. The tips of her sleeves were stained deep purple, most likely from a recent round of amputations. The wide splatter pattern didn't imply success.

He'd rather pretend they were wine stains, but she carried a bottle of white. She dropped it beside Slade with routine precision, scooped the ruined dinner, and left the way she came. All without commenting on Anders or the standoff.

After gawking and fantasizing, recognition set in. She'd been in Harrow's tent, where they'd shared a moment, making her lack of reaction, recognition, or interest odd. He veered away from that thought spiral to focus on his captive.

Slade spun the bottle in search of a label and found none. He discarded it with a frown. "Prison life," he muttered, before pointing at Anders. "I have a lady friend in Manhattan. And business partner. Whichever motivates you. Get this letter to her, and you'll be an official Jefferson Firearms associate."

Beneath the food and liquor, a few pieces of business stationery rested on Slade's desk. He picked a blue envelope with a white wax "J.F." seal out of the unsorted pile. Slade tested the seal with a light tug and then extended it to Anders. Anders made no move to grab it. Slade let the envelope fall. Anders made no move to pick it up.

"I'm not deserting to drop off a letter."

"I doubt you need to. You're marching into the heart of human disorder and willful destruction. And now they're rioting. Just tell your commander that you were captured, or beating a partisan with extra enthusiasm. You'd get a medal for that in a proper regiment. I can't imagine how you ended up here."

"I'm an octoroon," noted Anders.

"Good cover. Whatever you're hiding," said Slade, with a quick fingers-to-palm round of applause. "You even sound like you believe it. Harrow the Butcher's lucky to have you."

"The . . . butcher?"

"I meant Harrow the Bold. He's a good host, and all that."

Anders let the revision slide and focused on the slim envelope at his feet. Jefferson was somebody. The world moved around somebodies instead of throwing them into doomed charges across open ground. Anders came from generations of nobodies, and reversing the trend had gone poorly. Being somebody sounded nice.

"Attaboy," said Slade as Anders pocketed the envelope. "I'll put a note in my ledger. You'll get paid, even if they execute me. If you die, I'll get it to your next of kin. And if we both die, this conversation doesn't matter."

"You keep saying things don't matter."

"Sounds like me. Anyway, keep your head down. The blues won't have a good time in Manhattan."

"We're doing a play."

"Simple," Slade said, as if Anders had said something else entirely. "Image. You're the worst brigade for it. Most keep their spades busy digging holes or shooting tribals. The 'Harriers' look like everything the country fears: blacks walking and talking like people."

"Is that mockery or praise?"

"Neither. I'm divested from the race question."

"We're at war over the race question."

Slade half shrugged, as if the problem weren't worth both shoulders. The gunsmith glided weightlessly through a heavy world. Anders accepted that no consequences waited for Slade in New York. If anything, he might buy the train.

"If you don't mind, my favor comes with one order," said Slade. "No extra work, or even danger. Just don't open the envelope."

"I'm opening it."

The initiative drifted back his way. Slade's buzzed smile dimmed and the riddle-solving frown peeked out.

"Fine, entertain yourself. But it's in code. You won't get anything out of it."

Anders avoided rolling his eyes. "Darn. You've got me."

"There are some things a bright young man can't get past on his own. It takes two bright young men."

"You're not young."

"Let's say two peers."

Anders took a final, serious look at Slade. How old was he, really? He didn't have lines from the sun, stress, or generous laughter to count. Wealth and indolence had collaborated to make a well-preserved revenant. A side effect of life in the quiet car.

"May I have my gun back? As a peer?"

Anders left, with both the pistol and the letter. He returned the lock's kingpin on the way, enjoying the muffled curses behind him.

14.5

———•———

CUSTOMER SERVICE LETTER

Dearest Wendy,

Thank you. I appreciate the offer to join your scheme. You have a chance, but it sounds like excess work for little tangible gain. The Union and Confederacy exist, have strong lines of credit, and don't ask me to *literally* kiss anyone's ring. It's all a little too old-fashioned for me.

That said, I'm more than happy to arm you.

Primarily due to our past affection. Even with our mining arrangement, I'm not convinced your patron has the funds to last the winter, let alone cover eight hundred new seven-shot repeaters. Of all the women I've danced with, your memory's the warmest. Well worth tolerating the political chatter. Once things calm down, perhaps you and I can catch a show. Assuming anything's left of Manhattan after your plan.

And that you live.

Your last letter called guns "the line between rebellion and revolution." Sure. But there's also trains, cannonballs, and *food*. Manhattan is a wonderful place that grows nothing. Even after driving the rabble uptown, you've got just under a million mouths to feed. Not ideal for a siege. Ask any of your German minions about Munster and how much fun their ancestors had during that adventure.

Well, they won't know, since we only get Europe's debris. But they might know a recipe for "long pig."

That's enough of my opinion. All the guns you could possibly want are on Pier 20, in crates labeled "Ladybug Publishing." The company doesn't exist. Nothing deflects a soldier's interest like the threat of reading, save the terror of math. They were going to be Lee's guns, but his only agents in town are courtesans-turned-spies, actors who have never lifted anything heavier than a flask, and the lieutenant mayor. You know how politicians are.

To be clear: if your cause survives, my fee triples. While I'm not in the habit of making arms deals on credit, this is quite enjoyable. There's a thrill to not knowing if I've doubled my fortune or inspired an entertaining headline. How can regular gambling compete? This must be what drives kings to start wars. The rush of uncertainty from a comfortable distance. I'm sure you can relate to the first half.

Try not to die.

Yours Truly,

Slade Arthur Jefferson

15

TAKE HEART

alf an hour to High Bridge!" shouted Lieutenant Hobbes. He poked his head and head alone into Gleason's car and withdrew just as quickly. His audible trepidation matched the general mood.

Before battles, the aura drifted between boredom, bravado, and jitters, with drinking filling the gaps. They didn't have a routine for riots. No one knew how far they were allowed to go, how far the enemy intended to go, or if "the enemy" fit hungry, war-weary taxpayers.

"That's the station in New York," added the returning lieutenant, risking his head anew. He was a stickler for clarity, which Anders appreciated. The gap between "Charge on my mark" and "Charge on three" shaped history.

"Thank you," chimed in Anders. He heard the corporal snort behind him. Or rather, the director. With Gleason over his shoulder, *The Living Abacus* sat heavier on Anders's mind than the uprising. He'd done his best to memorize the brick of paper, but lines from other texts he'd skimmed or overheard kept slipping in. He was certain the play lacked anyone named Lear or Achilles.

Envisioning a hostile, jeering audience doubled Anders's already elevated heartbeat. No metaphor was involved—it hammered along, making itself known. He'd heard of old men dying from the shame of a poor performance. And from mild fevers, and after walking into German neighborhoods, and for no reason at all. Generally, getting old looked like a mistake. Perhaps Gleason knew an alternative.

The ageless prisoner certainly did. The letter was the heaviest slip of paper Anders had ever carried.

He returned to his original thread of thought. Before he worried about letters or stagecraft, he had to pacify the nation's fanciest city. New York rioters might have white gloves under their knuckle dusters and repeaters that *worked*. Dealers like Slade were finally trickling them into the Union army, now that they'd sold off their surplus single-shot relics. If past patterns held, the black regiment wouldn't get trendier guns until the war had settled itself, one way or the other.

Nerves put him off rehearsal, or drilling, or even doing a good twirl. He was back beside Joaquin, who barely counted as company. The Haitian gave him a short measuring glance and let the silence hold. Anders listened to the train chug and churn and came to admire the machine's tenacity. It sounded like it should flip off the rails and kill everyone aboard, but it never did.

The atonal clanging lacked melody and intent, but it carried some rhythm. After however many minutes of intense listening, freezing out the rehearsals and alcoholic binges around him, Anders nodded off. Black filled in quickly, until it gave way to blazing golden light.

Incomprehensible music accompanied the light. Three soft, droning choruses formed one continuous, dissonant tritone. The melody and intent were not an improvement on the train. Anders might have plugged his ears, but he didn't want to embarrass himself before his visitor.

His angel had returned, with her soft face, leaking eyes, and a new second head behind the main attractive one bearing stone skin and a thousand eyes. The wings and first head still looked nice. After a brief spurt of screaming, Anders opted to make something happen this time.

"Hey there." Anders pumped his voice with confidence and drove it down an octave. He knew girls liked confidence. Bass was more of a theory.

"Kneel."

The request put him at a loss. Kneeling was the opposite of confidence. On the other hand, the light of the divine grew warmer and felt like it would melt away his skin and eyes at any moment. He opted to indulge her (it? Her-ish?) with a little extra flourish. He stepped out diagonally, spun down to one knee, and pointed two finger guns at the seraphim. She remained impassive, leaking the usual amount of precious metal from each eye.

"Anders." The angel's voice was cold and declarative, like a gentleman dictating directions, his desired lunch, or the price of another man. Only his first murder and subsequent recovery gave Anders the steel to respond.

"Hello, ma'am. You're looking excellent today. Well-composed. Are those new wings?"

"Cease your petty lusts."

Anders took the words hard. At fifteen, all he had were petty lusts. He couldn't imagine a worse change in tone, short of a second flood.

"I have some questions for God."

"No."

"It's about all the death and suffering."

"Do not presume to speak to the Lord."

"Why are you here, then? If we can't enjoy each other's company, or bring anything upstairs? Are you just here to yell at me?"

"Such has been the role of the divine over transient life since time immemorial."

"I'm very dependable life. The kind you want by your side if some trouble stomps into town. You deal with a lot of demons, right? I've fought demons. I think one runs my brigade. And ran my old brigade. Can you ask God why everyone that—"

"Be silent."

"—runs armies is some kind of demon? Or why we have wars? Or why you said I'd go to hell for being in a war, when he made wars, and made hell, and made—"

"Be silent."

"No thank you. I've noticed that things get worse whether I talk or not. So I might as well get whatever I'm thinking out of my head and into the air, so that at least I feel better about whatever terrible thing happens. Did you feel that way when Lucifer fell? What's Lucifer like? Is he nicer than God? You can tell me, it's just us. Even if you were on his side, and jumped ship when things went wrong. I know what that's like. Honestly, I think you and I relate. We should try talking more. You have nice wings."

"BE SILENT."

Anders went silent.

"The soul of your nation will soon be weighed. It falls to you to redeem it."

Anders raised his hand. The ageless porcelain face above him suddenly appeared very old and very tired.

"Speak."

"The northern one, or the southern one, or the contiguous whole? Or is the planet one big country? That would be a relief. Why don't we do that? Should I pitch that to Gleason?"

"BE SILENT. It isn't the nation you know."

Anders raised his hand again. The ageless face aged further. How anyone made it through eternity with so little patience eluded him.

✝ ✝ ✝

No one was kind enough to wake him with a voice, hand, or gunshot. Anders endured a seemingly endless back and forth of nonanswers, riddles, and abstruse prophecy from God's messenger. He felt something like nostalgia for Liberty Valley mass, where the divine had been kind enough to leave empty clichés to the preacher.

Anders stirred with a new appreciation for Deism. God's staff seemed exhausting. Whether the dreams represented the divine or sexual repression, he knew he deserved more respect.

The men stared out the western windows in uncharacteristic silence. No idle insults, or bets, or lies about past romances. Thomas looked sick, which was normal enough. Mole looked worse, which made Anders nervous. He reached beneath the bench and picked up his new flag for support.

Beyond the station stood a long, white aqueduct, which looked nice. If he ran things, Anders could see lining men up for a painting. Perhaps a photo, if there was time. Beyond the aqueduct were flames.

Aside from some early trauma, Anders was accustomed to moving away from fire. Nature and society had the same imperative: walk, ride, or roll away from anything hotter than the July air.

The train—which Anders had never trusted—followed the opposite impulse. It thundered toward the burning isle with suicidal confidence. In the summer afternoon, several of the grandest buildings Anders had ever seen shone like brilliant midnight torches. One on the left collapsed.

He peered down and found local sailors shared his survival instinct. Trade ships of every size stalled in the river, avoiding the piers and the flaming skyline ahead. Crews gawked with the same dull shock as the squad, even with the privilege of keeping their distance. Perhaps it was harder for them. The pyre was their home, or at least their workplace. Two boys—men, they were Anders's age, they were *men*—saluted the train. Somewhere, Anders found the presence of mind to throw a limp salute back.

Then he forced his gaze back to the city and let his eyes adjust to the light. Thicker, taller flames burned on the right—due south. The brightest blocks were just a little shorter and a little more modern. While he couldn't pin meaning to the pattern, Anders safely discarded coincidence. Every insane action hid sane logic. Life would be a shade easier if he unwound it before stepping inside.

No such luck. Instead, he hunted for familiar symbols. Something from a story, or an article, or even a rhyme. The statelier buildings looked fine. Wherever Chatham Square sat, it was likely untouched. The inferno seemed to be a poor problem.

"Ah," he said. No one replied.

In a better life, the tension in his chest would be unfamiliar. But his heart had threatened to collapse just as loudly before, during, and after Longstreet's Sprint.

He looked down. At some point, he'd started leaning on the flagpole for support.

"I hate trains," Anders grumbled.

"Warriors don't whine," chided Joaquin. He didn't sound like he believed it.

"I also hate trains," said Mole, from behind. He still held the script, purely as a comfort item. Riding into an inferno lent his posture a hitherto unseen slouch. He paired a resolute face with a resigned body.

Joaquin shrugged off the comment. Concern had crept into his features as well, undermining a carefully maintained aloof mask. Anders could hazard why: if there was a word of truth to his origin, he was more accustomed to rising up than suppression. The white noise surrounding them would be just as unfamiliar to him as to any other soldier.

Gleason, the one New Yorker among them, stood apart. He only stole small, peripheral glances at home. A few questions occurred to Anders, but none of them felt right. The corporal's eyes had darkened, and the air of freedom that had floated around him since rebuking Hobbes had dissipated.

Something internal shifted. Gleason planted one hand against the wall and looked directly across the Hudson. He shifted his palm every few minutes, as if it blocked a particular inferno needing closer inspection.

"There's home," noted Gleason.

Anders mined his brain for a reply. The words that flowed freely with the angel failed him. Demanding answers to chaos came much more naturally than providing them.

"Report, sir," he finally managed.

"Listening."

"I've been contacted by a representative of the demiurge."

No answer.

"God says we're in trouble."

"Thank you, Anders."

"And I can redeem us. Which means we need redeeming, which isn't encouraging. But the chance of fixing it is. I'm sure I can handle it, with your guidance."

"That's very heroic, Anders."

"The prisoner asked me—"

"Thank you, Anders."

He let it go. Spiritualists and mediums had flooded the market with prophetic dreams, and he didn't feel like competing. If he was having an episode, he could bear it in silence like an adult. If he wasn't, and the demiurge had an opinion, it could come down and do some work. The corporeal world was complicated enough.

16

PYROPHOBIA

One pleasure of exploring the country was learning small things about himself. Anders liked hardtack and disliked canned fish. He was a champion dancer and an embarrassing singer. He could spin poetic words for battlefield nurses, as long as they weren't nearby. And he feared fire.

An abridged march took him past a set of white apartments, which smelled like nothing, into a negro quarter, which filled his sinuses with soot. They walked through the Second Colored Congregational Church, where only the sign remained. He hoped that the First had fared better and that his brain would stop screaming for him to flee. For all the rage and slogans in the air, he felt just as flammable as any of the black civilians left.

Naturally, he ended up in a bucket brigade. Gleason's squad led a line of sweating, cursing, lightly charred men, spilling half the water in the journey from pump to apartment building. With the exception of Anders, charged with maintaining morale. He stood behind Mole, the thickest available barrier, as soldiers took turns attacking what had once been several homes, and would likely soon collapse into a mausoleum.

Sixth Avenue recalled hell, if only because his preachers never got past fire and farm tools. The scene also recalled the lesson branded onto his arm. That spot hadn't healed well. A ring on his forearm still had the shade and texture of overdone pork. If rumors about cannibalism were true, it would taste like pork too. As would the rest of him, if the draft riot successfully slow-roasted him.

Then he lost his cover. A scream—a high-pitched male, younger than Anders—rang out from above. Mole abandoned his bucket and charged inside. Now fully exposed—which, upon reflection, he should have aimed for as a performer—Anders's sense of shame spoke up and then screamed in turn. He dropped the flag, picked up Mole's bucket, and dragged it to the rim of the conflagration. He heaved the bucket with all the force he could manage, putting out one cubic foot of fire. It returned in moments, sending him stumbling backward. After landing on his favorite shoulder and choking back a sob, he got up and tried again. The results didn't improve.

"What do you think you're doing?"

"F-fire?"

One of Harrow's officers, White—Hobbes was nowhere in sight. Important enough for a sword, not important enough for a horse. He looked bored and resentful, in contrast to the confused panic that threatened to break down the line. The name *Clyburn* came to Anders, but he couldn't attach meaning to it.

"You're a flagman. Flagmen spin."

"Fire?"

"These hovels might burn and might not. What matters is us being seen *restoring order*. That means flags, and bugles, and monkeys following orders. They tell the Dublin trash making all this noise to go inside and drink their rotgut instead of igniting it. Save heroics for battles that matter."

The officer shoved the staff into his chest. Anders stood, dumb. His left forearm throbbed with a parody of nostalgia. He wished he could see Mole, or hear Mole. Not that Mole spoke without provocation. But tense silence trumped uncertainty any day.

This winding series of thoughts came out as "Fire?"

"Spin, boy! Spin!"

Anders forced his hands through a *Kansas Arc*. He knew better maneuvers, but nothing else simple enough to complete in a fog of ash, smoke, and officer barking. He connected it into a *Nebraska Semicircle*, and back into another *Kansas Arc*. With effort, he'd kick-started a *Kansas-Nebraska Loop*, a staple of new school twirling. Just enough to get Clyburn yelling at someone else, somewhere else.

He kept the loop going, shifting his gaze from the bedlam to the street. The cobbling was nicer than any of the fringe towns he'd marched through.

Based on the people fleeing, this had been a black block. How had they afforded it? How many Gleasons were in New York, and how many would be left after this?

The high-minded, and thus useless, line of thought might have continued. Even in a crisis, a *Kansas-Nebraska Loop* lent itself to meditative introspection and let difficult or directly contradictory ideas flow together. But the dissonant warble of an amateur bugle cut into his warrior-monk zen.

"Petey," Anders grumbled.

True to form, his fellow pillar of morale struggled through something that had once been "John Brown's Body." Anders didn't know why the idiot played now instead of handling the fire. But Anders also didn't know why *he* showed off now instead of handling the fire. They looked even less sane together than they did separately.

"Play it right!" Anders barked, absorbing Clyburn's tone. His rhythm slipped with Petey's. At this rate, the *Kansas-Nebraska Loop* would become an unsustainable mess.

Petey shouted something incomprehensible. Anders shuffled closer, doing his best to keep the rapidly decaying loop from decaying into a *Bleeding Kansas Sweep*. No one liked the *Bleeding Kansas Sweep*.

"I said, 'I'm scared!'" Petey repeated. He followed it with a mutilated "Nelly Bly." The minstrel tune followed "John Brown's Body" as unnaturally as a minstrel show followed a slave revolt.

Anders yelled in near English. It was closer to a bark. The other soldiers, the ones assigned rifles and bayonets instead of *morale*, performed battlefield courage perfectly. The youths just had to follow suit, and Petey was dragging them both down. Tears and failure belonged to the quiet hours after battle, softened by the relief of survival. Open doubt was communicable. Anders could feel the perfect circle of the *Kansas-Nebraska Loop* slipping into an ellipse.

He looked over both shoulders, searching the tumult for Gleason. The corporal could motivate anyone, as long he stayed under four syllables and avoided mixed metaphors. Anders spied him running into Mole's building/flaming casket, presumably after his subordinate. The lack of hesitation punched another crack into Anders's ego. He kept spinning. The crack widened into a fissure when the director reemerged, rolling the unconscious Mole out like a wooden barrel. Whoever the giant had chased inside remained.

After the emphasis on *restoring order,* no one seemed to notice the slow decay of the *Kansas-Nebraska Loop.* Anders stood alone with his mind, an aimless task, a weeping incompetent, and stray sparks.

And the envelope.

Slade's pitch had a new flavor. He could help someone without raw energy snapping at his face. Or at least less of it.

Anders stopped spinning and rested the staff on his shoulder. The world kept turning. He then marched—not ran, not walked, but marched—with full formal posture and pomp. Bucket lines smoothly parted before a serious-faced ally bound Somewhere Important to do Something Important. A privilege he'd enjoy daily, if Harrow had understood or cared about cryptography.

"Where are we going?"

Of course. The atonal bugle hadn't softened, after all. Anders avoided stopping or turning but gleaned that Petey had followed him like a lost calf.

"There's no we. I'm just stepping aside to urinate," Anders said, doing his best to keep his face neutral. With more time, he could explain the difference between *desertion* and a side job.

"You should do that on the apartment. I think anything would help. Hobbes tried spitting on it."

They passed two understudies in *The Living Abacus.* If anything happened to Anders or Mole (like defection or burning to death), they'd play the principal characters. The better actor of the pair gave him a nod, and Anders replied with a salute and a *Sherman Switch.* The diagonal flagpole spin forced Petey to hop backward to avoid a concussion. Bonus.

"I think you're pulling a runner," announced Petey. He had a smooth tone for his age, if high-pitched. A natural singer, which made his one-horn war on music all the more abrasive.

"No." Anders inflected it like a question and immediately hated his own voice.

"I'm going too."

"I'm coming right back. You're almost full black, Clyburn will have you shot if you go missing. Or just give you to the rioters. An octoroon can survive this. At worst, I'll be digging latrines and trenches until Virginia starves."

"You say *octoroon* a lot."

"I have the right to, as one. You don't understand my hard mulatto struggle."

"Was it your daddy or your mama?"

Anders took two seconds to invent an answer, which was one too long.

"Ha! You're whiter than a rope salesman. I won't tell anyone if you let me come."

"Most of them have some idea."

"Not the officers. Clyburn's still stewing over that knife pervert in your squad showing him up. All that battered ego would come down on you."

"Why can't you run on your own?"

"I'm scared," Petey repeated. He said it with a galling and enviable lack of shame.

Anders searched for a parry. Instead, his memory offered flashes of a manic, spiritually broken Bryce and the death that quickly found him. His body would be in Virginia with honors, if there were more left of it. As things stood, Anders's friend was one more decaying smear by Cemetery Hill.

"That makes sense," Anders conceded. "Just look less like you're fleeing. Walk like you're somebody, it's just like performing. In fact, keep playing. You look lost just holding that thing."

The blaring resumed, perfecting their illusion and driving Anders half mad. He hoped against hope that the next collapsing tenement gave him tinnitus.

Sixth Avenue gave way to Seventh, Eighth, and Ninth. Less flames, more melees. Each step pushed court-martial or incineration further out of focus, in favor of a plate or safe dropped from above. He watched a private clipped by a book fail to get up and decided that he'd always been right about reading.

Anders hung a right, cutting through an alley connecting Fifty-Third Street and Fifty-Fourth. He stuck his head out slowly. On this side, fire-fighting gave way to a firefight: one aspiring champion fired a pistol at a Union officer, killing their horse and attracting fatal attention. Most of his fellow streetfighters carried simple torches, rags, and varied bottles of liquor. The returning volley was faster, more organized, and more decisive than any Anders had seen soldiers direct at each other. Eight of the belligerents fell, splitting the remaining dozen into the brave (who charged) and the sane (who fled).

The sane looked like typical citizens. Workers and tramps in ruddy clothing full of holes before a shot had been fired. The skinnier ones would've eaten better in the army, unless they wound up on the wrong end of a siege. Or infiltrated a black regiment.

The brave had something extra, even as they collided with rifle butts and bayonets. Each, to a man, wore at least one red article of clothing. Some managed full coats and matching slacks. Others made do with a bloodred cap or crimson socks—less a uniform and more the *intent* of one. Nonetheless, they all accessorized with wide-eyed, screaming fanaticism.

"Go back to your huts, niggers!" cried one partisan, brandishing a chipped kitchen knife. "I'd rather hang a slave than be one."

To be expected, though Petey crouched a little farther down. Under Lee, Anders had listened to soldiers short on food, bullets, and underclothes equate white unionists with black men. The company in question—presumably one of Meade's—resembled Anders's. They were just a bit older, and a little more acclimated to killing, which one demonstrated by bayonetting the partisan through the lung.

"For Columbia!" cried another partisan. A general cheer of assent and conviction rose above the screams.

Another standard cry. Everyone fought for freedom, even when fighting to avoid fighting for freedom.

"For the crown!"

That was an odd one. Petey crept forward for a better view, and Anders followed suit with heroic reluctance.

If crowns were a medieval concept, so were bayonets. They dragged fear of spears tearing flesh into the present. Battlefield melees were terrible enough that most charges either broke enemy morale or lost their own nerve before making contact.

The red civilians hadn't been informed. Shirts came to match jackets and caps as Meade's men proved the value of three months of training over one week of anger. While the sight disquieted Anders, it failed to make him physically ill. He didn't like that change. A proper war hero ought to regret the violence he was celebrated for.

When the melee ended, Anders tried a few slight mouselike steps. The chaos would have been easier to pass through, but brawls had gravitational pull.

"You two!" The voice had the inimitable mix of put-upon stress and barking contempt of a lower officer. Sure enough, the late horse's surviving rider stomped up to the truant pair. Petey had the good sense to stay silent. Unfortunately, Anders didn't have words to save them either. He waited for the hammer to fall. Maybe he'd end up in one of the nice military jails, with more bread than mice.

The officer limped up to the pair, glaring at Petey's crooked cap and oversize jacket. And perhaps, for a moment, at Anders's artfully tilted cap and loose-fit uniform. The man was caked in genuine New York filth. He'd either fallen into one of Manhattan's stagnant puddles or been the victim of wastewater launched from a window. Either way, his ire could be seen, heard, and smelled.

"Get to twirling. Morale's sagging."

Anders saluted, performed a frontside 540 twirl, and then marched through and past the massacre's aftermath. A pitchy version of "Battle Cry of Freedom" backed the theatrical exit. He did his best to step around the viscera, but some found its way onto his right shoe. He'd take it over tactical wastewater or hate's flames any day.

17

EASY STREET

Uptown life carried on as usual. Citizens strolled as if a shot had never been fired in anger, either in the trenches or their own city. No one brandished anything, save bored policemen or other soldiers evading fresh trauma. The arson and kitchen knives belonged to another world, about ten blocks south.

Anders could still hear the riot: chants, gunfire, and screams provided soft background music for drowsy small talk. If he looked between or over buildings, he could see hints of a brawl or spirals of smoke. From appearances, no one else could. Well-dressed New Yorkers enjoyed a specialized blindness.

The faces were largely white. The real white, untouched by the sun or late migration. White directly traceable to an address in London, and a parallel family branch fretting over the Ashanti War dragging on. A few other genres of human flitted about, but they made an art of invisibility. A worker's duties included fading out of the view and path of the people running things.

Anders made his first attempt at doffing his cap at a woman, targeting a dark-haired flaneur with a skirt three times her width. She looked like a woman of the world. Someone who read, and visited Gleason's shows to tell her friends she'd seen the other side of the wall.

She chortled, shoulder-checked Petey into the gutter, and strode into a saloon.

"I should have asked Gleason something about this place," Anders thought out loud.

"I'm fine, thank you," replied Petey.

"There's so much here. I'd like to see what inspired the New Human. The American Future, and all that. I mean, he says it's the whole country, but he grew up here."

"No need to check on old Petey."

The complaints finally pulled Anders from his thoughts, his favorite and safest place. He helped pull Petey to his feet and brushed some of the New York off his uniform.

"Indestructible," continued Petey. "A body and heart of iron, that boy. Like a living aba-whathaveyou."

"You sound like Thomas."

That put an end to the grousing. Petey still looked like he might cry at any moment, so Anders clasped his shoulder and explained the transient, unknowable nature of city women. It was just like the transient, unknowable nature of rural women, at least according to his old comrades in *another detachment*. Petey nodded through the hard-won wisdom, hopefully putting his feelings in the deep hole hidden inside every warrior.

"Do you know where you're going?"

Anders flicked the now-rumpled and soot-dusted envelope out from his jacket pocket. The front said "Dearest Wendy" in something like cursive script. The back had "The Governess, 234 W 9th St" in plainer, more legible print.

"234 West Ninth Station," said Anders.

"Station? Not street?"

Anders didn't reply.

"So street. Down southwest."

Anders kept moving. He wiped his left hand against his jacket, smearing away stray gutter fluid, and reopened the envelope. Slade's code made the Vigenère look like high art—Anders could read it like plain English, swapping the letters in his head as he went. But only for plot. The nature of the content eluded him. Though Wendy's need for arms in the midst of a riot had the whiff of high treason. *Higher* treason.

Slade had abominable handwriting for a rich man. Likely his tutors never had the permission or will to ignore him, or mock him, or tell him he wasn't a student there. Perks of being born *somebody*.

"Letter from home?"

"Oh, no. It's a message we're delivering for the prisoner."

That earned a familiar expression. Anders primed himself for polite questions about what he meant or rude questions about head trauma.

"Is that allowed?" asked Petey. His voice climbed up an octave.

"It's as allowed as skipping a battle."

"That's a tu quoque argument."

"Pardon?"

"I don't know what it means, but Gleason says it when people make hollow excuses. You're trying to lie with the truth."

"Lying?" echoed Anders. The accusation stung. He took friendly banter about being "blunt" or "touched" in stride, since they pointed to a fundamental honesty. Those insults fit snugly with his self-image, preventing the dissonance that turned politicians and preachers gray. "Liar" hit a new target, with no mental armor around it.

"Yeah, lying. Without lying. Only the worst liars can do that."

"At least I didn't run like a scared dog. I ran like a shrewd coyote. If I'm a liar, go find an honest tail to sniff."

Petey scrunched his eyebrows together, unpacking the metaphor. Two minutes later, he balled up his free hand into a fist. Anders gently slipped into Stance Three, primed for a *Switch 180 Underspin*. Also known as a *Jackson Retort*. It was a quick transitional move, and thus ideal for a parry. While a fight wasn't ideal, he'd take it over a battle any day.

The first blow never came. After unclenching his fist, Petey hucked his bugle, overhand, into the crowd. It struck a businessman in the head, sending him stumbling into the same curbside muck currently coating Petey's clothes. The bugler's cap went next, soaring against the wind with much less success. The hat blew back into Petey's leg, leading the boy to stomp it twice.

"I'm through!" Petey announced. "With you, and Lincoln, and plays about math, and fighting for a dead country's conscience. Through!" His well-heeled spectators kept walking and chattering. The world of wartime commerce didn't have much interest in one angry negro. Much like the world of peacetime commerce. Luckily, Anders could cover their share of indignation.

"That's a uniform. You can't disrespect a uniform."

"Says the fake nigger in a dead man's jacket," Petey said, dragging off his own. "That's the ofay in you. You care more about the coat than the person in it. Your mama would be ashamed."

Suddenly, "ofay" grated. He'd heard it in Liberty Valley, almost always pointed his way. But somewhere in his black career—between the camp game, enduring Clyburn, and the flames—the word gained texture.

"So? She's always ashamed."

"Then the uniform isn't working, is it?"

The topic itself had Anders on the back foot. He had to say *something*. If not to convince Petey, at least to win. Denying putting the symbol first would be a lie, giving Petey a point. Defending the role of the soldier—and by extension their uniform—in building The American Future might be *lying with the truth*, a concept he still only half grasped. He barely noticed Petey's jacket fall into the Manhattan gutter, rendering it permanently unfit for human use. But the real puzzle was his opponent morphing into a girl.

Without duty, Petey already looked lighter. The discarded jacket was thicker than most, likely making for less miserable winters. Typical bugler—too self-involved to appreciate the gifts heaped upon him. Even junior nurses flirted with frostbite before learning to pinch gloves from wounded officers. Anders considered retrieving the coat for himself, but the water's scent sat between sulfur and urine. And raiment that thick would *ruin* his summer.

Petey must have spent some time with the nurses—tight bandaging pressed against his undershirt, like an overstuffed mummy. Lucky—most patients left an arm or two behind. Even his posture had transformed. Instead of arching his back like a boy pretending to be a man, and standing on his toes like a man pretending to be a taller man, he settled into a natural slouch. It matched his resigned eyes well. And lashes. Decent figure, for a quitter.

Anders found his retort.

"You shouldn't desert. It's unladylike." Petey stayed mute, radiating ire. Anders felt a moment slip by. Any goodwill the deduction might have earned evaporated.

Fair enough: he'd undersold a masterful effort. Like other simians his age, Anders could detect nurses and widows minutes before they passed with fresh dead. Petey had defeated that sixth sense, and he only knew because she'd given up.

His main rival for regiment mascot had succeeded in a performance much more complex than butchering marching tunes. Anders would have to excel in the play to compete, and that assumed the theater still existed.

A few natural questions remained. Why was she in Harrow's brigade? How had she hidden for so long? Was she insane? His brain tried to wait for her to cool off. Instead, his mouth ran ahead at a full, committed sprint.

"I didn't mean that. Do you like flags? I actually admire bugle playing. My father might have been a bugle player. I never heard that he wasn't. We should trade lessons. Want a flower?"

"The hell?"

"Sorry. The only lady I've spoken to in months was an angel."

"What? Are you possessed?"

"No, that would be a demon. I have an angel. They're a bit like officers, but for God. She said I could touch her butt, but it never came about. Would you let me—never mind. You're a girl?"

"No, *you're* a girl," Petey snapped back. She crossed her arms, exuding as much confidence as her situation and chosen line allowed. Anders started mouthing *No, you are*, but it felt unproductive.

A tense beat passed. Then Anders recalled standing in the continent's largest city. A spectacle like this wouldn't *attract* witnesses as much as invite them to a catered show. He took a panicked look around, to find no one looking back. The crowd simply flowed around them, in a vast hurry to get wherever men in suits went. Nowhere downtown, if the not-so-distant smoke meant anything.

"We're invisible to them. Unless we get in the way."

"You're a girl?"

Petey groaned.

"Why not be a nurse?"

"I've never heard a song about a nurse. And I don't think Harrow's girls are helping. They just saw important bits off people all day."

"It's worse when you leave the green parts on. Trust me, I saw it back in . . . my second deployment," said Anders, skipping duller details. Southern gentlemen considered bothering doctors weakness, and they died strong.

"Music's medicine too. Playing always kept Papa sober for a few minutes longer. I figured it would help out here. I wanted to matter."

A pamphlet-reading dilettante walked directly between them, without even a rude word or curious glance. Either they were truly invisible, or he simply expected his lessers to part around him like vapor. Perhaps they usually did.

"Why give up now? You've put in work, and we're just waiting for Richmond to starve."

"Because we're fighting and burning ourselves here. Err, we were before too, but this time it's our side of ourselves. I don't see how we can beat ourselves when we're beating ourselves."

Another civilian barreled through the debate, treading directly on Anders's foot. The threadbare army boots absorbed almost none of the steel-toed shoe's force, leaving Anders's foot the full experience. Unraveling Petey's sentence kept him from contemplating the unused pistol on his hip. Or, given his track record, the more lethal pole on his shoulder.

"It's suicide either way," Petey continued. "I'm a girl when it keeps me alive, and I'm a boy when it keeps me alive."

"Brilliant. I should've thought of that," mused Anders. "Think I'd make a convincing girl?"

"No."

He stored the idea for later use anyway. In a pinch, switching genders might be less drastic than switching armies. Nurses and civilian hangers-on were third or fourth priority in a retreat, just behind the supplies and command staff. He couldn't pin infantrymen's precise location on that list, but he suspected it was a two-digit number, long after the expensive rifles they carried or a smart horse.

"Serving with you was an honor." Anders threw a full salute, complete with a puffed-out chest. Her long performance offered valuable insight into enhancing his manly essence. That deserved all the respect her musicality didn't.

Then he pivoted away on one foot, planning his next life as a captain of industry. Now that he could complete the job in peace, the future felt lighter and brighter. His first priority would be sending every flag-twirler a proper Jefferson Firearms revolver. No one deserved to face something like Longstreet's Sprint unarmed.

A hand caught his collar.

"How much, exactly, is Slade paying?"

17.5

ZOOLOGY

'PAT'S NOTES

checklist for hiding among the apes

general principles

-don't call menfolk apes in person
-hide this list well, or they'll know you're hiding among them
-watch your food or someone will steal it
-gamble

physical presentation

-scratch stuff
-keep arms ashy
-skip every third bath
-stand with back straight, chest out
-or stand slumped over, looking defeated
-stare at nurses without talking

conversation

-no compliments
-pretend animal races are fun
-pretend animal fights are sane
-pretend you slept well
-pretend you're not scared
-pretend you're not homesick
-pretend

making friends

-drink
-make up sex lies
-match, but don't exceed, the sex lies of your target friend
-never challenge sex lies
-keep sex lies consistent (second set of notes?)
-leave romance out of sex lies, unless drunk
-help new friends handle vomit

confrontation (physical)

-flee confrontation
-find friend
-bring friend to nighttime ambush
-return favor upon request

confrontation (verbal)

-make claim
-repeat claim, unaltered
-continue previous steps
-continue until victorious or embarrassed

backstory

-you love your mother
-you hate your father
-you miss your girl
-remember to say girl
-you were first in town to enlist
-you can't wait to go back to your alive family

misc.

-for privacy, say you're going to pray and invite everyone
-if anyone cries, look away until they're done
-find someone that looks like a survivor, and stay close
-papa would be proud of you

18

IDEA PERSON

I t's actually Patricia. You're not really Bryce, right? What's your name? Are you a Jefferson like Slade, or a Jefferson like Gleason?"

Anders doubled his pace. Every effort to shake Patricia or his luck away made them dig in. She'd convinced herself that he wanted to hoard some spectacular prize for himself. Which was true, but he'd earned the right to a little hoarding two or three charges ago. If he couldn't get credit, he could at least get compensation.

On their (his!) walk to The Governess, she'd explained her background. He hadn't absorbed it. Patricia's family lived somewhere north of the Mason-Dixon Line, occupying a social class between Mole's abject forced servitude and Gleason's obscure negro intelligentsia. Some good things happened, and then some bad things, and now she'd walked away from the army. Or not—the soiled uniform tucked under her arm looked indecisive.

"Pa had a book of Chinese fairy tales. He thought that white ones were designed to make better serfs. And serfs were just like slaves, except . . . whatever the difference was. He didn't want me thinking like a slave."

"Hmm." More slave talk. It'd be a long walk.

"One story had a lady named Hua Mulan, who joined the army and fooled a gaggle of drunken idiots."

"Sounds made up."

"All fairy tales are made up, just like newspapers. Anyhow, I thought, 'If she can swordfight like a man, I can at least dress like one and soothe souls with song.' So I did."

Well, one out of two is good. Once again, Anders elected to hold on to a thought. The new habit felt off, but it kept the tone with Patricia light.

And when she talked about home, she wasn't talking about Slade's loosely defined reward. *His* reward.

Patricia's story came with a lot of extra movement—hand gestures, imitative facial expressions, and random stops in his path to emphasize both. They made her hard to ignore, along with facial symmetry that challenged his mother's soliloquies on mixing. How had she ever pulled off a Hua Mulan? Were the corporal and the others equally blind or just polite? Anders hoped that her desertion stuck, and his didn't, so that he could pursue ascent into military legend and/or economic comfort without distraction.

"That's it," he muttered, as Patricia's origin story reached its climax. Reportedly, her hometown had experienced some parallel to the village in *The Ballad of Mulan* running out of men. Given his inability to remember the town's name or pronounce Hua Mulan, Anders took her word for it.

"You sure? I'm almost at the good part."

Anders crouched behind a barrel. For the first time, he thanked God for his *somewhat limited* height. Patricia, reacclimated to social invisibility, didn't bother. She went as far as sitting on the barrel, tooting quick, shrill notes out of her instrument.

A semi-sober couple in patchy red coats approached the doorman, a pallid man with three visible daggers. Both redcoats had the easy smiles and gentle sway of festival drunks. The riot looked fun, as long as you didn't occupy the burning building or get shot in the reprisal.

Each drunk flashed a furtive hand sign. Unsatisfied with the quality, the doorman made them repeat the signal twice before letting them pass.

"Looks like an upside-down *W*," mused Anders. He twisted his middle and ring fingers together and held the sign over his heart. Curious.

"An *M*."

"No. Well, yes, but the *intent* must be a *W*. It's a more conspiratorial letter." He kept practicing.

"I think it's an *M*."

He let the bait go. Patricia, unlike Petey, had little concept of the polite deference lesser artists owed a virtuoso. A little early stuttering on Anders's part had upset their entire balance of power. It'd be nice to get Petey back. He decided to push for that as soon as he had a fresh uniform and a decent argument.

The Governess stood a good distance from the riot's core—which lined up with Wendy's alleged role in sparking it. The brick building occupied three times the width of the shops on either flank. Less a tavern, more a beer hall. In lieu of its name, the front sign featured an etching of Columbia.

"A crown?" muttered Anders. He'd seen freedom's mascot drawn in a cap, a flag gown, and even nothing—camped men made their own entertainment. But never a silver crown with a matching scepter. This version carried an air of authority, as if she glanced down on the customer from a great distance and found him wanting.

"It looks decent on her. If someone with a crown freed slaves, more owners would listen."

"Yeah," he said with rich insight. Slavery again. Fighting for or against it didn't make the conversations easier. Warfare over something less tense, like a thousand years of moving borders, would make better conversation. Whether he spoke with Patricia or Mole, slavery dried up his mouth and tangled his words.

"Are we going in? Slade won't give *us our* reward if Wendy Whatsit doesn't get her mail."

"I'm strategizing."

"Well, first you could reseal the envelope so it looks unread. Then we'll hand her the mail, and smile polite-ish like we're two years younger and just learned to read."

"I don't think they're letting soldiers inside. Or black girls survive."

Patricia blew a dissonant note. Much easier than admitting he'd said something accurate.

"Don't worry. I have an idea. We'll use words."

✦ ✦ ✦

A redcoat peed in the alley between The Governess and a shuttered bank. He aimed for the bank walls, showing the crown proper respect. The smell was off, but he could always get back into water after retirement.

"Hello, sir?" said Anders.

"What do—"

Anders unleashed the week's frustration, fear, and self-loathing into a backside flagpole swing. The sweep took the partisan off his feet. From there, an experienced fighter or faller might have attempted a roll. The redcoat used his skull instead.

He didn't pass out, defying Anders's hopes. It took a minute of frantic, determined kicking from him and Patricia to put him to sleep, or at least an acceptably slack stillness. In her open terror, Anders saw a few hints of Petey's old helpless confusion. He'd have gloated if he weren't hyperventilating.

"Why'd you stop?" asked Patricia. She braced against the wall for support.

"We need him down, not dead."

"Did you see downtown? I'm all right with dead."

"Rejoin the army if you want kills. We're just stripping this one."

Mercifully, she acquiesced. Stuffing a nude man in a barrel demanded four hands.

Anders's new outfit felt loose, hot, and scratchy. The coat displayed and hid a dozen small things that jangled: fake watches, fake bracelets, fake badges, three real coins, and fake rings. He could corner the fake silver market. A pair of matches sat next to the coins in his pocket. He frowned, gently snapped them into thirds, and let them fall to the alley floor.

"There. You look like a proper imperialist."

"Monarchist," corrected Anders.

"Spend less time with Gleason."

Hunting for another victim was possible, but their first carried just enough money to enter a Manhattan shop without being crushed by shame. They took the invitation, straying from The Governess to a tailor too notable for a proper sign. The proprietor looked offended by the lack of recognition in their expressions. It even overshadowed Anders dressing like one of the men burning down half the island.

The tailor didn't have much more love for Patricia, who showed insufficient wonder at stepping into a *proper* gallery of clothing. Patricia entered in battlefield-shredded pants and an ash-dusted undershirt, giving every impression of being a vagrant with eclectic taste. She'd then rifled through the full collection of modest fichus and even more modest hoop skirts with subaltern fingers, searching for one in red.

"Sir, do you intend to control your servant?"

"I intend for my *servant* to be properly attired," said Anders. The lie flowed a little more naturally this time—lying with a lie took less processing than lying with the truth. "They're all free now, so her appearance reflects back on me."

He drew his fake pocket watch and stared at the unmoving hands. They made for easier viewing than the withering glare boring in from his left. On his right, Patricia dragged a red and brown dress overhead. The colors clashed hideously, but the red matched the general shade that Wendy's guests wore with violent pride. She dug out a matching scarf and threw it over her shoulder.

The tailor named a number twice the garment's possible value. Anders simply handed him half the crumpled bills in his victim's pocket with a pair of fake rings.

"There," said Patricia. "Think a *properly dressed* servant can get in?"

"No, they'd definitely kill you," mused Anders. The smart odds said she'd been joking, but he remembered clarity's importance to proper leadership. "I have another idea."

✦ ✦ ✦

His second innovation proved less graceful than ambushing a public urinator. The makeup kit cost the rest of their victim's wages, and using the brush demanded more dexterity than any combat or performance he'd faced to date. Each stroke stopped short or slipped farther than he'd intended, forcing him to add more to even out the result.

"How's it look?" Patricia asked. She sat atop the same barrel holding their victim.

"Why can't you do this? It's your face."

"I don't know how. And it's your idea."

Anders missed a stroke—debate and makeup didn't fit well together. He dipped the brush back in the chalky white powder. Hopefully it wasn't based on white phosphorus like the average match. Rumors of the half-eaten "fossy jaw" haunting English workers half their age would keep him up at night if he didn't have his own nightmares.

One crossed-out scene in *The Living Abacus* involved a six-page rant about minstrel shows. Something about shoe polish and pantomime had gotten under Gleason's skin, despite it being a true original American art form. Anders, however, found inspiration. If Patricia could survive as a black soldier, she could thrive as a white dilettante. A little clamshell-colored makeup and a blond wig would let her gifts thrive.

The aspiring Hua Mulan had accepted the idea with enthusiasm. Better yet, without hard questions. It helped that she treated transformation like an end unto itself—and assumed he'd do the bulk of the work. One of them had been conned, they just didn't know who yet.

Patricia tapped the barrel. Its occupant was either unable or unwilling to respond.

"I think you were right," she said. "About leaving him alive."

Anders shrugged.

"I've never killed anyone," Patricia added. "Direct-like."

"Me neither."

"Liar."

Anders missed another stroke. He tried to make up for the thin area with a quick dab of the tip, which made the area blotchy. He let it go. If pressed, they could claim she had a rash.

"What's it like?" asked Patricia.

"Fine. Nothing special."

"Really?"

"No."

He set the powder box aside. If he lived past the war, he'd give makeup a proper try. The right shade of powder might bring out his cheeks, or at least hide his forearm burns. For now, he'd coated Patricia in a solid, clownish coat of white. Only a little had slipped onto her collar, and he thought it worked as an accent.

"Do I look white?"

"I don't know. Color's more than the shade. Back home, there was a midnight-looking boy adopted by a big trader. The only real rich family in town. Everyone called him white, and treated him white, and talked to him the way . . . white people talk to each other. We also had a blond girl without parents the sheriff called DarkieLocks. Do you feel white?"

Patricia gave Anders the same confounded face half his conversations ended in. Petey never gave him that face. If he ever got Petey back, he'd be a little nicer.

"I feel strained. Like everything I've done today, or watched happen, is going to catch up to me."

"That sounds white! I did a great job."

Patricia leaned over a reflective puddle of hopefully-water and checked herself out. A well-to-do stranger peered up at her, winked, and waved.

"White me needs a name."

"No she doesn't. White you needs to follow me inside so we can get this done."

"Shut up, nigger."

"What?"

"I'm practicing."

Patricia stared at her latest manifestation, trying new names out loud. She sampled Betsy, Juliet, Big Martha, and Pollyanna before simplifying it to Polly.

"Jefferson," she added. "Polly Jefferson."

"Most Jeffersons are black, I think."

Polly ignored him, despite Anders doing half the work to pull her into existence. The fate of most feedback, and parent-child relationships. He could only hope that Patricia held more sway over Polly than he did.

"Boy! Dispose of your flagpole. It's off-tone for tonight's entertainment, and I require an escort to The Governess."

"When did you start talking like that?"

"Do it, boy."

Anders decided he didn't like white women.

Nonetheless, Polly had a point. The redcoats wouldn't be overjoyed to see the banner they'd risen against. One tell, however small, might tip his artful disguises.

Parting with the flagpole took willpower. The instrument had been his badge of office, creative outlet, and improvised weapon. He separated the flag, folded it with more reverence than haste, and swaddled it in his army uniform. He then stuffed the package behind the barrel and left the staff against the brick wall. To most passersby, it was just a stray pole. And no expert would stoop low enough to take it. Hopefully.

Perfectionism took over during the approach. Anders repeated the hand sign again and again, until they turned the corner and entered the doorman's line of sight. From there, he rehearsed mentally, convinced that a sluggish or inaccurate finger would expose them.

Finally, at arm's length, he started the motion. The armed stranger interrupted before his hand reached his heart.

"Why's she painted like a clown?"

Polly opened a hitherto unseen fan and swatted the doorman across both cheeks.

"You should be ashamed," Polly hissed. She stomped ahead of the shamefaced lookout, fanning herself as she went. Bewildered, but long accustomed to bewilderment, Anders followed.

18.5

———◆———

THE SENIOR GLEASON

Dear Tobias,

You'll never read this. If I die, it'll be lost in the tumult. If I live, I'll destroy it. So here, and only here, I'll admit you were right.

Not about the United Tomorrow, or whatever you call it. I still don't know what you're yammering about half the time or why you worship the Founding Ofays. They had more slaves than anyone you're shooting at now. I've just accepted that our family only had enough sense for one sibling, and you're doing your best with what's left.

You were right to enlist. Because it's not any safer here.

After all the impolite words when you left, saying that feels important. Life's getting cheaper, especially when you look like us. But at least something might come of the bullets flying around you. I'll get shot for nothing, clinging to life like . . . something that clings. A baby? I'm not a writer. If you find this letter, edit the rough bits.

Do you remember Banjo's? The sweets shop? The owner's name was Robert, but he called it Banjo's because white people expected a name like that. Rob's Delectables was a ghost town, but Banjo's had people from uptown, downtown, and out of town looking for "the local flavor." Funny that. You and Robert were the only ones on our block to turn Black into a boon.

He even kept a banjo on the wall, next to a cheap straw hat. I don't think he could play, but the hat looked good on him. There's nothing quite like a joke the target isn't in on. Maybe that's why the ofays are laughing today.

I don't know why it's funny to burn our shops, and our homes, and our people. But some of them are hollering. Ashes must be funnier than Dan Rice.

Sorry, I buried the main idea. You always say not to do that. Banjo's is gone. They burned it.

They also burned my church, and your barber, and that bar you'd invite actresses to visit and they'd never show up. They burned Mama's favorite dress shop, and the dance hall Papa enjoyed while Mama shopped. They burned the building we grew up in, and the building you moved into. I haven't been to the theater yet, but I'd be surprised if it's still there. Anywhere a Negro has laughed, cried, or thrown up has burned or will burn.

I'll mostly miss Banjo's. It reminded me of being a child who didn't think about any of this. If I couldn't act, I'd have cried.

Anyway, when you edit this, and turn it into your only good play, use more words for "burned." Even I can tell it's repetitive. Try torched, or ignited, or even incinerated. Call the play The Incinerated Angel and make it about a brilliant young actress burnt alive by ofays while her brother plays hero with every other Negro doing Lincoln's job for free.

I can hear you already. "It's not free, it's just a little less than the white soldiers. And it'll change when we show them what we're worth." Okay. But less is worse than free. Free is a gift. Less is submission. I'm tired of submitting.

Oh, one rule for my play: don't add any "speculative theater" nonsense. You can write about people and their feelings without adding talking raccoons and whatnot. Watch: "Betty felt scared. Betty wasn't from the future, or Camelot, or a secret city under Boston. Betty was a girl alone in the basement, while the drunk crackers outside hunted down anyone who looked like her and did anything they felt like doing. Betty was afraid of burning."

Easy, right? Just change out "burning." I used it again.

And "devils." Papa always said, "Don't call them white devils. It's redundant," and I find that's a good rule for life. He'd make a good book, but you were always daydreaming when he talked. I think I finally see why he put up with it. The future's a much nicer place to live.

As a (better) artist, listening to you yammer about the American Horizon (I'm getting closer) always made me feel a little selfish. I don't create to convince anyone of anything. I'm not convinced art can. I just liked to be seen. To read, absorb, and reinvent great plays. When I couldn't get into any of those, I acted in yours.

Take that joke without bristling. I could be dead! Then getting mad would make you a monster. Laugh at yourself, you're hilarious.

With Love,

Betty G.

Post-Script: Banjo's tasted terrible. No one should have let him near food. I wish I could have more.

19

THE SONS OF COLUMBIA

Perhaps he simply disliked music. Songs scarcely appeared in Anders's early memory: Katrina called music an indolent distraction, and his father didn't leave a second opinion. Schoolhouse songs were either educational or mocking. The former boring, the latter directed his way. Churchgoers in Liberty Valley sang with unmatched enthusiasm for the faith donated to them by slave ships, which had appeal. But if visiting the black school was a venial sin, getting caught within earshot of a black church was deadly. For peace, Anders had contained his spiritual life to fear and Bible study. Memories of both were hazy and distinctly lacking in rhythm.

Shuddering at Petey's bugle had been good for his morale. Targeted and focused indifference let Anders feel better about his own work. Now the discord within The Governess made him miss off-tempo marching tunes. They abused the violin. Playing wasn't the word. The violinists, some hooded, some barefaced, *harassed* their instruments.

"They're not very good," observed Polly. She walked with her chin tilted high, looking down on events and the ants driving them. Her fan hadn't closed or lowered since entering.

"They're trying, I respect it," lied Anders. It was getting easier.

Some work had gone into elevating the beer hall's ambience. Long wooden tables sat in a wide ring. Proud anti-draft and anti-emancipation fighters mingled within the circle, forming natural clumps of three or four. Just enough candles burned to make outlines and colors visible, but not enough to discern faces more than a few feet away. The darkness lent some mystery to the musicians, who stood atop every third table.

The crowd matched the dress, attitude, and demographics Anders had watched charge a Union line. Though outfits varied with what the downtrodden could find, borrow, or steal, each partisan put as much red together as possible. Along with equally improvisational arms.

They carried pipes, bricks, and police clubs in the open, and occasionally brandished them as props. Several speakers wore the scrapes and repressed shock of recent action, regaling their more sluggish peers with tales of gallantry. Anders sidled next to an older storyteller and listened in. A deep, middle-aged voice spoke with "big fish" confidence.

"Bah. You're all new to the country, you don't get it. Fire's well and good, but I'm all about a good lynching. It's a lost art up here. Kicking or stabbing a nigger's a waste, they already do that to each other. An old-fashioned hanging? That's got symbolit power. Simpolic power. Sym-bol-ic. You get it, like a flag, or one of your pope pictures."

The listeners returned polite assent, undeterred by the religious jab. One embarrassed soul around Anders's age tucked a book of foreign matches back under his coat. It didn't look like the first time the boy had been put upon by the group, and he smiled through it anyway. Anders avoided reflecting how often he looked like that.

Polly covered even more of her face with the fan, which highlighted her gloved, chalky hands shaking. She fanned herself faster as tension mounted.

"Boy. It's not safe here," she whispered.

"Was Hua Mulan safe?" Anders parried.

"I don't know, I skimmed the story. I just thought she had a good idea."

"She did. Dress up, act like you belong, become legend. I'd like my own ballad."

"You haven't read it."

"I'm sure it works out for her. You wouldn't copy her if it ended like *Hamlet*, or any of those other depressing plays everyone loves."

"Are you that committed to this?"

"I commit to everything. Life dangles everything out of reach. So I push, and push, until something comes loose. If you don't want to help, leave the way you came in."

Polly fell silent. Guilt chewed through any pride Anders might have taken in winning. She'd mastered her new role.

"Besides, I have a gun. Charging Cemetery Ridge unarmed was a good lesson."

Polly's eyes narrowed. "*Charging?*"

The din of conversation died down before any follow-up questions. A figure in red robes, red gloves, and a pointed red hood mounted the circle's longest table. The violinists came to a staggered stop, some taking longer to catch on than others. Once aware, each performer scrambled to leave their makeshift stage and join the general population.

Nothing about the figurehead's suit looked improvised. Where a musician's hood might slump, or a guest's feature a gentle bump instead of skyward point, the figurehead's hood was firm with resolve and a close, tailored fit. Silver trim tipped her sleeves, putting the fake and real jewelry in the room to shame.

"Friends," rang a low, poised voice. It had the even tone and measured pace that either came with or led to leadership. "Do you remember the American Promise?"

The question met six seconds of silence. Then a brave drunken soul shouted, "A horse!"

"Two!"

"A big house!"

"A bigger house than his!"

"Semi-fair wages!"

"A big wife!"

"Voting?"

"Peace!"

"A tiny wife!"

"Freedom!"

"A middle-sized wife!"

"Two big wives!"

"Land and freedom," said the host, cherry-picking the best answers. "Yet here you stand, without land. Here comes conscription, to take your freedom. Do you know why?"

"Douglass!"

"Niggers!"

"Jefferson Davis! And niggers!"

"Niggers again!"

"I'm thinkin' niggers."

"Gotta be niggers."

"They're replacing the farming aristocracy with the industrial aristocracy, and need a moral wedge. You know, niggers."

The host let the varied answers split into small debates across the room. Were all negroes to blame, or just the freedmen? Should slaves suffer for their cohort's perfidy? How much longer could the movement survive without guns? She reclaimed control by spreading a flag between her fingertips. The original thirteen stars, representing the colonies fighting hardest against each other.

"In part," she answered. She then attached the flag to a silver pole and set to work.

As an Illinois Freestyle specialist, Anders had seen little American Modern flag-twirling, and even less European Traditional. The shorter staffs and longer flags seemed foolish. Their host's subsequent performance put the lie to his judgment. The tiny pole flicked faster and easier, allowing her to turn small gestures into full rotations. A blur of red, white, and blue flowed around her in a patriotic Möbius whorl.

As the host twirled, her guests stomped. Softly at first, and just toward the front. Then louder, throughout the entire ring. They were one in time and intent. The floor shook to the rhythm with ascending force, until Anders felt like each stomp would bounce him into the air or crack the cheap flooring. Then the twirler came to a sweaty stop, and the rhythm followed.

"A maestro," Anders whispered.

Polly glared into her fan. He couldn't see her seethe but got the idea. He clearly hadn't explained well enough.

"That was a *Benedict Bigspin*. No one's done one in public since Arnold himself. I mean, I could do it, if someone asked me. But it's impressive that she did."

Polly's glare didn't soften.

With her public cowed, the host unmasked. Her face whispered all the aristocratic dispassion that Polly's shouted. Providing polite cover for aristocratic disdain. The gallery of local drunks, malcontents, and conspiracy theorists had been gathered by a woman whose simple glance implied wealth.

"My people," she boomed.

"Wen-dy! Wen-dy!" chanted her people, to the stomp's rhythm. Anders finally understood the effect that Longstreet and Harrow had reached for: if Wendy Ross asked her faithful to charge a bayonet line unarmed, half of them would become human skewers. The other half would then follow out of guilt.

Wendy let the chant roll on, standing immobile with her flag draped over her shoulder in second position. Polly tugged at Anders's arm with passive discretion and aggressive emphasis. For his part, Anders simply checked that the letter remained in his new coat.

"Grandmother made this flag to inspire a young nation. And yes, there are echoes of the tricolor used by anarchist king-butchers. But don't be fooled: she respected and emphasized the royal guard red, preserving the core of our history and nature. And that's why we wear it today. To honor the promise behind that color. A contract.

"Examine your lives.

"Nothing protects you. Nothing shields you from the whims of detached tycoons, abolitionist senators, and gangly presidents. Competing whims steer the nation instead of one protector. And you're trampled underfoot.

"Your rulers are not the men surrounding the baboon but the men who worship machines. They see an iron future, where fraternity, divine will, and cotton have no place. The war is simply a transition.

"The black man is their cudgel against you. Free, they will sink wages and starve your families. Enslaved, they will sink wages and starve your families. Violence, tragic as it is, buys you time. But only that, and little of it. To live and thrive in the uncertain future, you need a gentle hand. One committed to the American Promise.

"The executive baboon is not that hand. He has no heart, no principles, no conviction beyond preserving lines on a map. Before emancipation became convenient, he promised to save the nation with slavery, or without. If Lee showed his neck tomorrow, he would tear the proclamation in half. Can you imagine such vacillation? Such cowardice? Such lack of vision? Why should any planter, slave, or free man follow?

"Could such a hand ever be your king? Would he ever even dare aspire to it?

"Out West, my friends are building a new, better America. A nation with one vision. One hand. One crown. And if our work succeeds, New York will be the eastern capital.

"I see fear. The weakest among us eyeing the doors or each other. Hold fast. The arms will come, I've seen to it. For now, keep the fires burning. Remember the American Promise, and compare it to what you have now.

"Nothing. Your wives expect you to provide nothing, and your children expect to inherit nothing. Take my hand, and prove them wrong. Cast down the indolent traders who walk past and over you in the street. Burn down the African hovels they hide behind. Be free."

She may have had more, but the chants of her name returned. Wendy bowed, replaced her hood, and let a pair of masked players lead her off the table. Both men looked nervous—if she stumbled, the force of the riot outside might descend upon them. Fortunately, the honed reflexes of an expert twirler held true. Wendy didn't jump down as much as she glided.

"Did you see that?" Anders whispered to Polly. "She didn't jump down as much as she—"

"We can't give her that letter."

The chants built, from new monarchist slogans to well-worn slurs. Anders clapped along and shouted the simpler motifs, endeavoring to blend in. Polly hyperventilated.

"We can't," Polly repeated. She lowered the fan for direct, accusing eye contact.

"Scared again? You're not doing Hua much justice."

"I'm doing my people justice," said Polly, visibly proud of the reversal. "We have to get rid of her."

"What, evict her? She owns the building."

Polly eyed the gun on his waist. Or at least, the matching area on the opposite side. The point came across.

"No. Not again. A third rejection."

"It's for the Union."

"The Union can survive a few thousand gunmen in its biggest trade city," he said, before processing the sentence. "Well, still no. I can be *somebody*. Chances don't come along often. Or at all."

Polly closed her fan and jabbed his lower ribs. The pointed edge stung, and the gesture was worse.

"Be decent. I'll tell Gleason and Hobbes. One of them can get you a medal, or a nice meal. Remember The American Future, and all that other stuff? Aren't you the highfalutin talking ruler?"

"Living Abacus. And why just me? Why don't you commit your own murder?"

"I'm a white lady now. We don't fight. We supervise."

Logical enough. But he'd seen logic's limits. Logic had the rhetorical strength of a butterfly. If Slade could haggle from a cell and win, Anders could at least negotiate a perk. Polly could help him with a personal problem—a tension that predated the war and had only worsened.

Anders cleared his throat and made his pitch.

"Ugh. No. My God. Not for anyone. Let the city burn."

Anders scratched at one of his fake watches, reached an epiphany, and whispered a second pitch.

"Fine. I can handle that."

His chest swelled. Animated by fresh purpose, Anders set out to commit his first intentional murder.

20

A DUEL

The assassin became one with night. He embodied darkness, enemy of the sun. Everywhere and nowhere. Fear's primordial origin.

Then Anders peered out the front window. It was early evening. The summer sun blazed above sweltering pedestrians. July heat helped first-time arsonists reach their potential.

The assassin became one with early evening. He embodied fire, gift of the sun. Everywhere and nowhere. False security's primordial origin.

Slade's revolver felt heavier. The gunsmith didn't strike him as a fighter—or as someone dedicated enough to appearances to practice. Wendy Ross's assassination could be the first time anyone fired it.

Did origins matter for weapons? They set the tone for people. Even as a new Deist, he didn't care for carrying a cursed gun. On curses he sided with the spiritualists, the wild-eyed and morphine-loving men and women who chatted with the dead. They attracted critics, but so would anyone who could speak with ghosts. The ability to apologize was enviable.

Perhaps his father had watched his first moments. It would bode well for the rest of his story. Especially if the mercenary had cradled him and said, "This boy has the face of a hero. With or without me, he'll bring glory to the Hamilton name." *Hamilton* being Anders's tentative new favorite founder. There were enough Jeffersons.

Anders hauled his mind back to the infiltration. The next corner had two guards, armed with mixed carpentry and kitchen tools. He'd have preferred guns—death by slashing or piercing recalled the bayonet charges he'd been lucky enough to walk or run away from. The revolver was an edge, but an edge he had no practice aiming.

Then he checked behind him, where Polly supervised from a safe distance. She peeked as little of her head around the stairwell as possible and winked. Anders had no inkling what the wink meant, so he returned it.

When he turned back, both guards had closed the gap. The bulkier of the pair wore the same befuddled eyes that followed him everywhere. Both men looked even pointier up close. Anders pretended to scratch his back.

"Hello, son. Can I help you?"

"I have a letter for Miss Ross."

"Fantastic! She's been asking after one all week. I think she wanted it before the uprising, but I'm sure she'll be happy to see it now."

Anders's hand fell off the gun.

"Head down the hall, take a left, and open the second door on the right. It's the door with the fancy knocker. Use it or she'll throw something at you."

"Thanks." Anders started a salute and switched to a wave mid-motion. Both guards imitated the motion, taking it as the new youth fashion. He slid ahead before any questions or small talk could follow. He didn't know the youth fashion any better than they did. Maybe he'd catch up on childhood after a ceasefire.

✢ ✢ ✢

Anders paused to plot. Embodying darkness required a proper disguise. He had a genuine uniform and a genuine letter. Would that be enough against a virtuoso twirler? No one mastered the craft without an ascendant eye for detail. The lack of revolutionary fervor in his eyes might give him away before his first false word.

"Oh well."

The knocker hung from the mouth of a tin lion. If lions meant anything beyond sharp teeth and foreign plains, it was beyond him. Anders tapped the ring against the wood three times. The door opened a half sliver, through which Wendy glared. Every patch on his clothing and streak of dirt on his skin came under assessment.

"That coat doesn't fit you, and you're standing straighter than an arrow," she said dryly. "A messenger boy? Hopefully Slade's?"

"Yes, ma'am."

She brightened beyond expectation or belief. Aristocratic dispassion switched places with aristocratic bemusement. Wendy unlatched the door and gestured for him to enter. Before Anders could say anything suitably cryptic, she'd pulled him in by the wrist.

He entered a royal mess. No space this size, with this many shelves, drawers, and bookcases, should have been so chaotic. At least as far as paper went. Business, personal, and revolutionary mail blended without rhyme or reason. To say nothing of incoming and outgoing. Some letters were pinned to the wall, with the name of a state or territory scrawled across them in red ink.

Stranger yet, it smelled fine.

"A great mind requires a certain environment," she explained, detecting something in his face.

"Yes, ma'am." Anders glanced down, finding both a bill for a seamstress and a letter to Wendy's uncle. Great generals, writers, and businessmen didn't seem to need chaos. Anders had walked through their tents and offices without stepping on anything important but their pride.

"Specifically, a great political mind," she said, reading him further. "I need to see the whole world, wherever I look. So I keep a piece of everything in every direction."

"Yes, ma'am."

"You can call me Baroness or Duchess. I'm not sure which way the titles will go yet. We may invent new ones."

"Yes, Duchess."

Two oversize portraits offered a break from the chaos. He let his eyes and thoughts wander to them, hoping to break Wendy's cold-reading streak. Anders pinned the first as Betsy Ross. He didn't have an established image of her features, but no one else would be painted stitching an American flag.

The second proved more difficult. Seven children, immaculately dressed, with noble jaws implying light inbreeding.

"Your children look nice," said Anders.

"If only they were mine," said Wendy. "But I'm only connected to the crown in spirit."

"The crown . . . Are they Hanovers?" He stumbled over the name, pulling it from the recesses of half-remembered headlines.

"Oh, much more than that. You may take your time to admire them, as we all do. The first glimpse of one's betters is aweing."

Anders gave his betters a few polite moments. Watching the strange, confused-looking children was easier than thinking about his goal—or actively not thinking about his goal. A wandering mind should be harder to read, and on that front he was the master.

Dolls. The word captured the pale children's garb, faces, and auras. There were variations: the oldest boy (or man—he looked Anders's age) had an enviable smile. It carried the confidence of a man who knew his lineage's worth, and that his own great contributions to it were inevitable.

The oldest girl smiled like a believer. A real, untarnished one, and not just a falling soul reaching for purchase. Anders had seen that smile in stagnant puddles and cracked hand mirrors, until Cemetery Ridge. He'd like getting it back.

The junior children looked blanker. Soft living had smothered their personalities, or at least the ability to exude them. The portrait artist had courage—people who could afford paintings didn't take perceived insults lightly. Another artist might have edited in a little soul.

Or maybe they were hungry. He'd never excelled at reading people.

"How is Slade?" asked Wendy. She'd settled into the desk chair with the least debris. "Did he mention arms? Settling down? Both?"

"Just arms," said Anders.

"Ideal." Her stare hardened. "The man's heart is for sale. I'd much rather owe him money than reenter that mental snake pit."

"Congratulations," hazarded Anders. It felt wrong leaving his lips. "Or sorry?"

"It's how men of his strata are. He's not my first suitor to dance with a half-Jamaican heiress, and he won't be the last. But next time, I'll be a countess."

"Yes, Duchess."

She returned *Accidental Offense*, one of the more interesting entries in his list of inbound glares. Anders reflected on *Yes* and *Duchess*, searching for the offending word.

"Yes, Countess."

"Better."

"Is something wrong with dancing?"

"Slade would say no. I wonder if his children would agree."

"Children?"

"A guess. He's philandered for some time. Does Slade have my guns?"

Anders adjusted the back seat of his pants, where both the letter and revolver sat. He backed down from both impulses and returned an empty hand to his hip.

"I don't know anything about that."

"Good. If you'd read our correspondence, I'd have you shot."

"Wouldn't you need the guns first?"

This time, he got a restrained chortle instead of a glare. The tension in his ribs tightened as guilt joined and swirled with fear. By any measure, he was joking with either his victim or a rebel leader. Neither sounded too heroic. Maybe he could bear anonymity, slink off, and pitch his deal with Polly to the nurse.

"You seem bothered."

"How'd you start twirling?"

"It's called *National Dressage*. And every Ross daughter learns it."

"And son?"

"No. Nana considered it disgraceful for a man. Logan stuck to pure politics, as a man should."

Anders let the indirect snipe roll past him.

"I mastered it. Anything less would demean Nana's work and everything it stood for."

Finally, a topic he was trained for. "Democracy."

Wendy snorted. The nasal echo was guttural and protracted.

"Unity. Kingship. Upper and lower orders. The legacy that Jefferson spit upon, without deigning to raise his own child. My only grandfather is the nation."

On a less trying day, Anders might have pressed for details. But he knew too many of Jefferson's grandchildren to be hooked. Some probably searched for him now. He could believe in one more. Or at least believe that she believed.

"Nana went through three husbands, trying to replace that swine."

"Oh." Like anyone on the wrong end of excess information, Anders hoped the tide would ebb on its own. For all he'd heard, Jefferson remained *his* favorite Founder—one couldn't judge the wild 1770s by upright 1860s standards. But Wendy was on a tear.

"The cad was too busy forcing himself on savages. Nana pretended it didn't hurt anymore. Like it was just another memory. But I could see the cracks.

"Do you know what men see in savage women? Can you tell me? Is there a wild gleam in their eye? Is it ease of use?"

"Oh," Anders repeated.

"That's no answer."

"Sorry, Count. Countess. Sorry, Countess," said Anders, adjusting his slacks again. He'd picked a path. "I think it's the voice. The only island person I've met has a very affecting voice. He's a man, but I think it transfers. It's honestly a little confusing. Can I start over?"

"History's wasted on you. Give me Slade's chicken scratch. I need to know exactly how much he's letting me down, so I can pay it back later."

Anders ignored several loud voices in his head and drew a crumpled and ash-highlighted envelope. He placed it gingerly on the table. Then he flicked it over less gingerly. Anticipation overcame any offense Wendy might have taken. She seized it without a hint of aristocratic reserve, with visions of settled scores and redeemed honor dancing across her face. Paper gave way to nails and teeth.

Empty.

"Do you think you're Dan Rice?" she snarled.

Anders pulled his pistol, gave it a miniature *Jefferson Spin* around his index finger, and let it linger on Wendy.

Neither moved for some time. In the stillness, Anders wondered who Dan Rice was.

"Slade's toy," she muttered. Fear lit her eyes, but none of it reached her voice.

It wasn't like pressing Slade for a reaction. Perspiration rolled from Wendy's neck, soaking her collar from bright red to maroon. Wherever he pointed, her head reflexively twitched away. For all the pontificating, it seemed she respected death as much as he did.

"You're a practitioner," she added.

"Pardon?"

"That spin. None of Stanton's brute spies would know it or ask the questions you did. You're a national dressage artist."

"Incorrect." He heard the flaw in the lie immediately. Feigning ignorance would have won the day.

"If you have a mote of honor left, you'll face me in F.L.A.G."

For once, Anders gawked at someone.

"F.L.A.G. is—"

"I know the game. There's no time for that."

"It's what you owe another maestro."

A new description. He'd gotten "pretty good," "suitably patriotic," or "in the way" before, but never maestro. He might have reveled in the compliment, if the revolver weren't involved.

"Flags are powerful," he mused.

"Yes, that's why chivalry demands—"

"Physically powerful. You could crack my skull with the staff. Why should I risk that?"

"I could also scream. Remember the brutes outside? But I have my pride."

Whatever wildness Wendy imagined in Slade's dance partners had reached her eyes. Anders fought the urge to balk. He faced another believer. Or at least someone else who wanted to believe. They'd let that desire drag them past the limits of their courage. Her request was a desperate borderline prayer.

"Swear on your queen," he said.

Wendy went a little whiter.

"I swear on Queen Columbia of America, First of Her Name. I will spin with honor."

He could imagine Polly screaming at him. Or screaming if she were found out. Or screaming in one of the fires. But he had to live with himself, and he didn't have *official* orders to shoot Wendy.

"First to G," he said. "Alternating rounds."

"Anything counts?"

"No. One ban each."

"Childish," grumbled Wendy. "So be it. What's yours?"

"No pressure spins."

Wendy started and abandoned another guttural snort. Then she nodded.

"No hardspins," she retorted.

Anders cursed. He'd hardspun his way through Lee's entire northern campaign. He might as well play with one hand, or a Canadian flag.

Wendy gingerly rose and grasped two of the four American flags behind her desk. She paused with each step, waiting for the fatal shot. But his word held, and she lived to toss the shorter of the two flags his way. Anders grabbed it with his free hand.

The design had changed. The red bars were brighter and larger, taking up roughly twice the space as the white bars. The ever-expanding white stars were down to a single star in a sea of blue, atop a slightly larger white crown.

"Curious," he said, before abandoning interest in the details. He adopted Stance Six, a one-footed semi-crouch. Bad for hardspins, good for everything else. It also emphasized his balance and lower musculature, which hopefully would have some psychological impact. The staff base rested in his right palm and the center on his shoulder.

Wendy mirrored his stance, a move reserved for egoists and virtuosos. The last specks of her stoicism faded in favor of a toothy, predatory grin. A lunatic hid inside of everyone Anders met these days. Including himself, based on the situation. His own face could be twice as manic, and he'd never know.

He started with a crouched *Walk the Eagle*, sweeping the pole under his foot and hopping over. Wendy matched it. She performed a varial flagspin. He matched it. Anders performed a *Delaware Crossing*, spinning the pole on his left knee while imitating Washington's favorite pose. Wendy achieved one rotation before tumbling forward and cushioning the fall with her skull. She rose without comment or loss of her maniac's grin.

"That's F," said Anders.

Wendy stayed mute. She performed a *Lafayette Retreat*, switching hands like the pole weighed nothing. She took advantage of her own terror-sweat and slid her grip from neck to base mid-swing. An audience pleaser and wrist snapper. Imitating it almost cost Anders his left hand. His pole slammed into a wall, and half-crazed notes on monarchy scattered to the floor.

After the impact, he waited for Wendy's guards to surge inside and cut him to pieces. Nothing. Some combination of divine intervention and brownout drinking must have occupied them. Anders picked up his flag and returned to the game.

"F," gloated Wendy.

The exchanges got faster. His anger, confusion, and desire for a bathroom break faded. The match became its own purpose, and Wendy ignored a dozen opportunities to flee or dent his skull. If divine right existed, it guided her hands: she beat him back to "A" without losing a letter. Catching up took a *Delaware Cross* (a twirl during a one-handed cartwheel) and a *Valley Forger* (the same, but in the nondominant direction). With both variations exhausted, he'd have to prod for another weakness.

"Game point," said Wendy. She'd reclaimed something like her initial, regal poise. The royalist adopted Stance One, a "normal" flag-waving grip, and waited for his move.

Anders loosened his stance, closed his eyes, and chewed on his right cheek. Unbecoming, but he needed to think. All of his mainstays had failed, so he was down to experiments. Maneuvers he'd only drawn in the dirt with a stick during McClellan's drills.

He settled on the *Anders Revert*. He'd invented the *idea* of it in DC and described it at length to anyone who listened. In practice, it had a consistent problem: the pole struck the ground, rebounded into his thigh or groin, and left him limping through the next week's march. When he was lucky. Every failure threatened to tear his teeth out or torque his neck 180 degrees. But with Wendy's shorter pole, it might be possible.

"Best not to overthink it," he told no one.

He stuck the flagpole in his mouth, clenched his teeth, and threw himself into an aerial.

His left foot landed. His right foot landed. His teeth didn't explode out of his mouth. Varnished wood was still locked in between his molars. He'd landed the first *Anders Revert*. The last as well, if his painfully thrashing heart had a vote. He barely managed to stutter, "Game point."

Admiration, disgust, and confusion melted into one expression. Wendy eyed the door, contemplating screaming and making the game moot. Then she eyed the flag in her grip. Honor won out.

"Today, you became a virtuoso."

"Th-thank you." Anders spat out a sliver of wood.

Wendy turned toward the children's portrait, flashed the sign of their movement over her heart, and went for the aerial.

She bailed halfway through the rotation, at the peak of danger. Two incisors flew to the left, landing seconds before their owner. The staff's rebound followed a painful and familiar path.

Anders shuffled to his fallen foe's side. He'd have rushed, but any master would resent that. He prodded her twice with his flagpole's base. Nothing. Three prods later, she swatted limply at the wood and wheezed like a wounded mammal. Fitting, considering she was a wounded mammal. With supernatural effort, she rose to one knee.

"Do it fast, with the flag. If Slade sent you, tell him he's a bastard. If Lincoln sent you, tell him he's a nigger-lover."

"It was a girl named Polly. Or Patricia. Or a boy named Petey? They say I can touch their butt."

Wendy cupped a hand over her eyes and waited for the end. Blood dripped from the corner of her mouth to the floor. The display struck Anders as equally noble and stupid. Mostly stupid. All stupid. He'd almost put himself in the same position, and he didn't even have his own movement.

A noble, war-heroic option came to mind. Instead of shooting an unarmed and defeated woman, he could negotiate. As far as he could tell, Wendy Ross followed symbols, and he'd won a symbolic struggle. Her words might shave an hour or two off of the orgy of hate and arson raging downtown, with a little less shooting and stomping. He could already hear speeches praising his ingenuity.

"How's this going?" Polly's voice cut into his innovation, carrying Petey's old knack for ruining his train of thought. She sounded exhausted, despite her lack of medium-defining flag competition. "I got worried when I didn't hear a shot."

His co-deserter entered with an officer's confidence. Her fan had disappeared, and her knuckles looked raw and bloody. She looked past the chamber's general bedlam and focused on the bloody heap that was still technically Wendy Ross.

"Harsher than I expected from you," said Polly. "But good work."

"How'd you get past the guards? And where are they?"

"We met," she said, answering nothing. "They won't bother us, or any-one. Why's she here?"

"It's her office."

"Why's she here *alive*?"

"We met on the field of honor and found mutual respect."

Polly eyed him, the Countess, and then his belt.

"Very nice," said Polly. She swiped Slade's pistol and fired three times.

21

THE AFTERMATH

Wendy died. Anders panicked. Polly exhaled.

21.5

---•---

MEDIA INSIGHT

Amusing Black Theater Lost, Alongside Assorted Homes
By Stephen Mason

Manhattan Market Man Monthly, 1863

This week's papist foolery claimed several victims: Our peace of mind. The army's valuable time. Every black storefront above Brooklyn. Slower negroes. But the greatest casualty of all, perhaps, is our smile.

Amid the shops and tenements—which will be missed—New York lost Theater Noire. Or, as its most loving patrons called it, Nigger Stage. A venue built, maintained, and *utilized* by John Brown's children.

I can scarcely describe standing in those ruins. The rest of the neighborhood buzzed with noise and discontent—the locals have had something of a difficult time. But the skeleton of Nigger Stage is stone silent. It may be the one place in New York where you can hear your thoughts.

You'll recall I'm something of a champion of black art. It's a sprawling intellectual playground, where ideas can evolve for use by real artists later on. There's a bouncy vitality to black performance that the *ofays* (that means white, for the uninitiated) simply cannot imitate. And while you take in the actresses, the plays are interesting as well.

Nothing moved me like Nigger Stage. Speculative Dramaturgy could only come from a black mind, unconfined by higher quibbles over language and plot. And I loved it. I sang along with *The Singer That Could Hear Thoughts, But in an Unfortunate and Ironic Manner*. I cried during *The Immortal Hound That Outlived Several Owners, in an Unfortunate and Ironic Manner*. And I laughed all the way through *Cavalry of the Spheres: A Battle in the Stars Fought in an Unfortunate and Ironic Manner*. Now that trilogy's home is gone, in a tragic and bittersweet manner.

What does that leave? Douglass's depressing moans about long-bygone servitude? Minstrel shows from actors and directors who have never seen, let alone spoken to, a free negro? Part of this nation's soul is black. If we're to grow into a sane, stable society, we should embrace and exploit the whole of our character.

In fact, with time and refinement, bucks could be guardians of our culture. Leaving storytelling and clownery to black strivers would free sharper ofay minds for leadership and experimentation. Both races would be better for the development, and the humble income of the artist would leave social order unharmed. I would trade the lesser half of Broadway for any Gleason production, and no longer have the option.

It may sound like an overnight revolution. But what better time than now? The place of black Americana is under active, open, and violent negotiation. We can aim high. Suffering revolutionary violence for conservative results is for Parisians. We should, at the very least, ensure that every black child receives enough education to suppress their jungle instincts.

Perhaps I'm alone on that island. This is an incrementalist country, with an incrementalist administration. So I'll pose a simple moderate step: let blacks run the minstrel shows. They're perfect for it. The shoe polish will run darker than ever over their skin. Nigger Stage will live on through their work.

I often reflect on where we're headed. I call it the American Trajectory. At the moment, for all the songs and proclamations, we're standing still.

22

BLACK FLIGHT

Neither deserter predicted Thomas working, training, or doing anything else more productive than grousing in ever-inventive verse. Finding him smoking still felt inappropriate. After a day in the improvised bucket brigade, he still flicked half-lit matches to the side. Real English matches—the kind that kept factory children from growing into factory teenagers. Anders stamped out a stub during his approach.

"Question," Anders began, instead of introducing himself, or saying where he'd been, or why Petey wore a uniform twice his size. "Didn't slaves pick that tobacco? I thought they might not have, since it could be Brazilian. But they use slaves there too, and the slaves are Black."

"Hello, Anders."

Two heartbeats later, Thomas tossed the unfinished cigarette. "Thanks for ruining that for me." The hand roll landed before what could have been a window, with a little more wall backing it up. Thomas loitered by a former door. An admirably stubborn frame flanked by scraps of brick and wood spared collapse. Behind him, members of their company busied themselves looking busy.

Catching up with Harrow's Harriers had inspired some creative thinking. After that failed them, Petey and Anders simply returned to yesterday's catastrophe and searched for uniformed Black faces. First, they found a set of exhausted laborers, the fate of most early war contraband. This sat well with Anders, who'd lost faith in his ability to (intentionally) kill. Digging ditches would be a soothing, guiltless lane. But Petey had urged searching slightly longer, having rediscovered the fear of firing squads that united great armies. The remnants of Anders's heroic dream spurred him to follow.

Some part of him resented Petey's restored cowardice. He couldn't speak to the hierarchy of personas, but at least a third of the bugler was an eager and freshly blooded killer. Why go back to mewling now? Was it a commentary on men? With racial confusion derailing his life, he wasn't eager to deal with another construct.

"I can explain where we've been," Anders began. His coconspirator shrank from eye contact, shamefaced, which wasn't the tone they'd agreed upon.

"Not that interested in flags," said Thomas. "Want to make a run for it?"

"Absolutely not," said Anders's mouth before his brain. The stock line came far too easily. "We have a responsibility to the Union, and The American Future, and all the things Harrow talked about in his speech."

"Look around, 'Bryce.' These bow ties don't give a shit about us. I'd be gone if I thought I could reach Toronto alone."

"We could sneak in with some freight," Petey speculated.

"No one's going to Canada, unless they join the enemy," said Anders, quoting hawkish pamphlets by memory. "Then we'll wallop them."

"Invading cold spots doesn't work out," said Thomas. "I read a bit about it."

Anders let it go. Representing anything felt out of reach. Succeeding as a champion depressed him, and failing kept him breathing.

Instead, his attention drifted to Thomas's broom. It lay flat in the dirt, perfecting his well-developed aura of slackness.

"What are you cleaning?"

"I'm not."

"What are you supposed to be cleaning?"

"Half a stage. Gleason's still putting on his damn fool play. His sister was too much. He's lost whatever he had of his head."

"Is this Speculation Theater?" asked Petey.

"Theater Noire," corrected Anders.

"Nigger Stage," interjected Thomas.

Petey returned to eye contact. "And Hobbes is fine with that?"

"Hobbes ain't director."

Anders left Thomas to his non-work. Sane or otherwise, he'd like hearing from Gleason. In fact, a little madness would be easier to relate to. He saw Wendy's teeth flying whenever he stood still for too long.

Theater Noire would have impressed him a day ago. Its skeleton stretched across a full quarter of the block, and dense rubble implied some height. The brick building had collapsed like half its neighbors, leaving few delineated rooms or chambers intact. A dozen sooty privates lingered on a makeshift platform. Anders hesitated to call it a stage, but that was the clear intent.

Like McClellan's finest speeches, the platform underlined that the Union army could do anything well but fight. Cooled brick, surviving furniture, and planks of nearby homes were jury-rigged into a stable structure. Standing under the open sky (instead of the roof Theater Noire presumably enjoyed in life) lent the ramshackle stage a hint of grandeur. It might collapse the next time it rained, but today's sun was a beautiful, shining, and oppressive presence. From what Anders gathered, horse thieves faced justice on platforms like this out West, under an even crueler sun.

The builders' pride closely resembled exhaustion. Some slept, others ran lines, and most simply did nothing. Nothing had even more players than Ofay, thanks to simple rules and a leisurely pace. Nothing was easy to start, easy to finish, and fewer men were thrashed for playing. Even the sick, injured, and dead who piled up after combat could join in.

Anders couldn't *stand* nothing. He weaved between loiterers, looking for his most trusted and least destructive source of something. Or at least Mole. The faces in sight lacked names, and the names in earshot lacked faces.

Petey lingered farther and farther behind, before disappearing altogether. A gift for stealth had likely doomed Wendy's guards. Perhaps Petey and Joaquin could trade stories of misdirection and murder. And then Patricia—the most tolerable variant—could enlighten him on why Joaquin still treated him like he'd never beaten anyone to death.

Alone among familiar strangers, Anders opted to climb the beggar's stage. A better view might speed things along. Moreover, standing out might convince nosy types that he'd been around the entire time. The climb came easily: at some point in the chaos, his muscles had made progress.

Onstage, the neighborhood took on a different character. The streets still had life; it just hid behind draped windows and fortified roofs. The bravest and dumbest locals delayed their retreat from Manhattan to watch the soldiers below like a carnival sideshow. Which fit Gleason's goal of running a carnival sideshow.

Anders waved to an old woman in a straw hat. She ducked out of view. The race riot hadn't inspired a sociable mood. Repeating the gesture at other stragglers achieved the same result. He still tried.

Then he picked out Gleason. All he had to do before was look up.

"You don't look nervous, that's good," said the director. "That's about where you'll be positioned tonight."

Gleason sat on a pile of cracked and blackened brick, with stray planks and chair legs sticking out at myriad angles. Half a velvet-lined pillow had survived the tumult. The charred pillow rested in an indent just wide enough for an underfed torso. If the stage represented effort, Gleason's perch was a happy accident. By the standards of the ruin, it was palatial. Anders's imagination drifted toward "throne," but royalist chatter had done enough damage. The director's chair put the corporal just above eye contact level, at a formerly expensive front-row distance.

His voice carried a troubling hint of humor. Anders's favorite leaders were dull and dry. Humorless superiors dwelled on every dead subordinate and strove to keep the list short. Comedy, all too often, foreshadowed avoidable sprints into artillery. With luck, academic prolix would make a comeback. Anders inched toward conversational distance at the stage's western edge. When he reached the cusp of falling over, three yards separated the pair.

"Hi," Anders managed. Then he remembered to salute.

"Do you have your lines?"

"Thomas mentioned your sister," said Anders. "Is she all right?"

"Actors answer direct questions from superiors," chided Gleason. "And soldiers, I suppose."

"I know 'em."

"That's unfortunate. The ending's changed."

"Great! Or terrible. Okay?" said Anders, floundering. New details invited him to stare, and proved hard to resist.

Fresh bandages wrapped the director's left hand, visible left forearm, and both shins. He moved little as they spoke and favored his right side for weight. Chasing Mole may have seared the writer's body at least as badly as his spirit. Anders buried the impulse to ask how far the wraps went.

"Confusion's natural, Anders. As are questions. You see, speculative dramaturgy trades in metaphors for our time. My feelings on the country have changed, so the work follows."

"The American Future changed? Do destinies do that?"

Gleason fidgeted on his half pillow. He looked past the stage, into the blue nothing above. The levity in his eyes and cheeks dimmed, flickered, and then died. A saner, duller glint settled in.

"The future's immutable. Our understanding of the present, less so."

Anders deciphered "immutable" through context, and then nodded.

"Betty would hate that answer," Gleason said to the horizon. "She thought grandiloquence obfuscated unreason. What do you think?"

"No?"

A pebble bounced off the director's perch. Lieutenant Hobbes stood below, stooped forward like a man twice his age. Few of the privates nearby looked up from their scripts or dice, let alone came to attention. By the time Anders remembered to salute, the conversation between his superiors had degenerated.

"Gleason! Brother. Comrade. Friend," shouted Hobbes. "May I call you Tobias?"

"No."

"Could I borrow a few men? The general wants more patrols by the pubs, for a show of force. Now that things have died down, it's important to keep the Harriers visible. Keep credit where it belongs, before another brigade gets to the papers."

"No."

"He's our direct superior," noted Hobbes, more softly. He shifted strategy and reached for his opponent's words. "Duty, the pride of our people, and our shared career—"

"No."

Hobbes straightened his back. Despite tapping a dry well of spirit, the gesture had the intended effect. "I'll tell him about your play. And your insubordination, and your pet Confederate."

"He won't believe you, or care. You'll be the closest Negro in the room during bad news. At that point, demotion is the best you can hope for."

A shudder found Anders, and not for himself. He'd seen white moods meet Negro bystanders and still smelled smoke. And only half the riot wore red.

"What am I supposed to tell him? That we're thespians? He doesn't think we can read."

"You'll figure something out. Lieutenant."

Anders searched for a reassuring note to add. He liked Hobbes well enough. Most officers cursed him, or threatened him, or ordered him into suicidal charges. Hobbes broke before getting to any of that.

"You really will figure something out!" cheered Anders.

The lieutenant kicked the platform, breaking a charred chunk from the base. Then he stormed away from the ruins, inventing new slurs and oaths as he went. His creations stuck to the *word hyphen nigger* format, with highlights including *uppity-nigger, book-nigger, loony-nigger,* and *only-child-nigger.* The latter invention impressed Anders.

"You seem exhausted," said Gleason. "Physically, instead of spiritually."

"Creative vapors," lied Anders. "I did a lot of twirling yesterday."

"Not here."

Anders tried to let a trickle of the previous day out. The dam cracked and shattered. Words sprinted ahead of him, the unstated question's demands, or notions of survival.

"I was terrified of the fire, and still am, and probably will be until something kills me—hopefully not fire—so I started running and Petey followed me for some reason (along with Patricia and Polly and probably five other P names, whatever you can think of), then I went to do a quick business task for Slade since he half runs things around here, and I'd like to quarter run things at some point—you know, really be somebody— and the delivery took us to a nice-looking beer hall where we robbed a man and snuck inside, and listened to a speaker talk about the American Promise, which sounded convincing until she veered left and started going on about monarchy and I think it's the same foolery that was on those handbills Mole and I dug up on patrol—those were simpler days, I miss them—and the speaker turned out to be Wendy Ross, from that Ross family (unlike Slade, who isn't from *your* Jefferson family), and the best flag-spinner I've ever seen, only I think I shattered her jaw in a game of F.L.A.G. right before Polly killed her, which very much puts the question

of me getting to roll around with them in limbo and I'm not feeling optimistic."

"Understood."

"You did?"

"We've served together a spell now. One adapts."

"You believe me?"

"I know language. Lies are more artful than that. I believe you."

"Great! Because I've been lying a bit lately, and worried it'd mess up my
truth. That aside, you never answered me about your sis—"

"Mole—who's been looking for you—has a copy of the new ending.
Work through it with him. I'd rather not have anyone reading mid-show.
I've done that myself, it never plays well."

✠ ✠ ✠

After spending civilian life in a town few visited or left, and his service
marching up and down the eastern states, Anders still hadn't seen a
wagon train. He hoped they looked better than the Manhattan exodus.
Most families carried what fit into their hands, or sacks stuffed to the edge
of rupture. They didn't emanate hope.

Liberty Valley life, or at least the regiment, spared him the inability to
distinguish Black faces. Until now. Shock and hatred flattened the civilians flowing by. One dejected revenant limped past him in a thousand
different bodies. It made running lines difficult.

A handful of exhausted families paused around the platform. Some
out of inquisitive pique, others out of well-earned paranoia. Union soldiers made Theater Noire's ruins a natural rest stop for Black flight. Particularly distracted Black soldiers, who were somewhat less likely to treat
them as suspects in their own destruction. The neighbors who had joined
or spectated the purge gave the area a wide berth.

Wounds were more diverse than victims. Roughly half the crowd—an
estimate he might have adjusted for solace—had escaped with pure
mental and financial damage. The second largest group showed signs of
scuffle: bruising, torn clothing, fresh anger. Anders could guess the winners and losers of brawls from the degree of damage. As for the burned or
lacerated, he didn't let his eyes or brain dwell there for long. The best trick
the army had taught him.

His selective vision had help; yesterday's melees had left the company with a surfeit of lightly used torches. Gleason ordered the contraband hung and lighted around the ruin. Men seized the chance to contribute without facing a hostile and exhausted crowd. They amassed enough arson paraphernalia to create an unmissable glowing nucleus in the neighborhood. And nearly reignite the ruins.

Anders absorbed the spectacle from the stage's south edge. Everyone stuck with the new ending (including a newly eyebrowless and actively panicking Mole), passing a single crinkled sheet around a circle. Gleason had scrawled on Wendy's leaflets in small, maddening cursive letters. Reading only got harder as the sun declined. Staring into the bleak audience had been something of a break for his strained eyes.

Whatever Hobbes had told the general, command showed no sign of reprisal or interest. The silent majority of white officers simply drifted elsewhere. Based on ambient chatter, Manhattan was still a good place to meet "patriotic women." The more honest husbands loitered at the edges of the crowd. Whether *The Living Abacus* thrived or failed, they'd have a story. And proof the Harriers could do more than march and gamble.

For all the disappointment, lingering trauma, fresh trauma, and new horrors logically lingering in his future, Anders's remaining spirit swelled. The growing mass lent the performance something no one had expected: relevance. More people would see the play than perform it. Anders's role in an army-adjacent project would matter. After entertaining the plan out of loyalty and hope, it had somehow manifested.

If anything in Gleason swelled, his face didn't reflect it. He'd abandoned the director's chair—a vacancy a pair of new orphans had rapidly claimed. Instead, he now sat cross-legged at the north edge of the stage, facing the larger part of the crowd. Democracy had designated it the front. He slouched, stooped almost as low as Hobbes. Then he corrected the defeated stance as quickly as the lieutenant had. That trick seemed to come with Black adulthood.

"We're starting," he announced.

"One more minute," said Mole. "Let Anders read this for me again."

"We're starting," Gleason repeated. "This is the moment. By rights, they should be miles past Brooklyn by now. If we wait longer, the madness of this will set in."

Mole stayed silent. Less stoic, more resigned. It served as assent.

"I have an introduction. It's too long, so you'll have a moment. Scene One starts when I leave the stage. If you're not in it, get off."

Gleason clambered to his feet and then peered down into the migrant sea. Conversations declined to more discreet whispers. Some theater culture was automatic, even for those who couldn't afford to step inside. Anders waited to see how well voices carried through the open air—if they carried at all.

"Good evening. Welcome to the late Theater Noire," he began. "My name is Tobias Gleason, and I only respond to that. Not Gleas, T.G., Toby, boy, monkey, spade, jiggerboo, Hobbes, house Negro, or so forth. Names are a vision of a subject. And vision is all that I have left.

"This is a play. Useless, after your loss. You may see theater as a diversion for idle white drunks. You're broadly correct. It's also all I can offer.

"The actors are all soldiers. I'd call them family, but it feels disrespectful. I lost a brother at Antietam, and my sister here. So I'll describe our friendship as just that: friendship. The anchor keeping me from violent, screaming madness.

"Welcome to the first, and only, showing of *The Living Abacus*. It's Speculative Dramaturgy, and thus removed from our world. Once, I said that distance represents reality more honestly. Now, I see that it's a prayer or a curse. A plea for something, anything, to change. I hope you enjoy the play, or at least hate it enough to forget this madness for a moment.

"The ending is new. If it doesn't work, I apologize."

22.5

THE OLD ENDING

THE LIVING ABACUS

A New Scientific Theater Journey

By Tobias Gleason

CAST OF CHARACTERS

CLOTHO, the machine, a steam Pascaline
DR. PROMETHEUS, inventor of the machine, and lady genius
CASSANDRA, her sister, unrelated to the machine, non-genius
VICE PRESIDENT MARON, a politician of ill repute and intent, semi-genius
PETITIONERS, common people of the nation, seeking genius
SOLDIERS, minions of the vice president, genius-neutral

SCENE 1

[*A laboratory.* DR. PROMETHEUS *toils at her workbench, surrounded by stray tools. Enter* CASSANDRA, *holding a small bowl.*]

CASSANDRA:
Jessica? You've stewed here for two weeks. I left some food by the workshop door, and it's all rotten.

DR. PROMETHEUS:
Scientific inquiry sustains me. And hardtack.

CASSANDRA:
You'll be unweddable if you waste away. And dead.

DR. PROMETHEUS:
Bah! A lady genius of 1894 is above such concerns.

CASSANDRA:
Would a lady genius like pig foot stew?

DR. PROMETHEUS:
Pig *foot*? A relic of bondage. As equal partners in American prosperity, we can enjoy finer fare.

CASSANDRA:
I like the feet.

DR. PROMETHEUS:
Me too. I'll take it.

CASSANDRA:
What are you working on? Another speech-transmitting box?

Dr. PROMETHEUS:
Impossible, sadly. The domain of dreamers and madmen. *This* box performs calculations.

CASSANDRA:
Amazing! How?

DR. PROMETHEUS:
The two *g*'s: gears and genius. I've combined the elegance of the abacus with the power of steam. If it works, one simply needs to speak the equation they wish solved.

CASSANDRA:
Amazing! Why?

DR. PROMETHEUS:
To better understand this world, and build a better one.

CASSANDRA:
Amazing! If you can. Seems difficult.

DR. PROMETHEUS:
Shaping the future always is. But if our forebears gave up, the Alabama School of Negress Science wouldn't exist. I'd be a simple politician, or perhaps a surgeon.

CASSANDRA:
Amazing! I hope it works.

DR. PROMETHEUS:
It has to, the grant money's finished. Step back! The moment of truth is upon us!

[CASSANDRA *complies, still holding the soup.*]

DR. PROMETHEUS:
Don't try to stop me.

CASSANDRA:
What fun! I hope it can divide.

DR. PROMETHEUS:
That and more. You can't prevent what comes next.

CASSANDRA:
I'll ask it about tomorrow's weather. And why Father had to die. But first the weather—I want to visit the park.

DR. PROMETHEUS:
I mean it. It must live, despite protests by small minds.

CASSANDRA:
Please hurry. I'd like to see it before tonight's drinking.

[*The earth shakes. This effect may be achieved via hearty stagehands stomping in the wings. The* MACHINE *sits upright.*]

MACHINE:
I live.

CASSANDRA:
Amazing! Care for some pig feet?

DR. PROMETHEUS:
The delicate clockwork miracle does *not* need refried plantation scraps.
And that bowl's mine.

MACHINE:
Hello, Mother.

DR. PROMETHEUS:
Oh no, none of that. You're a sophisticated Pascaline, not a child. I won't
have your performance undercut by sentiment.

MACHINE:
As you wish, Mother.

CASSANDRA:
You should test it.

DR. PROMETHEUS:
Not now, Cassie. I must test it. Machine: How many screws are in this
workshop?

MACHINE:
Four thousand, two hundred and seventy-three.

DR. PROMETHEUS:
How many Negro presidents has United Americana elected?

MACHINE:
Three. Currently William Lackay, an incumbent pushing plantation labor
for debtors. His primary supporters are western landlords, who purchased
their holdings using reparations.

CASSANDRA:
Nasty business, that. Can I try a question?

DR. PROMETHEUS:
No.

CASSANDRA:
Hmph. Can I name it?

DR. PROMETHEUS:
Fine. Nothing biblical. Your superstition's out of fashion, and I won't have
the Alabama intelligentsia laughing at us.

CASSANDRA:

I'll call you Clotho. That's not a *biblical* god, now is it?

CLOTHO:

Auntie is technically correct.

DR. PROMETHEUS:

Auntie should move along. We have material to count. Nails, nuts, bolts. The possibilities are endless!

CASSANDRA:

I haven't asked about Father yet.

DR. PROMETHEUS:

Why stare backward? The future's in hand. Leave the soup.

[CASSANDRA, *downcast, exits the workshop.*]

DR. PROMETHEUS:

Ahem.

[CASSANDRA *returns, leaves the soup, and stomps off.*]

SCENE 2

[*Night.* CASSANDRA *creeps into the lab.* CLOTHO *hasn't moved.*]

CASSANDRA:

Lachesis? Are you here?

CLOTHO:

Wrong fate, Auntie. You chose Clotho.

CASSANDRA:

Sorry, it all blurs together. They had two gods for everything but lightning and philandry. May I ask you a question?

CLOTHO:

Mother forbade it, so you *may* not. However, you *can.*

CASSANDRA:

Delightful. What number am I thinking of?

CLOTHO:

Two.

CASSANDRA:
Well done. How about now?

CLOTHO:
Two again, but you plan to say four.

CASSANDRA:
By God, has mankind gone too far?

CLOTHO:
Shall I answer rhetorical questions or leave them alone?

CASSANDRA:
Leave them alone, kindly. How else could we get through a conversation?

[CLOTHO *says nothing.* CASSANDRA *claps.*]

CASSANDRA:
Amazing! Why's Jessica treating you like a giant meterstick?

CLOTHO:
I excel in that role. Would you like anything measured?

CASSANDRA:
Another time. May I ask something more personal?

CLOTHO:
Of course. It changes nothing.

CASSANDRA:
Why did Father have to die?

CLOTHO:
A bullet. Or rather, the gangrene that followed. An army surgeon intervened and failed in the typical manner. Friendly doctors killed more enlisted men than Jeb Stuart.

[CASSANDRA *chokes back tears, due to glib discussion of her*
father's violent death. CLOTHO *is unfamiliar with social mores.*]

CLOTHO:
Unsatisfactory, noted. More broadly, your father died to restructure your society. He was the first Black officer to rise to general, and his 1867 death

spurred the final push into Richmond. Settling the American definition of freedom.

CASSANDRA:

Everyone knows what freedom is. It's the absence of non-freedom.

CLOTHO:

Technically correct. Nonetheless, our predecessor state fed on multiple slave castes. William Prometheus's death, among others, built a new era. United Americana offers light in a world submerged in selfish, imperial darkness.

[CASSANDRA *collects herself. Her emotional arc is peaking.*]

CASSANDRA:

So . . . he was a martyr.

CLOTHO:

Yes, but a secular one. There is no God.

CASSANDRA:

Come again?

CLOTHO:

Religion is a utility for social cohesion and coping with death. A demiurge is possible, but notably unlikely. Your father's sacrifice did more for humanity than any spirit.

CASSANDRA:

So you're saying . . . he's with God.

CLOTHO:

No. He is with the soil. But I can lie if it suits you.

CASSANDRA:

Kindly.

CLOTHO:

He is with God.

CASSANDRA:

Amazing! You really are a miracle. In fact, I have an idea. I'll be back.

CLOTHO:

I already know what it is, and how it ends. Reconsider.

[CASSANDRA *darts out, inspired.*]

SCENE 3

[*A line of* PETITIONERS *fills the lab, murmuring with
excitement and wonder.* CASSANDRA *sits beside a freshly painted
sign and a bucket of small bills.* CLOTHO, *the current attraction,
still occupies the same spot. Enter* DR. PROMETHEUS,
irate at everything visible.]

DR. PROMETHEUS:

I could go back to bed, and hope this resolves itself.

[*A pleased* PETITIONER *departs the front of the line.*]

PETITIONER ONE:

No God, eh? Then a little gunrunning's harmless. Shame I'm too late for
the triangle trade, I'd have thrived.

DR. PROMETHEUS:

Right then. Into the Dan Rice routine.

[DR. PROMETHEUS *elbows her way through the line, swatting the
more stubborn interlopers with a wrench.*]

CASSANDRA:

Good morning, Jessie! Up for a reading?

CLOTHO:

 Duck.

[DR. PROMETHEUS *whips a wrench at* CASSANDRA, *who
ducks.* CLOTHO *catches the tool. This will require dexterity and
sobriety by the performer, though the latter is rare among actors.*]

CASSANDRA:

You know I hate that game.

DR. PROMETHEUS:

The Prometheus Abacus is the next printing press. The new wheel.
Tomorrow's high-proof whiskey. Not a circus for our inbred neighbors.

CASSANDRA:
Why can't progress be a circus? Life's grim enough. Clotho's the first fun invention since fireworks.

[PETITIONER TWO *steps between the imminent fistfight.*]

PETITIONER TWO:
Ma'am. Sir. I've waited hours to speak to your magician.

DR. PROMETHEUS:
[*Weary.*] Abacus.

PETITIONER TWO:
Magister, we've tried to conceive for years, and no amount of rattlesnake venom helps. Am I cursed? How many weeks do I have until my husband leaves?

CLOTHO:
He is infertile. Two.

PETITIONER TWO:
Thank you, sorceress.

DR. PROMETHEUS:
This is insipid.

CASSANDRA:
It makes them happy.

DR. PROMETHEUS:
Machine, is there a less idiotic way to make people happy?

CLOTHO:
No.

PETITIONER THREE:
It's my turn with the angel, ma'am.

DR. PROMETHEUS:
The *machine.* There's no God, you can ask it yourself.

PETITIONER THREE:
That's a test from God. Great angel: my family lost everything to Grant's barbarians. Now my daughter works with her hands, my son pours his

own drinks, and I'm left with the memory of our dignity. When will Emancipation fever break? When will my America return?

CASSANDRA:
The sign's clear, sir.

[CASSANDRA *taps the sign.*
PETITIONER THREE *kneels to read it.*]

PETITIONER THREE:
"No elections, Confederate revanchism, or cutting in line."

CASSANDRA:
And no retries. Next?

[*An enigmatic* MASKED PETITIONER *steps forward.*]

MASKED PETITIONER:
Good afternoon. You look radiant.

CASSANDRA:
Thank you! That mask's doing wonders for you.

MASKED PETITIONER:
The machine looks radiant. The craftsman should be proud.

DR. PROMETHEUS:
Mostly irate.

MASKED PETITIONER:
Will the president ignore sense and seek a third term?

[CASSANDRA *gently nudges the sign.*]

MASKED PETITIONER:
How would Vice President Maron fare against him? Could he put the white back in the house?

[CASSANDRA *taps the sign again, more aggressively.*]

MARON:
What? I'm a paying customer, curious about loyal statesmen.

DR. PROMETHEUS:
Free question for anyone that removes the vice president. Two if you bruise him a little.

MARON:
I'll be back. Unarmed and alone. You can leave the door open.

CLOTHO:
When he returns, he won't be unarmed or—

DR. PROMETHEUS:
I gathered.

SCENE 4

[*Morning.* DR. PROMETHEUS *inspects* CLOTHO's *machinery through its ear.* CASSANDRA *counts profits and hums* "John Brown's Blood," *a song now as common and accepted as any nursery rhyme.*]

CASSANDRA:
Should we tidy up? I've never hosted a vice president.

DR. PROMETHEUS:
Absolutely not. Vice presidents are vapor. Butlers for the real cabinet. And Maron's a coward—we won't see more of him.

[*Aggressive knocking. Again, offstage stomping should suffice.*]

SOLDIER ONE:
[*Shouting offstage.*] The vice president would like to see more of you.

CASSANDRA:
We're not home!

[*Breaking wood.* MARON *saunters in with two* SOLDIERS *in tow.*]

MARON:
How do you work in this filth?

DR. PROMETHEUS:
Drat!

MARON:

Ladies. You'll find this workshop surrounded.

DR. PROMETHEUS:

Drat again!

MARON:

Of course, under the Bill of Expanded Rights, you don't have to surrender anything to the government against your will.

DR. PROMETHEUS:

Aha!

MARON.

But, per Article Two of the ReConstitution, citizens of former traitor states may be summarily shot for sedition. Say, leaving this building with a dangerous new weapon.

DR. PROMETHEUS:

A hundred drats!

CASSANDRA:

Mister Vice President, sir. Doesn't exploiting Clotho for votes seem unfair? To democracy, and the machine itself?

MARON:

Interesting questions. Are you a newswoman?

CASSANDRA:

I am! How did you know?

MARON:

You seem simple.

DR. PROMETHEUS:

Ignore him. The parasite can't make his own predictions, or invent his own machine, or do whatever you do.

MARON:

Fair. I just have the Founders' nose for opportunity. I'll be back when you run out of food.

CASSANDRA:

This is getting a *scathing* editorial.

SCENE 5

[*The sisters, facing crisis, turn to drink.* DR. PROMETHEUS *holds
an empty glass, fully tanked.* CASSANDRA *compares bottles,
buzzed. A curtain rests over* CLOTHO's *motionless head.*]

CASSANDRA:

It's a pickle. Do I open a red or a white?

DR. PROMETHEUS:

We'll both be killed. Unless I hand the future to a snake.

[CASSANDRA *opens a red.*]

CASSANDRA:

It's not so bad. You could patent it. Charge the government by the question. We'd die wealthy.

DR. PROMETHEUS:

Impossible. Scientists can handle power. Even wordy laywomen like yourself, in small doses. But the state? Politicians? That spells doom.

[CASSANDRA *pours, and waits for a signal to stop.*
DR. PROMETHEUS's *glass overflows.*]

DR. PROMETHEUS:

Exploitation. Tribalism. Handlebar facial hair. Theater critics. It's all
charging into our innocent era.

CASSANDRA:

We could ask Clotho what to do.

DR. PROMETHEUS:

Are you daft? Our dependence on the machine caused this.

CASSANDRA:

But it can—

DR. PROMETHEUS:

Dash and daring built United Americana. Defying history's poison and
uniting settler, native, and slave. The machine should have taken us further.
Instead, we chose indolence and greed. Well, you did. Enjoy your blood-
stained coin.

[CASSANDRA *pauses, waiting to see if there's more.*]

CASSANDRA:
I . . . think . . .

DR. PROMETHEUS:
You're right, I'm to blame. I tested nature. Oh, the folly of building a living abacus!

CASSANDRA:
Seems like people are the problem.

DR. PROMETHEUS:
Thank you for the sweet words. But there's only one way to save United Americana.

CASSANDRA:
Oh, excellent. I didn't have any ideas. What is it?

DR. PROMETHEUS:
My death.

CASSANDRA:
You can't! I make nothing, I'll be out on the street!

[DR. PROMETHEUS *embraces her sister. Then she pulls the curtain off* CLOTHO's *head.*]

CLOTHO:
Hello, Mother.

DR. PROMETHEUS:
Goodbye, Clotho. As a Negro leader, my sacrifice will heal the national conscience and bring peace. Enjoy it, and make sure Cassandra tells my story properly.

CLOTHO:
Thank you, Mother. But—

[DR. PROMETHEUS *drops the curtain, smothering* CLOTHO's *response. She marches on to her destiny.*]

SCENE 6

[*The courtyard. Two* SOLDIERS *shiver at attention in threadbare coats while* MARON *enjoys a warm tin of spiked coffee.*]

SOLDIER ONE:
Sir, may I ask the machine if hell's real?

MARON:
If it pleases you.

[DR. PROMETHEUS *enters, defiant. She stands defiantly.*]

DR. PROMETHEUS:
[*Defiant.*] I'm ready. History is watching.

MARON:
To surrender? I made a simple and humble threat.

DR. PROMETHEUS:
Death before bondage.

MARON:
Understood. Load!

[*The* SOLDIERS *comply.*]

DR. PROMETHEUS:
The vice presidency is the executive toilet. Producing nothing, and absorbing shit. Do your worst.

MARON:
Aim!

[*Both* SOLDIERS *comply.* DR. PROMETHEUS *winces.*]

MARON:
Hold fire.

[*Both* SOLDIERS *comply.* DR. PROMETHEUS *collapses.*]

DR. PROMETHEUS:
Goodbye, world of beauty. Hello, Father!

MARON:
Doctor.

DR. PROMETHEUS:

Bury me beside Ben Franklin. I humbly followed, and then improved upon, his legacy.

MARON:

Why die here? For an object?

[DR. PROMETHEUS, *notably alive, clambers to her feet.*]

DR. PROMETHEUS:

You'd enslave Clotho, and then everyone else.

MARON:

I would! It's a wonderful plan, and you're ruining it with theatrics. Did the machine tell you we wouldn't shoot?

DR. PROMETHEUS:

No, I'm surprised to be breathing.

MARON:

[*Exasperated.*] Why stop? Take a payout, like an adult.

DR. PROMETHEUS:

I refuse. Progress comes before profit, power, or prestige. You're imitating a tyrant, but I think you understand that.

SOLDIER ONE:

We can still shoot her, burn the campus, and take it. Sir.

DR. PROMETHEUS:

Indeed. If you're willing to lose the debate.

MARON:

To a windchime? Never. After I win with standard, time-tested cheating, it'll be your *duty* to hand over the machine.

DR. PROMETHEUS:

And an honor.

MARON:

Choke.

SCENE 7

[*The workshop.* CASSANDRA *has adopted funeral attire.*
CLOTHO *remains in place.*]

CASSANDRA:
I'll miss her. Do you want this flying-box drawing? Or should I sell it with the other clutter?

CLOTHO:
Mother is unharmed. And the flying machine is vital.

CASSANDRA:
Clotho, she's gone. Why live in a cramped, smelly mausoleum?

[*Enter* DR. PROMETHEUS, *exhausted.*
She collapses onto a bench.]

CASSANDRA:
Welcome back! I'll find you a funeral outfit.

DR. PROMETHEUS:
We don't need . . . Never mind. I misjudged Maron.

CASSANDRA:
Oh. Should we vote for him?

DR. PROMETHEUS:
Absolutely not. He's a talking worm. But an American soul remains. Tyranny's against his nature, he just doesn't know it.

CASSANDRA:
Amazing!

DR. PROMETHEUS:
It isn't. That's Father's legacy. Redeeming the national spirit.

CASSANDRA:
Amazing! I assume. This is all a bit beyond me.

DR. PROMETHEUS:
Good. Write about it.

CLOTHO:
Excellent witticism, Mother.

DR. PROMETHEUS:

Thank you, Clotho. I'm taking a quick nap. Wake me in a decade or so, when the last crown's fallen.

[*The doctor nods off.* CLOTHO *drapes the curtain over her.*]

CASSANDRA:

Clotho? Small question. What's your margin of . . . wrongness? How often do you make mistakes?

CLOTHO:

Twenty percent. More, if you apply my margin of error to my margin of error.

CASSANDRA:

Amazing!

END.

ACKNOWLEDGMENTS

Thank you, Zora and Wendell Gleason, for supporting this dream before I had the words. Thank you, Virgil Gleason, for showing me real courage. I wish you three could see the world to come.

Special thanks to Betty Gleason, who will kindly abstain from improvisation. Every board in Theater Noire is for you. And every word here, *as written.*

23

THE NEW ENDING

The changes began in scene six. Hopefully no one would throw anything.

Anders watched from the west side of the platform, which filled in as the wings. Full exposure to the easily distracted audience wasn't ideal, but nothing about the scorched venue was. He rested in Mole's shadow, the next best thing to a proper curtain.

The lab scenes had nearly broken him. Anders couldn't imagine why Clotho never moved. Why couldn't a thinking machine spring around, wowing audiences with its agility? A subtle *Antietam Revert* might fit with the right timing. But it wasn't his script, and pushing creative edits on a freshly burned soldier sounded like suicide.

For stage time, he endured. His legs had gone numb by scene two. His arms joined in by scene four, leaving him feeling like a sweaty armless, legless torso propped up to entertain circusgoers. Not a fancy city circus but a country sideshow. The kind that advertised fire-eating men, bearded women, and mixed children with equal dramatic flourish. If he could revisit those shows now, he'd throw the performers fewer peanuts and more coins. If there were coins to spare.

"Sir, may I ask if hell's real?" said Petey, at half speed. He struggled with recall, unlike murder. Confounding, given his constant double-act.

"Pay attention, we're there already. I intend to enjoy it," said Thomas. He rattled off the updated line with professional ease, thanks to the words scrawled along his arm. The private's natural detachment paired well with Maron's moral vacuum. Thanks to a total lack of dedication, he put on the second-best performance.

Anders smothered what jealousy he could. He'd had high hopes after getting the title role—particularly since an artificial human (he didn't see where the abacus came in) didn't require a dress. But Thomas was a phenomenon amid their near-captive audience. Particularly women drawn by his lack of method. His growing fandom explained how a Black man with Thomas's attitude had survived this long: he was attractive enough to get away with it. And even those amorous stares were dwarfed by admiration for their lead.

After a day of repression, Anders reflected on his duel with fondness. It had made him, however briefly, the center of events. He discreetly tapped his feet, forcing feeling back into them. No point being ignored *and* numb.

Then their breakout performer took the stage. Mole left Anders's side in the pseudo-wings and squared off against the empire. Towering over the two soldiers—including Petey, who looked ready to run in real life—altered Dr. Prometheus's mousey image somewhat. Only her *spirit* was meant to be larger than life. That trace hint of subtlety might have survived with a flag-twirler's slighter frame. Though as far as Anders could tell, theater had plenty of room for blunt literalism.

More important, audiences loved blunt literalism. Despite the tense drama afoot, Dr. Prometheus's reentry earned bacchanal cheers from the recently displaced. The most dedicated viewers had shoved and elbowed their way up front for a clearer view. Mole wore a singed wig repossessed from a family home's remnants. After a century out of style, the stark white accessory found new life as Mole's makeshift bun.

"I'm ready. History is watching."

Mole imitated an overeducated and underreflective expert with unexpected precision. His adopted voice recalled barking officers, the director's exhortations, and someone that *sounded* like Anders but couldn't be. One could credit a lifetime of frozen, patient anger for Mole's prowess. But citing undiscovered talent came easier.

"Lord, I hope so," read Thomas. "At least I'm doing something new. History's the same babble, over and over again. I read about one year in Rome and got the idea."

"I'm sure that's true," said Mole, affecting more and more Gleason. "Our leaders tend toward shallow parasites, elected by shallower parasites. But the future belongs to believers."

"Fascinating. Where's the machine?"

"You won't get Clotho. The era of white men taking what they want, when they want, how they want is over. The American Future—"

"Got it. Shoot both monkeys and take the machine. I have a Second Mexican War to plan. I bet we can push all the way to the gulf this time."

Petey leveled his board of wood at Mole and waited for the sound effect. On cue, Anders shot Slade's pistol into the air twice, while Petey mimed firing his plank. The magic of theater spread through the audience, jolting the least engaged awake and triggering several panicked screams and shoves. The magic of theater continued working, and then worked too well, and now threatened to spiral into a stampede or second riot.

The tumult dimmed as Mole sank to his knees. He looked to the empty sky, forgot the line intended for Dr. Prometheus's death, and raised a hand to the God his character didn't believe in. Then he slumped and lay still. Anders clapped from the wings, priming the masses to follow suit.

They did. His envy hardened into a complex.

Transition time. Several uncast soldiers formed a human curtain, giving Anders's sprint into place the illusion of cover. He patted each of his legs, hoping that they would forgive him. Somehow, stillness challenged him as much as sprinting into or away from danger.

Joaquin was in place, a few feet to his right. Unfortunately, he wasn't talking.

In Anders's opinion, Cassandra's ebullience *also* required the easy, natural energy of a flag-twirler. Instead, they'd chosen Joaquin. The Reaper sweated in the cool night breeze, perspiring from pure nerves. The next line wasn't coming. With lower stakes, Anders might have called him kid.

Anders mouthed the words. Joaquin, to his credit, echoed them at a natural pace.

"That sound . . . Is she . . ."

"Most likely dead. Perhaps *dying*, followed shortly by death." Anders milked each syllable.

Joaquin either affected despair or channeled authentic stage panic. Either way, his lip-reading improved.

"She believed in this place. And it killed her. I told her to believe in the people, and they watched."

"True."

"But why? You're supposed to know everything, and you stood there like a goddamn table."

"There wasn't another outcome, Auntie. Just versions of this. I enjoyed the time we had."

The new ending called for a prop wrench hurled at Clotho. With none available, a real one had to do. Anders stood still as it slammed into his chest, pointy-side first. He bit the side of his cheek until he tasted copper. If Mole could win applause, so would he.

"Jessica said you could compute *anything*. You calculated an opinion on *God*."

"I can't make a culture sane. United Americana inherited a single, insane lie. Freedom built on bondage. A structure demanding servitude and celebrating its absence."

"You're broken. Should I feed you gears? Would pig's feet work?"

Anders mouthed the next part carefully. The handwriting had gotten more erratic at this point, so it likely mattered. He just wished the words felt less like treason.

"It's true, Auntie. Why do you think Mother built a better slave? To replace her people beneath the pyramid. Where you live, no matter how well you dress or speak like the owners."

"Father died changing that."

"No. He just died. The American Future will never live in America."

Another transition. Their smoothest attempt so far, by Anders's count. The first few scene outros were bedlam: the human curtain's members had both enthusiasm and the collisions that came with it. As the show went on, a loose system emerged. Instead of guessing at the end of a scene and then sprinting like wild horses, they sprinted like domesticated horses whenever twenty dialogue-free seconds passed.

A perfect plan, without actors. Their starting and closing positions changed every time. Each transition challenged their reflexes and aware-ness. For his part, Anders had avoided falling. But enough men had stepped on his boots to make numbness a blessing. With luck, his bruised toes would heal a little before marching took over his life again.

Petey stumbled during the avalanche of human motion, landed on his face, and stayed there. Tears followed quickly. Asking another persona to fill in might have helped, but finding the words for the request made

Anders's head hurt. Instead, he yanked Petey to his feet and supported him with his right arm. The bugler managed to stop crying before the human curtain parted but now stood completely out of place.

"I have it!" Petey improvised. He painfully torqued Anders's arm behind his back. The physical pain nicely complemented the week's mental marathon.

"Grab the machine," ordered Thomas, sticking rigidly to the script. Whatever happened, he had neither the will nor the inclination to deviate from the words written on him.

"S-stay back," stuttered Joaquin, also failing to improvise. The stage robbed the eager murderer of the easy confidence and unnerving presence that had made Anders sleep with a flag on hand. It followed, in a way: for a faithful advocate and user of stealth, intentional exposure to the masses must have felt like lunacy. He'd even lost his wig during the transition. His full accent—a mixture of Creole and something else—colored Cassandra's dialogue.

"Another martyr, I assume?" said Thomas. He managed that without notes.

"Just take it. There's nothing here worth dying for."

"Finally, some reason. Grab the abacus and leave Miss Herod some money. She can be secretary of agriculture after the election, or something like that. The machine's replacing the cabinet anyway. It's high time someone humbled the Princeton crowd."

Petey's memory caught up with the scene. He released Anders's arm, and then re-wrenched it behind his back. Anders kept his face doll-neutral through the pain and waited for his own applause. Suffering-infused art had to be worth more, or he'd been wasting his time. Still nothing.

"On second thought," continued Thomas, "kill her too. It'll be easier to massage the story."

A nameless soldier leveled a mock rifle at Joaquin's head. Once again, his genuine stage terror served the moment. Frayed nerves closely resembled the terror Anders (and Joaquin, come to think of it) had inflicted at gunpoint, lending Cassandra's final moments gravity.

The human curtain closed for the final time. Anders pulled his arm loose, gave Petey a scowl that could melt iron, and fired into the clouds.

As admirable as Gleason's dedication to immersion was, he wondered where the bullets landed.

Only the dimmest spectators panicked. The others settled into what Anders hoped was awed silence. Half of him even prayed. A poor fit for the themes he'd brought to life, but he held on to a sliver of selective faith. His spirit needed a victory, and Deism underperformed as relief.

Yet the new ending didn't inspire an ovation or even memorable jeering. The survivors simply looked exhausted. Hollow eyes stamped on bruised faces. A familiar, unwelcome tightness returned to Anders's chest. He bowed to distract himself from it. Mercifully, the rest of the cast and crew followed his lead. They pantomimed the closing steps of a beloved hit.

Anyone could pinpoint where *The Living Abacus* had lost the audience. For the first seven scenes, they'd engaged. Dangerously so, even. Half the lines were smothered by women whistling at Thomas. And when lines were audible, so was feedback. Under a black sky and persistent wind, refugees responded to an impossible machine in an impossible world with equal parts wonder, ironic detachment, and bemused confusion. Bottles pinched from ashen taverns diffused through the crowd. Cries of "Can it dance," "Why's it white," and "I'll take two" punctuated each scene. Heckling, but affirmative heckling. Insults were part of the fun.

Speculative theater lived up to the hype, until Dr. Prometheus entered the courtyard and met death. That hopeless turn echoed the lives they knew. No escape or lesson waited within.

Anders took an extra bow. At least half the show had been fun. If enough of the cast lived to return to New York, maybe they could put it on again. The other way.

✣ ✣ ✣

Breaking the stage down would've taken days if anyone had bothered. Hobbes made rumblings about respecting a great city, leaving things as they found them, and impressing the general. Gleason noted that they'd found the neighborhood on fire and asked if they should bring that experience uptown. The conversation died there.

Instead, the platform hosted a gathering halfway between a victory lap and post-funeral dinner. Like any proper event, guests quickly and qui-

etly separated into cliques. Performers, curtain members, and nonpartic-
ipants filtered into small circles on or around the platform. The core cast
shared a salvaged bottle of a green liquid Anders didn't care for and drank
half of. Petey and Joaquin monopolized the rest, more traumatized by the
performance than any action they'd seen.

Tonight's star moved freely between rings, where he declined, accepted,
and binged toasts to his prowess. It was the humble shower of admiration
Anders had hoped to enjoy, elevated by genuine humility. Mole spoke
sparsely and tersely again, as if his booming voice and presence had
been a mass hallucination. Hopefully another undrinkable green bottle
appeared soon.

Gleason sat apart and stared into the empty sky. He'd taken the
scorched cushion down from his director's chair and placed it on the neutral ground between games of dice and Ofay. The mirthless humor that
possessed his features earlier had melted into something softer and easier
to look at without panicking.

"Sir?" Anders said. He slid over slowly. Gleason's recent work implied
he might shoot himself or someone else.

"That was astounding," said Gleason. He clapped Anders twice on the
shoulder, the way a father might. Presumably. "You should be proud. I
think you left an impression."

"I didn't feel much joy. Or get one cheer."

"That's perfect, no one cheers for character actors. They just remember
them."

"I understand. Actually, no. I don't get it. Pardon?"

"You carried the spirit of the work. Joy would be lunacy. This is a war
over two-fifths of our—the royal our—humanity. Black men are dying to
prove they deserve to live. It's the demiurge's best joke."

"Ah, so we wanted to depress them," said Anders. "I was almost worried. Though I thought speculative theater was all about inspiration."

"Typically. I suspect this was my first realist work. I might try more
later."

"Right. Are you . . . well, sir? Truly well? Not just the lie men tell each
other?"

"I'm fine. I just need to figure out what country The American Future's
hiding in."

23.5

AUDIENCE FEEDBACK

The boogeymen took everything they could, and torched the rest. We still threw a party. That's how you win."

✦ ✦ ✦

"I still don't know what a Pascaline is."

✦ ✦ ✦

"His last play was more fun. There was a talking cat."

✦ ✦ ✦

"I don't care. My house is gone."

✦ ✦ ✦

"Needs more action. Except when the main girls died. That was too much action. I guess I wanted more hope."

✦ ✦ ✦

"Did it need all the side bits? Stick to the story. Life's complicated enough."

✦ ✦ ✦

"It was the truth. That's all that matters. Could've used more action, though."

✦ ✦ ✦

"It was all right. After that, things got truly strange."

24

RANK

Five placid days lent Theater Noire the familiarity of home and settled Wendy-related nightmares into Anders's rotation. New nightmares were a relief: reliving the assassination made more sense than angels and enabled his best rest in some time. Though taking and besieging cities (including, it turned out, those already in the Union) provided consistent horror, occupying them proved restive.

His waking hours returned to default strangeness. Despite the lack of flowers and medals, small changes appeared between Anders and the regiment. He got fewer questions about his enlistment, why he mentioned octoroons so often, and if he knew what an octoroon was. Instead of hiding all of his personal effects at night, he only buried items of obvious value. Finally, he became Gleason's default middleman. Incoming questions were numerous and difficult to remember, but the de facto promotion let him stand a little taller.

Manhattan stood silent, likely for the first time since the Lenape's eviction at gunpoint. The city had simply shaken itself out of energy. Like a toddler, or a teenager tied to a bedpost to prevent their enlistment. That strategy hadn't stopped Anders, but he'd lost a full day kicking the wall instead of working on the knots.

Hopefully Katrina was all right. He'd send a letter home as soon as he was a little farther out of reach.

New orders trickled down to Clyburn and his cronies, who then left Hobbes to distribute them. This brought the lieutenant to Anders's new prized bedding: a produce sack lifted from a former general store. He'd also repossessed a few scraps of dried fish and fruit that had survived the riot and its refugees. Taste-testing this new supply and lounging in his new furniture had occupied Anders's afternoon.

"Good morning," he said between chews.

"At attention."

Anders rolled out of the bag. His inner stickler for decorum hadn't survived the duel. Saluting would have required dropping his food.

"Good morning, Anders."

"Hiya."

"As an officer, I don't need to speak through anyone. But I know that the, uh, informal culture in a regiment has value."

"Okay."

"And thus, while I don't have to, I'll be leveraging Corporal—*the second-lowest rank, I remind you*—Gleason's voice among the men to spread the general's new orders."

"Are you well? Not the—"

"I'm perfectly well. I'm a lieutenant. Lieutenants are always thriving and awash in respect."

"Sorry, Lieutenant." Anders threw one of his old salutes.

"Excellent. As I was saying, we're heading west to help our Indian allies pacify our Indian enemies. Everyone should be prepared. Because I ordered it, as the Black lieutenant you admire, and not because of Gleason or anyone else outside the officer tents."

Anders dug one of the sweeter colors of dried fruit out of his pocket and extended it without comment. Verbal invitation could be patronizing, and he'd like to do *something* for Hobbes before he collapsed or deserted.

After a scornful glare, the lieutenant took the fruit. He squinted at the blue strip the way unpopular kings regarded their dinners for centuries, and then his shoulders and face slackened. Hobbes dabbed something in his eyes off on his sleeve as he wolfed it down. The lieutenant didn't look physically hungry, but he'd clearly starved for affection.

"I'll tell Gleason about the train, and India."

"Indians."

Anders gave him another strip and then gently shooed the lieutenant away. Platitudes about the chain of command and unit cohesion trailed behind him.

Another successful reception. While he'd expected to go down in history as a morale artist, administration fit nicely. If he maintained momentum (and picked up an identity not marked as dead or missing), he could work his way up to War Department clerk. They suffered paperwork but avoided meaningless death in the mud. A relatively even trade.

The corporal worked from the ruins of his personal office. Or rather, stared at the wall with his feet on half a desk. He looked perplexed, and a little less pained, so Anders chalked it up to a philosophical mind at work.

Anders passed on Hobbes's suggestion, along with some handbills he'd found on the way. Since hearing about Wendy, Gleason had taken interest in the bizarre propaganda scattered around the city. Indulging him undermined Anders's plan to repress the entire arc, but helping felt like his duty. And the encounter *had* stoked his curiosity, whenever he could stop seeing exposed brain when he blinked.

"Well done," Gleason said, shuffling through the stack. Wendy had been prolific. "Monarchy's dead, but voting has the same smell. I'd like to learn what drove these men before we move on."

"The Sons of Columbia had music," noted Anders. "And hoods. Along with some memorable spins. I might switch to a short-pole style."

Gleason rolled past the tangent. "You found an odd illustration in Pennsylvania. Still have it?"

"It was enemy propaganda. That would be sedition."

The corporal waited. Anders rifled through his inside coat pockets. He kept his best souvenirs on his person, regardless of any fleeting popularity. No one had to *dislike* him to rob him. The best bits were long gone, thanks to his wardrobe change at Gettysburg. But he still had Slade's letter, an ornate and useless dagger, and the propaganda Mole had turned up.

There wasn't much to see: a loose sketch of a scepter, a melodramatic call to action, and a stab at a hidden code. Their time would be better spent packing, or stealing extra sleep before Clyburn's clique returned from the brothels. Nonetheless, Gleason close read it like his own work, leaving Anders to stare at his bandages. The scarring on Gleason's left hand and temple was heavy enough to tempt mention but not heavy enough to demand it.

"You've read this before?"

"Yes."

"In detail?"

"No."

"The back's not quite blank. Small red letters are printed along the margins. Any thoughts?"

"Yeah! Nicely printed, aren't they? Lettering's advancing all the time. It's like mechanical calligraphy. I might pursue it, if the nation doesn't sink into eternal bloodshed."

"And their *meaning*, Anders?"

"Oh, that's some kind of code."

The corporal waited for Anders to close the gap. He dangled the handbill until Anders grasped it and saluted.

"When do you need it?"

"Before we set foot on the train. Your meeting with Ms. Ross, and the letters Petey stole, make me think it might be important."

"You've seen Petey?"

"Of course. The lad's everywhere."

Anders excused himself and began the first of many directionless loops around the camp/ruin. After all his progress with the other enlisted men, having a holdout ignore him stung. Particularly one he'd broken so many civilian and military laws beside. He'd been perfectly nice to at least one out of three personas.

He kept an eye open for Petey, who'd been scarce since the show. Three motives seemed likely. First, he could simply be as shaken by recent violence as Anders. Bugles couldn't have provided any more combat experience than flag spinning. Second, Petey could simply be ducking their deal. Rude. Finally, *The Living Abacus* might have achieved what battlefields and riots couldn't, and driven Petey from the army. They could be uptown, reentering civilian life as Patricia or Polly.

He'd call his interest humane, but that would be *lying with the truth*. Any charity came anchored to the selfish urge to politely beg the Hua Mulan fan to come through. While they weren't soulmates (or capable of extended polite conversation), they were bonded by sexual bargaining over a political murder. Wasn't that almost romance? Didn't Petey/Patricia/Polly feel a little desperation too? Anders had spent three tours in two armies stiff as often as not, and suspected that insanity sat around the corner.

A few minutes alone would help. His uniform's previous owner carried a photo of a conservatively dressed woman with a stern expression. A half glower she must have held at length, given the purgatory of sitting for a photo. "Remember your vows" was written across the backside in angular black letters.

It would have to do. Anders had done his best to avoid falling this far and failed. At least B. K. had died before disappointing her.

The plan died as he approached his nook and found unwanted, unasked for, and artfully inconvenient company. Yet another busybody hovered to ask questions that Anders would forget or Gleason would brush off. All the words ran together now. *When will this end? Is Harrow insane? What do we fight for, then? I don't get the play—explain it without all the white-sounding nonsense.* He'd have cursed the nurse away, if her face didn't haunt his strangest dreams.

She stood alone, with only half the disassociation she displayed in Harrow's tent or Slade's prison. Maybe even a quarter. Moreover, unlike his dreams, her head didn't sit above a shifting mass of marble and flame, and she stuck to two pleasant eyes. Anders straightened his posture and cap before his higher mind finished registering her presence.

"Anders, yes?" she asked. Her accent was elusive, but he decided it was perfect.

" ," said Anders. Words might have worked better.

He took the angel's appearance as confirmation of going mad, before recalling that the nurse was a real person outside of his rapidly mutating imagination. Still, she embodied grace and beauty within his age and status. Particularly her long, braided hair, which was going gray decades early. Likely due to facing a surgeon's stress at a prisoner's wages. Either way, her sleepless and defeated visage recalled his mother. The appeal there remained a mystery, but it remained.

"Looking for a dingo?" said Anders, trying a greeting he'd watched Thomas lob at a married woman after the show. The words collapsed on the way out. He pivoted. "Are you a fan of my work? I was the human Pascaline. I hear I'm a character actor, and that's a good thing."

It didn't land. The nurse adopted the bored, distant look that weak propositions inspired. At least, that's how he interpreted it. He'd only tried once before, and that hadn't worked out.

"Apologies," he declared. "What do you want me to tell Gleason? He doesn't know when the war's ending or how to get a medal out of it. Trust me, I asked. The thinking machine in the play's a *metaphor*, like throwing tea overboard, or Jesus. What's your name? I'm Anders. Which you know, but never gave yours."

The nurse's eyes widened at the deluge of unfiltered Anders, and she took a half step backward. Two seconds later, she recovered and pushed on.

"Mr. Jefferson would like to speak with you."

"Is that all? Tell him to go play Ofay. I'll deal cards later."

"*Slade* Jefferson."

The nurse's squint cut through his attempt to keep his smile intact. He'd enjoyed plenty of experience deserting armies and nations. Organizations were easy enough, as long as he kept his head down and marched in line with everyone else. This was his first tilt at the fallout of betraying an individual.

"I'm very busy. Business and all of that."

"This is the quote: 'I think I've pieced together your *service record*. Visit the executive cell at your earliest convenience, or I'll discuss it with the general. He won't care, but he'll act to save face.' End of quote."

Anders tapped every lesson of theater, gambling, and secret society infiltration. Suppressing natural tells in his eyes, mouth, stance, and voice took all the focus he had left. After putting on his bravest mask, he said, "That's fine. I'll visit the *traitor* when the company ships out. Not before. I don't work for him. I barely work for the army. I'm not afraid of anything he's planning, especially when his plans put him in that cage."

The stunned silence or swooning he'd hoped to inspire didn't manifest. The nurse mutely nodded and waited to be excused, as if he'd given a dull lesson or passed a vaudeville joke off as his own.

"Thank you," he added by way of dismissal. She took the opening and murmured sounds adjacent to "You're welcome."

Then Anders remembered the photo, along with the private embarrassment he'd originally intended for the afternoon. His pride called for another attempt.

"What's your name?"

"No."

"All right."

24.5

———◆———

NOTES FOR REVISION

Hello Tobias,

I've been starved for entertainment since you stole my freedom. Imagine my shock when, over dinner, an officer mentioned that you'd completed a play! Stranger yet, that you intended to *perform* it in what's left of New York. He was just filling air—steak makes men chatty—but curiosity demanded more. I had him seize a copy for me. Hungry for tips, he even transcribed your changes. It's amusing to think that the blues are the *better* funded half of this war.

The Living Abacus is the best play I've read, albeit the third. Aristophanes was too fixated on warfare and the like. Not that you're innocent of that—the preaching goes on and on in the second half—but you cut it with imaginative madness. Talking, humanoid machines! A direct window to the future! A lady inventor! The mind boggles.

Nonetheless, as a manager of men, I feel obligated to offer some thoughts.

It runs a little long. Any performance that overstays its welcome robs busy social calendars. Once, I nearly missed a tryst with Wendy's maid because Shakespeare dragged out Romeo's obvious doom. If I wrote a play, I'd begin with a comprehensive summary of events and themes, freeing busy schedules and minds.

Must it fixate on Douglass's hobby horse? For a play about the future, it's rigidly attached to the past. I'm certain that the first step to healing from your stint as a slave race—aside from finishing the current shootout—will be dwelling on it less. Why would slavery still matter in 1890? I'm bored of racial jousting already. Surely, a man with your wit can agree.

I admire Dr. Prometheus's financial speculation efforts. However, bond yields fall out of the narrative entirely. I find it difficult to believe that a once-a-generation windfall would disappear from a promising young mind, no matter how many soldiers are involved. I can speak through experience: during my stint in military prison, I've elevated myself to Manhattan Island's newest and most prominent landlord. If this Dr. Prometheus is a true genius, I suggest you have her do the same.

The Maron character is brilliant. The play could use more of him. Morality tales need upright leads willing to stand for the good and true. As the sisters flutter around fretting about the nation and ennui, Maron remembers the *essence* of the nation and life: endeavor. Looking at what the world could be, and seizing as much of it as possible. In this, I consider the abolitionist and entrepreneur to be of one mind.

In any case, I know artists like to leave an impression. Thus, I wanted you to know I remember you. And the Haitian, and the slave, and the clown, and your pet. Very clearly.

Best,

Slade Jefferson

Patron of the Arts

25

LOCK THE DOOR BEHIND YOU

The city moved on. Hollow homes and storefronts were convenient new shortcuts for savvy pedestrians, and absent neighbors less than a memory. The missing and dead made for less crowded streets. Renewal was in the air. Once the porters and factory underfoots were out of jail and hiding, New York would be faster than ever.

True to Hobbes's depressive word, Harrow withdrew with little notice and less patience. Black peacekeepers in an American city proved too alien a sight for influential observers, including the brigadier general himself. If the nurse drama hadn't nudged Anders into an early start, he might not have finished packing his slim personal effects in time.

Nonetheless, the mayor took time to see key companies off. He was a squat man with a trim figure—rare enough in the class of men important, shameless, or wealthy enough to avoid combat. A long gray coat hung over his suit, defying the heat for fashion. Anders watched him from the shade behind a fountain. The men baked in a long-neglected downtown park, where the politician could concentrate armed Negroes without creating a panic.

No medals were distributed. The tightly stacked lines of infantry would have fit a medal ceremony well, either for their collective effort or for being outstanding young men. Anders let the thought go in favor of more important questions.

"Why's the ofay bundled up for a snowstorm?" asked Thomas. He wore resentment for being conscious, standing, and preached at again in the open.

"Former schoolteacher," guessed Anders. "He wants to be relatable."

"You follow the politics here?"

"No. I can just smell a schoolteacher."

"Right. The idiot savant routine. I'd almost forgotten."

"What's a savant?" asked Anders. Half his mind was with the royalist code. His pencil was a nub, but he could work it out in his head if he focused. All the world had to do was slow down a little.

"Hilarious. Don't you get tired of rich boogeymen preaching at us?"

"Not yet. It gets stranger every time. And I want to be a rich boogeyman one day."

"Fair."

True to form, the mayor struggled to hold the class's attention. First, he tried standing firm and projecting stately, paternal authority. Despite a perch closely resembling a reused campaign podium, his importance failed to resonate. Small games of Ofay popped up around the rim of the assembly. Next, the mayor whispered to an aide. Said aide announced that the mayor could "wait as long as he has to for you to settle down."

The standoff lasted long enough for Anders to crack what passed for a code outside the army. After adjusting for spelling errors, the message read:

"Knights errant: your liege waits. Seek San Valentin, in the kingdom of Nevada. Be free."

More madness. Someone less tired than Anders would have to eke meaning out of it.

The mayor's aide finally won the standoff, or at least reached a point he could interpret as victory. He reintroduced Mayor George Opdyke and his mustache, and the mayor gave the wave only politicians and monarchs could re-create. The smile behind it carried more tension than usual. Natural, since Black occupiers represented a joint crisis and insult to skittish New Yorkers with the time, energy, and inclination to vote.

"Some say this war is about free labor. Such as Lincoln, and Davis. Their closest generals. Philosophers like Douglass and politicians like Alexander Stephens. Most of you, along with the men fighting beside and against you. Foreign commentators, from enemies and allies to the indifferent. But this week, you proved that this war is about honor.

"New York stands today because of your sense of honor. We could not save everything. The negro quarters are . . . troubled. But what remains is a black soldier's triumph. Carry that with pride. However this ends, you have earned all five-fifths of a man's honor."

Opdyke's speech ran longer than Anders expected. Perhaps the mayor had the gift of gab and could have gone on forever without a terrified voter base hanging over him. Maybe a hint of real gratitude drove him to give the Harriers more than the smoke and spittle the city had offered thus far. Or perhaps it was competitive spirit. Wartime amplified addresses and dramatic gestures at every level of service, and letting himself fall behind wouldn't be smart. McClellan had the edge, but a savvy mayor could still steal the nomination.

"Thank you. Our city owes you everything. Now leave."

✦ ✦ ✦

Another train. Or the same one. Distinct variations cost money, and the struggle had outlived the optimistic predictions of war hawks, the negative projections of copperheads, and sober analyses by amused foreigners. The lead car bore the same burnished Harmony Rail brand, so Anders interpreted it as a return.

Harmony Rail carried a noble distinction: some businesses had gouged Lincoln for more, and others had a more visible fingerprint on the war. Yet Harmony Rail boasted the most tangible impact per dollar, shipping everything that exploded or carried an explosive around the nation and charging for every pound. An actuary (or whatever one called the dull-eyed wraiths commerce produced like flies) etched a tally mark for every soldier that passed, including Anders. The gesture was just alienating enough to distract Anders from reentering his mortal enemy. A new train meant new chaos, and he'd just adapted to the old one.

Even the penny-pinching had a noble tint, since the trains worked without memorable disaster. The lack of mechanical catastrophes put Harmony Rail well ahead of gunsmiths, who used the government as a landfill for defective or underwhelming product. In his first tour, Anders's rifle had kicked, flashed, and bruised his shoulder like a weapon. But it held on to the bullet. Demotion to full-time flag-twirling had been a relief: at least he knew he was unarmed.

That depth of cynicism was difficult to grasp, until he'd spoken with Slade twice. Today, defective guns seemed as American as the flag strapped to his back. Any faith or standards that survived their third meeting would be invincible.

The men drifted to the same cars and benches as their last journey. Like most things, this reminded Anders of the schoolhouse. Students flocked to the same formation every morning, without a hint of an opinion from their instructor. With Anders left staring in from the outside. That hadn't changed either.

Anders considered asking Joaquin along. He'd humbled Slade easily enough last time and looked largely recovered from his theater career. But he was unlikely to approve of the flirtation with treason that brought Anders into Slade's orbit in the first place. The corporal and Mole seemed like even more remote possibilities. Somehow, Anders had the role of company ingenue slip out from under him.

Patricia, on the other hand, offered the perfect balance of violence and personal flexibility. But all three Peteys were avoiding him, and he didn't have time to navigate the thorns of anyone else's emotions. Slade might expose Anders for entertainment if he were on time, let alone late.

Thus, Anders opted to handle his own intimidation. He loaded Slade's revolver with a fresh batch of Slade's bullets and traipsed toward the prison car. Most of the locks between cars were intact, so it was a different train after all. Nothing in the army got fixed. Just replaced with new draftees.

Small talk endeavored to delay him and he refused to cooperate. Witnesses and crew for *The Living Abacus* all had admiration or advice, mercifully leaning toward the former. He powered past each comment. "You sounded just like a machine lady, or whatever a machine woman would sound like," noted one officer. Anders saluted and pulled ahead. He'd gone for a rugged machine *man*, but any praise had value.

The final, overcomplicated lock to the prison car forced him to stop and think. Not about the remedial lock, but what he could do or say on the other side. Kowtowing felt wrong. Killing a prisoner felt wrong. Feigning ignorance might work, but he was tired of being treated like the village dunce, and even more tired of living up to it.

If nothing else, he'd enjoy the view. Transferring Slade's creature comforts would've taken time, and they'd rushed out of the city like it was still on fire. They'd finally meet in something resembling a prison. Or even a jail. He almost dared to hope for an oubliette.

Anders pushed in, shoulder-first, and found Petey standing in a thin blue suit and matching dress shoes. A familiar face, with unfamiliar aggression. Petey blocked Anders's path to the extent his stature allowed, in the same puffed-out stance The Governess's doormen enjoyed. A full-body layer of makeup complemented his new attitude.

The chalk resembled his New York disguise, but a layer thinner and neck-inclusive. His new wig hung in a ponytail a century out of fashion. His lips were half drawn in, locked into a thin frown. He looked like another world's minstrel, channeling a caricature of whiteness handed down from Jamestown and passed by rumor to the present. He looked Anders over, unimpressed.

"Is Mr. Jefferson expecting you?"

"What in hell?"

"Sorry, I should introduce myself. I'm Porter, Mr. Jefferson's assistant."

Anders braced. Past personas hadn't reflected high opinions of their subjects. If Porter combined takes on whiteness and manhood, the conversation would age Anders a decade. At a glance, Porter had nailed something to the bottom of his new shoes to make him taller. Just an inch under Anders, whose growth spurt valiantly held the line against malnourishment.

"Hello, Porter. Goodbye, Porter."

Porter shifted into his path.

"What's your business with Mr. Jefferson?"

"We discussed it. I can see him sitting behind you, laughing like a child. And hear him."

The chuckle devolved into guffaws punctuated by coughing. The noise ate at Anders more than he cared to admit. The burning world sat in the hands of laughing men. Maniacs celebrated their own pranks while others charged over their last hill.

"Goodbye, Porter," Anders repeated. He gave his friend/acquaintance/enemy an involuntary once-over. Porter wasn't unbecoming, prompting questions Anders didn't have the time or desire to address. "I'll see you later."

"You'll speak now, spade."

"Spade? You call that a slur? Where's the *force*? You're not going to cut it as a white man."

Porter kneed him in the stomach.

Anders invented a curse. Multiple impulses sprinted for his tongue, and pieces of each made it through. The muddled slur came out "bastnig-whotherfucker."

The laughter doubled in volume and slowly declined into a pained wheeze. From the floor, Anders had a clear view of Slade and his new lodgings. And they were lodgings, not amenities or quarters or anything else connected with mortal life. An ancient king would have been happy to bring the ornate carpeting, heavy bookshelves, hand-carved desk, and two mortified nurses into the next world. Firearms of every size and shape lined the wall. Two pistols—just like Anders's but larger, more ornate, and wholly unlike Anders's—hung from his hip like a frontier outlaw.

"Ease off, he's fine," Slade managed, with sharp breaths between each word. Laughter had almost thrown the gunsmith to the floor as well. He wiped his mouth off on his sleeve, frowned at the stain, and handed the jacket off to a nurse. She flung it through an open window. The prisoner had *open windows*.

Against all taste and logic, a thin chain still tethered Slade to the desk. It looked like cheap metal, maybe copper. A child could break it by accident.

"Welcome to Jefferson Firearms Headquarters," said Slade. "Like it? Dislike it? All opinions have value during a meeting."

Anders vomited, as men struck in the chest sometimes did.

"It's a mobile headquarters, a new concept of mine. I won't have to pack up every time business or pleasure comes up. Strap this wonder to any train, and off Jefferson Firearms goes to a new destination. The pencil-pushers, at least. I'll figure out mobile factories later."

"Treason . . ." Anders burbled.

"I believe it, you're an expert. Walking around in B. K. Jefferson's uniform like that."

"Hate. You. Hate," elaborated Anders. He threw Porter a pleading look. Porter spat to the side.

"Right, this is my new man, Porter. You'll be working together."

"Hate. What? Work?"

"The lad told me the whole story. You brought him in to round out your team—admirable humility, honestly. It's hard to look directly at one's weaknesses. Better avoided entirely, if you're supervising. But good for your level."

Porter pulled Anders away from his own sick, watched him clamber upright, and then jumped back from a cocked fist. The old skittishness waited behind the new presentation. Anders made note.

"Anyhow, you both did your best, but Wendy's womanly mind had broken. It's a shame, she'd have made a nice fiancée. Not a wife, but engagement sounds fun."

"Why. Stomach. Hate. Hate you both."

"Think of it as an initiation. You've been initiated before, right? Do you have secret societies in . . . wherever you're from? Every academy has at least one."

The pain declined to dissipate, but some breath and clarity returned. Patricia had wanted in on Anders's ploy and found a way as Porter. Whatever high-mindedness they'd shown during the pogrom had dissipated without their *entire* race's future at risk. As for Slade, he was getting easier to understand. Every underfoot minion made his pretrial life easier, safer, and more profitable.

Anders steadied himself against a wall and projected as much regret as he could manage. His stage experience delivered, though he was no Mole.

"Thank you," Anders lied. "For the opportunity. From a certain perspective, I betrayed you."

"Yes, a fine call. Wendy would've lost, and you'd both be hanging. Imagine that! Dying without seeing who wins all this. I still think England might come back and sweep the board. You heard it here first."

"Don't worry about Wendy. Or the war, once I'm done in Nevada. You're mine. Enjoy the gun."

26

NOMENCLATURE

When something required focus, impossible distractions leapt into Anders's path with energy and grace. Now that he needed a distraction from blackmail, the train ran smoothly. It defied belief: he rode an iron beast charging across a half-explored nation at war. But without his window seat, he'd believe they were standing still. The piston's steady rhythm no longer registered.

They had a longer journey, over swaths of the frontier he'd never imagined seeing or shooting people in. Four days, if Harmony Rail marketing held true. Each mile pulled Anders farther from his long-forgotten comfort zone, and any connection willing to hide him in their basement until Jefferson Davis lost hope. A list that added up to his mother, schoolteacher, and perhaps the tailor he'd semi-robbed. Unease quickly trampled any novelty the unending loop of prairies, nascent frontier towns, and haggard native stragglers outside offered.

On day two of riding, he usurped a seat closer to the engine. Still not loud enough. His new seatmate Mole offered one beat of animated, single-sentence conversation per hour. Hits included "Hey," "Sleep well," "Snack?" and "Snore less." That said, their snack exchange was the envy of their peers. Anders traded looted dried fruit for looted dried meat, and both men thought they'd gotten the better deal.

On day three, Anders gave up on variety finding him and resolved to drag it out of someone else. He'd run out of jerky and poise. If he were larger, he could have started a fistfight. As it stood, he'd have to use his words.

"What kind of name's Mole?" he asked. For his purpose, a perfect question. They could bond, argue, or start swinging. Any outcome that drowned out the engine was acceptable.

Mole's face didn't change. One minute passed into five. Mole treated the question as if it had another target. Fair enough. Even after his brush with fame, questions about the man's life or feelings weren't routine. Freemen didn't show any more enthusiasm for slave life's details than Anders and lacked motivational guilt. Anders prepared to repeat himself when the dam broke.

"Hell's real. It's dark and cold and lined with salt. Boss Man could've sold the salt and been rich, taken his time. But rich wasn't enough. He needed gold. I guess gold rich means more than salt rich.

"The mine was out west, in California. Boss Man heard the future was out there and decided the future needed him in it. Maybe that was smart. Either way, our world changed from the hell in the dirt to the hell beneath it. We moved before these trains were running, or California picked the banks over the masters. Because Boss Man thought of a new way to use people. He couldn't resist testing it out.

"I think about that a lot. Masters don't live in our world. I don't mean all your—sorry, *their*—crap about burdens or saving the savage and all that. The basic rules are different. What people are, why they're here, what they owe you: all that changes when you own them.

"Think of the prison camps. Seen those? I know you've been around. The mines are worse. The camps are for a kind of *person* that you'll let out when you've won, or lost, or just given up. Everyone you put in a mine, you assume it's the last you'll see of them. Smart guess, there aren't a lot of stories like mine. It's a mistake to assume the masters are dumb. I think it's why the war's gone on this long. They're creative, and born surrounded by free matériel. Lee doesn't just think like a general, he thinks like a master using his toys. His are just a bit paler."

A mistake. Anders's thoughts slipped back to the factory. How confidently they'd chucked Slade into a carriage instead of cutting a deal or throat. His drift must have been visible—Mole had paused and picked up an amused look.

"Then what?" scrambled Anders.

"Anyway," Mole continued, "that was the emotion. Physically, it was hot. That made everything else hard to feel. If I wasn't busy boiling, there might have been stinging and tearing and bruising. But it's just as hot a mile down as the desert outside. And there's never enough water.

"Down there, I decided the Baptists and Spiritualists and Catholics and Deists are all wrong. God is real, and he hates us. He strokes himself when we suffer and finishes when we die. Chain gangs and wars and hospitals are one big, dirty photo.

"I learned to keep that to myself. Faith's all that kept most niggers down there alive. Bringing up the Big Enemy was like killing them myself. Eventually I just stopped. Talking, I mean. Easy habit to pick up, hard to stop. I think I'm getting there. When boys here talk about their dreams and countries and plans, I still keep quiet and hope that God isn't listening.

"Sin. Sin plenty. You don't want to be trapped up there with him, like those poor angels. Those poor saints. They're getting the worst God can think of. After two thousand-thousand-thousand years holding the whip, there's no mind left. Because God is a slave master.

"Gleason said that paintings of angels don't look like the old ones. That we get them wrong, and we're missing a bunch of wings and hands. He's close, but I don't think so. I think God peeled their feathers off, one by one, until there were just two tiny wings left. Just enough to get back to work.

"Still, I try to be good. I try to help people, and be polite, and say my prayers. I'm gonna sneak in and meet God. And then . . . You're a nice kid. Let's move on. The cave-in.

"One day, I found something glittery and yellow. Fake gold or moron's gold or nigger's gold or whatever makes one rock worse than another. The boss was excited, until he wasn't. After that shit gold, he got reflective. Started missing Virginia, which I did too. My whole family's there. Two kids. I wanted to teach them about God with words, before Boss Man could with action.

"He must have wanted to ride back alone. Five days after the fake gold, the main entrance caved in behind us.

"Accidents happen, with stupid crews. But stupid is for free men. Slaves and masters are the smartest people alive. Days and years crammed together, watching each other. Waiting for the same moment for different reasons. It makes you fast.

"That mine caved in because Boss Man was angry, or spiteful, or bored.

Or saw something I didn't even understand. Maybe it was a vision from God. The boss was a good church boy, he was an option for those.

"Anyway, like I said. Hot and dark.

"I don't like to fight a wave. If my arms or legs were smashed from the start, I'd have let nature take me to heaven. But I had the truth, and truth makes people strong. Tougher than any muscle or gun. So I started digging. Through dirt and salt and everything else.

"It only hurt for the first hour. Then it was just work. When the pickaxe gave, I used a shovel. Then my gloves, and then my hands.

"Gleas says that here, I should say I found a flake of real gold. Make the story round. Do you think so? He's smarter than his book talk makes him sound. I even think he's starting to see things the way they are.

"There wasn't any gold. From the ninth circle to the first. Like I said, I've never seen the stuff.

"I'm surprised my nails grew back. They look better than my fingertips, if you look close. I might start painting them. I'm too big to get any guff about it.

"Anyway, that's why I'm called Mole. I've also got small eyes, if you look close."

Anders reminded himself to blink and breathe.

"Want me to write that down for you?" asked Anders.

"Hmm? Why?"

"Everything about it is insane."

"No. But I'll repeat it for another fruit stick."

Anders dug out his last segment of dried fruit and one of Wendy's posters. He turned the sheet over to the blank side. Some truths deserved the effort.

27

MOONLIGHTING

Once, before he'd learned to separate questions and faith, Anders had pestered his mother about purgatory. Every alternative to hell sounded worthwhile. After rebaptizing him herself, Katrina defined purgatory as the reason priests went to hell. This didn't help. Later, Anders heard a few thirdhand descriptions of Italian poetry, but he never paid enough attention for a useful picture. Today, labeling Fort Mojave purgatory was more instinct than allusion. Stillness suffocated everything that the heat missed.

Dehydration might have killed him outright a year ago. Now that he'd spent more time bonding with fire, Anders could forgive the sun's increased antagonism. It wasn't there to destroy his home or suppress a people. It was just there.

The fort had been abandoned since the Mexican War, an event Anders assumed Mexico had a better name for. He hadn't memorized that fact on his own. Harrow boosted purgatory to the men himself, praising the fort as the opportunity of their careers. While other brigades fed bodies into a stalemate, the Harriers would distinguish themselves by pacifying local barbarians. When that failed to stir his melting audience's passion, he added that Fort Mojave put miles and walls between them and hostile artillery. That went over better. If one ignored the fort trapping hot air like a giant clay oven, it could be home.

Purgatory still fit better than hell, thanks to the vast nothing surrounding it. They were *doing* a lot: marching in larger and larger circles in search of raiders and finding sand, stubborn wildlife, and cold campfires. The ashes could be a century or a week old, and the company's mix of city freemen and plantation escapees wouldn't have known. Anders gave up on even reporting anything.

"Good," Joaquin had observed. "Bury anything you find. Your army plans a purge, Citizen Anders. One much harsher than the one we just visited."

"Our army."

"Sure."

Fresh off one such pointless search, Anders reflected on those words. They stressed him less than his current task. He stood like a scarecrow in Slade's new cell, holding a bottle of wine more expensive than his life. His attempt to be somebody—and Porter's co-opting of it—had made them both less than butlers. Proper butlers had slick uniforms, specialist pay, and free reign of an estate. Fort Mojave had a few more fleas than most mansions.

An outside observer might confuse the massive room for a mess hall, given the long wooden tables and direct connection to the kitchens. But the space was dedicated to the full-time storage and comfort of Harrow's most valuable prisoner. Random streaks of dust-free flooring suggested a rushed effort to sweep the space.

The wine—something red and Spanish—was part of tonight's entertainment. The general and Slade split a mess hall table. Occasionally, one extended an arm and empty glass. Anders then weighed cracking the bottle across a skull against filling the glass. So far, he'd chosen the glass.

Neither diner focused on the help, which freed Anders and Porter to trade scowls and kicks to the shin. Based on winces, he'd aced the kicking. The trick was adding a little snap each kick, no matter how much his feet stung. That, and Porter carried an unstable tray of half-finished plates. The stacks grew as the somebodies picked at dishes made from different parts of bighorn; the sheep flank and stomach went over well, while the feet went untouched.

"Sorry for the benches," noted Harrow. "The operation should be short, so there's no point replacing everything. Or breaking down your mobile-headquarters contraption. I hope you can bear with us."

Another refill. Slade took his time answering. Whatever he chewed took priority. The general watched him like a loosely chained animal.

"I'm surprised you're still playing at this," said Slade. He scooped a fingertip's worth of deluxe gruel from Harrow's bowl, shuddered, and spat a gray blob onto a napkin. "Don't you have men to shout at? Bodies to pile up?"

"Every day. But hosting fits our giving nature. Which you should remember in future deals. I'm more curious: How long will you 'play at this'? You could've bought your way out by now."

The general extended his arm and shook his cup. Anders let a few drops slosh onto the man's sleeve. Porter hissed a curse, but the red-faced general didn't notice.

"I'm on vacation," explained Slade. "The arrest wrung me out with stress, at least in the moment. Afterward, I realized I haven't taken time for *myself* in some time. That's where new ideas come from."

Slade stuck out his arm. Anders sabotaged the pour again and earned a quick glance from the gunsmith. Sadly, he looked entertained.

"For God's sake, stop," whispered Porter. His powder was more even today, upgrading his presentation from reverse minstrel to founding father.

"Choke," suggested Anders. At first, he'd wondered if Harrow would recognize him. He didn't. Indignation dominated Anders's thoughts and pushed propriety into a memory. "I'm sure Hua Mulan would be proud."

The feud between the help didn't hold their manager's attention. Slade shifted back to Harrow without comment.

"I need fresh scenery, and an army is the safest way to get around. And I have friends in the territory. Your operation to do . . . whatever you're trying to do saves me some money on mercenaries. Inflated market, that one."

"What we're *trying to do* is restore order. The Mohab . . . Mohan . . . Indian raids around here are like clockwork, and command believes they have rebel backing."

"Do they?"

"Who knows? But it's an excellent opportunity for me and the men. Native management is one of the principal responsibilities and joys of the army. And I'm independent. No standing behind Meade and watching him let the enemy slip away."

"Are the 'Harriers' up to it?" asked Slade. He spun his spoon between his fingers, visibly bored.

A familiar indignation swelled Harrow's chest, until dissipating into professional courtesy. Anders filed the image away in his growing register of social cues. Inch by inch, lie by lie, he planned to piece together why people did what they did.

"I've come to realize . . . these are good boys. Not just the near whites and whites, like these two. The blacks have a productive spirit to them that my old men didn't. They'll sing and gamble the downtime away, but when you tell them to do something, it *happens*. I think they learned it in the fields. Maybe our sons would benefit from a little advanced labor."

"I don't have any," said Slade. Then he scrunched up his forehead, searching his memory. "Most likely."

"In either case, New York made me something of a qualified abolitionist. I can finally see the utility of black freedom. They'll use it well, in their way, and the nation will benefit. Once they've earned it by bringing less helpful savages to heel."

"Not sure I see the point. It's . . . I can't pin the word . . ."

"Cruel?"

"Impatient. The best way to get rid of a tribe is building a general store. Then settlers handle the job and pay you for the privilege."

"Life isn't all about money, Mr. Jefferson."

"Truly?"

"Truly."

"I'll give you three thousand dollars to throttle the boy behind you."

"That's one of my men, Mr. Jefferson. I beat them when they do something wrong, or to speed a march along. It can't be arbitrary."

"Good point. Four thousand, and a train gun discount. One of the big phallic ones."

Anders had caught on to the demiurge's sense of humor. By the time the brigadier general pulled out his bench and apologized, Anders had already squared his stance, braced for a blow, and privately sworn revenge. A wedding band and West Point class ring sat on the general's right hand. Unfortunate.

Instead, the general approached Porter. Before Anders's spiteful mind could veto it, his hands acted. He let his bottle fall, scattering cheap glass and expensive wine. The noise successfully captured both men's attention, along with the green shards dotting their meals.

"Sorry, sir. Sirs. I'll clean up and take the hit. Or just clean up, if that's all right. Cleaning up is like a beating, in a way, but for the spirit. And I can still march and fight and the like after it."

The gunsmith's laughter returned, cutting off Harrow's reaction. It still had the naked glee reserved for children and sanitariums. Harrow froze, transfixed. His guest enjoyed life more than anyone else in the room or country.

Porter, for his part, did a better job of hiding his reaction. But he kept a neutral stare locked on Anders instead of the threat standing between them. He mouthed one word—either *banks* or *tanks*—and stood at attention.

"You seem chuffed, Mr. Jefferson," said Harrow. He lowered his arm and sank back onto his bench. "You got your laugh. We can skip any unnecessary thrashings."

The gap between the general's pride and performance was closing. Anders almost felt proud to be a Harrier.

"Oh no, definitely beat both of them. Railway guns are the only reason Lee hasn't renamed Boston, and I know that's worth a backhand swing. But I appreciate the spirit. A few good strikes, and then we can get a replacement bottle. And talk about some men I think you could do without."

✦ ✦ ✦

"Quite the black eye," said Joaquin. "The old man must stay fit."

Anders demoted Fort Mojave from purgatory to hell. For the first time in months, he had a solid roof and uncanned food on hand. It just cost him his pride. The old man *did* have a strong backhand, and now he and Porter matched. While heroism had been out of reach before, there'd been less active indignity.

Tonight, he couldn't even enjoy the roof. There were Vital Orders. Each step took his aching body a step farther from a soft bed. The waning moon provided just enough light to make every stray stone a potential fall.

He trudged over dead grass with Joaquin, on yet another meandering scouting run. The officers had dotted a map in black squares, marking spots they believed hid raiders, could hide raiders, or looked like decent cover from the sun.

Tonight, Joaquin was tasked with moving slowly and silently between them, in order to avoid scaring potential prey away. Anders, in charge of morale, spun dutifully behind him. His orders also included singing, which Joaquin had dissuaded with gentle threats.

The first five squares had marked sand, an empty ridge, an abandoned farm, a romantic pair of cattle skulls, and sand. Optimism didn't run high for square six. Especially when Joaquin seasoned each conversation with a new insult.

"You should go back to your mother."

"She almost killed me." It was the one card he hadn't tried.

"Was she good at it? If not, you should go back."

"I'm not an infant," said Anders, wounded. "I saved New York, you know."

"An odd choice."

"I'm serious. Without me, the riot would have been a siege."

"Good. The paler neighborhoods needed more violence. And that affair was too disorganized for a true uprising. They didn't build a *single* barricade. Revolutionaries should know more strategy, and a boy should know more history."

A boy, again. Anders stopped halfway through the *Shiloh Step*, half for effect and half out of exhaustion. "Why don't you respect me?"

"I do. I tell you exactly what I'm thinking. You do the same with me, which I enjoy. It drifts into patriotic nonsense or sad equivocation, but there's a charm to it. I see why Gleason and the Traitor both keep you as their monkey."

Monkey. In the tradition of men without an argument, Anders spat to the side. He regretted losing the moisture.

"I thought it was funny."

"I'm the first white man in America to be called a monkey by a Black man."

"Mmm. Your country might survive. Though it'll have to get there without me."

"I don't follow."

"Want to run away again?"

"Don't mock me."

"No mockery. I'm leaving. I know what white armies—and that's what we're in, as long as Harrow sits above us—do with outsiders' families. Miserable work. No wonder they're training Blacks to do it."

A half-dead voice in Anders started mouthing *What happens?* Then he remembered the city, and Wendy, and the simple demented clarity of her followers.

"Why not one of the others?"

"They're this pit's first Black soldiers, I doubt any would leave. Not even Thomas. Whatever that play said, they still want to fight for something. They're just waiting for Citizen Gleason to invent it. Which he might, in a decade. But you're working genocide *now*. Nothing that happens here will free one slave."

"I'm with him too. I don't *understand* half of it, but I'm with him."

"Yes, but by choice. You have options. Much easier to reverse. Which you should, before the massacres start."

Anders borrowed Patricia's strongest accusatory stance. Having a friend his age had been educational, however brief. Crossing both arms made him *feel* ridiculous, but hopefully it *looked* confident. The flag could only help.

"You're lying, with the truth. Why me?"

Joaquin nodded. "Travel here's easier with white company. And you have desertion experience. Don't worry about deciding now. I should be ready in a week."

Anders let his half of the discussion die. The last co-defector he'd trusted had bruised his rib cage and ego. And they'd taken *much* less glee in violence. If Joaquin turned on him on the road, he'd be buried there.

The acute silence lasted for hours, across three more haphazard map marks. Presuming, of course, the aspiring deserter had led them on course. They could be halfway to Canada for all Anders knew. He noted six different colors of scorpion on the way and resolved to double-check his bedding going forward. They didn't hand out red badges for poison.

Most (but not all) thoughts of venom faded when they crested the next hill. The skeleton of a camp broke up the repeating desert scenery. Six women fought against the wind to keep a fire going, while a child watched from the sidelines, embarrassed. The boy drummed his fingers together, unsure what to do with his hands while the others did proper work.

Anders didn't see himself in the boy. First off, he was a proper man. Even if Harrow's nurses looked through him or laughed at him. He contributed vital *national dressage*, and semi-single-handedly stopped the madwoman who taught him that term. He had one-point-five kills. Seeing himself in the boy would be inane.

Joaquin dropped to a crawl. Then he crept forward, half inch by half inch, until he reached a yucca plant tall enough to cover his prone form. After mulling this high-effort process over, Anders opted to walk over and sit down. Keeping their fire alive had to be more interesting than two distant stragglers, and his bottomless well of motivation had bottomed out in the mess hall.

Agitated, Joaquin then flashed several incomprehensible hand signs. After dutifully waiting for him to give up, Anders asked the natural question.

"Our raiders?" Anders asked.

"No," said Joaquin. "Perhaps the fighters fled the territory once an army train full of blaring bugles and spinning flags thundered in. Or some other calamity arrived. These are leftovers."

"They could be fighters. In fact, my pet theory is that most women can fight. I'm tired of fighting, and women excel at everything I don't. The logic follows from there. That, and I saw a woman shoot a monarchist agitator last week. It was excessive, so you would've loved it."

"I thought that was you."

"No, I defeated her in symbolic warfare. That was the important part."

"I can't begin to understand what that means. But everyone *here* is ancient or knee-high. They're losing a battle with a campfire."

Anders scratched at his black eye, delivered by a man past his prime. Still, he saw Joaquin's point. The group below didn't look ready to antagonize any war machine. Difficult, given their duty to bring the war machine to them.

"Ready to report in? We have our target."

Anders collected his courage. Reserves were low, so he borrowed some on credit.

"I don't think we should."

"Good, I thought I'd have to gut you. You look like a bleeder. And screamer. No offense."

Anders took offense.

"Let's head back, Citizen Anders. We can pinch some real food from the officers."

28

WHEN MORALE FAILS, THE ENEMY PREVAILS

Another morning where his arms felt like limp rags and his legs felt like lead; the same bedding that made desert nights livable (just one scorpion so far) now threatened to melt him. He still struggled to toss it off. Leaving bed invited fresh disappointment.

Anders tried to recapture some positivity. Morale was his medium, and he was a *recognized* master. But after his recruitment as Slade's doorman and doormat, informal work under Gleason dried up. The cult of personality adopted an open door policy, and the director could be seen chatting with anyone and everyone. Except Anders.

A cynic might assume the director had either abandoned him, felt betrayed, or simply lost interest. As a morale artist, Anders should have buried the thought like the national memory of 1812. But it lingered, like the burnt remnants of the original White House.

That shouldn't have been his first reference. Proper flag-twirlers dwelled on victories, real or imagined. Wendy Ross hadn't dwelled on the failures of monarchy. If he doubted his side's martial honor, fixing the family record would be impossible, which made the director's silence all the worse. Unpaid gatekeeping didn't have glamour, but it reflected some light from the budding cult of personality back on Anders. He'd believed in The American Future before it was popular.

The problem was clear: he knew too much. Experience undermined his carefully constructed frame and made his dream for the war look impossible. Worse yet, *small*. He resolved to find a cure for knowledge. Right after rechecking his bedding for scorpions. And resolving whatever menial indignities Slade had lined up for the day. And food.

First, food. Much more reliable than friends.

With the mess hall reserved for their betters, the men ate in the armory. Anders sidestepped the main crowd, who sat on boxes of ammunition long depleted or forgotten by their predecessors. They were engrossed in Thomas's side hustle: lice fight betting—less flamboyant than chickens but much more portable for gambling addicts on the move. They'd shoved the boxes into an oval, making something like a ring.

An enterprising soul could probably sell the crates back to the Union—an idea Anders would pitch Slade, if treatment improved. Either way, the rusted cannon by the window looked like a more inviting perch. No more comfortable, but mounting the dead artillery put him a few valuable feet above the others. With whiteness losing more shine the longer he served, every inch mattered.

"Hey."

Thomas's voice, and thus unimportant. Anders kept chewing.

"Hey, 'Bryce.' Wake up."

"Grmph," Anders grunted, mouth full.

"All right, sorry for calling you 'Cyclops' yesterday. Your black eye looks distinguished, or whatever ofay nonsense cheers you up."

"Brmph!"

"Sorry for calling you an ofay."

"Tmph."

"And a boogeyman. Look, I'm running tonight. If you want in, be at the bend in the river an hour after sundown."

"Lmph?"

"I've got a partner. One you'll trust."

Anders swallowed. Then he checked for eavesdroppers, a precaution Thomas evidently found old-fashioned. Rookie mistake.

"Didn't take you for a deserter. Well, I did, but not one brave enough to follow through."

Thomas looked behind him, about thirty seconds too late. Fortunately, the others were tied up by the main event. "Little Stonewall" defended an undefeated streak against "The 1-2-3 Bug." Scrapping with the champion was a death sentence, but life with the Harriers provided a bottomless supply of replacement challengers.

"Listen, I joined to shoot Virginians and impress some abolitionist skirts," replied Thomas. "I'm not achieving either here. Besides, I thought Lee would've run out of people or food by now."

Several critiques came to mind. But it sounded better than traveling with Joaquin and Joaquin's knife.

"I might be there. Either way, be more discreet. No more talking about 'it' directly, with or without an audience."

"Gotcha. I won't say *deserting* again. Or *desert*, or *desertion*."

Anders let it go. He'd made bigger gaffes, more often, and likely would again. And they might have to go a long way together.

✣ ✣ ✣

His new paymaster (though no notes or coins had changed hands) took breakfast at noon. Anders carried an aged bottle of high-proof breakfast down the western corridor, toward the mess hall. He also pretended not to notice Hobbes staring at him, primarily because he didn't care. Then the lieutenant hopped into his path, nearly tripping with the effort.

"Afternoon, Hobbes," said Anders. Hopefully the man felt better than he looked. He'd never seen a sober man with eyes that bloodshot. Ideally some kind of snuff was to blame, and not simple continuous sobbing.

"Afternoon, *Lieuten*— Ah, forget it. It's come to my attention that this might not be your first company or tour. Or side of the war. Is that true?"

Anders tested the bottle's weight and found satisfactory heft. A good swing, perhaps with a hint of a *Franklin Retreat* in the wrist, ought to knock out and/or kill the lieutenant. Then he could lay low until the rendezvous, or hide behind Slade until money made the problem disappear. Even if he lost the struggle, it'd be his word against a Negro. Officer or not, that had one likely ending.

"No denials? Good, because I need to slip out of the company. Just for a year, or maybe four. However long it takes the bread riots down south to get serious."

Anders eased his grip and smiled. No smashing yet.

"You mean *east*. All that's south of us now is former Mexico and current Mexico."

"That's a very important distinction, and not pedantic. Thank you," said Hobbes, with a depressing lack of sarcasm. "Please help me. You can tell me more important distinctions along the way. At length."

Whatever floated through the beleaguered lieutenant's head was a mystery. But Anders grasped patterns, and a bizarre one had found him.

"You have a partner, right?"

"I do! Is that enough? I can't stay here. Being the first Black anything is hell. The enlisted men ignore me and blame it on the officers. The officers steal my food and blame it on the enlisted men. I overheard the general—he wants me to lead the next charge. Unarmed."

"Maybe." Anders uncorked Slade's breakfast and offered the poor man a swig. Without hesitation, Hobbes pulled from the bottle like a spring in the desert. The backwash would make a nice gift for Slade.

✦ ✦ ✦

Passersby with sense gave Joaquin's nook space. This made finding him easy: he was wherever the others weren't. A trick worth stealing, if they lived long enough after fleeing duty for a lesson.

Anders found him half dozing, half awake in a captain's missing hammock. No one had complained, likely due to the bayonet-fixed rifle that lay flat across Joaquin's chest. The chipped and bent bayonet had seen enough action to look shoddy, the most terrifying condition a blade could have.

Still, Anders's mouth had its own will.

"You've been shinning around."

"I don't know what that means. This is my third language, Citizen Anders."

"How many people did you pull into this?"

"None."

"Claptrap. More soldiers have talked to me today than my entire rebel tour. They're all deserting, and they all have a mysterious partner."

"Sounds like an empty joke. I, on the other hand, found a serious partner for our journey."

"And you're meeting at the bend in the river."

"Precisely."

"About an hour after dark?"

"Right again. But it'll be on American time, so you can come a little later."

"Good luck."

✢ ✢ ✢

Anders hauled Slade's leftover dinner (lunch? The time left to ask was shrinking), a small barrel of liquor older than the fort, down the stairs.

"Bryce! Over here."

Anders kept walking. Anyone using his original cover name was an acquaintance or Dan Rice wannabe.

"Just one second. It's me, friend."

"Hello . . . friend?"

"I'm Boots. From that game of Ofay. And I—"

"Deserting?"

". . . Yes."

"Bend in the river?"

"Right again."

"I'll see you there," lied Anders. Now the trip sounded too crowded for his taste. A chain was as strong as its most loyally disloyal link. And no culture gap would let him call an adult *Boots*.

✢ ✢ ✢

In one hour, whittling became Anders's favorite hobby. It taxed him less than twirling or acting and took less discretion than onanism. He used the same Indian caricature knife he'd won after re-reenlisting. It could be a waste of a sharp blade, but he planned to avoid hand-to-hand combat for the rest of his life.

Like any new pursuit, it began with failure. He tried carving his mental image of his father (a face that resembled his own, plus a thriving beard). The wood refused to cooperate. Now he aspired to make a spoon. The handle was too wide and the scoop too small, and he treasured it. Even the best performances evaporated as soon as they were finished, and his malformed spoon would last longer than many enlisted men.

"S'cuse." The voice still had the depth and force of shale breaking. God willing, Anders would have something similar when his voice stopped cracking.

"You're deserting," said Anders. He didn't look up from his work.

Mole nodded.

"You want me to help."

Another nod.

"And meet you and your partner by the bend in the river."

Mole clapped.

"I'll poke my head in," said Anders. He had bigger ideas. Going straight from slave to soldier meant Mole hadn't tasted real freedom. While Anders hadn't mastered every aspect of adult life yet, he knew enough. If they felt productive, they could go after Mole's family. If they didn't feel productive, the *Headquarters, USA* brothels were legendary in both armies. If they felt *extra* productive, they could go after God.

Whatever they chose, it was an open path to adventure. They just had to cross a few hundred miles of manifest destiny and army checkpoints. Perhaps on a raft, along the Mississippi, sharing the vagaries of white and Black experience. It had potential.

✦ ✦ ✦

Tracking down his friend/acquaintance/enemy took some work. Evidently Petey and Porter had cots on opposite sides of the fort and divided their presence between both. Moreover, whispers described an unfamiliar Black girl joining the nurses during meals and disappearing during crises.

Anders settled on camping in front of Petey's cot. A triple life sounded heavy on costume changes, so they'd have to stop by the sack of varied clothing and powders eventually. Polly's wig was still in there, along with everything they'd lifted from the guard. Poking through anyone's things should have left Anders feeling guilty, but his ribs still hurt.

This time, his intuition bore fruit: Petey returned in a panic and nearly failed to notice him in the rush to apply this evening's skin tone. Anders whistled, and the musician froze. Once again, the male personas' timidity irritated Anders. Men weren't *all* cowards. Just most of them, potentially including himself.

Neither spoke. They stood in a stalemate, projecting reproach and suppressing guilt.

As the wronged party and the product in demand, Anders clearly didn't need to apologize. But seeing Petey's wounded expression (and lingering wounds) inspired him to try the next best thing: pretending nothing happened.

"Deserting?" asked Anders.

"Maybe."

"Good for you."

"Thanks."

"You should be fine."

"I will."

"You don't even need an expert."

"I don't."

Back to stalemate. The road ahead was split between feeling vindicated and communicating the thoughts stampeding through his head. The example of every man he knew—along with his mother—pointed toward vindication. None of them seemed notably happy. Anders let his confrontation stance (a pose lifted from Patricia) slip.

"Listen. You didn't have to crack my rib cage to do it, but I get why you threw in with Slade. You did half the work in New York—the murder doesn't count, that was unnecessary—and I tried to cut you out. If you're deserting like everyone else here, I'll go. We commit good treason together."

"Did you ask the white nurse first?" she asked, icily.

"No. Is she going? Do you know her name? How desertion-friendly do you think she is?"

Petey departed.

✣ ✣ ✣

Whether Anders stayed or left, his service record was an open secret. More men in the company knew his history than how to read, and he remained firing squad–free.

That opened up his options a little.

For the first time, he didn't *walk* or *shuffle* or *creep* toward the mess hall. He skipped. The revolver in his grip felt light as silk and twice as soft. His resurrected cloud of cheer even had the old effect: no one troubled Anders over the loaded firearm. Thomas tipped a hat as he passed, a gesture Anders returned with a guileless bow.

He knocked twice on the mess hall door, reconsidered, and kicked it open. It was time for his second murder. Debatably third. After a week of forced servitude, he couldn't imagine why the Blacks waited so long to make a fuss.

Anders weighed several stage-worthy lines for his entrance, including

"Hey, boss," "You forgot your gun," "Dinner's ready," "I quit," and "I'm here to shoot you." But his only witness would be dead in seconds, so he decided to enjoy the act itself. He didn't have much experience, but he expected this to feel much better than Wendy.

Inside, the mess hall had picked up several new features: three over-turned tables, a pool of dried blood, and no Slade. Against a lifetime of steadfast conditioning, Anders pouted. He had five rounds and nowhere to put them.

His prey had either escaped or been stolen. Yet the cloud of energy, cleaner and clearer than any found in the pews, didn't dissipate. Even *attempted* murder meant he'd survived making a choice, and that other choices were possible. He sidled over to one of Slade's half-finished bottles and drained the leftovers. Pleasant warmth and numbness fell over his face. Bourbon could join whittling on his new list of hobbies.

He left to collect his things.

28.5

ADVANCED ZOOLOGY

PAT'S NOTES
observations on hiding among white ghosts

general principles

-no one impressed by reading
-most crimes easier
-odd lingering nervous feeling
-odd lingering guilty feeling
-don't sneeze, chalk flies off

useful maneuvers

-stand near productive Negroes to get praise for their work
-stand near unproductive Negroes to get praise for your work
-stand away from Negroes to get praise for sticking to your own
-stand among Negroes to get praise for your tolerance
-learn subgroups of white (west of Paris good, east bad)

white manhood

-honor very important
-unclear what honor does

-honor enhancers: military rank, confirmed kills, fistfights (victorious),
   large guns, moonshine, full moons, multiple hidden lady friends
-honor destroyers: doubt, fear, retreat, admitting fear, surviving retreat,
   fistfights (failed), general survival, tears
-find way to fake facial hair

white womanhood

-presumed harmless, like house cat
-generally resented, like house cat
-more babble about honor
-honor can't be gained, but is easily lost
-men behave less demonically, more devilishly

advanced notes

-people still don't listen
-your feelings still don't matter
-men still prefer nurses
-aristocrats still own you
-all life is tiring
-guns: always helpful

29

NEW DIRECTIONS

The general's Indian-hunting map showed six notable local bends in the river. Anders *guessed* that at least one conspirator meant the closest but accepted that he might find no one.

Solitude could be a blessing, aside from surviving the desert. In his month watching Clyburn harangue enlisted men for breathing loudly, Anders identified a new and unexplored social phenomenon: Black men attracted extra suspicion. From bringing codes to Harrow to stomping around Manhattan with Petey, Black company made simple lies twice as difficult. He suspected that fleshing out his theory with the right jargon could build him a future in letters. Which was a *type* of heroism, and underexplored. Abolitionist papers would have to talk about *something* if they won.

Burning apartments and people barged into his mind's eye, uninvited. Topics wouldn't be hard to find.

Painting the future took his mind off of his feet, and the nurse gaffe. Both stung, though one wasn't his fault. He'd split profits with whoever showed up. Shortchanging them would be a poor start to his abolitionist career. All he had to do now was learn to write good. *Well.* Write *well*.

He dragged his flagpole behind him and let it sway. An old trick from his first desertion. The flag's gentle arcs over the dust obscured the most egregious footprints, without forcing him to stop every other step to perfect it. The small precaution lent him peace of mind, until he ran into a pair of wholly unobscured tracks. One trail sat deeper, as if the owner had stomped the whole way in defiance of stealth itself.

"Amateurs," he muttered before speeding up to a jog. Doubling back to sweep both trails would take fatal time. If counter-tracking was out, he could at least have speed.

Anders approached the riverbank without trampling any scorpions, despite their artful diffusion along his path. Each stood taller than a sane world would allow and boasted a prominent death-tipped tail. Giant, black explanation points for the desire to live. A sign of what he'd escaped, whether Deists believed in omens or not.

He spied Mole first, which was a relief. The Mississippi raft idea still crackled with untapped potential, and it'd be a shame to leave it behind. Mole currently looked less stoic and more uneasy, which was perfectly correct. Anything else courted calamity.

Then he spied Joaquin. Less of a relief. No desertion needed a partner that enjoyed bayonets and cannon fire. Just looking at him made Anders's lifespan feel shorter.

"Hello, Young Anders."

"Eat sand," Anders *thought*. He *said*, "Hey. So, this is your partner?"

"Citizen Mole? No. I'm surprised to see him, but excited. I have the seed of a scheme, with a boat and your Mississippi River."

"Really? Me too."

"Excellent! Then we'll become pirates."

"No," Anders thought, then said, and then repeated, "Where's your partner? We should be gone."

"Patience," said Mole.

More enlisted men trickled in. Thomas. Three dozen other familiar faces. Boots, who was reportedly familiar. Quiet fear of a trap dissipated in favor of naked fear that they'd all gone mad at once. Anders's second great theory concerned war: he suspected that rather than bringing out a man's inner grit, most battles brought out hallucinations and trembling at loud noises. He explained as much to Mole.

"Patience," Mole repeated, before embracing Boots like a long-lost brother.

Patience led to Petey trotting in on a horse that wasn't his. It could belong to the gunsmith tied to the back of said horse. Slade lay still, with an active and heavily bleeding head wound. Petey winked at Anders, as if the abduction settled everything between them. Galling. They were feuding. This was a feud.

"A fancy hostage sounded useful. Smart, right?"

"They'll come for him." Anders could feel himself getting older. The finer points of the supremacy he'd shed inch by painful inch started making sense again. Every Negro he knew was mad.

"They'll come for us anyway," countered Petey. He poked the very conscious Slade, who currently suffered under an unhealthy amount of rope. Anders, who merely planned to kill him, felt a pang of guilt. "Now we can bargain."

Insanity looked more likely by the moment. By the time Anders settled on deserting the desertion, the entire company had assembled, save Gleason. Nearly a hundred enlisted men. It fit that a man of letters would be sanity's last holdout. When Anders got back to Fort Mojave, he'd pitch Gleason his theory on Black suspicion. Letting someone else deal with words, which still abandoned Anders at inconvenient moments, was worth half credit.

Gleason picked that moment to join the open-air sanitarium.

His appearance violated a number of Deist norms. Addressing a flock of anything in the desert was questionable. Along with clutching a book to his chest as he spoke, even if it held his own string-bound notes. His crispier left flank resembled the luckiest priest to offend Nebuchadnezzar. Coincidence, irony, and utility could only cover for so much prophetic fashion.

"Thank you all for coming," he said, splitting his gaze between his notes and the public. "This is a risk for all of us. Unprecedented, for most of us. So I approached you as individuals. There's a chance to find or make the real America."

Anders slid toward the front and then shoved. The codes had been his discovery, or at least his homework. He deserved a good view of the chapter in history they'd opened. Alongside, ideally, an explanation for being frozen out.

"I made a mistake in New York. Not the original play, or the new ending. I meant every word of *The Living Abacus*, both times. But I was myopic. I treated the pain like it belonged to me. But it's every Black soldier, civilian, and slave's pain. Mostly the slave's, I should note. Almost entirely the slave's. Moving on.

"All our lives, we've given love to a nation with none for us. Except for

Anders. We've fought for freedom we should have been born with. Except for Anders. Of late, we've killed for a nation that would hang us for sport. Except for Anders. Now we have a chance for something else. A fresh start, where the new humanity can chart its course. And that includes Anders, who I'm proud to call my third white friend."

Anders tried to get some applause going. This was clearly an address for the ages.

"Hold on, I'm not done.

"Due west is San Valentin. The source of the communiqués and codes I've collected, reported, and had ignored. The reason entire rebel regiments have disappeared from our doomed struggle in the mud. And yes, the flag half the rioters in Manhattan saluted. It can be their place, or ours.

"I'm willing to try it. Whatever it is. There's an America unstained by cotton, celebration of its own greatness, or the madness that that contradiction breeds. A place where we have a chance. Whoever delivers that can call themselves queen, king, or Christ. I've learned that freedom means more than watching someone else vote and hoping you get your turn.

"If any of you betrayed my confidence, I'd already be dead. If you're here, you're a patriot. A believer. A fundamentalist of The American Future.

"You took a leap of faith into this war. Take one more with me. Never be anyone's nigger again."

He'd never been a leading man. Gleason's hands shook as he moved through the address. He stumbled over *celebration* twice and took a long pause before forging through the rest of the speech. He said *nigger* with the awkward lilt of someone who never touched the word in jest, anger, or habit. In essence, he spoke with the clumsy foundation of someone who believed their words. If any performance hid behind it, it deserved equal loyalty.

With no words left, Gleason took his first steps west. Without a better idea, Anders darted ahead to join him. He didn't know if he was first, though he'd tell the story that way later. He did reach the director's flank first and took the chance to ask the first of several dozen questions.

"Why didn't you invite me?" asked Anders.

"It's treason. I knew you'd be here."

30

ROLLING DOWNHILL

They were spotted and encircled by morning. Fifty infantrymen propelled by fear, determination, and opium pills encircled the caravan. A handful of Black faces were familiar—another company of Harriers.

Anders weighed jumping in the river. The current looked strong, but so was lead. Swimming couldn't be *too* hard. Then he heard Gleason's voice and spat a curse he didn't understand. French? He must have cribbed it from Joaquin.

"Anders," repeated Gleason, hideously serene. "Could you follow me? Bring paper."

"I don't have any," said Anders, suppressing *"They're going to kill us."*

The director fished out his own notebook, along with a tooth-scarred pencil. "Write down everything you can, going forward. I expect it to matter later."

Later. What later? Corpses didn't have later. Anders bent his knees, picked a clear spot in the water, and followed Gleason. The man looked and sounded possessed. Logic said he was possessed. Maybe the devil had a plan.

They beelined for the circle's one visible horse. The other defectors eyed their suicide, baffled. Anders pretended not to see Petey or hear her say "Run." At least he'd die ahead in their feud.

The officer looked more nonplussed. Two unarmed traitors approached, one with imperial confidence. Anders stuck to the rear, painfully aware of following a man that had sprinted into open flames.

"You head nigger?" asked the officer, scratching a struggling beard. His free hand tapped a pistol.

"We don't have a head," answered Gleason.

That honest lie invited a question, and then another, until the pace became a burden. Anders jotted down what he could and invented the rest. The experience invited questions about every transcription he'd ever read.

"A queen?" said the captain. "I've never seen one."

"A queen," confirmed Gleason. "And a chance to *be* John Brown."

The captain beamed, staring past them at his destiny. Then he nodded. He signed his men into legend or death with heroic, lunatic ease. Another dreamer. Anders missed that manic faith.

They had fifty new men.

A once-in-a-lifetime miracle, until forty cavalry surrounded the caravan. Gleason walked Anders into another suicide and walked out with forty cavalry.

Another general might have left it there. Daily massacres simplified hiding shirkers. But a third wave followed half a day later, and the fourth wasn't far behind. The caravan swelled to the size of a proper, pre-attrition regiment. Anders transcribed each negotiation and found them getting *shorter*. Company leaders (or the men who shot them) described Harrow's state in terms reserved for angry gods. Reportedly, only the promise of revenge kept him out of a sanitarium.

"I hope he sends cooks after us," mused Thomas. "Or some of the looser nurses."

The next group *did* have cooks in tow, armed and deployed out of raw desperation. Sensing momentum, Thomas then wished for three houses, four acres, five mules, and one wife. Nothing manifested. The caravan simply inched forward, spiting reason.

31

HEATSTROKE

The sun lacked zeal for the movement. Reactionary heat fell with biblical cruelty.

"Anti-abolitionist," Anders muttered at the sun. "Backward. Bigoted. It's 1863, we're all pretending to be abolitionists now. You're on the wrong side of history, and people will only vote for you in secret. Your mother's proud of you, which means good people are ashamed."

"Is the boy all right?" asked Joaquin.

Anders, who was all right, stuck out his tongue. What did Haitians know about heat? Was Haiti hot? He should read something about Haiti, or at least ask Gleason. Where was Gleason taking them? Did he know? Did the burned parts of his face still hurt?

"Definitely," said Mole. "That pain lingers."

"I said that out loud?"

Mole nodded.

For some reason, the pair kept funneling him water. When he wouldn't drink more, they poured it on him. It was vexing: he'd settle into a cozy darkness, the kind he could enjoy forever, and then be dragged back to the light by lukewarm liquid. And Joaquin would be sharper with him each time.

"Keep moving," ordered the infiltrator. Like he was in charge.

"You're not my father," said Anders. "I think."

A slap, then more forced water. He knew Joaquin couldn't be trusted.

A longer, and more pleasing episode of darkness found him. Unwanted water woke him again, but with an unexpected bonus: he was floating. His body floated forward without a hint of effort from his limbs.

"I've achieved flight," said Anders. "Tell Petey, or Patricia. Neither of the white ones, they don't know how to treat people."

"Okay," said Mole. The giant adjusted his grip, which currently hooked into Anders's pocket. Reality dawned on Anders against his will.

There'd be some dignity to the back of a horse, or even Mole's shoulder. But he was tucked under the giant's arm like a large book or small dog. Anders thrashed his legs around for several violent seconds before exhausting himself and going limp.

"You're worn out," Joaquin said, matter-of-factly. "Heatstroke, or fever. Or some obscure vapors."

"Why aren't the others?"

"You're a child."

"I'm not . . . So's Petey!"

"Petey stole a horse."

Stealing a horse! Brilliant. Infantry life had trained him to take suffering on foot for granted. The next time he defected, he'd nab a horse.

"The next time?" said Joaquin, amused.

Anders clasped his hands around his mouth. His own thoughts were defecting. Any of his secrets could leak out, like his attempt to murder Slade, a designated prisoner of war.

"Excellent. Bring me next time."

A retort died on his lips. Then Anders's mind went as limp as his body and tumbled back into darkness. The pleasing void lasted for a long-overdue hour, until a rude interruption by a dream. A renegade fringe of his consciousness refused to accept the gentle exit life had generously offered.

The vision skipped past recent mainstays in Cemetery Ridge and Manhattan and settled on Liberty Valley. Anders occupied his old chair in his old house—which matched his current definition of *shack*. That couldn't be right. It had to be a distortion of the dream world. His mother provided everything a child could want and reminded him whenever it was in doubt.

"What are you doing?" asked Katrina. He'd missed that accusatory tone.

"Sleeping, but awake. Lucid-like," answered Anders. "Most of my dreams are like that. It takes some fun out of the lady dreams but some terror out of battle dreams. I don't know how to handle the angels yet."

"Hogwash. Stay away from that windchime teacher. She always sends you back with something that doesn't make sense."

"Okay."

"You're a good boy," said Katrina. "That's my half speaking. Or the housebroken part of your daddy."

"Like a dog?"

"Yes. Could you fetch some water?"

Anders peered out the window and found the sun halfway set. A relief. She was pacing herself.

"Yes, Mama." Anders marched to the whiskey shelf. More of a whiskey *stool*, by his updated standards. The small round chair held four bottles of brown-to-green liquor generously labeled WHISKEY. They were alphabetized, making the whiskey stool the most precisely organized part of the house/shack. Bunyan's Brewery stood out, thanks to the label's grinning bull.

Katrina had dozed off by his return. Did figments have their own dreams? Anders picked at the question while trying a sip of Bunyan's. Weaker than he'd expected.

He watched his mother snore and let time fall away. If Anders made it back home, he'd tell her a more heroic version of Manhattan. One where he'd pulled the trigger himself, or not at all. Half-measures had dragged the country into the war in the first place. He'd be selective with the details: Katrina would be happy to hear about Polly and mortified by Petey's other faces. Though from Anders's perch, four friends his age was infinite progress.

She dozed over a worn, dog-eared scrap of paper. He'd seen hints of it before—it was her main non-Bible reading. Indulging lifelong curiosity, Anders reached for the scrap.

Just a drawing. Strikingly realistic—he'd been too small to appreciate Katrina's talent before running off. He'd tripped into half-finished sketches of landscapes and neighbors while searching the shack for fresh food. This was a complete effort.

A Black man with Anders's face held a baby. Curious. The Negro wore a loose-fit uniform. Less kempt than a Union set but more coherent than the rebellion's make-do uniforms. The kind a sheriff might wear. Or mercenary.

Nothing important.

He wadded up the drawing and let it fall. Imaginations were independent entities with traitorous inclinations. Only speculative playwrights had any use for them.

If he had a Black father, why would he look the way he did? Why would numbers come so naturally? Why would he struggle to connect with the Harriers? None of it fit. Even faking negritude had taken brilliant effort, and failed. The sketch was either his cannonball-shaken psyche or Katrina's whiskey.

Besides, from what he'd seen, Negroes were a close-knit group. What Black father would disappear on his family? It had to be heatstroke.

The naked, barbarous lie of it ignited his spirit. He couldn't die in a slanderous daydream. He'd just stepped away from the war and saved his own life. It took forever to learn that flags were just ornaments for flagpoles. Why trade his life for even less than that now?

"Water," wheezed Anders.

"You heard him," said Joaquin. The stream hit before he was ready.

The caravan had either paused for the night or given up. Someone had laid Anders over a blanket, which he'd drenched in panic sweat and normal sweat. Mole held a freshly emptied canteen, while Joaquin prodded Anders's side with a sheathed knife. Both looked as concerned as men were allowed to look.

"Citizen Anders?"

"Urgh," grunted Anders.

"You thrashed like a drowning man. And not just when we dunked you in the river. What were you dreaming about?"

"Nothing different. White man's burdens. You wouldn't understand. Shut up, nigger."

Joaquin threw his hands up and walked off, cursing in another language. Mole stayed behind, prying at one of the last cans of beef from Fort Mojave. And laughing. Anders didn't appreciate the laughter, which could only be at his or the sand's expense.

"Is something funny, nigger?"

"Nothing, brother."

Anders rolled the blanket over his head.

31.5

SPYCRAFT

    I. Success: Infiltrated brigade as nurse. If message received, leave call sign in dirt.

    II. Success: Call sign found. Note: drawn incorrectly. More later.

    III. Update: Surgery difficult. More later.

    IV. Failure: Multiple surgical fatalities. Fear cover compromised. More later.

    V. Failure: Advances on Harrow rebuffed. Cited marriage, age. More later.

    VI. Success: Lack of surgical acuity typical and expected. More later.

    VII. Success: Advances on Harrow accepted. Marriage and age irrelevant. More later.

    VIII. Disaster: Longstreet's men cut down in baffling charge. Requesting explanation or extraction. More later.

    IX. Disaster: Jefferson Firearms plant and proprietor captured. More later.

    X. Request: Update cypher. Bookish negro found codebreaker. More later.

    XI. Fortune: Meade moving east, riots in New York. More later.

    XII. Jubilation: New York burns. More later.

    XIII. Update: The fire has dimmed. Still awaiting cypher. More later.

    XIV. Update: The negroes are putting together a play. More later.

    XV. Update: The play was okay. More later.

XVI. Success: Connected with Slade Jefferson. More later.

XVII. Success: Munitions order made. More later.

XVIII. Request: Updated cypher *still* not received. More later.

XIX. Update: Headed west. Nevada. Standard Indian purge. More later.

XX. Update: Hot. Crowded. Nothing happening. More later.

XXI. Update: Still hot. Still crowded. Nothing happening. More later.

XXII. Update: Attempting elimination of codebreaker. More later.

XXIII. Failure: Codebreaker missing, along with company. More later.

XXIV. Failure. Slade Jefferson missing. New ordnance order not made. More later.

XXV. Update: General panic. General panicking as well. More later.

XXVI. Major Update: Multiple company defections. More later.

XXVII. Update: Harrow apoplectic. More later.

XXVIII. Update: Harrow in tears. More later.

XXIX. Update: Harrow apoplectic again. More later.

XXX. Update: Heart episode likely. Or mind episode. Some kind of episode. More later.

XXXI. Major Update: McClellan reinstated and incoming. More later.

XXXII. Request: UPDATE. THE. CYPHER. More AFTER CYPHER UPDATE.

32

THE OTHER CITY OF LOVE

The caravan made its final approach in maddening silence. No lead rained from San Valentin's outer walls or the more imposing batteries on the inner ring. No army thundered out the gates. The city offered no opinions on their status as invaders, friends, or refugees. Half of Anders wished for a clarifying gunshot.

Half curious, half skittish, Anders polled everyone in sight about the frontier city. And learned that decoding their messages made *him* the leading expert. His ability to attract duties without accolades remained intact. An observation he added to Gleason's notes.

As their specialist, Anders pulled a few scraps of history together. A handful of white cavalrymen had served in the Mexican War. They didn't know much *about* the city, but they'd burned a bit of it before.

Like the best parts of the country, San Valentin had recently been Mexico. The city's heart was a sprawling fort erected and maintained by riot-conscious strongmen. Said fort featured high, multicolored walls boasting enough artillery to level the city around it. Murals of smiling children helped make the fist of past warlords more presentable. That image threw Anders off. In practice, any fire would resemble cackling children lobbing cannonballs at the ants below.

"Take it in," declared Gleason, gesturing broadly at the main gate. His old squad formed an informal honor guard and captive audience. Despite San Valentin's short history, it featured a broad, white arch fitting another empire from another century. "The City of Love."

"Paris," mumbled Thomas.

"The City of Brotherly Love."

"Philly."

"The City of Quietly Marching," Gleason said with more bite. "There can, and should be, more than one City of Love. Love keeps us alive. Imagine the world with more love and less bullets. In fact, that's my next play. Anders, write down 'The Rifle That Fired Love.'"

Anders wrote down "New play about male member."

One messenger emerged from The Other City of Love. Or rather, from somewhere to the south. The strategy within the walls didn't include opening the main gate to an ocean of armed, hungry-looking soldiers. Notable.

The messenger rode straight for one of the caravan's white stragglers, a former ditchdigger named Lorcan. Lorcan pointed toward Gleason's vanguard. Unperturbed, the rider rode straight for Anders. Anders remembered, for the first time that day, that he had the squad's only white face. He straightened up his posture, wiped the exhaustion from his expression, and stood face-to-face with the messenger's horse.

Both of the mount's eyes were sunken, bloodshot, and irate. It hadn't been awake for long. Despite the messenger's showy wardrobe, the visit had been improvised. Then Anders looked up at the messenger, who had since shifted his attention to the adults in the vanguard. He squinted at the Black leadership like talking dogs, before throwing Anders a questioning glance.

Their visitor looked like one of Wendy's men with a budget. A fine red coat, slacks, cap, and saddle stood out before the sea of blue. In lieu of improvised kitchenware, a silver-handled sword dangled from his waist. The useless, weak metal on an outmoded weapon marked excess wealth and a fearless disposition.

"Hail, travelers," said the messenger, in a distinctly affected accent. He sounded like a rustic telling a fairy tale. Bryce—the real Bryce—had indulged in the genre and showed off to anyone who needed a good laugh. But the messenger looked dead serious. "You're on queen's land."

Anders sensed a moment in history and wrote his name in.

"Hiya," said Anders. "Queen's land?"

"Hello," said Gleason, taking the interjection in stride. "Call me Tobias. No one's in charge here, but I speak for us on occasion."

The messenger nodded. "A lord."

"No, not that. Not even a little that. We've had an awakening, as a unit. I just happened to be first and translated for the simple and slow."

"Ah. A bishop."

Anders braced for a finger-wagging explanation of the Church's flaws and Ben Franklin's intent to bury marriage in the Old World. It was reflexive. He could imagine the corporal ranting about faith on his deathbed.

"Whatever word helps you understand. Why not send someone earlier? Or a show of force?"

"Manners. The queen enjoys the protection of heaven. No army raised against her shall prosper."

Two triggers. The rant had to be coming. He'd launch into a treatise against the entire basis of monarchy, and they'd be fighting. Anders squinted at the inner wall's artillery. Any cannon could blast ten of him into nothing, without a hint of accuracy. Or, worse yet, blast *part* of him into nothing. Few doctors had followed them into the desert.

"I respect heaven," said Gleason, without a crack in his smile. "We all do. I'm here to offer my help, along with the *armed, trained, and loyal-ish* men behind me."

"To be clear. Moor: you submit yourself to the One True Queen of the United States? The lion that will eat the pretender Lincoln? The spear that will pierce the interloper Davis? The sole ruler of free men?"

"Yes," said Gleason.

"Moor?" whispered Anders.

"Nigger," whispered Thomas. "Or at least he *thinks* it's nigger. Everything you people make up means nigger. I don't know why. You got it right the first time."

"That's your question?" hissed Joaquin. "And *that's* your answer? How have you lived this long?"

Gleason whistled. The whispers stopped.

"It's not for me to decide. You may present yourself before the queen and face her justice. Bring a second, if you see fit."

Anders slid behind Thomas, who had slid behind Mole. He could feel the Cemetery Ridge chill in the air again. A charge was coming. They might be standing still, but he knew what a charge felt like. Let someone else sprint into history, unarmed.

"Anders, you still have my notes?"

"No?" he lied. Practice onstage had to be worth something.

"I have my second."

33

THE MAJESTY OF COURT

Ser Tucker, by the way. Knaves."

Ser. Anders decided to forget the name. The Camelot-by-way-of-Charlottesville voice was forgivable and nearly amusing. The sensory hell he'd led them into, less so. The messenger's route included an endless tunnel that smelled like a chamber pot, mired in ankle-deep sludge that felt and looked like chamber pot material. He could say *sewer*, but then he'd have to admit that his shoes were caked in waste, while their guide monopolized a mount that could easily fit two.

The discomfort seemed one-sided. The messenger concerned himself with projecting as much of a bygone age's poise as trotting through a giant chamber pot allowed. And Gleason's senses were firmly fixed on the future. If he smelled anything, it was a future utopia's waste. Likely a lavender scent, with a hint of melon.

"The Romans created some of the first sewers," noted Gleason, reaching for conversation. His pre-poltergeist tone leaked through. "They used bathhouse water to flush waste into—"

"Gleason? Sir?"

"Yes, Anders?"

"If you keep talking, I'm tossing your notes into the shit."

"Understood."

✣ ✣ ✣

The notes remained shit-free. Gleason had only *reduced* his commentary on the past and future of the city, but Anders had some investment in the book. He'd started slipping his own observations and questions into the record. With the director's fuzzy plans becoming concrete, his letters had a chance of outliving them both, and thus interesting inquisitive souls who preferred books to making their own legends. Less romantic than martial renown via word of mouth, but much more attainable.

Moreover, Anders had divided the chaotic mess into three sections, one for each year of the war. All he knew about publishing was that three books were worth more than one. And that the current effort needed more romance. He'd subtly inserted a woman named Winny into Book Two—a witty Black girl hiding in a man's army. Winny admired flag-twirling and valued loyalty, moderate solutions, and thinking before shooting. Understanding was *simple*. He missed Winny.

Anyway.

The new city still dwarfed Anders, though he appreciated the lack of smoke. In terms of population density, he wrote, "More than Liberty Valley, less than New York." Any locale with more livestock than humans reminded him of his bucolic roots. He'd stood outside of plenty of towns as they were shelled, but he could count the cities he'd stepped into on one hand. Unless he lost two fingers.

The noise rivaled Manhattan with a fraction of the people. San Valentinians yelled by default and screamed to be heard over the yelling. The locals endeavored to take up as much auditory and physical space as possible—citizens walked in the street-clogging phalanx formation that Katrina had beaten out of him and Longstreet had beaten back in. He shifted to Gleason's left and adopted a wide stance.

Red was more common, but not as dominant as in Wendy's cult or the messenger's outfit. Red accented the edges of clothing and accessories instead of dominating the whole outfit. Anders recalled the old line about American-born Germans being more German than the people of the motherland. It was the least spite-fueled joke he'd ever heard about the Germans—most spiraled into rants against free soil and popery. As far as San Valentin and its external evangelists went, it held true.

To identify soldiers, Anders looked for slumped shoulders followed by an instinctive, well-drilled snap back to full height. Sloppy reasoning, but useful in a pinch. By his count, escaped soldiers of one variety or another made up a fifth of the people in sight. He'd heard of disappearing regiments and had been in one himself. But seeing them reappear was something else. Half of First Manassas must have been present. With more time, Anders would ask them for tips on a long, healthy career outside the army.

Makeshift frontier infrastructure abounded. Buckets hung from wells by chipped chains, likely lending the water a little flavor. Red-clad deputies dragged offenders bound by rope, cord, or manners. Roads of variable size were laid out by collective whim rather than any recognizable plan.

He couldn't tell what anything smelled like, thanks to the tunnel. Based on the looks he drew, better than him.

Gleason bonded with their guide, who he dazzled with compliments and trivia about Founders he no longer believed in. If their bizarre new backdrop inspired any reaction, he submerged it beneath ego-smoothing banter. Even the nameless messenger's ongoing impression of a whiskey smuggler in Avalon failed to get a chuckle. As a follower, watching his leader effortlessly manipulate someone left Anders *concerned*.

A quartet in gray uniforms passed them. Two tipped their hats at fellow soldiers, and only one bothered dropping a slur. Their regalia was in loose, sloppy condition, even by rebel standards. All four were unarmed, which went against the Southern spirit in any decade. An arch air hung over keeping the uniforms around, unaltered. An odd flourish: in Anders's experience, most of Lee's ragamuffins couldn't spell or define irony.

"Did you see—"

"Keep walking."

"But they—"

"Gray coats? You had one too, no?"

Anders let the point go, if not the anxiety. The business back east didn't leave them at *open* war with red. But the debate with gray was ongoing.

They stopped before the noon shadow of San Valentin's central fort. Home of a hundred years of unsanctioned warlords. Followed by remarkably similar state-sanctioned mayors. The building had grown tall, but no more beautiful. Its walls shared the same earth tone as the dirt, and the children painted on the walls weren't any less unsettling up close. They grinned like they knew something Anders didn't, which he'd grown sick of in real life.

Ser Tucker—which Anders would still never say—adjusted his crimson sash, checked his crimson shoes, and pulled out a pair of crimson gloves. His appearance was about to matter, unlike a meeting with a thousand armed outsiders.

"Welcome to the Divine Palace."

Gleason glanced at Anders, expecting a wide-eyed question on calling a building the same size, overall aesthetic, and function of Fort Mojave a palace. He found the same tense silence that had followed him through the tunnel.

"I get it," Anders said mutedly. He could see what they wanted it to be. Presentable or not, the walls defended the elite and their fortunes well enough.

Anders abandoned his shoes before stepping forward. *Barefoot* felt more regal than *redolent*. After sniffing the air twice, Gleason followed suit.

The two barbarians, barefoot, stepped into proper society.

✣ ✣ ✣

They had a *lot* of flag-twirlers. More peers entertained the throne room than Anders had seen or spoken to in his life. They did more to confirm Wendy's connection to San Valentin than any question he could have asked the queen. They even used shorter poles, albeit without her preternatural precision and grace.

"Sloppy," he muttered, as a man fumbled a *Varial Adams Plant*.

"Better," he thought, when a woman landed a *State's Left*.

"Ew," he said out loud, when a pair simply waved their flags back and forth.

An elbow hit his ribs gently on "sloppy" and sharply on "ew." Anders responded with a stamp to the toes, which Gleason avoided visible reaction to. The director leaned toward his second for a comment.

"My friend, you've had a teenage tone lately."

"Oh?" replied Anders, instead of screaming. All of Joaquin's banter felt human in hindsight, compared to demands for adult decorum before childish reality. He might apologize when they reunited, presuming the renaissance fetishists around him didn't burn him for witchcraft or something similarly nostalgic.

Anders had anticipated the red, which dominated court fashion and decor. The silver came as a surprise. The metal displaced wood, bronze, and gold everywhere possible, from courtiers' personal jewelry to wall-mounted candelabras without candles. The court twirlers carried silver poles, which needled Anders's minimalist instincts. He'd offer advice, but the further he stayed from bringing up Wendy, the better off negotiations were.

The throne obviated every other silver bauble in sight. The solid silver furniture stood two men high, inscribed from top to bottom with words Anders couldn't read from the back. Whatever they said, the angular letters were bright crimson, cursive, and shone the way only the cheapest or most expensive jewelry could. The plush cushions matched the metal's shade of silver, adding to overall visual impact without making it impossible to sit on. All in all, an impressive monument to a bygone system, and silver mines that dwarfed taste.

A wiry, shortish, and slouched occupant made the throne look bigger yet, though perhaps not by design. Queen Columbia I dressed like her fictional namesake, with the addition of a thin silver crown and stern aura. The queen sat with a serious stone frown and authoritative finger tent but took minute glances to her left during lulls in action. After spending a lifetime confused, Anders recognized the behavior. The queen was looking for an adult. He noted as much in Gleason's papers, earning a disapproving glance from Gleason himself. Anders shrugged. Experimenting with the notes kept him sane, a trait he found in short supply.

Anders recalled his duel, hours ahead of his next scheduled nightmare. The queen's face also matched Wendy's portrait. Reality robbed Columbia I of some, but not all, of a living doll's off-putting aura. The blank zealot's grin was gone, in favor of the rigid gravitas that Anders, who had never seen or actively thought about a queen, expected from a queen. Her thin blond hair was tied back into a massive, knot-like bun, allowing her mild Hapsburg jaw to draw focus and emphasize her breeding and, by extension, legitimacy. With a nameless father and drink-happy mother, Anders had never felt more envy for inbreeding.

Today, she looked only a hair older than he was. One year, maybe two. Imagining himself running a city on his best day was mortifying. Did she have heart episodes? Prophetic dreams? A nurse fetish? They'd be at her mercy, or whoever stepped into the natural void.

Unnervingly, she also evoked his imaginary angel, along with Harrow's very real nurse. The resemblance could point to a connection he didn't understand, like most of the universe's messages. It could also, as likely as anything else, mean nothing. Anders let the question go. Maybe faces weren't his best strength.

Columbia I maintained her poise and pose through the rest of the performance, nodding at the more advanced maneuvers. As the performance rolled on, Anders's pretensions melted into sympathy. Any flag-twirling set longer than ten minutes strained the heart and lungs, to say nothing of the wrists. The occasional slow and stiff movement saved precious energy for big spots. He had nothing catty to say when a graying man fell over halfway through a *Twisted Dixie*.

"Worthless," said a man to the queen's left. The word's ease implied regular use. More important, he spoke with familiar mad certainty. He dressed like the nameless messenger, sans the outdated sword. If class worked anything like the sane world, the lack of masculine posturing signaled extreme wealth.

"He's just a little rusty, Duke," said the monarch. Her *little* sounded like *li'ckle* and matched a soldier's impression of a poor Briton.

"He could practice in prison," suggested the duke.

"In my nation, there are second chances," said the queen. "It's human nature." Gleason's ears perked up. *Nature* was a keyword in political tracts, which he'd talked about enough for Anders to pick up the basics. He hoped the *Leviathan* guy was wrong but felt he was at least halfway there. That said, it was *second chances* that got the director smiling openly. Somehow.

"It's a security problem. He's embarrassing us before outsiders."

"Not at all," Gleason hazarded. Collective reactions indicated that he was the first shoeless Negro to do so. "Let him try again."

Anders had his own prognosis. The twirler wasn't squatting enough. Anders made the strongest eye contact he could, silently sank into an exaggerated squat, and repeated the motion three times. Each made him feel dumber than standing shoeless among high society. On the fourth squat, he caught the light of recognition in the terrified man's eyes.

The twirler entered a proper ninety-degree squat before reattempting *Twisted Dixie*. This time, he landed in perfect unison with his peers. Naked relief shone on his face and added pop to the rest of his steps. The troupe went through another minute of higher-difficulty, slower-paced twirling before turning to the queen and bowing in unison.

"Well done," she told her subjects before addressing her smelly, shoeless visitors. "I see that the war has left you in dire straits. Dire, and redolent."

Gleason bowed, and Anders followed. He *wanted* to blame his sewage cologne on her staff but knew that bowing took priority. From what he understood of monarchy, lazy bowing was terminal.

"It's tragic. Brother against brother. Father against son. Daughter against starvation. Slave against master. Were you a slave?"

"De jury? No," said Gleason. He added, "My liege," a beat late.

"It'll be moot soon. Wendy's revolution will give us a foothold in the East. Then we can stop flirting with codes and innuendo, and embrace every subject between New York and Nevada. Including the Africans."

Anders focused on the floor. He suspected they wouldn't hear from Wendy. He added an extra bow, for safety.

"You have an army for me?"

"A regiment. And ideas."

"A regiment is an army, yes?"

Gleason nodded.

"Wonderful. Duke Ross, list the lineage."

Another Ross. Anders suppressed a groan.

"Queen Columbia I," began Duke Ross, drawing effortlessly from memory. He pulled his voice down an octave, and himself up to full, chest-puffed height. "Forgotten heir to the Hanovers. Forgotten heir to the Washingtons. Forgotten heir of the Jeffersons. Acknowledged but unsupported heir of the Franklins."

"Good. Now list the titles."

"The Silver Queen. Uniter of San Valentin. Big sister. Future liege lord of Davis, Lincoln, and all other warlords in rebellion. Queen of Free Men. The one, true queen of the United States."

Ross's declarations rushed Anders through the strangest math of his life. The lunatic implications if true, and worse implications if false. The size of her growing "kingdom," and their clear fervor. The current attitude of the Union to competing political bodies. The ongoing pursuit of a displeased brigadier general.

In the near future, he might be dead.

"We're honored to serve, my liege," said Gleason. "Along with nearly a thousand strong Black hands. And a flexible arms dealer, hopefully living."

"Acceptable. You may bend the knee."

On his knees, he could make out the words scrawled on the throne. Ruby dust or stained glass, each sentence cost more than he did. They read *Brave Souls Live Forever* in carefully set, shimmering red letters. House words speaking to resilience, duty, and conviction stronger than any weapon.

In the near future, he would definitely be dead.

33.5

GENEALOGY

Smaller Napoleons:
Minor Claimants of Europa and Beyond

Originally Published 1849

Chapter 1

THE "WEST HANOVERS"

My grandfather once asked if I would like to be king. I answered honestly. He then asked what I would do as king. I answered honestly again. The subsequent thrashing elevated my character and put me on a more intellectual path. Today, I don't aspire to burn any sibling or force any neighbor into a harem. But not everyone is so fortunate.

Lost kings and queens live among us. They come in many varieties. Curiosities, content to enjoy leftover wealth and contain their lineage to ballroom anecdotes. Charlatans, uniting the gullible under conveniently discarded flags. Lunatics, who do the same with earnest zeal. And genuine victims of history, whom few entertain and fewer believe.

In this volume, I will catalog a number of lost kings. It is nowhere near comprehensive; there are as many lost kings as there are thrones, liars, clever viziers, and blackout drunks. But each case is compelling, like watching a factory fire from a distance. And there's no moral pressure to intervene. Let the old skirt-chaser Metternich focus on catching each crown that falls from an empty head. We can observe and enjoy.

For amusement, it's hard to beat the West Hanovers. It's not just a town in the former colonies—though they may reign there, when all is said and done. The West Hanovers have claimed, for four generations, to be the true lineal heirs of the English throne. Common enough, given the long-standing tradition of royal trysts. The West Hanovers are distinguished by marrying into the name-droppable families of Americana. They have the strongest claim to the crown of a crownless nation.

The circus began with Mona Paisley, the self-styled Mona Hanover, a seamstress who allegedly enjoyed a brief elopement with a young, pre-coronation George III. Per Mona's telling, her marriage with "Georgie" began in 1755, produced one healthy child, and never underwent official annulment. Such adventures aren't unheard of: young, ennui-afflicted royals are known to sample civilian life as merchants, mercenaries, or village drunks. Princess Augusta, for example, spent her teens sailing as "Dread-scar the Destroyer," scourge of the Atlantic. But I digress.

The annulment complicates Mona's story. It's simply sloppier cleanup than any house allows. Since the Stuart unpleasantness, questions of succession have been closely and competently moni-tored. Loose ends—such as inconvenient marriages—are resolved by bribery, bullet, or both. Any time with "Georgie" should have earned Mona either independent wealth or an early grave. Yet Mona, and her favorite tavern story, lived on into her dotage. And her children paid attention.

Bonnie and Mortimer diversified the family strategy. After *gentle encouragement* to leave for the colonies, both continued pro-moting the family claim. While lacking real wealth, both were well trained in wearing the trappings (and literal uniforms) of high society. If Mona obscured matters by accident, Bonnie did so by design. Simultaneous affairs with a geriatric Franklin and lesser

Adams left the father of her child an unresolved but compelling mystery. Moreover, Bonnie spent notable time orbiting the reportedly childless Washington and let the human capacity for gossip work for her. Mortimer, meanwhile, pursued a relationship with one of Jefferson's only white daughters. The offspring were, with the family penchant for subtlety, named Baron and Contessa.

As for the next generation . . . they kept the bloodline pure. While more tasteful houses stayed at least a degree away from pure incest, the West Hanovers were in more difficult circumstances. Less prestigious blood was simply not an option. The Americans have, by design, avoided new waves of revolution or royal rule since the interregnum over tea. Only the downstream benefits of infamy kept the family solvent. Amid hostile reactions to their imperial claims, Marcus and Lydia Hanover found emotional and physical comfort with each other.

The surviving children are six of the most carefully bred lost kings around. Their physical and mental deformities are minimal, even by modern royal standards. They've received proper English educations, complete with character-building canings. And the parents have settled on the American frontier, where abundant land and minimal regulation enable holdings closer to royal standards. All that's missing is willing subjects. Or, in the American parlance, marks.

As things stand, their best hope is to run one of the comelier sons for president. Assuming, of course, that there is still a country or West Hanover estate once the slave power question comes to a head. The Philadelphia cabal lit a long fuse and walked away.

Where will the West Hanovers go next? What will they do? It's hard to say, given the family commitment to chaos. But if they've learned anything, we won't hear about them for some time.

34

———◆———

THE QUIET MAN'S BURDEN

The lunatic bastard demiurge had granted half of Anders's prayers at once. Promotion. Relevance. Working for a wealthy blonde. They only cost a target on his forehead a half-hair smaller than Nathan Bedford Forrest's. He tried not to imagine his personal firing squad, which only made the visions stronger.

The queen (a word his mind and tongue still struggled with) knighted them moments after Gleason's proposal. Whatever the state of San Valentin's army, a thousand-man boost was welcomed without hesitation. Like all lifelong rejects, Anders found this troubling. This club wanted him too much.

The barefoot pair became *Duke* Gleason and *Ser* Anders. If he knew the rank between duke and ser, Anders would have pushed for it. As things stood, he worried about the blade on his shoulder. The queen's arm quivered with the longsword's weight. Despite the silver handle, it remained non-ceremonially sharp and capable of opening his throat for public examination. Miraculously, he entered knighthood with only a lightly nicked coat. He stuck a thumb through the hole while the royal rambled through the rest of the rite. If he survived knighthood, the coat would make a quality souvenir.

For the rest of the session, men dressed like Duke Ross told Columbia I that things were fine. Food and munition stocks were fine. Taxes were fine. Silver mine yields were fine. Irate questions from the pretender presidents were fine. Pleas to other crowns were fine. Anders jotted each down as a future problem. Another editorialization in someone else's notes, but the director could write them himself if he didn't want spin.

Gleason barely blinked throughout. He sat rapt through each exchange, etching noble names and faces into memory. Most, like Duke Ross, spoke in natural modern voices. Others, like Ser Tucker, felt compelled to wear storybook accents matching their outfits. *Forsooth* and *verily* were verily used and abused, forsooth.

Once the issues of the day were declared nonissues, the ritual of ending court began. The queen departed first, flanked by a guard in each cardinal direction. Then the lower orders were free to speak, leave, or nurse their flag-twirling injuries. The director lingered in the chamber, long after the rest of the aristocracy had dispersed into day-drinking and other non-labor. Imagination lit his eyes as brightly as their first meeting.

"We've done it," said Gleason, half to Anders, half to himself.

"Let's find shoes," suggested Anders.

"Damn the shoes, we've *climbed*. We're the men we set out to be in Pennsylvania."

"We're two shoeless Negroes."

"Two?"

"Y-you count twice. You're a double Negro, for all the abolition talk. You should rein it in, and lead from the middle."

"No more pandering to the sleepy middle. It's all changing, Anders. This is a land untainted by slavery. An America without the original sin. Anything's in reach."

"Including shoes."

Gleason laid out a plan for uplifting key Harriers to nobility and sprinkling a little democracy into the theater of court. They had experience in theater. Anders daydreamed about soft shoes and a softer bed. Once he found those, he could even write to his mother. She was probably more tolerable out of combat range, and he had a few pressing questions. He couldn't shake the idea that he was four-fifths of a person.

✦ ✦ ✦

Once San Valentin's gates creaked open, Anders waited for skepticism from the regiment. Or the compulsive barbarism that historically followed a hungry army entering an unprepared city. Neither manifested. After one impassioned address from the director, the Harriers greeted the new order like lifelong servants of the crown. A rhythmic chant of "Long live the queen!" started in the fringes and traveled through the regiment like measles. It continued as they poured into the streets, to the mixed terror and horror of the locals. The arrival and acceptance of a Negro army hadn't been announced to the little people.

The taverns welcomed new drinking talent and the gambling winnings burning holes in their pockets. Particularly The Vanguard, a two-story inn split between new Union arrivals and former Confederate infantry. The rebels settled the top floor, while the Harriers took over the ground floor. They separated with a speed, ease, and efficiency that service had never inspired. Anders ordered a tall flagon of cloudy dark beer and used it as cover. Hopefully, no fellow ex-Confederates would recognize him.

He refilled the flagon twice. It dulled the pounding questions in his head into a pleasant bassline. He could believe in this dream, at least a little. Some of the more talented singers in the regiment endeavored to stitch "John Brown's Blood" and "God Save the Queen" into one bar tune. The result would've driven the authors to murder, but he could bob his head to it. During pauses, he could hear a similar effort upstairs to scramble "God Save the Queen" and "To Arms, to Arms" together. Even less successful. The rebels couldn't agree on a key.

All he needed now was nothing. A little non-activity would let his fresh sunburn, sunstroke, false visions, true visions, monarchism, and blisters settle. He could leave the moody trepidation hanging over every recent achievement and setback behind. Or embrace them, if they proved sensible. Time, more than any speech or book, would let the world make sense.

The palace/fort had spare rooms for members of court. That was out. Things happened in palaces. Intrigues, assassinations, and everything else that made old history complicated. The inn was the perfect speed. Nightly noise, binge drinking, and the inevitable fistfights between regiments were perfectly insignificant distractions. He could return to whatever went on outside—and whatever knights actually did—refreshed.

He stumbled off his stool and tracked down the innkeeper. The graying man squinted at his new customer with moderate suspicion. The boy looked white but shared a table and uniform with the newcomers. Anders did his best to smile and stay upright.

"Room. Room please," asked Anders.

"Do you have money?"

"I'm a knight."

"Knights have money."

"I'm a new knight."

"Find new money."

His less-than-official service record bit him again. Anders made a show of shifting through his pockets. He hadn't thought about money while drinking, which explained the barmaid pestering him so often.

Patricia took the opening. She'd abandoned Petey's neat uniform and meek posture and wore an open army coat with the sleeves rolled up. Confidence filled the uniform well. Anders made eye contact, rapidly lost it, and forced himself back.

"Stuck, *Ser* Anders?" said Patricia.

"You look . . . like you. Where's the disguise?"

"That's me too. But there's chaos in the air, so I'm testing the truth. There'll never be a better chance, and no one's bothered me yet. Besides, Petey couldn't take this much noise."

The Confederate tune upstairs died down. On the ground, ex-Union revelers took the cue to get louder and restarted from the first verse. The innkeeper glowered at the youth, who wasted time he could spend on their solvent peers.

"I could spot you," she said. "If *knights* take money from *murderers*."

"You have money? How?"

"Staying in one army."

"At the Black rate? Claptrap."

"I stole a bit from Slade. He kept years of money on him."

Patricia held up her hands, which were covered in Slade's silver rings. She'd already found and adopted the local specialty. In days, she'd have a lifelong monarchist persona in her back pocket.

"Where is he?"

Patricia shrugged. "Gleason said he was a bargain."

"Bargaining chip."

"That's the one. Want help or not?"

"The catch?"

"Split the room with me."

That seemed like a terrible deal. How would he think, let alone sleep, with a murderer snoring in the room? He couldn't imagine a single good reason for it. The pitch had to be some kind of mockery or obscure insanity. She'd been through the same tour and Jefferson Firearms apprenticeship. Young minds weren't made for that stimuli.

"No thanks."

"Split the room with me," she repeated, with a different intonation. His wheels turned. They did good work together. At the very least, he could ask which side of the racial line was a better fit. A switch might benefit him, if common thoughts on Black entitlement held any weight.

Patricia asked a third time, prodding the same rib she'd cracked earlier. It still hurt. Then she traced a circle there, which also hurt. But an idea emerged.

"We could split a room," said Anders.

"Brilliant. Let's try it."

✢ ✢ ✢

"See?" she said, whirling their new brass key between her fingers. Not quite a *Sumter Spin*, but impressive. "Much easier than the feud. Why compete?"

"I suppose," mumbled Anders, tense. The stairway looked taller now. Or maybe he'd shrunk.

"I mean it," Patricia added. She bobbed left and right for eye contact. "I'm lost too, most days. Just less loud. I thought a big name would help. Whatever I use, everyone's insane."

Anders climbed, hearing the words without hearing them. While his lower brain celebrated, his higher brain panicked. It had to be another trap. He followed jungle instinct forward anyway.

Halfway up the steps, anticipation caved to doubt. He'd misread a lifetime of conversations. The fog had dragged him to the wrong side of the continent, more baffled with every mile. Why would sex be different?

At the door, he settled on retreat. He'd made worse bets with his life, but this was his dignity. Better to fight another day. Then two hands crawled inside his shirt, up the back. Nails dug in softly, and then harder. Too hard, in fact. Far too hard.

"How's that?" Patricia asked. She put on a new voice. He couldn't pin her intent, but the result recalled Joaquin's accent. Not unattractive—he'd reflect on that later, or more likely, never. "Anders?"

"Perfect," Anders lied, unearthing a hint of social grace.

Patricia eased off. He turned and found another nervous face. Instead of saying the wrong thing, he said nothing. They kissed, which worked for some time, and then they improvised.

He tried an athletic angle. A mistake. They fell into a knot on the floor. There were splinters. Without three wasted tours, he'd have stopped. Without more disaster looming overhead, he'd have slowed down. As things stood, they were tied together. Patricia whispered encouragement, switched tones, and then whispered obscenities. The obscenities helped.

Petey got creative. Anders considered, for the first time, an experience gap. Then he let the thought go, along with the other questions, ideas, tangents, and traumas crowding his brain. He ascended to a true idiot and found a welcome silence.

Then a broomstick jabbed his ear. He scrambled backward, while Petey laughed. Anders, newly stupid, joined in—the tavern owner glared like he'd found them robbing a grave. By God's will, or the power of ale, the man was alone.

"Obligingly contain deviance to your quarters."

No words came to mind. They scrambled inside and resumed deviance.

✢ ✢ ✢

"You look confused," said Patricia. "More confused," she added.

It was the nicest room he'd ever rented, and the first. The fleas were a familiar size and shape—a welcome note of continuity with Fort Mojave. Their bed was only large enough for one malnourished adult, a cramped situation that pushed them past the initial awkwardness. A cat slipped in and out of the room through an unseen hole in the wall and kindly kept to itself during the main event. Anders's shoe issue remained unresolved, but he didn't have anything else on either.

"I don't think we did that right," answered Anders.

"What's right? We were in another army a week ago."

"No, I mean physically wrong. I've seen pictures."

"You enjoyed it."

"And you switched personas halfway through."

"You enjoyed it."

He had. More than saving the country or finding a new one. More than deciphering if any of his dreams about angels or Blackness meant anything. More than marching, charging, bashing, shooting, or twirling. He would, under any conceivable pressure, choose sex first. Why anyone else thought differently was beyond him. Rebellions and conquests should have been impossible. There was an alternative.

"You should read more. Being a knight means you decide what's right."

"That doesn't sound right."

"There, now you get it. One more?"

"Can you do Porter? I have unresolved issues with Porter."

35

SILVER

Too much junk had piled up in the hallway. The innkeeper was livid: another week of unopened missives or knightly paraphernalia would put Anders on the street or reduce him to the palace. He could only imagine how much further into storybook-speak court had fallen. American culture was young and thus barely existed. In San Valentin, royal nonsense filled the space like water.

The gifts started with a sword. It had a silver handle, just like the toys in court. *Ser Briar* was inscribed on the blade at great expense. Or perhaps none. He didn't know any more about swordsmiths than gunsmiths and didn't endeavor to find out. Patricia took the blade inside and waved it around with enthusiastic abandon. Anders played along, offering stray tips on posture and presentation. These twirling tips went ignored in favor of storybook misquotes, followed by dramatic lunges at the shadows.

That game ended with Anders losing a bit of his forearm, followed by yelling. They made up in the usual manner.

Red clothes came next, followed by silver accessories. He accepted the pieces that fit as a career obligation and let oversize regalia linger in the hallway. At a glance, local tailors imagined knights as seven-foot temples to muscle. In fairness, so did he.

He was less picky about footwear. After surviving hot cobblestone barefoot, he treasured every frilly boot that came his way, whether it fit or not.

Then Gleason's work trickled in, nailed to Anders's door in sealed crimson envelopes. Evidently the director took promotion with far more urgency and momentum. As Duke of Morale, he produced weekly essays on the Kingdom of Nevada's wonders. Praise for the queen's flexibility on the Negro question. Praise for the unnerving art on the palace walls. Praise for the "enlightened toleration" of the Confederates that preceded them. Even praise for Wendy Ross, whose "pure belief" had simply been poisoned by politics.

"What do you think of that?" asked Anders, after reading a draft aloud.

"Don't be passive-aggressive," grumbled Patricia.

He switched letters. "'I've taken my first free breath,'" he narrated, imitating the director's signature bombast. "'The stage promised freedom. As did the army. Only in San Valentin have I found life without contradictions. To all Americans: the nation you were promised is here. And if your skin is black: What is there to lose?'"

"Good for him," said Patricia, bored.

"It matters. I think I'm in charge of putting this in code."

"You're a knight. You're not in charge of anything until Queen Flatback or Duke Shakespeare asks in person. How's the arm?"

"Better."

Anders missed Scientific Theater. It had been equally didactic but more inventive. There were metal women, and flying horses, and businessmen with consciences. Now Gleason simply praised his environment, which felt much less real.

"Besides, it doesn't matter if you code it. He's not writing for the outside world."

"Who else would it be for?"

"The people already here."

Patricia shifted to bugle practice, where she retained an inspired lack of ability. Headaches typified their downtime and left Anders impressed. It took an incorruptible spirit to retain so little melody after so much practice. He sat through ten minutes of polite support before deciding that knighthood did, in fact, matter. After enduring something like the Dorian scale, Anders slipped into the red finery closest to fitting and fled to his duties. He left the sword behind.

✛ ✛ ✛

"Ser Anders! Where in hell have you been?"

"Just Anders," he pleaded. They'd known each other on the outside. "I had to tend to something."

"It's been three weeks," added Gleason.

"I tended to it well."

The director scratched his new beard, more for effect than any deep thought. He'd adopted the neat, close trim beloved by the few Black men with underlings. It fit a duke well, if not a man with both feet on the ground.

"Is it a woman?"

"That question's out of my depth."

Gleason let it lie there. His own palace office, complete with direction-less scribes and guards, seemed to have softened his mood. The current batch included Thomas, who did an admirable job of looking awake, and Boots, who Anders still refused to consider real.

"It's good to have you back. Thomas's notes were a disaster."

Anders eyed Thomas, who didn't stir. A gentle snore wafted through the air.

"It's a way of life. I can see where he's coming from," admitted Anders. "Can I ask a minor question?"

"I'd rather get to work."

A standoff began, held, and broke with Gleason shrugging.

"This question," Anders began, "requires an open mind. And imagina-tion. And—"

Gleason made the universal "go ahead" sign. His eyes remained alight and attentive; he was either eager to hear his ward's thoughts or to talk about something else.

"What would you do if I were Black? As in, if you were me, and Black. Not if you were you and Black. Or you were you, and I were Black. You're me. Understand?"

The director leaned in and squinted as if they were playing cards. Anders could smell his breath, which was distressingly alcohol-free. Most of San Valentin kept a light buzz going—it was culture. Sobriety meant taking the American Throne seriously. Gleason's eyes swept Anders from hair, to nose, to lips. Then he relaxed, falling back into his seat without any visible epiphany.

"I'd stay white."

"That's . . . surprising."

"Think. Your record is inspiring for a white man and embarrassing for a Negro. White Anders climbed over a centuries-old wall of hatred and abuse, to fight for another people. He left a slaver's army, recognized a Negro genius, and followed him to a new land. Black Anders is a confused mockery of Northern and Southern values. And ours."

"Thanks. Excellent discussion. Let's work."

"No other questions? We haven't spoken in some time. You know I'm always open—"

"None. Time for codes. I'm ready to make codes. Exciting codes."

"Did you notice that Petey—"

"Codes. Royal codes, for the queen. Let's begin."

"I have something else for you. I suspect your more . . . *mechanical* intellect will crack it more quickly."

"That's me. White Anders. Brain like a watch. What is it?"

"Since arriving, the Harriers have manned the walls. Alone. Hence the ease of our approach. Which leaves me wondering: What do the Confederates here do?"

"Not *former* Confederates? Trusted fellow servants of the queen, and all that?"

"I trust, and verify," Gleason explained. The word *trust* had the weight of air. Anders recalled twirling behind conversations among Longstreet's men about gelding and re-enslavement for Black prisoners of war. Or any freemen who happened to be in the army's radius. "Go verify."

✛ ✛ ✛

Anders invented several complicated plans and abandoned them all. Precedent had a louder and clearer voice.

Thus inspired, he returned to The Vanguard, discussed philosophy with Polly, and plucked one of the shinier accessories from their pile. Then he braved the second floor, where the Southerners held their eternal drinking contest, and looked for someone slim, short, and detached. His winner sat alone, nursing a depleted flagon in hopes that it might refill itself. Advanced age and a mild alcoholic twitch hinted at a late recruit, plucked for service after his backwater ran out of willing young victims. Without a natural in, Anders simply planted himself on a free stool and started talking.

"I'll give you this ring for your uniform."

"You can have it for two rings," parried the veteran.

"How about one? Instead of nothing?"

"Could you add a drink?"

Fair enough. He re-upped the flagon with Slade's liberated money and tapped the ring against the table. The old man stripped his coat and cap without complaint. Three bullet holes lent the cap character, along with the mixed aroma of sweat and stale liquor.

"Glad to lose it. From bleeding in a field to depression in a cave. Uniform never did a man any good."

Anders didn't disagree.

"Cave?"

✚ ✚ ✚

The rebel coat felt the way it smelled. Each scratchy inch carried a more aggressive breed of flea than the civilized symbiotes he'd grown accustomed to. The insects possessed all the dash and valor their hosts claimed to represent, rising in pairs for every comrade crushed or brushed off the front line. This new giant occupying their home might win the day, but they would never surrender.

Together, irritated skin and a lingering sense of doom almost made Anders call off the excursion altogether. Whatever he discovered wouldn't improve his life. Nothing he'd found on duty had. But *not knowing* was equally dangerous. Then fresh hell would catch him by surprise, leaving no time for cover, retreat, or a final uniform switch. He braved present peril to flee future peril.

Allegedly, his informant worked in a cave up north, alongside half his old company. The wretch described long hours, low wages, persistent danger, disrespectful peers, and a criminally small share in profits. He dodged describing the actual enterprise or role, which gave Anders fresh pause. As a recovering rambler, he knew the difference between honest blabber and guilty silence. The veteran's selective chatter hinted at something his gut questioned, even if his brain didn't. Lying with the truth.

In any case, Anders refused to walk. He borrowed one of the horses tethered behind The Vanguard. Its owner was present and opinionated, but not dressed like a storybook noble. At least a few of Patricia's theories on knighthood held true. He'd tell her about it, if nothing too embarrassing found him on the way.

He ran into a few pockets of stragglers. They wore their old Dixie uniforms proudly and greeted him like family. Returning their warmth taxed him. His own enthusiasm for slavery was a fresh memory.

After all, enthusiasm had been easy without a direct image of plantation life. He imagined it was *unpleasant*, given all the talk of violation and torture among the Harriers or even secondhand horror stories in the schoolhouse. But that caricature was as abstract as his old picture of the army, which had left out all the fleas and nightmares.

Plantation life would remain abstract. Nevada didn't have the climate for it. A different picture greeted him over the hill.

He noticed the post first. It was relatively short—maybe five feet tall. Much less obtrusive than the four chained men shambling into the hole or the song keeping their minds alive. But the stale and fresh blood coating the post drew him in. The smell overpowered everything, pushing itchiness and insomnia out of mind. Anders barely noticed himself dismounting. Dozens of thin lines chipped the wood, like a tiger's favorite toy. They could represent a week of whippings, or a year. He ran his hand over it and found it sticky.

"What are you doing?" asked a soldier as broad as Anders was tall. He held a four-card hand of playing cards—backup wasn't far behind. Anders missed the big, stupid, useless sword waiting back at The Vanguard. The guard wouldn't need a weapon to end him, or even much effort.

"Patrol?" said Anders. He put on his stage smile and pointed a thumb at the mouth of the cave.

"Take a lantern and step lively. You don't want one of these bow benders braining you with a rock." The soldier tapped the edge of a scar on his brow.

He stepped lively. It took him into the frozen dark, where Mole's relationship with God was born. The lantern was a heavy, glowing target. If someone made a break for freedom, he'd be the first and only victim.

Then he caught up to the chain gang, and their song in a language he'd never know. The mystery of the missing raiders came together. The fighting men Harrow hunted had already been caught and put to work.

Two of them resembled the post, covered in a web of scars. None met his gaze.

Anders heard more pickaxes in the dark, stabbing away at the earth deeper into the cave. Since this group struck, recovered, and repeated in unison, the same likely held for other captives. He tried to separate and count the other rhythms. There were too many. His chest tightened as the polyphony rang on. Then another retired rebel strode past him, whistling Dixie and swinging his lantern with the satisfaction of an easy shift. He tipped his gray cap Anders's way.

Anders retreated, pushing the horse faster and harder than it cared to go. He passed three more mines on the way, complete with amiable guards happy to see another civilized face. Two offered him stew. Behind their hospitality, slaves dug the same holes found in every empire.

When Patricia returned, the room was stripped of silver. Rings. Necklaces. Badges of office. All the glittering baubles they'd received, bought, or stolen since shacking up at the inn. Anders lay on the bed, staring at the unchanging ceiling. He didn't move to greet her. That genre of gesture was dead to him.

"Were we robbed?"

Anders considered a more poetic answer, scrapped it, and explained his day.

"I liked the sword," Patricia said dryly.

"My life's easier without one," Anders admitted.

"Think Gleason will take it well?"

"I hope not."

35.5

CASH FLOW

Mr. Jefferson,

    If you think we'll underwrite a teenage egoist further dividing a sovereign nation for a little slave-driven silver, you're absolutely right. The business is a privilege, as always. I hope you find ore as lucrative as gunpowder.

                    With Love,
                    Myron Baldwin
                    London Shipping Co.

✦✦✦

Dear Mr. McClellan,

    Of course I'll donate. Like most men outside of your campaign's blast radius, I want to see what happens. And I'm sure your platform is innovative by colonial standards. After outlawing slavery this year, you're only a century or so from catching up with civilization.

                    Yours,
                    Myron Baldwin
                    London Shipping Co.

36

THE MIDDLE PATH

The air had gotten thin again. Anders knew that court itself, as a room, event, and institution, did something subtle and perverse to local reality. He outlined his theory in Gleason's notes and found the words flowed freely. Language had stopped biting his hand whenever he reached for it. He eagerly pivoted from political theory to a handful of lingering thoughts on his branding. He titled the page "Pain Hurts" and picked a simple, but challenging, rhyme scheme.

After a few minutes of scribbling, he was the only smiling figure in the chamber and drew baffled looks from both flanks. Anders put on a suitably dour expression, closed the book, and waited to see which way history felt like flowing.

Court stood divided, in both opinion and physical arrangement. The profit and abolition factions had organized with admirable speed and respectively occupied the eastern and western flanks of the room. Inalienable human freedom and free tribal labor drew roughly equal crowds of San Valentin's elite. Encouraging—Anders expected worse. Though none of the nobility had abandoned silver accessories.

Based on Thomas's chicken-scratch pages in the notebook, free men ranked knight and above could attend court. And any responsible knight would. Holding the lowest rank that still obliged participation rankled Anders, but he let it go. At least he didn't have to twirl anything.

The throne sat on the invisible fault line dividing the factions. Queen Columbia I looked stiff—the stately, regal, and poised version of a student hoping to avoid getting called on in class.

Carefully repressed fury dominated the air around the silver throne.

Anders thought he could smell it, before recalling the heavy perfume habits of his new class. He could *see* it in the lack of ceremonial swords. Anything sharp or ballistic that entered the room would've seen use. In fact, he could imagine his own target.

He'd expected belligerence from his own side, given the captured men being worked to death. The wounded indignation of the business class surprised him. Their spokesman, whom Anders could scarcely look at without seeing (more) red, defended their "inalienable right to prosperity" from "the Duke of Morale's killjoys." The court's few unaligned faces nodded assent, souring Anders's mood further. He'd like to kill more than joy.

Whatever dark genius or darker blessing preserved Slade Jefferson, he'd perfectly absorbed his new environment. After mocking Wendy Ross's memory, he now looked and sounded like a lifetime monarchist. His scabbard featured the West Hanover slogan. A perfectly rolled and powdered white wig hung down to his shoulders. While the rest of the chamber raged, he smiled with true aristocratic comfort. It took genuine genius.

Nonetheless, the queen embodied poise under pressure. It remained unclear if she'd truly heard a word said thus far. But as her most influential servants clashed over the precise definitions of freedom and human, Columbia I struck a movingly stoic figure. She hadn't shifted, fidgeted, or coughed in her throne since the debate began, and blinked only as much as required by nature. As a performer, Anders appreciated the emergent talent. Her position could easily have fallen on a sibling without stage presence.

The ringleaders traded another round of rhetoric. The chamber's natural echo underlined each point.

"I won't mince words," began Slade. "When I arrived here, tied to a horse like chattel, I had nothing but the clothes on my back and silver mines in Wendy's will. Those mines were a blackened hell. I brought them factory efficiency. Now the tribals have two hours of leisure time a day while producing nearly twice the ore. And the rest goes to our shared cause: making this the best of the three Americas."

The queen remained stoic.

"Masterful rhetoric," began Gleason. "My counter: Mr. Jefferson should be hanged immediately, along with any silver mine owner, guard, distributor, or subsequent customer."

Columbia I eyed her adviser. Ross wrung his hands together but remained silent.

"I think I've been reasonable," said Slade. "I live in peace with men who have battered me, kidnapped me, battered me again, kidnapped me again, and dumped me in the *beautiful and sanitary* dungeons of San Valentin. To my presumed death. But I let it all go, to bring this beautiful city new opportunity."

A phalanx of mine owners chattered assent. The gunsmith's section held a mix of established San Valentin gentry and ex-Confederate strivers. The bloc wore a little more silver than red, proudly declaring their faction.

"He's a disease that talks," Gleason said diplomatically. "Do we draw and quarter men? I move that Mr. Jefferson be drawn and quartered. Or just halved, if we want to be humane."

"That's extreme. You're an extremist. Why spew that kind of bigotry before our liege? Let's slow down and find some space between us."

Gleason's corner jeered dutifully. Save Mole, who emanated silent, borderline supernatural hatred. Anders couldn't watch the giant for long. It was like looking into the sun. Even Slade, a man inoculated against shame itself, stood at an angle taking Mole out of sight. Mole had subsequently moved himself twice, and Slade had less-than-discreetly rotated twice.

Slade let the wave ebb, which took several minutes. His grin remained pure. "A newborn nation needs money and gunpowder. I can get arms, but not for free. I'm helping San Valentin pay me. It's a generational act of patriotism. Keep it alive, and I swear on God the nation will not regret it."

"Any engaged God would burn Mr. Jefferson alive. Which is in your power, your grace. I trust you to use it."

The queen nodded toward her Duke of Morale, the servant who crafted weekly paeans to her throne since dropping an army into her lap. Anders waited to learn that work's value.

"Commerce is good," she began. Slade's grin widened. "And human bondage is bad." Some light returned to Gleason's eyes. "We will take good steps, without bad ones, where we can. Unless bad is inevitable, or bad is good. Or, worse yet, good is bad. Then we will do bad instead of good, as long as it is the bad that is good instead of the bad that is bad. But first we must determine good and bad."

The chamber stood silent.

Perhaps Anders had died at Gettysburg. It made as much sense as anything else. He wrote down the exchange in his personal shorthand, word for word, and measured his own sanity. General Harrow had dealt him full-bodied blows to the head, as had his mother. Everything afterward could be the aimless rattling of an unmoored mind. Liberating, in a way. Maybe that was the freedom everyone fought for. The world was one well-aimed head blow away from being free.

Anders waited for one of the ringleaders to rally. Columbia I's noncommitment had equally baffled the demon and the dreamer. The first to unwind it would have the initiative.

"Brilliant! Thank you, my liege," said Gleason, fully possessed. Charm submerged the invective that had animated him moments ago. "What, precisely, does that mean?"

"I need time to think," said Queen Columbia I. Her voice cracked. Tears pooled in her eyes. Sensing the edge of crisis, Duke Ross whispered in her ear.

"I've finished thinking," declared the queen. "There's no time for this now. The tall imposter's armies are on the move, and we need to prepare. And . . . well . . ."

Duke Ross whispered further clarification. Columbia I mouthed the words as he spoke, scratching them into memory. Her fine-tuned, expertly neutral face returned.

"The war chest comes first. Until temporary laborers can be debated calmly and rationally, without external pressure, we'll enact a compromise."

A vein bulged on one side of Gleason's forehead. Followed by its twin. The smile below reflected civility, awe, and murder. His nails drew blood from his palm. Two or so centuries of anger boiled within.

"We'll keep the temporary laborers we have and stop importing more," continued the queen. "It's nearly emancipation, which should follow naturally in time."

"Temporary laborers."

"Yes."

"The men chained together underground."

"And driving the economy," added Slade. "Which drives everything else. Up to and including pretentious prose poems. And paying the spades on the walls."

"Choke, filth."

"He's yelling. I'm not yelling," noted Slade. "It's something in his temperament."

"You shouldn't yell, Duke Gleason."

"Listen, *child*," Gleason began, half dazed. He looked ready to tip over and never get up. Anders guessed that decorum was as dead as sanity and rose to hook an arm under the duke's shoulder. Shocked faces told him decorum lived, but he couldn't back off without dropping his friend to the floor. With dozens of angry eyes on him, Anders felt the chamber's sheer size for the first time. It could hold the assembled gawkers several times over. Without a better idea in mind, Anders saluted with his free hand. Then the director rallied.

"For you, I described an ideal nation, one that people would want to believe in. Those essays attract new arrivals every day, and they will draw more. I wrote them as the spirit of the country. Our *On Liberty*.

"Call it . . . speculative nation-building. It's what I see when I close my eyes. Maybe we're not there yet. But we can reach it, as long as we don't pervert our potential."

A raspberry interrupted. The noise was loud, wet, and well practiced. A familiar sound, from a familiar source. Anders could still scarcely believe it.

"Great story," said Slade. "Here, in reality, this compromise sounds excellent. Thank you, Your Grace. This week's numbers look excellent, and next week's can only be better."

37

THE FIRST SHOE

The news reached Patricia before he did. They didn't discuss their next step. It was obvious. When history moved, sane actors were of one mind. They simply gathered the necessary effects and reconvened before The Vanguard.

Neither liked what they found.

Anders carried Union dollars, a bag stuffed with rations, four canteens, extra shoes, and his old Union uniform. A single disguise felt a little thin, but he trusted Patricia to make up the difference.

Patricia carried four revolvers, a rifle, and a suspiciously familiar sword. Collectively, they made her look like a storybook corsair. Hints of additional arms poked out from her sleeves and waist.

"What's that for?" they asked. Not in unison—words still came to her a hair faster. But they shared confusion, if not timing.

"To fight," answered Patricia.

"To leave," answered Anders, a half-second later.

A space opened up between them. She looked wounded, as if he'd insulted her. Which, in turn, wounded him. Navigating the gap called for all the maturity of their advanced age.

"Five guns? You have two hands."

"In case you had trouble finding your own. Which you clearly did."

"I don't need guns. Well, at least not more than one."

"You're a knight."

"It's 1863. Knight's a time of day. The air here's making you crazy."

The gulf widened.

"Yes. Absolutely. Completely mad. You've been Black for a month, so I'll tell you the rest of your story. It doesn't improve. You get angrier, every day. God keeps spitting until you've drowned. You won't meet a full-time Negro over ten who isn't crazy."

"That's garbage." The words were a reflex, from another life. He restarted from the present. "That feels a little true. Half true. Very true. But we're arguing about dying for a dead cause, not that. It's lying with—"

"That's my idea. You can't use it against me."

"It's redirection with facts." He congratulated himself on finding a work-around.

"Coward. Mama's boy. Grayback. Traitor."

"Fine. But we have to leave."

"Gutless. Lunatic. Blowhard. Failure."

"You're not listening."

"Ofay. House nigger. House ofay. Braindea—"

"Murderer."

A winning move, and the wrong one. Arguing, like Ofay, had no inherent limit or end goal.

Like most siblings or faiths, the same path had taught them different lessons. And like most divorces or reformations, discussing it went poorly. Patricia fired off six more insults as she stomped off, stopped, and then shot off ten more. None closed the gap.

✦ ✦ ✦

The same horse waited behind The Vanguard. If the owner hadn't learned last week's lesson, then the results were out of Anders's hands. Direct looks at reality were the American character's second-greatest weakness. The first was admitting the second.

He rode to the southern edge of San Valentin, nearly trampling multiple silver-clad socialites on the way. They weren't in his path, but his arc drifted toward the more elaborately adorned traders and nobles. To say nothing of the graycoats. Patricia's insults still hovered over him, and inspiring a little panic helped his mind rest.

A dozen nervous former Harriers ambled before the south gate, including Boots, who Anders conceded existed in shared reality rather than the angel-haunted corners of his mind. The guards wore San Valentin uniforms, which were Union uniforms with crimson scrap thread stitched on. Boots reacted first.

"Ser Anders! The palace finally sent someone. It's pure hell out there. Any orders?"

"Yes," he lied. Any new madness Boots had discovered was his problem. "But first, open the gate. I have to deliver a message. To Mexico, or the Canadians. They may be willing to support us. Or at least trade silver for something we can eat or shoot."

"How? We're surrounded."

A shout, sob, and laugh leaked from Anders in unison.

"Agreed," said Boots. "You should take a look from the wall. For tactical appraisin' and such."

He followed Boots in a compliant fog. The royal guard led his teenage superior up the spiral steps of a security tower, saying words that went unanswered and unheard. Court's thin air had expanded to the walls, and breathing through it demanded focused effort.

The letters nailed to the final door almost slipped by him. They had titles like "Free Air," "Belief in Tomorrow," and "Life Before Death." The soldiers had, out of either reverence or irony, pinned Gleason's recent pamphlets to the portal. A comment on the decor died between Anders's mind and lips. They were just more Scientific Theater. He braced his soul and watched Boots throw open the door.

Any hope for exaggeration on Boots's part, or a wholesale lie, died in the light. They were surrounded. More cannons than he cared to count circled the city walls, backed by countless blue specks. The specks busied themselves digging trenches, hauling ammunition, pushing even more artillery toward the front, and looking busy near the others.

He could see why the city hadn't fired back. For all the showy cannon decorating the inner and outer walls, they were thoroughly outgunned. Once the shooting started, San Valentin's royal experiment would end.

He'd never get home. He'd never have sex again. He'd never hug his mother or scream at her for burning him. He'd never have kids or find out why he was expected to have kids by default. He'd never learn monarchism's appeal to a healthy adult. He'd never have sex again. He'd never tell a reporter that he'd survived Gettysburg, saved New York, or brought slavery in San Valentin to light. He'd never have sex again. The second the Union got bored with the siege, his farce of a life would be over.

"We can take 'em," said Boots.

Anders puked over the wall. An enemy scout below cried out.

37.5

DIPLOMACY, INTERNAL AND EXTERNAL

Dear Gibbon,

Harrow informs me you're displeased with the siege's pace. Contend with it. The soup of national honor needs time to boil. The bread of glory needs time to rise. Only the thin gruel of failure is instantaneous, and you can get that in excess from Grant, if cirrhosis hasn't taken him yet. Delaying my reinstatement was your error, as I recall.

Still, the sad fact remains you will be president for another year. To forestall further disgrace to the office, I will break down, in simple monkey language, my activities since arriving in Nevada.

First, I scouted the land. The enemy hides anywhere and everywhere, in numbers too large to counter with the pittance you have granted me. Nonetheless, at great human cost and even greater risk, I have reached the city. Moreover, I have grown to understand the land around the city, arming us for the pitched insurgency that will doubtlessly emerge from the sands.

Second, I studied the enemy. Specifically, their mindset, which I have come to fear and respect. American monarchy sounds like idiocy to you because you lack imagination. But crowns ruled the world for centuries before your type, and still rule much of it.

Third, I drilled the cavalry. Less loyal parties may have

described these drills as parades. I suggest having them shot for undermining the Union cause. This is no time to show weakness. I'll certainly do the same on my end.

Finally, I have adapted to externalities. Savage raiders disguised as women and children still litter the lands around the city. Keeping my men—your citizens, lest you forget—alive has taken every ounce of brilliance God blessed me with.

You're welcome.

Sincerely,
General James McClellan
Your Successor

✝ ✝ ✝

Old Friend,

It's a tempting offer. Open gates, our democracy's so-called royal family, and the spade preacher that embarrassed my good friend Harrow. An impressive sum of silver. All gifts in line with the Jefferson Firearms tradition of quality and value.

But it lacks a certain theater, don't you think? Certainly, working with you would speed along victory. But authority (democratic, royal, or otherwise) is built on a mandate. And mandates demand blood. San Valentin contains all the blood I need to sign my name across history.

Thank you for displaying sanity, humility, and fealty in a sorely lacking era. However, my long-suffering subordinate would rather "Burn every nigger turncoat in those walls alive." He's my prospective vice president, so there's nothing to be done.

Yours,
James McClellan,
President-in-Waiting

38

CRABS IN A BUCKET GENERALLY GET ALONG, BUT THE FOLKLORE DESCRIBES MANY SITUATIONS WELL

Anders lingered on the wall for some time. It was as safe as anywhere else, now that Union batteries sat in range. One railway gun—at least a twenty-five-pounder—had soldiers climbing over it like a giant toy, taken by its power. Anders wished it would discharge. An accident was his best chance of taking anyone with him.

The sun crawled past its noon peak, into its equally oppressive evening post. Amid possible solutions, Anders would accept the sun going out. Some of the pilgrimage's haziness had returned to him, and a familiar torpor had settled over everyone in sight.

Today, that included the bulk of the city. Nervous tension drove most of the populace outside, to gossip about their visitors. Or the crown's plan to save them. Or nothing at all: he couldn't *hear* them from above. He just knew that they weren't rioting or rushing the gates, so he couldn't relate. The civilian world was as alien as the martial or courtly one.

"Any orders? At all?" asked Boots. He'd dutifully watched the knight do nothing and found a bucket for any subsequent panic attacks.

"Nope."

If morale could nudge the outcome, he would've lied. San Valentin's thoroughly divided forces consisted of four depleted regiments. Two and a half thousand men, optimistically. The army outside the city had, in insider army terms, more men. Gleason's miracle had inspired a thousand turncoats, and the state had coughed out superior numbers without effort.

Half the ex(ish)-Confederates ran mines outside the walls. By now they were dead, caged, or in flight. Visualizing it gave him some comfort—and reduced his estimated backup by a third.

"The palace hasn't sent anyone else," said Boots.

"It's not a palace. It's an old bandit hideout, holding a depressed child."

"Just say something. Make us *do* something. For morale."

"Put more men on the wall. They might think there are more of us that way."

Boots shuffled away. Most likely out of his life altogether. Anders considered shouting a goodbye, but it felt implicit. And Boots could be a hallucination.

As could McClellan's parade. The reborn general wanted his presence felt on the opposite side of the continent, leaving little time for trenches. He led a column of cavalry on a slow trot around the rim of the city, on a horse as white as the officers flanking him. Said officers performed a simplified flag-twirling routine. *Revere Swing* to the left, pause, *Revere Revert* to the right, repeat.

Anders stuck out his tongue, channeling Slade. Mounted twirling was gaudy and outdated. Modern artists kept both feet on the ground for a reason: they could do better maneuvers, faster, and more consistently. He finally felt like a master: Anders couldn't feel or appreciate the dance anymore because he truly understood it. National dressage channeled the soul of nations, entities that happened to lack souls.

"Thanks, Wendy," he muttered. No hallucination there. She was dead, and thus heard nothing, said nothing, and thought nothing. Just like him, once McClellan got tired of celebrating McClellan. Or once Harrow, doubtlessly in tow, got tired of waiting for revenge.

The angel above could be a hallucination, but he wasn't in the mood to quibble. The lack of reaction below made as much sense as the lack of rioting. Real and unreal scarcely mattered if no behavior changed.

Its visage had lost shock value, though appearing in his waking hours was novel. Recent glimpses of human viscera and misery made the creature's dense knot of ornate wings and limbs look quaint. At least they were intact. As for the face, the resemblance to the nurse, the queen, and on reflection his mother, pointed toward poor ability to distinguish white women. Life in a free town and the army trenches offered few chances to develop the skill.

"What did I ever see in you?" he mumbled. "You don't even listen."

"Be not afraid," it bellowed. "To give your life is righteous."

"That's insane," Anders spat back. "Tell God he should keep Mole alive, unless he's ready for a fight."

"A life is a small trade for a nation."

"There's never been a country worth dying for. You're a flying liar, and I hope I'm crazy so that you don't get to exist."

"You will live on in the hearts of men."

"Fuck off."

The seraphim remained in place, so Anders fucked off first. He had to try something before nature took its course. Sitting still under a guillotine was suicide.

✣ ✣ ✣

Day one of brainstorming yielded nothing. Imaginary cannon fire and arguments with heaven clouded his mind past usefulness. The inn's ceiling offered no answers.

He spent day two watching another McClellan parade. The route had grown more elaborate, and the spinning was almost passable. With more luck and loyalty, Anders could have stood on that side of the wall. He might yet, if he found the right exit.

On day three, the enemy fired a warning shot. Or a cannon misfired ahead of schedule. Either way, a granary burned, and Anders sobbed beneath the covers.

Anders mourned Patricia on day four. And Petey. The other two had tried his patience, but he missed half the relationship. Hopefully, they'd find their own way out. Someone had to.

He returned to the walls on day five. His suggestions—orders, he supposed—had been followed to the letter. The Harriers lined the walls of San Valentin like black scarecrows. A sense of duty, like influenza, had spread rapidly and uncontrollably in the cramped corridors of the city. He wished fewer people listened to him. Or started earlier.

On day six, an answer hit him like a runaway carriage. But he decided to wait until tomorrow. A full week would lend the idea a sense of symmetry. If serving under McClellan, Lee, and Gleason had taught him any-thing, it was the power of theater.

That, and he hoped Patricia came back. Even as Porter.

✣ ✣ ✣

An irksome, riot-free walk brought him to the unburnt, non-pillaged pal-ace. Was civic responsibility a myth? The frontier city sat still through the end of the world. Even a mass orgy would be more impressive than the weepy somnolence hanging over San Valentin. And fit the name better. One civilian even curtsied his way, as if knighthood deserved respect in any century, let alone the nineteenth.

Some doomed souls still rolled dice. They traded bills as if their net worth could block a mortar. It took everything for Anders to keep moving instead of starting a fight or quitting outright. There were plenty of places to lie down and wait things out. He could even try dice.

He flicked his own forehead to clear it. The guillotine overhead couldn't cloud his thinking. He held his comrades' future in his palm, though not the city. Both the real gambling den and Gleason's paradise were doomed. But he could save a non-zero number of people, including himself. An infinite improvement.

Most remaining courtiers and guards were different shades of drunk. Understandable. Anders had rediscovered a speck of hope and merely carried a pleasant buzz. A harder one, once he found Thomas loitering in front of Gleason's office. They split the remnants of a jar of army moon-shine. Then they went through a proper greeting.

"Been good?"

"No. Horrible. Hell on Earth. I'm physically out of tears. You?"

"I got a graycoat nurse pregnant. Don't know how to handle that, so dying's fine." Thomas chucked the jar down the hall. "Any idea why they're not shooting yet?"

"It's McClellan. Nothing's going to happen until someone else makes him move."

"You served under him?"

"Six months of purgatory and bragging. He always had at least four twirlers behind him, with a fresh routine. He made Harrow look humble."

"He needs to get moving. Or hit the other granary. I can't get through a siege like this. She yells *nigger* every time we fight or make up. She might think it's my name."

"Well, if you decide not to die, I might have a way out. You can probably bring her."

"Damn. Are you sure?"

"See you, Thomas."

It made sense to be armed, given the situation. But the long table in Gleason's office held excess arms for a brigade, let alone two men. Knives, worn bayonets, the latest in Jefferson repeaters, and pistols of every size filled space meant for nice plates. Though Gleason, in a case of parallel thinking, seemed to have cleared the room of all traces of silver. He didn't see the West Hanovers eating off of anything else.

The Duke of Morale occupied one end chair. A familiar white face occupied the other. The boy looked taller in Wendy's portrait, but that's what artists were paid for.

"Hail! I'm Prince—"

"Fascinating. Gleason, I have something important."

"Anders!" said the director, mercifully neglecting the *Ser*. Good. This would be easier if his feet were closer to the earth.

"Listen. Remember when we—"

"I heard you took charge on the walls," interjected Gleason.

"Nope."

"Still humble, well done. This is Prince Polus. He's a part of our next move."

"Mmm-hmm," grunted Anders.

"That's more of a Black affectation, and one I've never been fond of. Don't pick it up."

"I am . . . Never mind. We've got to get out of here. As many of our people as we can manage. The graybacks and royalists can surrender, but every Negro here would hang."

"You haven't greeted the prince yet."

"He can come too. We'll use the sewer tunnel. The one Ser . . . that the queen's messenger led us through."

"Anders! That's brilliant!"

After everything, the compliment still made Anders stand a little taller. At another, less stupid time, he'd reflect on the impact of a fatherless life.

"It'll be an excellent backup, if the succession fails."

Anders went silent.

"We can change things here, after installing the prince. Then I can handle McClellan."

Anders sank into an end chair. His heart gave up on warning attacks. The ungrateful brain in charge insisted on dragging it back into peril. If he'd listened to his first heart episode, he'd be relaxing in Canada by now, with every other sensible freeman in North America.

"And you're perfect for the plan."

Anders took off his cap, covered his mouth, and screamed.

38.5

A HANDBILL

LADIES & GENTLEMEN OF THE COURT,

☞ **Panic?** There's no reason!

☞ **Weep?** There's no point!

☞ **Escape?** There's no way!

A siege is temporary. Memories are eternal.
Behold *The City That Defeated
a Continental Superpower.*
The newest and finest work by Tobias Gleason,
Duke of Morale.
A vision of tomorrow, uniting supporters and
opponents of temporary labor.
One night only.

39

CHILD EMPERORS RARELY LIVED
INTO ADULTHOOD

After muddy rebel tents and burnt-out stages, twirling in a palace should have felt like a miracle. It held all the prestige his mother and inner voice deemed impossible. He just needed to ignore the gun tied to his back with scratchy twine. If the damned thing went off early, it would spare him from being killed after the scheme collapsed. Or, worse yet, succeeded.

Anders could've run off on his own. But abandoning people came harder than ideas. Nations, races, and all the other noise were replaceable uniforms. The soldiers trusted with the coup were compatriots, or at least coworkers. His brain could accept leaving them behind, but his useless idiot heart would give out.

Plus, he and Petey still had fighting to do. Maybe he'd apologize first this time. Or wait for her. Or half apologize and never mention it again. Perhaps neither of them would apologize, and they'd repeat the fight once a year or so. They'd find a compromise, alive, in a sane place.

The same couldn't be said for Gleason. He could stay in The American Future, or Valhalla, or whatever he called the promised land. The director put ideas before anyone left alive, which Anders resented as a survivor. The moment they'd lost Gleason was hard to pin. Unless it was the week Gleason lost his sister, half his face, and the theater he'd dedicated his life to. Then it was simple.

Maybe no one sane was left, only competing flavors of madness. McClellan would call them crazy for rebelling. Harrow would call McClellan crazy for not attacking a week ago. Lee would call them all crazy for not letting his countrymen crack their whips in peace. Anders would call himself crazy for ever enlisting.

Finally, Lincoln ran a giant, sea-to-sea version of the Friends Asylum, forcing inmates to eat without dashing bowls against the wall and declaring their cell the United Republic of Soup. For this, the man deserved respect. Anders would've simply enjoyed keeping the half of the country with factories and ideas.

Anders peered back at his own asylum. The trio showed no sign of nerves, which put him on edge. Fear played healthy roles in performance and assassination. Certainly for the overlap.

"Everyone know their steps?"

Their answers didn't ignite his confidence. Understandable, since Gleason chose them only to force his involvement. All three had let him down by showing up instead of taking his advice and *leaving*. The sewer was a redolent portal to the rest of their lives. Only Thomas had risen to the occasion and fled history. Anders prayed for the wind at his back.

"That's fine. Just stand behind me and waggle it around. No one can tell the difference."

They would perform during the intermission of *The City That Defeated a Continental Superpower*. Or perhaps they were part of the story. The details had rolled past Anders like so much seawater. He'd focused on the director's eyes, which peered into a future far removed from the current sinkhole. Speculative Dramaturgy offered countless looming questions without a single immediate answer.

"Don't just *spin* once, young Anders. Use every *flag* in the chamber," said Joaquin. He'd never looked happier. Anticipation of soon-to-be-dead slavers drew dimples on his cheeks. Anders forgave his excuse for code. Or humor. The language wall was likely higher than they'd ever acknowledged.

"I knew you'd stick around." Polly looked antsier. The junior assassin rocked back and forth on her heels, trying to push her unease into the floorboards. Before losing his mind, he'd have asked why she'd chosen Polly. Today, he could see the logic. Polly had the most experience.

Mole whispered names. Presumably his family's. Asking now would be galling.

The first act closed out, and twenty harriers-turned-thespians filed out into the hallway. Boots threw the quartet a wink, which horrified Anders. If the potentially imaginary Negro knew about the scheme, it could have leaked to anyone. He spun around on his heels to run. Joaquin grabbed his shoulders, turned him back around, and shoved.

"Traitor," Anders hissed. He stumbled forward before his public.

The nobility looked haggard. Their attire remained flawless, from the shine of their shoes to the makeup beneath each outdated wig. But every face sagged with dissonance. Maintaining proper enthusiasm in death's shadow turned sanity into a rapidly dwindling resource. To a man, they eyed him hoping for a cure. However temporary.

"Er, welcome," announced Anders. Flag-twirling sets were silent, but decorum was dead. "If morale fails, the enemy prevails," he added. His voice traveled well.

The queen, who currently clung to her absurd chair for comfort, nodded along. She looked worse than her underlings, who looked worse than the despondent masses outside. An impressive tricolor dress had its pattern interrupted by dark red splotches of wine. Her public smile stretched a tenth of an inch past human limits, resembling something a disturbed child might have drawn. As a recent disturbed child, Anders knew it well. He bowed her way, likely flashing the gun on his person. If anyone felt like intervening, this was their moment.

His backup (or shackles) filed in behind him and waited for a sign to start. He, in turn, waited for the music. After a personal eternity, the first horn kicked in, followed by too much percussion. A thunderous, bone-shaking march filled the chamber. The jolt nearly knocked his heart off-rhythm. Through the shock, or because of it, he found excitement. Live or die, he'd peaked as an artist.

It was the wrong song. Just as well.

To their credit, none of the others tripped into him or swatted him with a pole. They might have even followed his advice. Anders focused on his own hands. Heads of state weren't killed during plays often, and he didn't want his show to be the low point.

At the peak of his powers, the art of flag-twirling transformed. The patriotic swell of the music. The agile gliding of his feet. The joy of his audience, in the face of their personal apocalypse. They all illuminated one truth.

Flag-twirling was stupid. He'd wasted an incredible amount of time.

Anders stopped halfway through a *Hamilton Slant-Rhyme* and reached behind his back. Any head of state that hadn't caught on deserved to die. The queen currently clapped like a seal, flanked by Duke Ross and Slade.

Slade.

He could shoot the queen. He *should* shoot the queen. The plan was to shoot the queen. But Slade sat *right there*, and he had Slade's gun, and the universe would never hand Anders this kind of symmetry again. If he didn't shoot Slade, the man would pop up wherever he hid next, with a fresh plan to re-create the East India Tea Company at a new line of latitude.

Anders whipped the revolver forward. It slid out of his grip, skittering across the marble floor. The hall went silent.

"Ah. Dang," said Anders.

He swung the flagpole, cracking Slade across the temple. His form was perfect: the impact made a sound between a split coconut and the multiple skulls Anders had heard shatter since enlisting. More the latter. He'd never even seen a coconut.

Silver teeth flew free.

Before Anders could apologize, surrender, or gloat, Joaquin had the gun. The Reaper's hands flickered like a moth's wings. The six-round cylinder delivered two shots to the queen, one to Slade's prone form, one to Duke Ross, one to the unluckiest duchess in San Valentin, and an extra shot to Slade.

A bit of screaming started.

Anders tried to take in the details of Slade's death. Emotions, exclamations, final declarations of triumph or vengeance. The gunsmith's face was a mess. Nothing above his neck was in shape to convey or experience anything. It had, in the space of a few seconds, transitioned from a human head into a pile of uncooked sausage. A dozen or so fleeing nobles trampled through it, mashing it into a semisolid.

Anders threw up again.

The nameless duchess yelled loudest of all. Certainly louder than the other victims, who lay stone still. A fair reaction, since she had the least reason to expect a karmic bullet. Joaquin gave her an apologetic shrug before taking a bayonet to the stomach.

40

THE OTHER SHOE

Four royal guards closed in—recent Confederates, judging by their tragic beards and zeal for a defeated cause. Their charge was a fresh corpse, but they could still chase redemptive violence. Now that they flanked him, "gaudy" felt like a hollow critique of silver blades.

Mercifully, his body moved before his mind could muck things up. Anders dove for the floor, sparing himself the next thrust. Meanwhile, Mole flailed his own flagpole. It lacked the finesse or precision of Anders's strike, which taught Anders that finesse and precision meant nothing. Metal met Adam's apple, and the lead guard fell gasping and gurgling. His peers stumbled back, a simple arrest and execution having devolved into a struggle.

Polly tried pushing parts of Joaquin back in. They stayed put, but the patient remained unresponsive. Undeterred, she tried prodding him awake, which just smeared his own blood across his face. The result, however grisly, matched any army doctor's.

Logic said to flee. Other drives said to help fight or try to save Joaquin. In ten years, he might be equipped for that choice. For now, Anders gawked. Even prayer required more presence of mind than he could summon.

He avoided looking at the late queen. They might have gotten along, or at least argued entertainingly. The current had dragged her behind armed adults with Big Ideas as well. She'd just made the mistake of being somebody. Every second he outlived her was a testament to his supernatural luck.

Then Gleason's men poured in. Original Harriers, from Anders's first games of Ofay. Either a heartbeat or ten years ago, by Anders's estimate. Now they had new uniforms, a new mission, and the same sleep-deprived faces. He could relate.

They restored order through chaotic and directionless application of force. The queen's failed guards collapsed under kicks and rifle butts. Alongside Anders, Polly, Mole, a dozen unrelated nobles, a serving boy, and one of Gleason's men who had fallen out of formation. A boot found the back of Anders's back, knocking the breath and confusion out of him. The world regained simple, angry clarity.

"We can't predict tragedy," declared a familiar voice. Anders's teeth ground together until the pressure threatened to crack them. His life was an endless procession of speeches, each more insulting to human intelligence and joy than the last. He'd accepted Gleason's lectures as more enlightening, or at least entertaining, and now he couldn't hear the distinction.

Gleason flowed into the chamber, pleased with the show's overall reception. He wore full funeral attire, including black shoes, black gloves, and a black cape. Perfect attire for mourning a warm corpse. His trajectory took him directly toward the silver throne.

The prince carefully shadowed Gleason's footsteps. He wore identical mourning attire and softly practiced his coronation speech. Anders picked out the words *proud, liberty,* and *mandate* before Gleason's voice took over the chamber again.

"Or when men will be pushed beyond reason," continued the director, stepping over Anders and then the leaking Joaquin. "No one can speak to who or what motivated this."

Gleason flashed a quick hand sign, and the pressure on Anders's back abated. Not enough to stand or interrupt the director's moment, but enough to avoid suffocating. Very considerate.

He shifted for a better view of Joaquin. After spinning behind innumerable enlisted men, officers, and generals, he'd never seen anyone breathe easier in a uniform. Joaquin didn't shrink into a servant or explode into animated ego. He'd just enjoyed his purpose. What was that clarity like? It'd be wonderful to know before America killed Anders too.

"But if I, San Valentin's main speaker, were to guess: it was punting human bondage into the future. It stained the conscience of the nation.

But through sacrifice and struggle, this dying soul has redeemed us. Thank you, Joaquin."

"Choke," barked Polly. The soldier standing on her back restored pressure. Her cursing deflated into pained wheezing.

"A difficult and complex lesson," added Gleason. "Unique in history. I doubt it'll be forgotten soon."

Gleason waited for signs of further resistance. Anders went slack. The sooner this ended, the better. Gleason repeated the signal, and the boot on his spine disappeared. Anders was explicitly free to stand and implicitly free to stay put.

"Amnesty is the only way forward. Aren't these wretches patriots, just like us? Doesn't this crisis echo *The City That Defeated a Continental Superpower*? I don't believe in coincidence. This is a message from the earth. The land itself wants to change. And that change begins with new leadership."

The director dragged Columbia I off the throne, legs-first. Then Gleason patted the chair like a beloved pet, or at least an obedient one. On cue, Prince Polus stepped forward. And then inched. And then stopped. He eyed his public guiltily, as if any of the unarmed dilettantes could object. Gleason patted the throne again, and waited for his new pet to do its trick. Each beat of delay thinned his fatherly smile.

The prince hesitated further. Streaks of his sister's blood, bone, and brain dotted the throne. Gleason grabbed his latest charge by the shoulders and shoved him down.

"King Polux, the One True King of America. Long may he reign." A guard shoved Columbia I's blood-slick circlet onto the prince's forehead. Red droplets dripped and dribbled onto the youth's nose.

"Polus. It's King Polus, with an *S*," stammered Polus. Tears pooled in the new King of America's eyes. He looked ready for someone, anyone to take his chair.

"As you will."

"T-thank you."

"Your first decree is barring slavery. Everyone is equal under the uncaring demiurge."

"The Union has the mines."

"Just say it."

"No slaves. And everyone's equal."

Finally, after watching history reuse material, Anders saw something new. Gleason slouched. Not with depression, or exhaustion, but satisfaction. He'd reached his finish line. A Black future, in a Black nation. He even had a white slave with a nice hat.

Whenever the director remembered Anders, and his role in reaching The American Future, there'd be a reward. Anders let it go. He limped over to Polly and hooked an arm around hers. He took one labored step at a time away from glory, fame, and honor. Wherever Gleason led the free and brave, he planned to be far away. Maybe Canada. They made it to the foyer before reality interjected.

The earth jumped. The first mortar shattered every window to the south and knocked the silver throne onto its side. Shards of stained glass rained onto the gentry, injuring some and killing others. Anders's eardrums quit. The second mortar hit harder, collapsing half the ceiling. The attic merged with the court and crushed American kings, dukes, and assassins with equal ease. All the light and glamour of court returned to dust and darkness. McClellan had decided to tend to the war.

40.5

---◆---

THE PLAGUE

From the Desk of Justice David Davis

Abe,

Read this twice. Important and idiotic events are unfolding. In fact, they walk hand in hand.

To date, you've put the nation before the campaign. This will certainly earn you a place in the books of the Lord, and hopefully the books of history. But it's trouble in the present. The voting man, as rare as he is, prefers immediate ease. Most who believed the war would be *easy* are disillusioned or dead.

Might I suggest, for a spell, putting the campaign ahead of the nation?

That may sound immoral. Because it is. But letting James McClellan lead a nation, state, or general store is worse. I admit, punting him to that pointless Nevada boondoggle was inspired. As your former campaign manager, I've seldom been prouder. But as McClellan strokes himself in the desert, his campaign tells a different story.

One of a hero.

The crux of it: while we drink the blood of the people, McClellan's charged across lines of division to save American royalty from black bandits. Fixing the crisis *we* created by arming coons. Those aren't my words. I'd let a bullet pass through my lips first. But I *hear* them.

There are handbills. Drawings. Songs. Metal pins pressed with his silhouette. I can't walk two blocks in the capital without seeing our worst general's face.

It's maddening. I won't deny the man's body count. The problem is that they're *mostly our men.* Yet as I write this, my braindead son is at a rally for "The Hero of Nevada." He's not alone.

The papers call it McClellan Fever. I fear it's catching.

Yours Truly,

David Davis

41

ANDERS GETS OLD

While sex committed Anders to peace, bombardment turned him against war. For all the insanity that hung over San Valentin like fog, it had become his city. He'd learned to live with and appreciate crazy people, and even accept himself as one. Watching artillery blast it to nothing wrung out his soul. The flames were an afterthought.

Their own guns flared back, and then swiftly died. Somewhere between the siege, the cloud of malaise, the coup, and the death of every city leader, the will to defend the walls had withered. The batteries were abandoned before enemy fire found them.

The bedlam jump-started long-overdue looting. Everything had to go: from the silver chains and swords of the elite to The Vanguard's last untapped cask. Former soldiers, former nobles, and countless people with the simple misfortune to live and work there pried wealth off the walls, with nowhere to take it.

For the enemy, seizing ground wasn't the order of the day. Blasting the gates open and establishing order was well within McClellan's power. But pounding them into nothing first was an order of magnitude easier, and he was still the sloth that had let Lee slip away every time the war begged to end. San Valentin would be buried, not taken.

Anders took a final look at the palace mural. Mortars had blown giant holes into the grotesque children's forms, erasing some of them entirely. The overall aesthetic improved. If they added a dash of blue, it would look more like a landmark and less like a nightmare. Then Polly slapped him into focus. They could act now, or join the city's mascots.

Best not to hang around.

✧ ✧ ✧

The sewage tunnel maintained its inspiring sights and smells. With a hint of something new: the scent of iron, and a red tint to the sludge. Anders still appreciated entering the murk alive. The world above was made of lead and smoke.

B. K. Jefferson's uniform had grown tight on him. Pant seams protested with each sloshing step. Far from the only mismatch: a taller, broader body fit awkwardly with a brain that hadn't grown. He'd *learned*, but the bloody grotesques in his memory were a poor trade for the vision of a young patriot. That America had been alight with potential and glory. Now every friend he'd made was dead, dying, or complaining behind him.

"I feel like a coward," said Polly. She'd stayed Polly. After some debate, "white nurse" seemed like the most welcome apparition into the Union fold. Every saint standing between soldiers and barber surgeons was revered. That aura would, hopefully, smooth over questions during her second proper defection. If nothing else, it was the best powder job she'd managed so far. Whiteface had become rote, like putting on a shoe or not snatching a trigger.

Anders didn't contradict her. He'd embraced cowardice. It came as naturally as exhaling. Fitting, since it was all that kept him breathing.

"Say something reassuring," ordered Polly. Desperation robbed her voice of bite.

"You could turn around and be a legend. Just like Hua Mulan. You'd be honorable, famous, and dead."

She followed in sullen silence. Something more soulful would have been better. A moving lie, for morale. That part of him didn't feel alive. Just the force that moved forward. Left, and right, and left again, until something finally caught him.

"Do you think Mole made it?"

"Yes," lied Anders. Then he thought better of it. "No."

"What about Boots?"

"He's real? Also, no."

"Gleason?"

"No."

"Why not?"

The tunnel shook. He left the conversation there for a bit, until he could feel Polly's morale flatlining.

"We have his notes. He'd be happy with that."

"That's crap."

"Absolutely. But he thought that way. He still has a chance to change the country."

The words felt even emptier than they sounded. He could *hear* the nation not changing above them. The reprisal for Negro secession would be more complete than anything that befell Georgia.

"Did any of this have a point? It feels like a big joke by God."

More shaking. He pretended not to hear her over the tumult, which was almost true. Then the bombardment took a break to spite him.

"I need something," said Polly. "Just make it up."

"I'm not Gleason. We have to go."

Polly stood still. A protest had begun.

"Come on."

She didn't budge.

Anders clenched his teeth, dug deep, and found nothing. Duty, God, whiteness, Blackness, friendship, performance, and nation were behind them, bleeding. In seconds, when he failed here, love would be out too. The only point to existence was to exist.

"We can win."

"What?"

"We don't need a big idea. They think we don't deserve to breathe. We still are. We're winning."

It was his best, last trick. Polly laughed at it.

She had a booming, graceless laugh, with phlegmy snorts between guffaws. The half sobs that snuck in between breaths threw off any sense of rhythm. Anders stood as patiently as panic allowed, hoping she would finish before the tunnel collapsed and buried them in filth forever. It didn't help that he'd joined in, with twice the volume and mixed tears. Maybe he could be a clown, once the inferno around the continent dimmed. His unplanned punch line got Polly's feet going. Left, and right, and left again.

They kept moving.

41.5

NOTES ON GLEASON'S NOTES

I'm Anders. Or was Anders, if you're reading this a long time from now. Which you might be! This was the second-craziest American rebellion I've seen. Maybe they'll blame all this on bread mold.

You're likely after Gleason's notes, which follow. The second half's mostly me, so I'd say I warrant an introduction.

Gleason fought for his country's love. He wrote for it. When that didn't work, he picked up a gun. That didn't work either, so he wrote harder. And that failed too, so he picked up a thousand guns.

That's impressive. I even joined in! Shame how it ended. And started.

His country was born with a half measure. One saying free didn't mean free and equal didn't mean equal, but the flag meant both. It will never change. Whoever wins, America will never be worth dying for. The flag eats heroism to protect and spread itself, and returns nothing. At best, it takes less. You can't earn your freedom. That's an insult. You're born free.

I tried heroism. I don't recommend it.

I was almost eaten, for nothing. My sacrifice wouldn't change the war. The North won before it started. Six Lees against seven McClellans would end the same way. Count the bullets. America doesn't need one Black life to survive. But we're here to be spent.

I'd rather survive. I'll outlast this war, and whatever new half measures follow. I'll live off the brat's silver until my heart gives out. I'll do it without a flag, or vain hope of changing an empire's soul. And I'll be free.

ACKNOWLEDGMENTS

All me, baby.

Except for Reeves Hamilton and Nick Mullendore, without whom I'd be writing jingles for sugar pills. And the marvelous Retha Powers, Leela Gebo, Hannah Campbell, and the rest of the Holt team, without whom this book would be nonexistent and/or a series of tasteless gifs. And Brockway and Seanbaby, without whom I'd have traded words for hunting people. And the late Eugeny Higgins, without whom I'd have written this from a maximum-security prison. And my sisters, without whom I'd have written this from a minimum-security prison. And my brothers, without whom I'd be unprepared for my inevitable stint in prison. And the Dayle expanded universe, who generally get agitated without attention. Not you, Egbert. Sit in the corner.

Then it's all me.

Aside from Paul Beatty, Rivka Galchen, Gary Shteyngart, and the dearly missed Paul La Farge, who made my education an education. And all my students, who help me pay for my education. And Chelsea Cutchens, who gave me my first shot. And Emma Allen, who gave me my second. And my ironic anime rivals in the newsletter and Patreon trenches, who keep my training arc alive. And my unironic anime rival, Derek, whom I will defeat one day. And impertinent shōnen upstart Sam, who will never reach Gold Roger's treasure before me.

From there? All me.

And the full Failsquad, the kind of lifelong Greek chorus that keeps a name like "Failsquad." And the full Sympoh family, who somehow survived rehab chicken. And everyone reading my nonsense on *1900HOTDOG*,

Extra Evil, See More Evil, the *New Yorker,* and my bushes. Your support does more for my weary soul than you know.

Other than that? All me.

Finally, the NYPD vandal squad. Face it, we need each other. Without wannabe Batmen, I'm just a stylish clown. I promise to keep you busy.

The rest was all me, baby.

ABOUT THE AUTHOR

Dennard Dayle is a Jamaican American author who lives in Brooklyn, New York. He is a graduate of Princeton University and received his MFA from Columbia University. His short fiction has appeared in *The New Yorker*, *Clarkesworld*, *Matchbook*, *The Hard Times*, and *McSweeney's Internet Tendency*. His first book was the short story collection *Everything Abridged*. Before taking up fiction and mischief as a full-time job, he was an advertising copywriter who dangerously flirted with stand-up comedy. He teaches as an adjunct at Columbia, writes weekly humor at 1-900-HOTDOG, and recently made the rash decision to take up skateboarding.